It isn't ~~...~~
It's eyeshadow !!

by Cathy Guisewite

Selected Cartoons from
WHY DO THE RIGHT WORDS ALWAYS COME
OUT OF THE WRONG MOUTH?
Volume 2

FAWCETT CREST • NEW YORK

Cathy ® is syndicated internationally by Universal Press Syndicate.

A Fawcett Crest Book
Published by Ballantine Books
Copyright © 1988 by Universal Press Syndicate

All rights reserved under International and Pan-American Copyright
Conventions. Published in the United States by Ballantine Books, a
division of Random House, Inc., New York, and simultaneously in
Canada by Random House of Canada Limited, Toronto.

No part of this book may be used or reproduced in any manner
whatsoever without permission except in the case of reprints in the
context of reviews. For information write Andrews and McMeel, a
Universal Press Syndicate Affiliate, 4900 Main Street, Kansas City,
Missouri 64112.

Library of Congress Catalog Card Number: 88-71102

ISBN 0-449-21772-8

This Book comprises a portion of WHY DO THE RIGHT WORDS
ALWAYS COME OUT OF THE WRONG MOUTH and is reprinted by
arrangement with Andrews and McMeel, a Universal Press Syndicate Affiliate.

Manufactured in the United States of America

First Ballantine Books Edition: May 1990

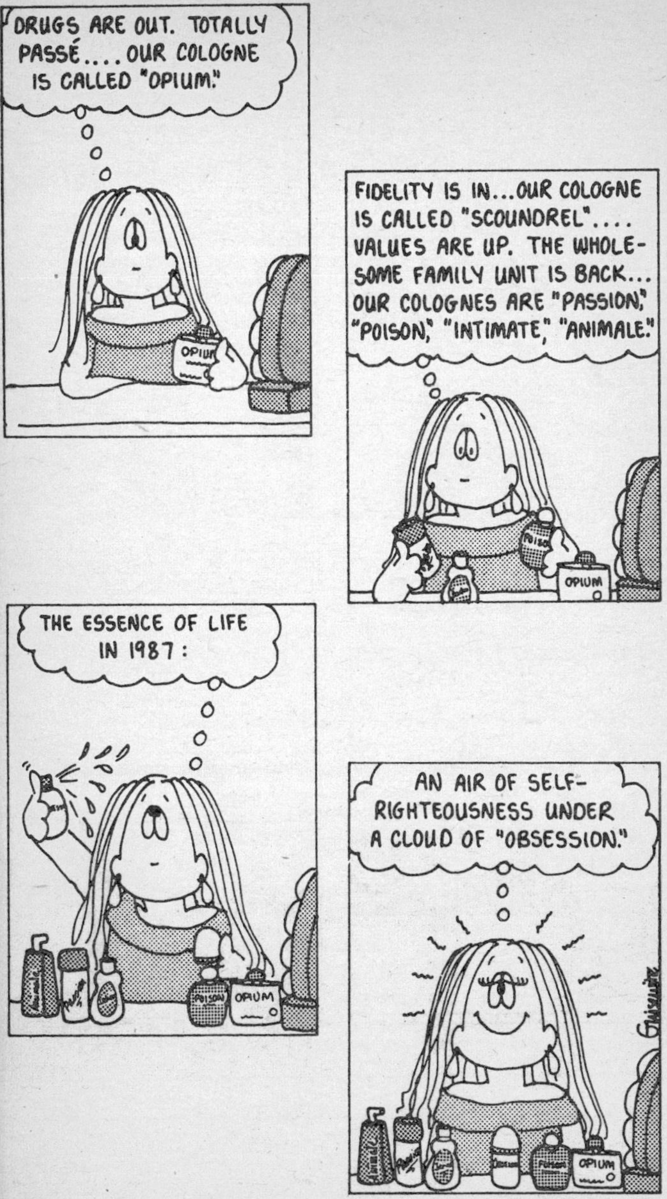
DRUGS ARE OUT. TOTALLY PASSÉ.... OUR COLOGNE IS CALLED "OPIUM."
FIDELITY IS IN...OUR COLOGNE IS CALLED "SCOUNDREL".... VALUES ARE UP. THE WHOLE-SOME FAMILY UNIT IS BACK... OUR COLOGNES ARE "PASSION," "POISON," "INTIMATE," "ANIMALE."
OPIUM
THE ESSENCE OF LIFE IN 1987:
POISON
OPIUM
AN AIR OF SELF-RIGHTEOUSNESS UNDER A CLOUD OF "OBSESSION."
POISON
OPIUM
Guisewite

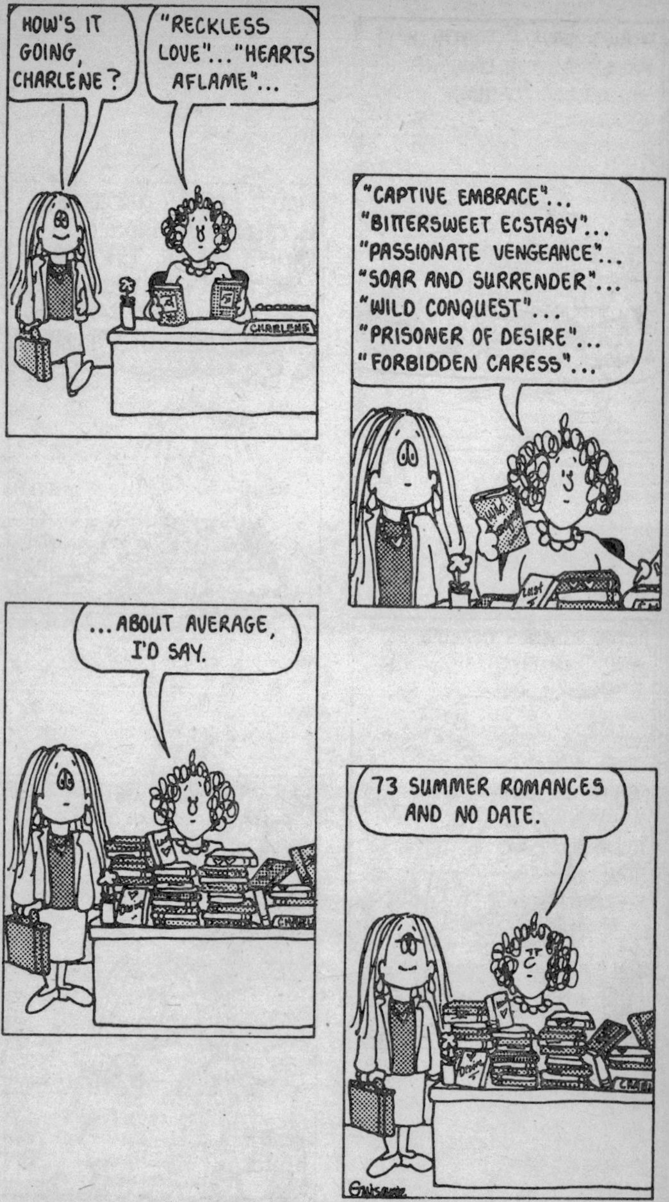
HOW'S IT GOING, CHARLENE?
"RECKLESS LOVE"..."HEARTS AFLAME"...
"CAPTIVE EMBRACE"... "BITTERSWEET ECSTASY"... "PASSIONATE VENGEANCE"... "SOAR AND SURRENDER"... "WILD CONQUEST"... "PRISONER OF DESIRE"... "FORBIDDEN CARESS"...
...ABOUT AVERAGE, I'D SAY.
73 SUMMER ROMANCES AND NO DATE.

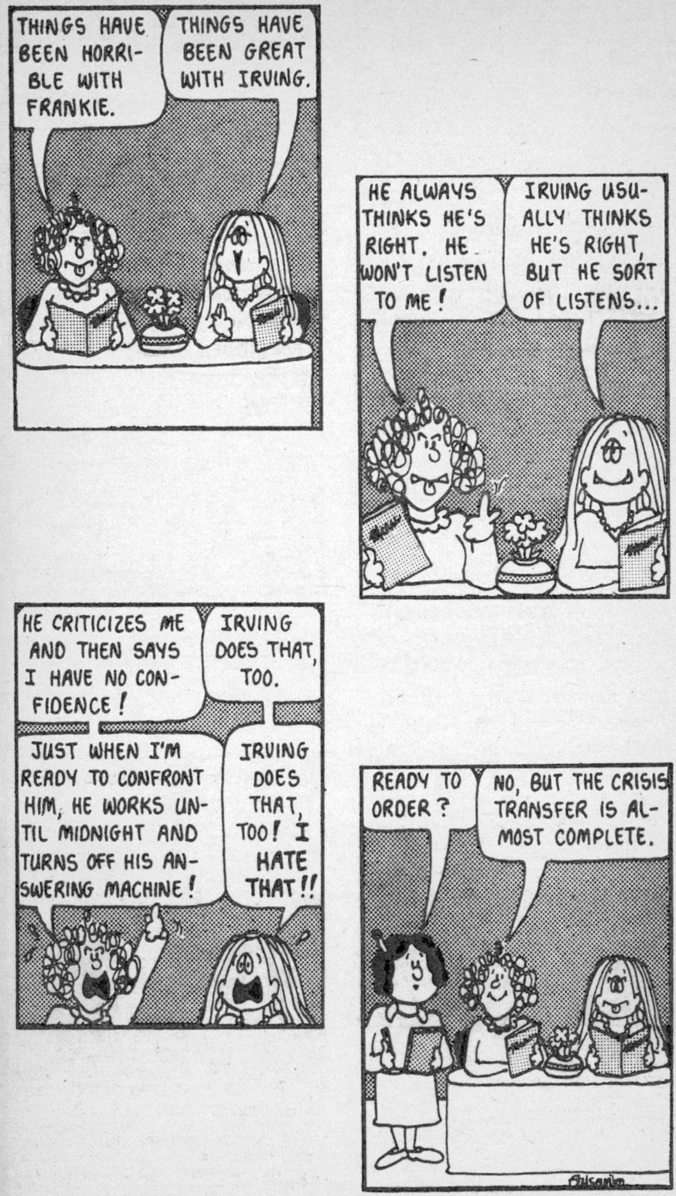
THINGS HAVE BEEN HORRIBLE WITH FRANKIE.
THINGS HAVE BEEN GREAT WITH IRVING.
HE ALWAYS THINKS HE'S RIGHT. HE WON'T LISTEN TO ME!
IRVING USUALLY THINKS HE'S RIGHT, BUT HE SORT OF LISTENS...
HE CRITICIZES ME AND THEN SAYS I HAVE NO CONFIDENCE!
IRVING DOES THAT, TOO.
JUST WHEN I'M READY TO CONFRONT HIM, HE WORKS UNTIL MIDNIGHT AND TURNS OFF HIS ANSWERING MACHINE!
IRVING DOES THAT, TOO! I HATE THAT!!
READY TO ORDER?
NO, BUT THE CRISIS TRANSFER IS ALMOST COMPLETE.

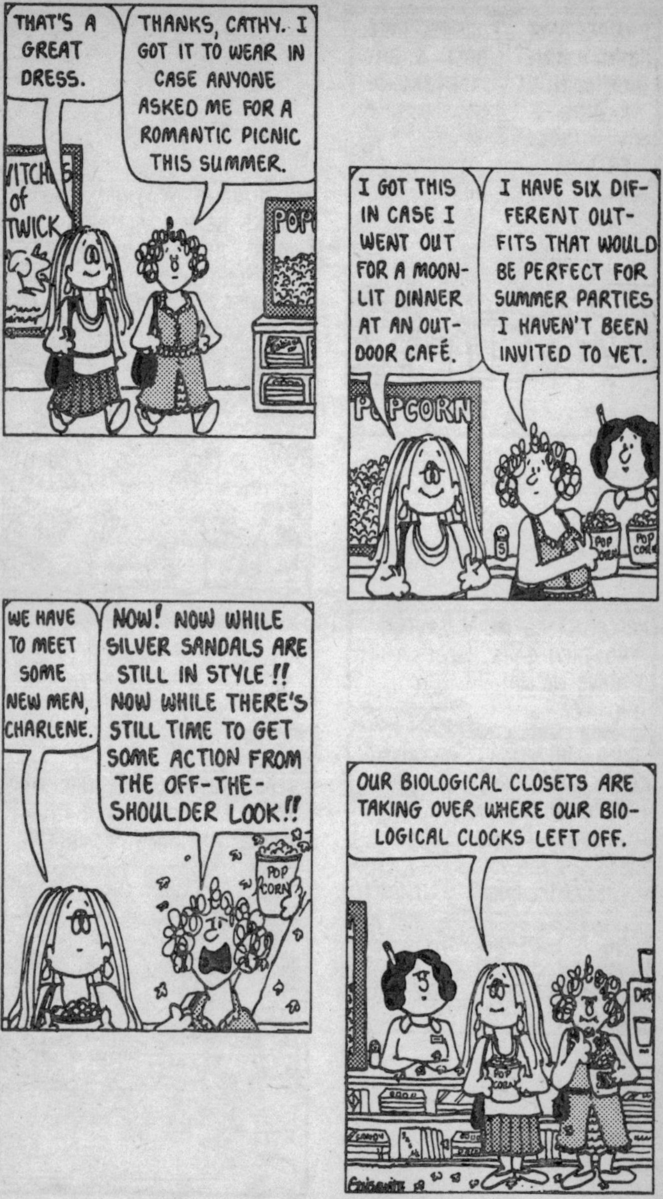
THAT'S A GREAT DRESS.
THANKS, CATHY. I GOT IT TO WEAR IN CASE ANYONE ASKED ME FOR A ROMANTIC PICNIC THIS SUMMER.
I GOT THIS IN CASE I WENT OUT FOR A MOON-LIT DINNER AT AN OUT-DOOR CAFÉ.
I HAVE SIX DIF-FERENT OUT-FITS THAT WOULD BE PERFECT FOR SUMMER PARTIES I HAVEN'T BEEN INVITED TO YET.
WE HAVE TO MEET SOME NEW MEN, CHARLENE.
NOW! NOW WHILE SILVER SANDALS ARE STILL IN STYLE!! NOW WHILE THERE'S STILL TIME TO GET SOME ACTION FROM THE OFF-THE-SHOULDER LOOK!!
POP CORN
OUR BIOLOGICAL CLOSETS ARE TAKING OVER WHERE OUR BIO-LOGICAL CLOCKS LEFT OFF.

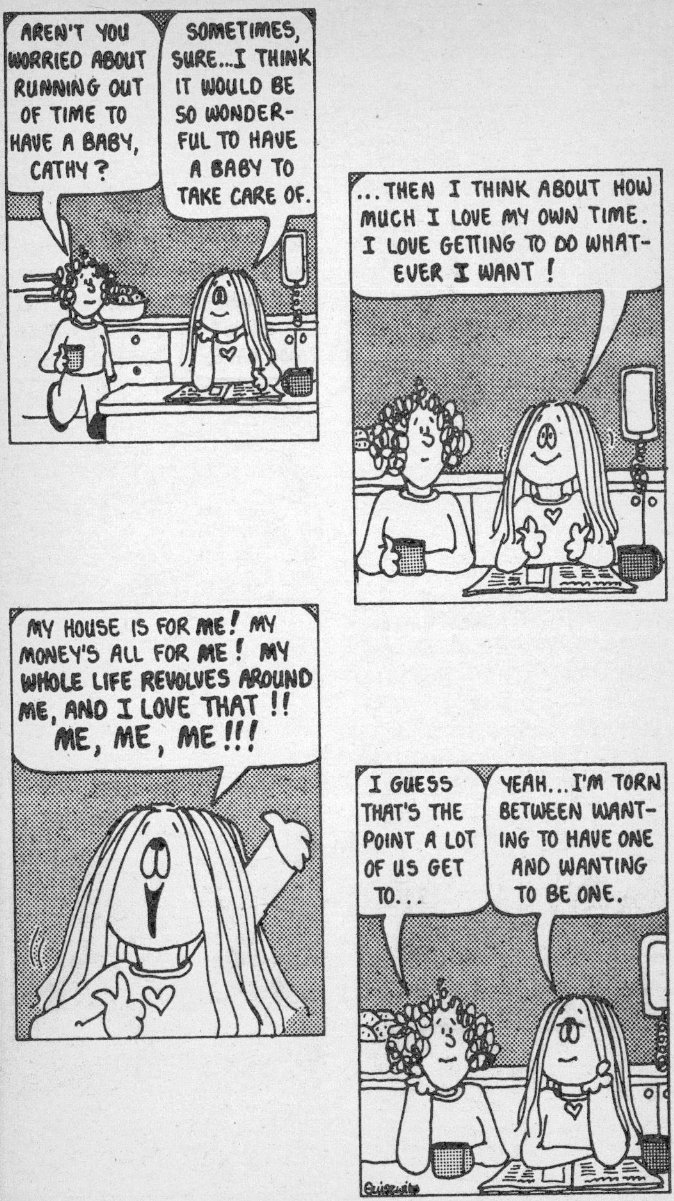
AREN'T YOU WORRIED ABOUT RUNNING OUT OF TIME TO HAVE A BABY, CATHY?
SOMETIMES, SURE...I THINK IT WOULD BE SO WONDERFUL TO HAVE A BABY TO TAKE CARE OF.
...THEN I THINK ABOUT HOW MUCH I LOVE MY OWN TIME. I LOVE GETTING TO DO WHATEVER I WANT!
MY HOUSE IS FOR ME! MY MONEY'S ALL FOR ME! MY WHOLE LIFE REVOLVES AROUND ME, AND I LOVE THAT!! ME, ME, ME!!!
I GUESS THAT'S THE POINT A LOT OF US GET TO...
YEAH...I'M TORN BETWEEN WANTING TO HAVE ONE AND WANTING TO BE ONE.
Guisewite

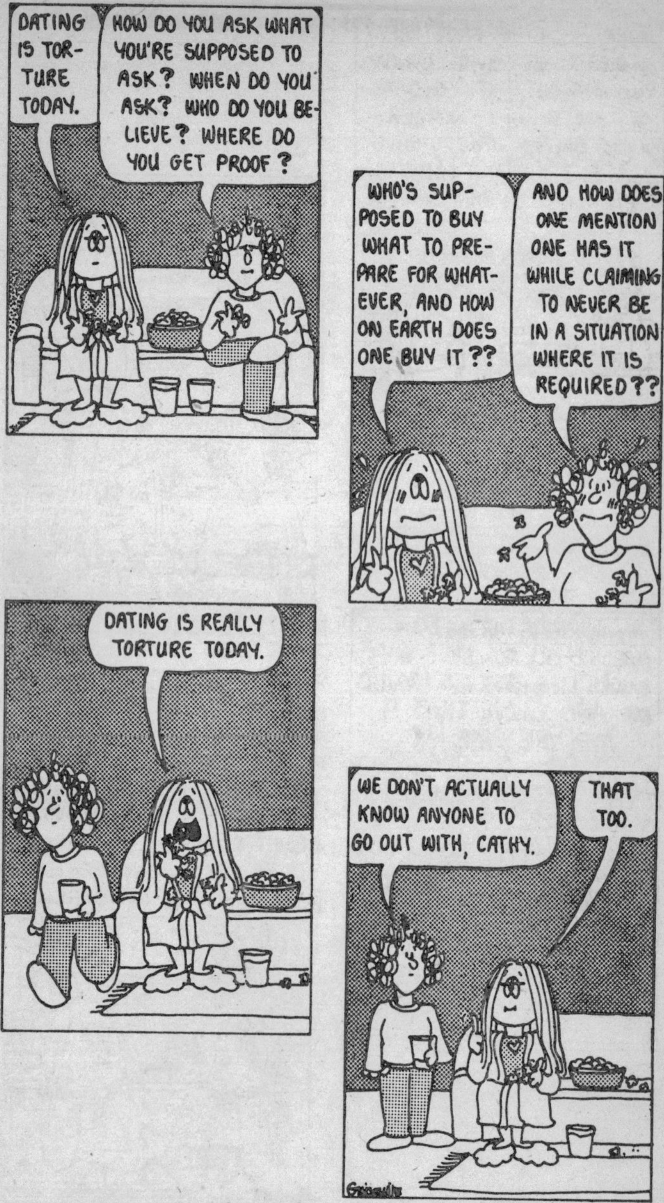
DATING IS TORTURE TODAY.
HOW DO YOU ASK WHAT YOU'RE SUPPOSED TO ASK? WHEN DO YOU ASK? WHO DO YOU BELIEVE? WHERE DO YOU GET PROOF?
WHO'S SUPPOSED TO BUY WHAT TO PREPARE FOR WHATEVER, AND HOW ON EARTH DOES ONE BUY IT??
AND HOW DOES ONE MENTION ONE HAS IT WHILE CLAIMING TO NEVER BE IN A SITUATION WHERE IT IS REQUIRED??
DATING IS REALLY TORTURE TODAY.
WE DON'T ACTUALLY KNOW ANYONE TO GO OUT WITH, CATHY.
THAT TOO.

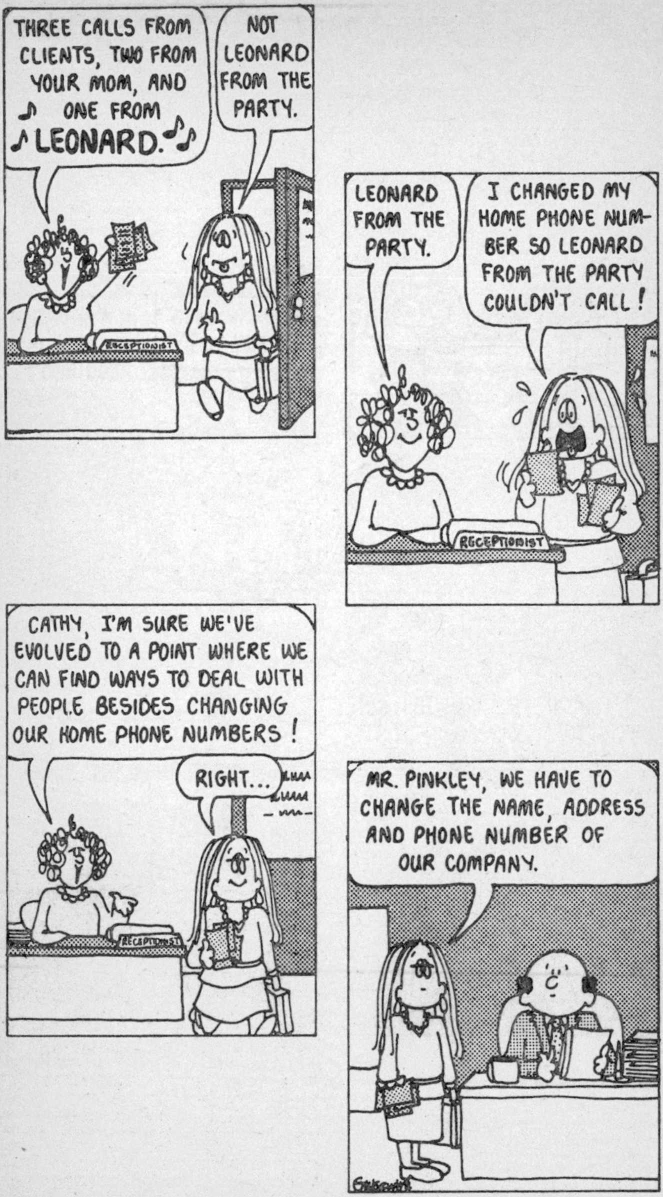
THREE CALLS FROM CLIENTS, TWO FROM YOUR MOM, AND ONE FROM LEONARD.
NOT LEONARD FROM THE PARTY.
LEONARD FROM THE PARTY.
I CHANGED MY HOME PHONE NUMBER SO LEONARD FROM THE PARTY COULDN'T CALL!
RECEPTIONIST
CATHY, I'M SURE WE'VE EVOLVED TO A POINT WHERE WE CAN FIND WAYS TO DEAL WITH PEOPLE BESIDES CHANGING OUR HOME PHONE NUMBERS!
RIGHT...
MR. PINKLEY, WE HAVE TO CHANGE THE NAME, ADDRESS AND PHONE NUMBER OF OUR COMPANY.

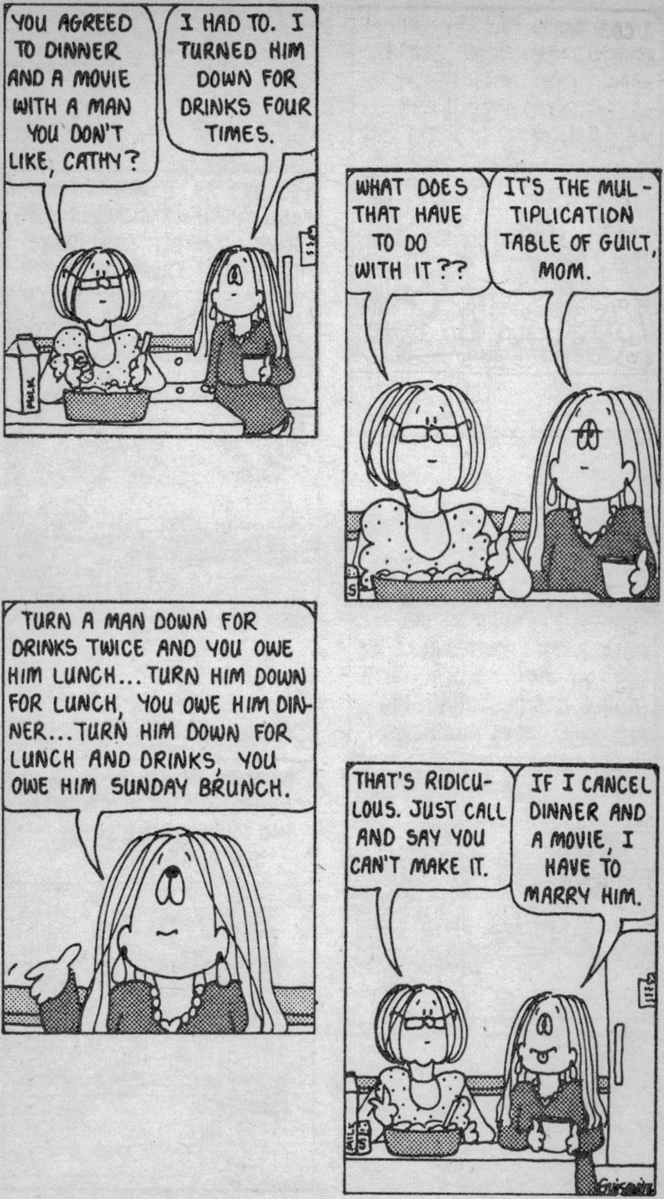
YOU AGREED TO DINNER AND A MOVIE WITH A MAN YOU DON'T LIKE, CATHY?
I HAD TO. I TURNED HIM DOWN FOR DRINKS FOUR TIMES.
WHAT DOES THAT HAVE TO DO WITH IT??
IT'S THE MUL-TIPLICATION TABLE OF GUILT, MOM.
TURN A MAN DOWN FOR DRINKS TWICE AND YOU OWE HIM LUNCH... TURN HIM DOWN FOR LUNCH, YOU OWE HIM DIN-NER... TURN HIM DOWN FOR LUNCH AND DRINKS, YOU OWE HIM SUNDAY BRUNCH.
THAT'S RIDICU-LOUS. JUST CALL AND SAY YOU CAN'T MAKE IT.
IF I CANCEL DINNER AND A MOVIE, I HAVE TO MARRY HIM.

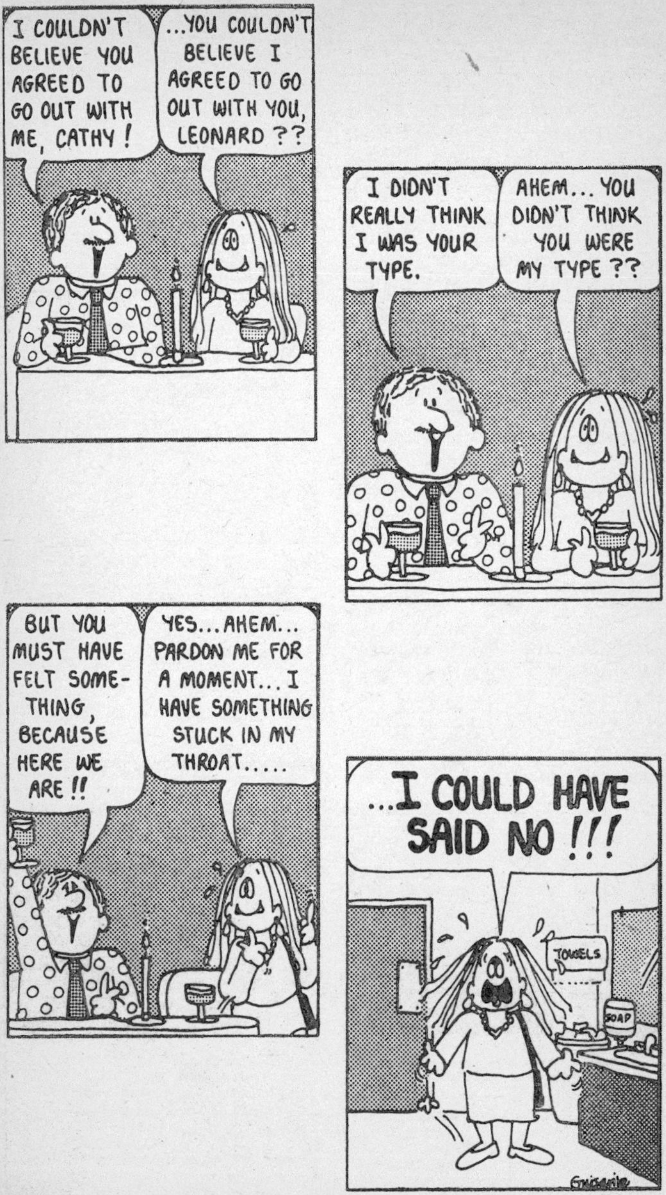
I COULDN'T BELIEVE YOU AGREED TO GO OUT WITH ME, CATHY!
...YOU COULDN'T BELIEVE I AGREED TO GO OUT WITH YOU, LEONARD??
I DIDN'T REALLY THINK I WAS YOUR TYPE.
AHEM... YOU DIDN'T THINK YOU WERE MY TYPE??
BUT YOU MUST HAVE FELT SOME-THING, BECAUSE HERE WE ARE!!
YES...AHEM... PARDON ME FOR A MOMENT... I HAVE SOMETHING STUCK IN MY THROAT.....
...I COULD HAVE SAID NO!!!
TOWELS
SOAP

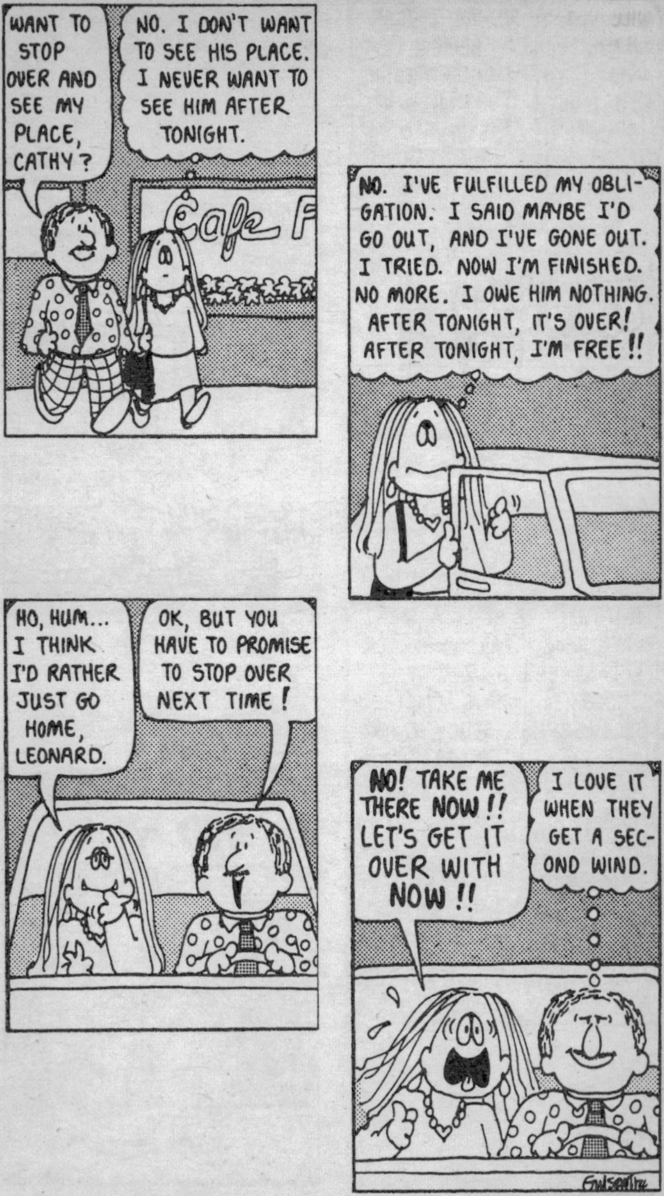
WANT TO STOP OVER AND SEE MY PLACE, CATHY?
NO. I DON'T WANT TO SEE HIS PLACE. I NEVER WANT TO SEE HIM AFTER TONIGHT.
Cafe F
NO. I'VE FULFILLED MY OBLIGATION. I SAID MAYBE I'D GO OUT, AND I'VE GONE OUT. I TRIED. NOW I'M FINISHED. NO MORE. I OWE HIM NOTHING. AFTER TONIGHT, IT'S OVER! AFTER TONIGHT, I'M FREE!!
HO, HUM... I THINK I'D RATHER JUST GO HOME, LEONARD.
OK, BUT YOU HAVE TO PROMISE TO STOP OVER NEXT TIME!
NO! TAKE ME THERE NOW!! LET'S GET IT OVER WITH NOW!!
I LOVE IT WHEN THEY GET A SECOND WIND.

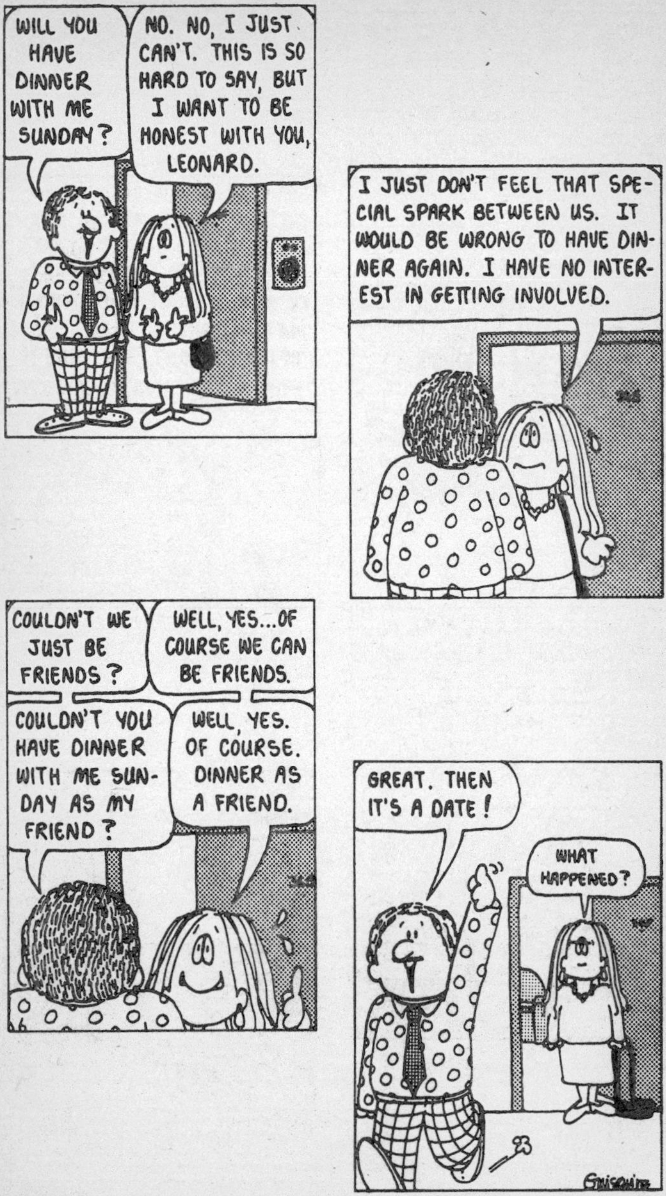
WILL YOU HAVE DINNER WITH ME SUNDAY?
NO. NO, I JUST CAN'T. THIS IS SO HARD TO SAY, BUT I WANT TO BE HONEST WITH YOU, LEONARD.
I JUST DON'T FEEL THAT SPECIAL SPARK BETWEEN US. IT WOULD BE WRONG TO HAVE DINNER AGAIN. I HAVE NO INTEREST IN GETTING INVOLVED.
COULDN'T WE JUST BE FRIENDS?
WELL, YES...OF COURSE WE CAN BE FRIENDS.
COULDN'T YOU HAVE DINNER WITH ME SUNDAY AS MY FRIEND?
WELL, YES. OF COURSE. DINNER AS A FRIEND.
GREAT. THEN IT'S A DATE!
WHAT HAPPENED?

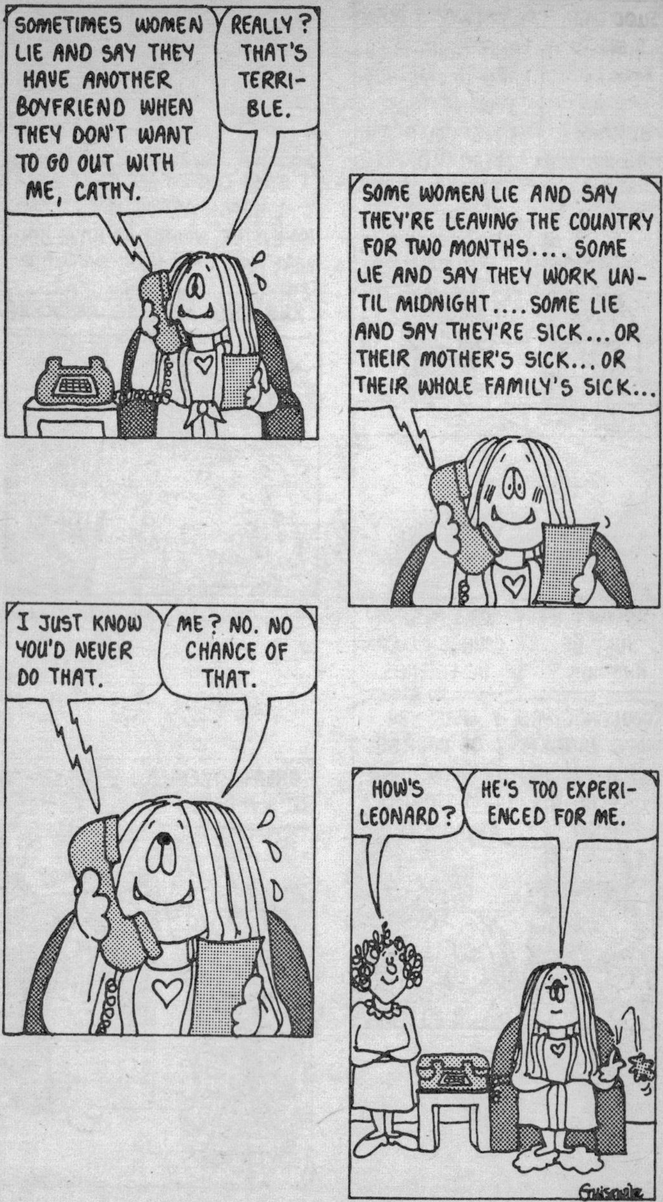
SOMETIMES WOMEN LIE AND SAY THEY HAVE ANOTHER BOYFRIEND WHEN THEY DON'T WANT TO GO OUT WITH ME, CATHY.
REALLY? THAT'S TERRI-BLE.
SOME WOMEN LIE AND SAY THEY'RE LEAVING THE COUNTRY FOR TWO MONTHS.... SOME LIE AND SAY THEY WORK UN-TIL MIDNIGHT....SOME LIE AND SAY THEY'RE SICK...OR THEIR MOTHER'S SICK...OR THEIR WHOLE FAMILY'S SICK...
I JUST KNOW YOU'D NEVER DO THAT.
ME? NO. NO CHANCE OF THAT.
HOW'S LEONARD?
HE'S TOO EXPERI-ENCED FOR ME.

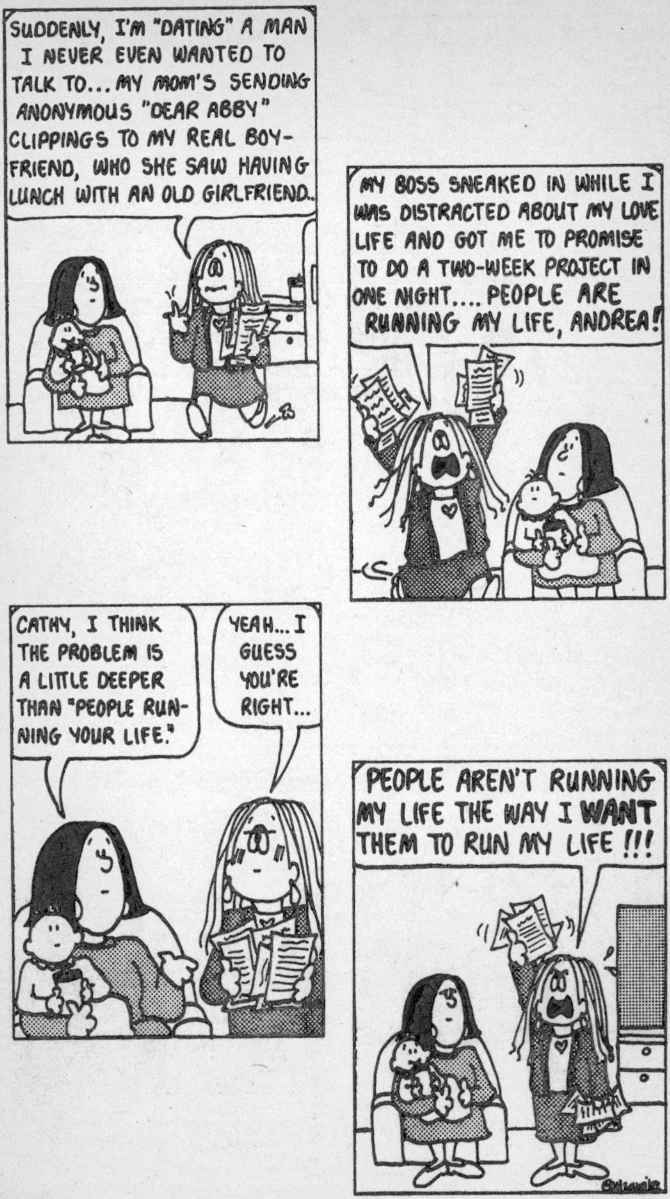
SUDDENLY, I'M "DATING" A MAN I NEVER EVEN WANTED TO TALK TO... MY MOM'S SENDING ANONYMOUS "DEAR ABBY" CLIPPINGS TO MY REAL BOY-FRIEND, WHO SHE SAW HAVING LUNCH WITH AN OLD GIRLFRIEND..
MY BOSS SNEAKED IN WHILE I WAS DISTRACTED ABOUT MY LOVE LIFE AND GOT ME TO PROMISE TO DO A TWO-WEEK PROJECT IN ONE NIGHT.... PEOPLE ARE RUNNING MY LIFE, ANDREA!
CATHY, I THINK THE PROBLEM IS A LITTLE DEEPER THAN "PEOPLE RUN-NING YOUR LIFE."
YEAH... I GUESS YOU'RE RIGHT...
PEOPLE AREN'T RUNNING MY LIFE THE WAY I WANT THEM TO RUN MY LIFE !!!

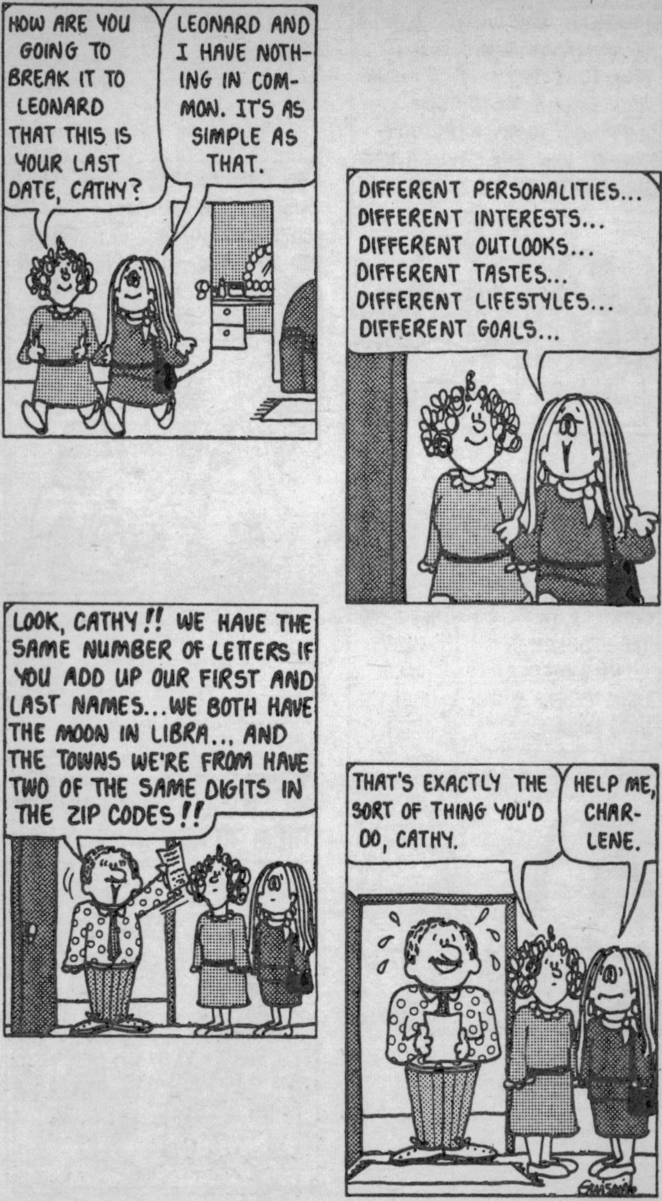
HOW ARE YOU GOING TO BREAK IT TO LEONARD THAT THIS IS YOUR LAST DATE, CATHY?
LEONARD AND I HAVE NOTHING IN COMMON. IT'S AS SIMPLE AS THAT.
DIFFERENT PERSONALITIES... DIFFERENT INTERESTS... DIFFERENT OUTLOOKS... DIFFERENT TASTES... DIFFERENT LIFESTYLES... DIFFERENT GOALS...
LOOK, CATHY!! WE HAVE THE SAME NUMBER OF LETTERS IF YOU ADD UP OUR FIRST AND LAST NAMES...WE BOTH HAVE THE MOON IN LIBRA... AND THE TOWNS WE'RE FROM HAVE TWO OF THE SAME DIGITS IN THE ZIP CODES!!
THAT'S EXACTLY THE SORT OF THING YOU'D DO, CATHY.
HELP ME, CHARLENE.

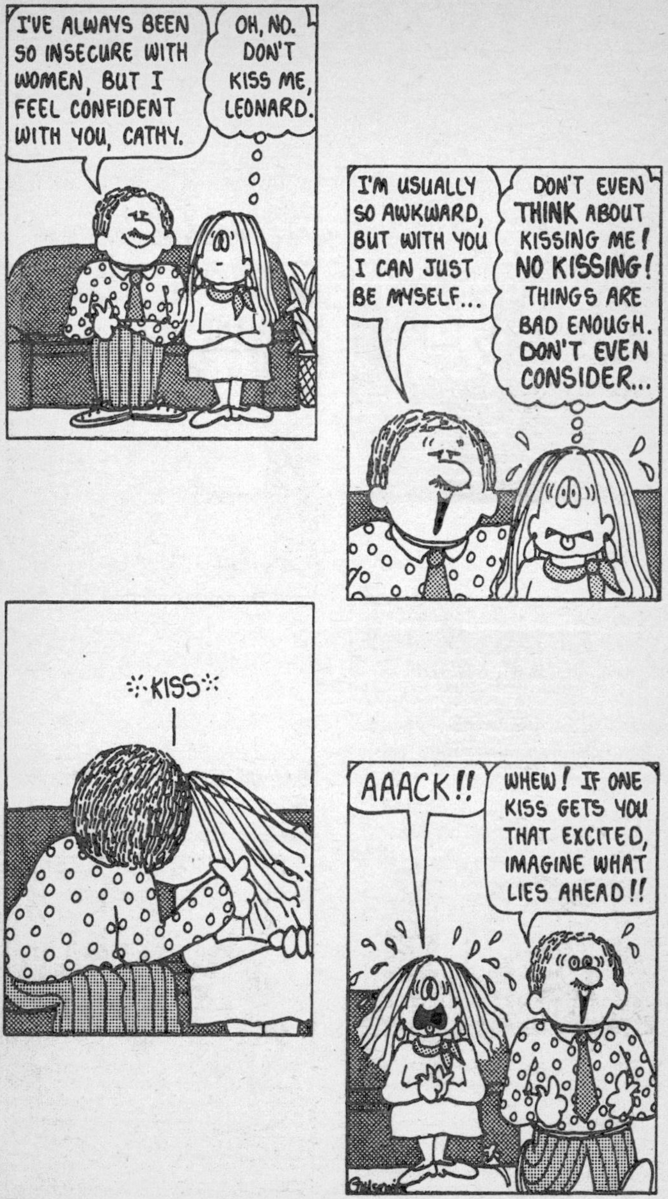
I'VE ALWAYS BEEN SO INSECURE WITH WOMEN, BUT I FEEL CONFIDENT WITH YOU, CATHY.
OH, NO. DON'T KISS ME, LEONARD.
I'M USUALLY SO AWKWARD, BUT WITH YOU I CAN JUST BE MYSELF...
DON'T EVEN THINK ABOUT KISSING ME! NO KISSING! THINGS ARE BAD ENOUGH. DON'T EVEN CONSIDER...
KISS
AAACK!!
WHEW! IF ONE KISS GETS YOU THAT EXCITED, IMAGINE WHAT LIES AHEAD!!

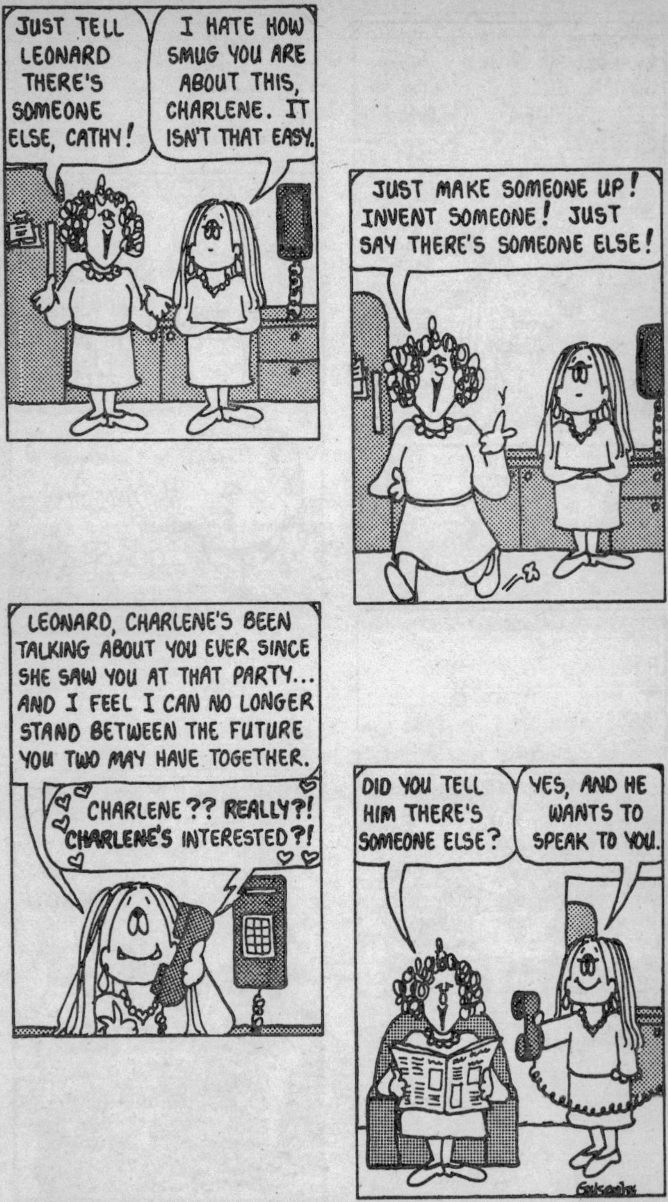
JUST TELL LEONARD THERE'S SOMEONE ELSE, CATHY!
I HATE HOW SMUG YOU ARE ABOUT THIS, CHARLENE. IT ISN'T THAT EASY.
JUST MAKE SOMEONE UP! INVENT SOMEONE! JUST SAY THERE'S SOMEONE ELSE!
LEONARD, CHARLENE'S BEEN TALKING ABOUT YOU EVER SINCE SHE SAW YOU AT THAT PARTY... AND I FEEL I CAN NO LONGER STAND BETWEEN THE FUTURE YOU TWO MAY HAVE TOGETHER.
CHARLENE?? REALLY?! CHARLENE'S INTERESTED?!
DID YOU TELL HIM THERE'S SOMEONE ELSE?
YES, AND HE WANTS TO SPEAK TO YOU.

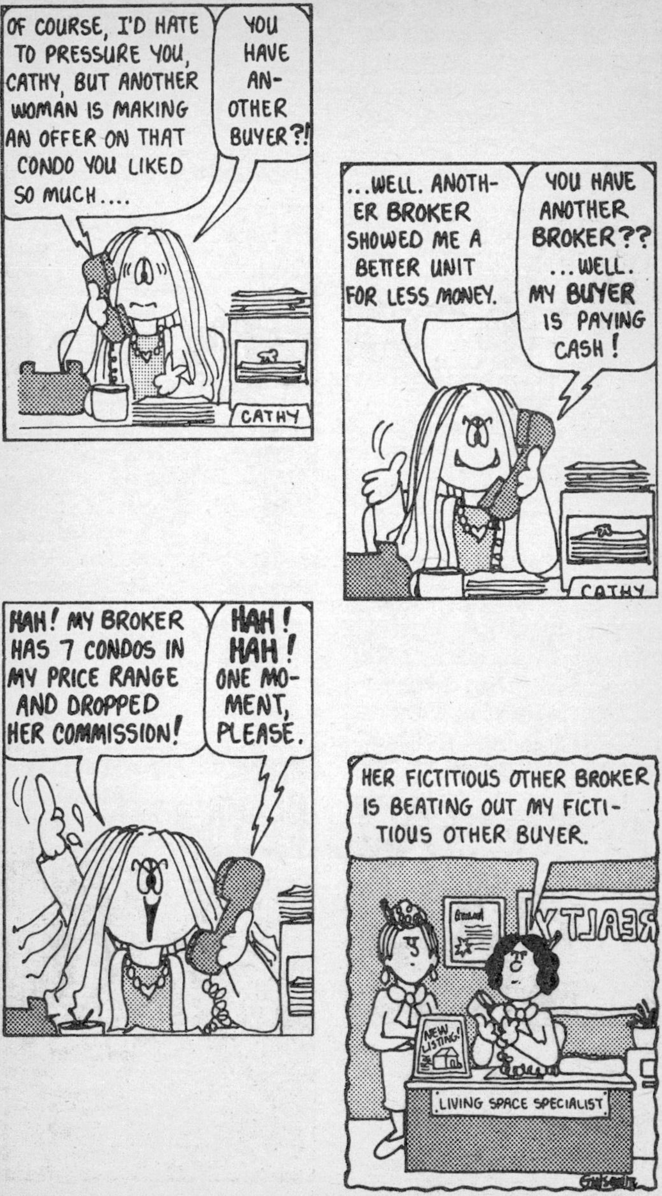
OF COURSE, I'D HATE TO PRESSURE YOU, CATHY, BUT ANOTHER WOMAN IS MAKING AN OFFER ON THAT CONDO YOU LIKED SO MUCH....
YOU HAVE AN-OTHER BUYER?!
CATHY
...WELL. ANOTH-ER BROKER SHOWED ME A BETTER UNIT FOR LESS MONEY.
YOU HAVE ANOTHER BROKER?? ...WELL. MY BUYER IS PAYING CASH!
HAH! MY BROKER HAS 7 CONDOS IN MY PRICE RANGE AND DROPPED HER COMMISSION!
HAH! HAH! ONE MO-MENT, PLEASE.
HER FICTITIOUS OTHER BROKER IS BEATING OUT MY FICTI-TIOUS OTHER BUYER.
NEW LISTING!
LIVING SPACE SPECIALIST

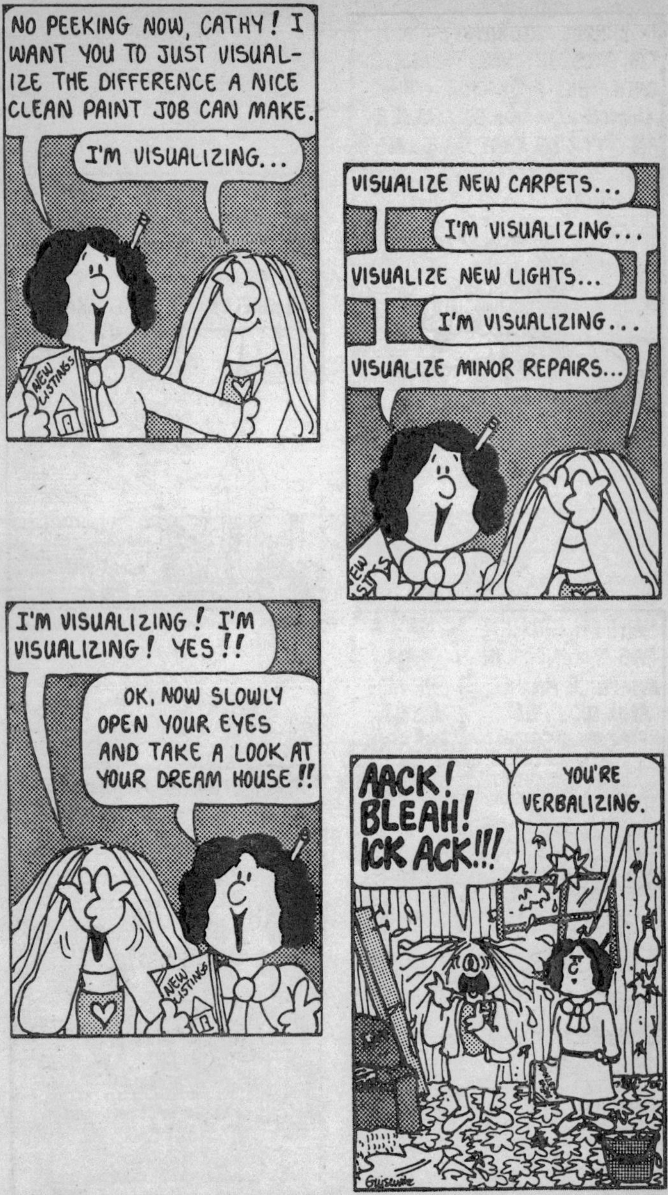
NO PEEKING NOW, CATHY! I WANT YOU TO JUST VISUALIZE THE DIFFERENCE A NICE CLEAN PAINT JOB CAN MAKE.
I'M VISUALIZING...
NEW LISTINGS
VISUALIZE NEW CARPETS...
I'M VISUALIZING...
VISUALIZE NEW LIGHTS...
I'M VISUALIZING...
VISUALIZE MINOR REPAIRS...
I'M VISUALIZING! I'M VISUALIZING! YES!!
OK, NOW SLOWLY OPEN YOUR EYES AND TAKE A LOOK AT YOUR DREAM HOUSE!!
NEW LISTINGS
AACK! BLEAH! ICK ACK!!!
YOU'RE VERBALIZING.
Guisewite

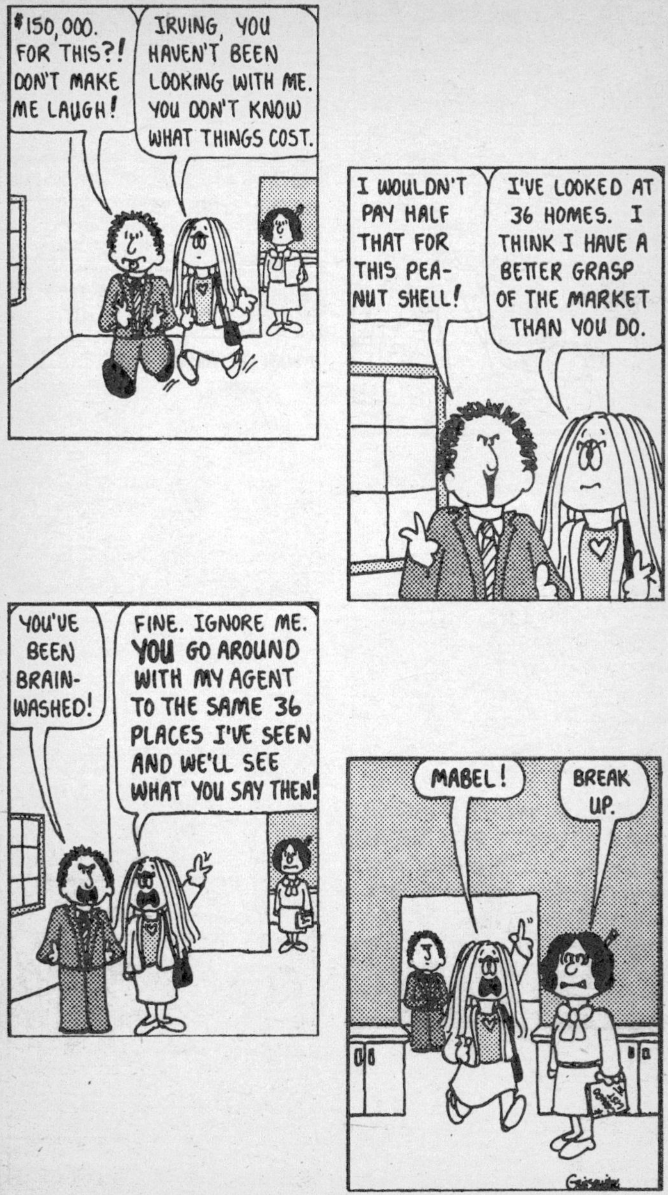
$150,000. FOR THIS?! DON'T MAKE ME LAUGH!
IRVING, YOU HAVEN'T BEEN LOOKING WITH ME. YOU DON'T KNOW WHAT THINGS COST.
I WOULDN'T PAY HALF THAT FOR THIS PEA-NUT SHELL!
I'VE LOOKED AT 36 HOMES. I THINK I HAVE A BETTER GRASP OF THE MARKET THAN YOU DO.
YOU'VE BEEN BRAIN-WASHED!
FINE. IGNORE ME. YOU GO AROUND WITH MY AGENT TO THE SAME 36 PLACES I'VE SEEN AND WE'LL SEE WHAT YOU SAY THEN!
MABEL!
BREAK UP.

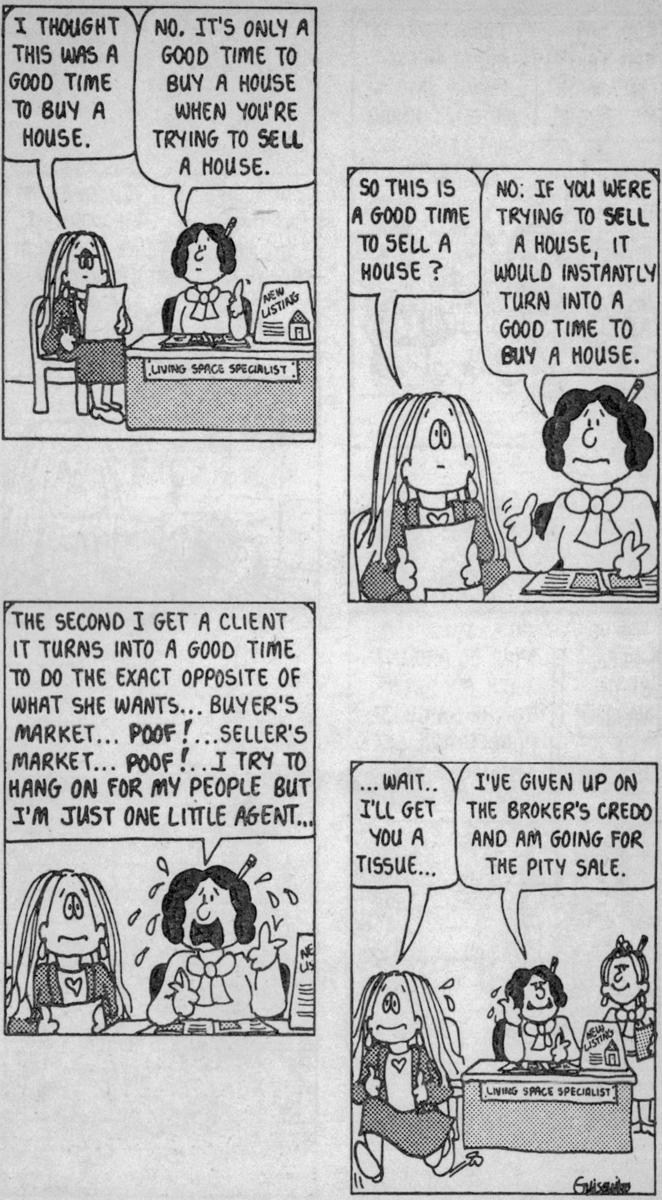
I THOUGHT THIS WAS A GOOD TIME TO BUY A HOUSE.
NO. IT'S ONLY A GOOD TIME TO BUY A HOUSE WHEN YOU'RE TRYING TO SELL A HOUSE.
NEW LISTING
LIVING SPACE SPECIALIST
SO THIS IS A GOOD TIME TO SELL A HOUSE?
NO: IF YOU WERE TRYING TO SELL A HOUSE, IT WOULD INSTANTLY TURN INTO A GOOD TIME TO BUY A HOUSE.
THE SECOND I GET A CLIENT IT TURNS INTO A GOOD TIME TO DO THE EXACT OPPOSITE OF WHAT SHE WANTS... BUYER'S MARKET... POOF!...SELLER'S MARKET... POOF!..I TRY TO HANG ON FOR MY PEOPLE BUT I'M JUST ONE LITTLE AGENT...
...WAIT.. I'LL GET YOU A TISSUE...
I'VE GIVEN UP ON THE BROKER'S CREDO AND AM GOING FOR THE PITY SALE.
NEW LISTING
LIVING SPACE SPECIALIST
Guisewite

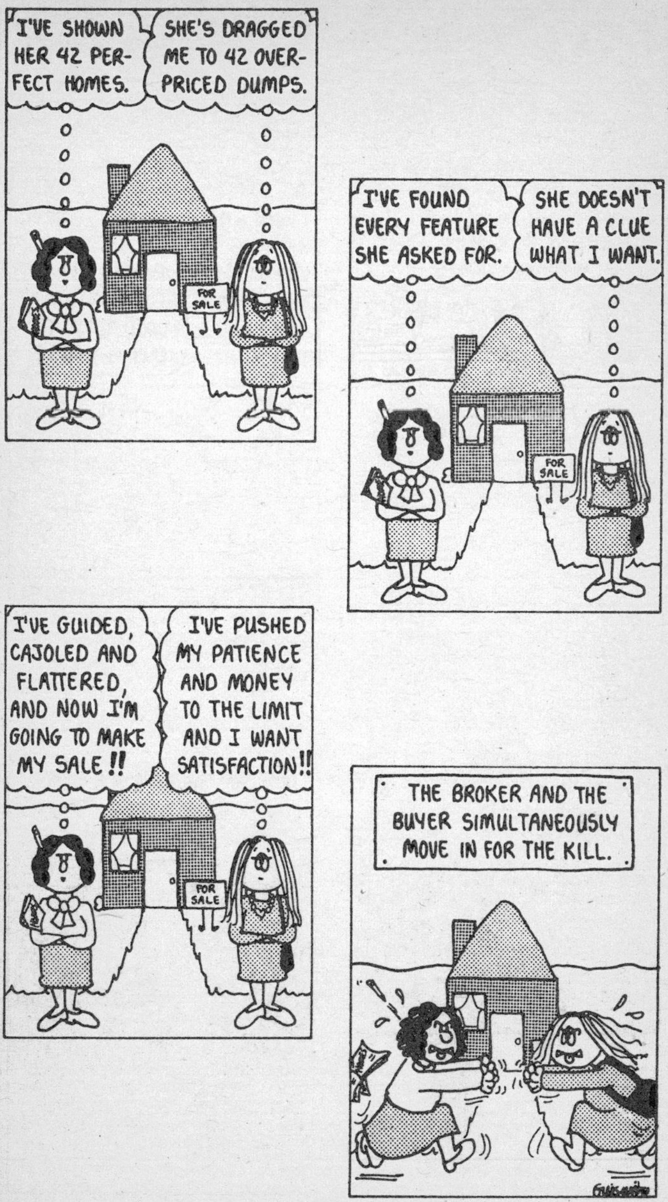
I'VE SHOWN HER 42 PERFECT HOMES.
SHE'S DRAGGED ME TO 42 OVERPRICED DUMPS.
FOR SALE
I'VE FOUND EVERY FEATURE SHE ASKED FOR.
SHE DOESN'T HAVE A CLUE WHAT I WANT.
FOR SALE
I'VE GUIDED, CAJOLED AND FLATTERED, AND NOW I'M GOING TO MAKE MY SALE!!
I'VE PUSHED MY PATIENCE AND MONEY TO THE LIMIT AND I WANT SATISFACTION!!
FOR SALE
THE BROKER AND THE BUYER SIMULTANEOUSLY MOVE IN FOR THE KILL.

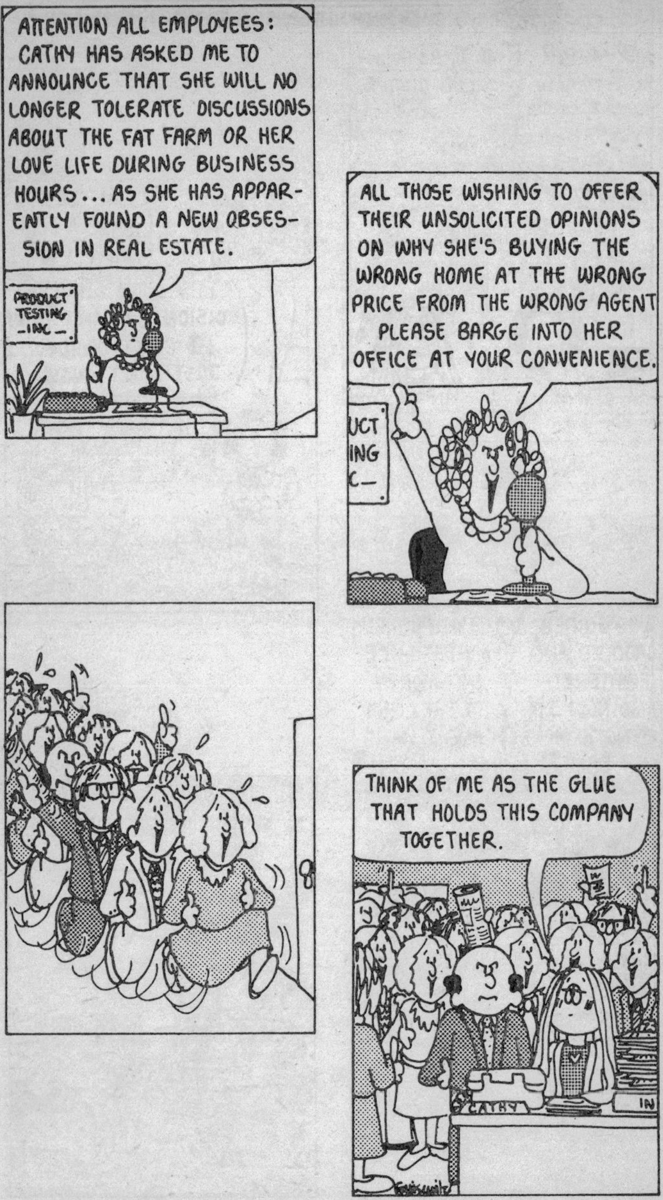
ATTENTION ALL EMPLOYEES: CATHY HAS ASKED ME TO ANNOUNCE THAT SHE WILL NO LONGER TOLERATE DISCUSSIONS ABOUT THE FAT FARM OR HER LOVE LIFE DURING BUSINESS HOURS... AS SHE HAS APPARENTLY FOUND A NEW OBSESSION IN REAL ESTATE.
PRODUCT TESTING -INC-
ALL THOSE WISHING TO OFFER THEIR UNSOLICITED OPINIONS ON WHY SHE'S BUYING THE WRONG HOME AT THE WRONG PRICE FROM THE WRONG AGENT PLEASE BARGE INTO HER OFFICE AT YOUR CONVENIENCE.
THINK OF ME AS THE GLUE THAT HOLDS THIS COMPANY TOGETHER.
CATHY
IN

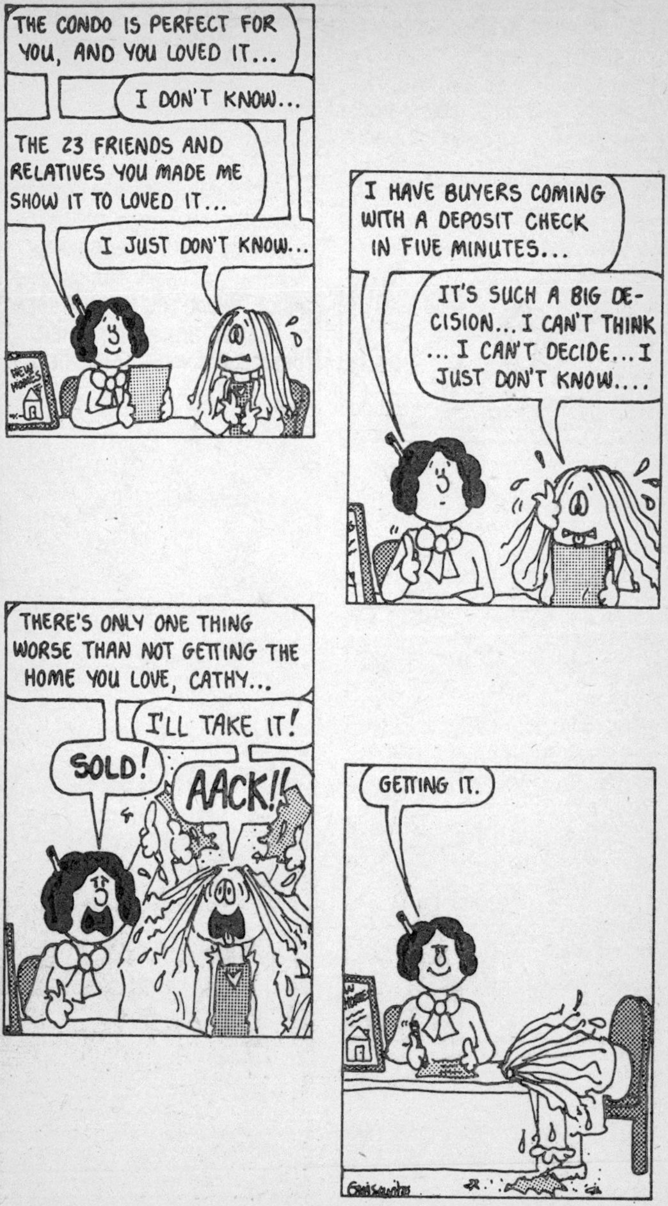
THE CONDO IS PERFECT FOR YOU, AND YOU LOVED IT...
I DON'T KNOW...
THE 23 FRIENDS AND RELATIVES YOU MADE ME SHOW IT TO LOVED IT...
I JUST DON'T KNOW...
NEW HOMES
I HAVE BUYERS COMING WITH A DEPOSIT CHECK IN FIVE MINUTES...
IT'S SUCH A BIG DECISION... I CAN'T THINK ... I CAN'T DECIDE... I JUST DON'T KNOW....
THERE'S ONLY ONE THING WORSE THAN NOT GETTING THE HOME YOU LOVE, CATHY...
I'LL TAKE IT!
SOLD!
AACK!!
GETTING IT.

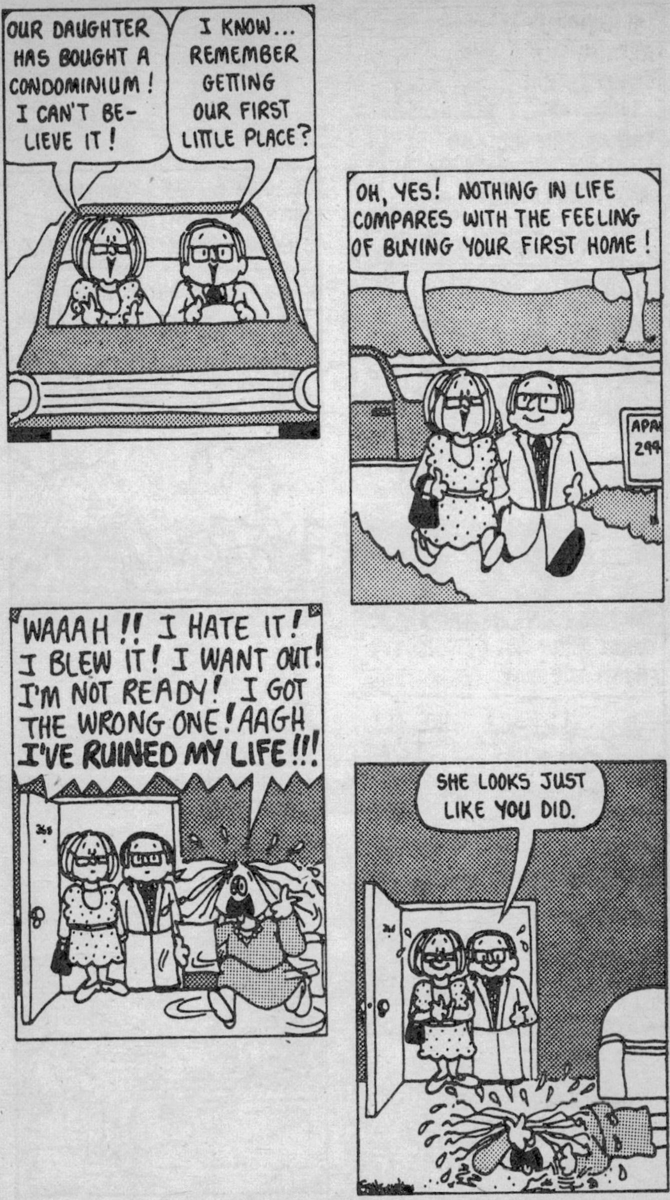
OUR DAUGHTER HAS BOUGHT A CONDOMINIUM! I CAN'T BE-LIEVE IT!
I KNOW... REMEMBER GETTING OUR FIRST LITTLE PLACE?
OH, YES! NOTHING IN LIFE COMPARES WITH THE FEELING OF BUYING YOUR FIRST HOME!
WAAAH!! I HATE IT! I BLEW IT! I WANT OUT! I'M NOT READY! I GOT THE WRONG ONE! AAGH I'VE RUINED MY LIFE!!!
SHE LOOKS JUST LIKE YOU DID.

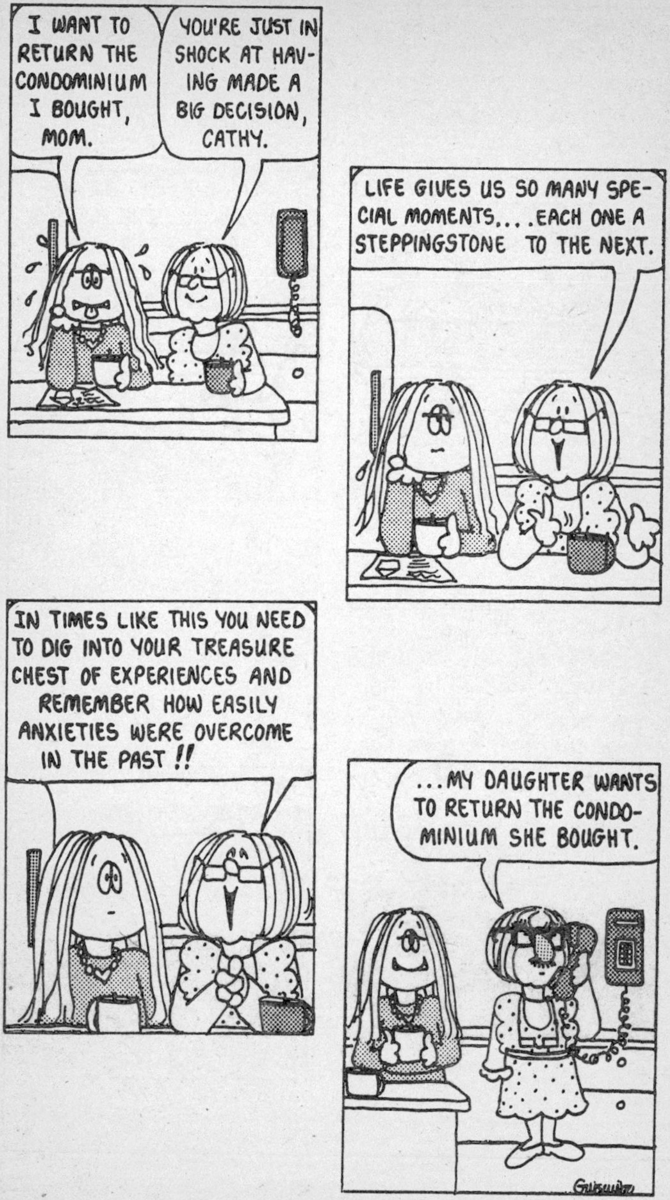
I WANT TO RETURN THE CONDOMINIUM I BOUGHT, MOM.
YOU'RE JUST IN SHOCK AT HAVING MADE A BIG DECISION, CATHY.
LIFE GIVES US SO MANY SPECIAL MOMENTS....EACH ONE A STEPPINGSTONE TO THE NEXT.
IN TIMES LIKE THIS YOU NEED TO DIG INTO YOUR TREASURE CHEST OF EXPERIENCES AND REMEMBER HOW EASILY ANXIETIES WERE OVERCOME IN THE PAST!!
...MY DAUGHTER WANTS TO RETURN THE CONDOMINIUM SHE BOUGHT.

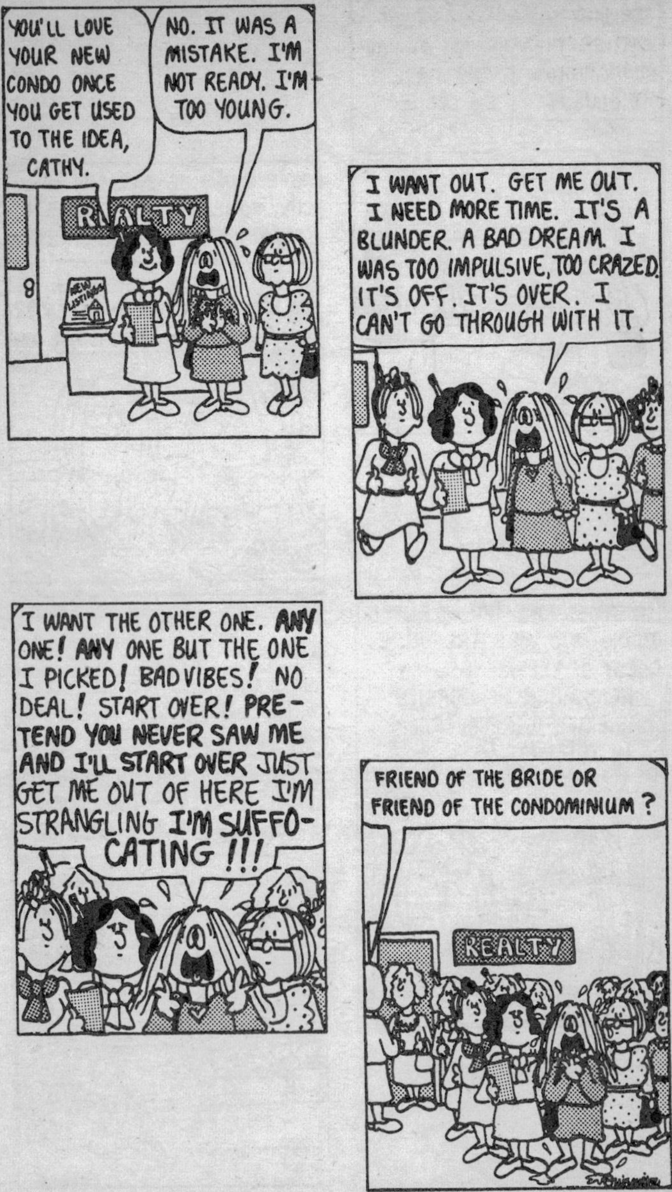
YOU'LL LOVE YOUR NEW CONDO ONCE YOU GET USED TO THE IDEA, CATHY.
NO. IT WAS A MISTAKE. I'M NOT READY. I'M TOO YOUNG.
REALTY
NEW LISTINGS
I WANT OUT. GET ME OUT. I NEED MORE TIME. IT'S A BLUNDER. A BAD DREAM. I WAS TOO IMPULSIVE, TOO CRAZED. IT'S OFF. IT'S OVER. I CAN'T GO THROUGH WITH IT.
I WANT THE OTHER ONE. ANY ONE! ANY ONE BUT THE ONE I PICKED! BAD VIBES! NO DEAL! START OVER! PRE-TEND YOU NEVER SAW ME AND I'LL START OVER JUST GET ME OUT OF HERE I'M STRANGLING I'M SUFFO-CATING !!!
FRIEND OF THE BRIDE OR FRIEND OF THE CONDOMINIUM ?
REALTY

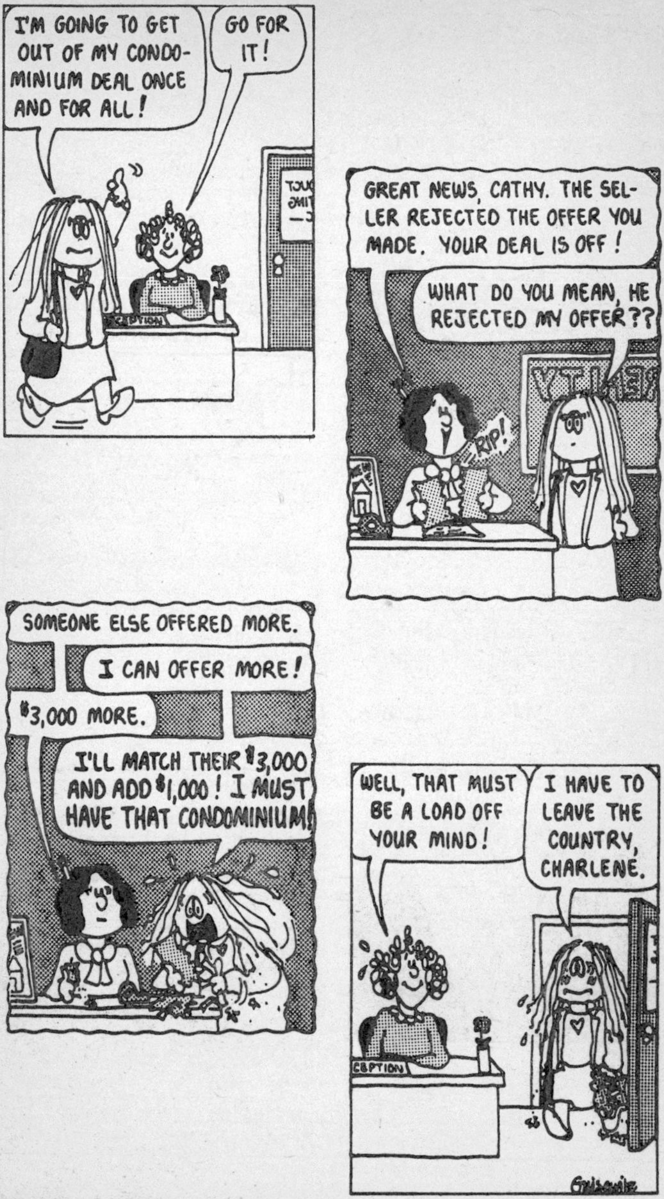
I'M GOING TO GET OUT OF MY CONDO-MINIUM DEAL ONCE AND FOR ALL!
GO FOR IT!
GREAT NEWS, CATHY. THE SEL-LER REJECTED THE OFFER YOU MADE. YOUR DEAL IS OFF!
WHAT DO YOU MEAN, HE REJECTED MY OFFER??
RIP!
SOMEONE ELSE OFFERED MORE.
I CAN OFFER MORE!
$3,000 MORE.
I'LL MATCH THEIR $3,000 AND ADD $1,000! I MUST HAVE THAT CONDOMINIUM!
WELL, THAT MUST BE A LOAD OFF YOUR MIND!
I HAVE TO LEAVE THE COUNTRY, CHARLENE.

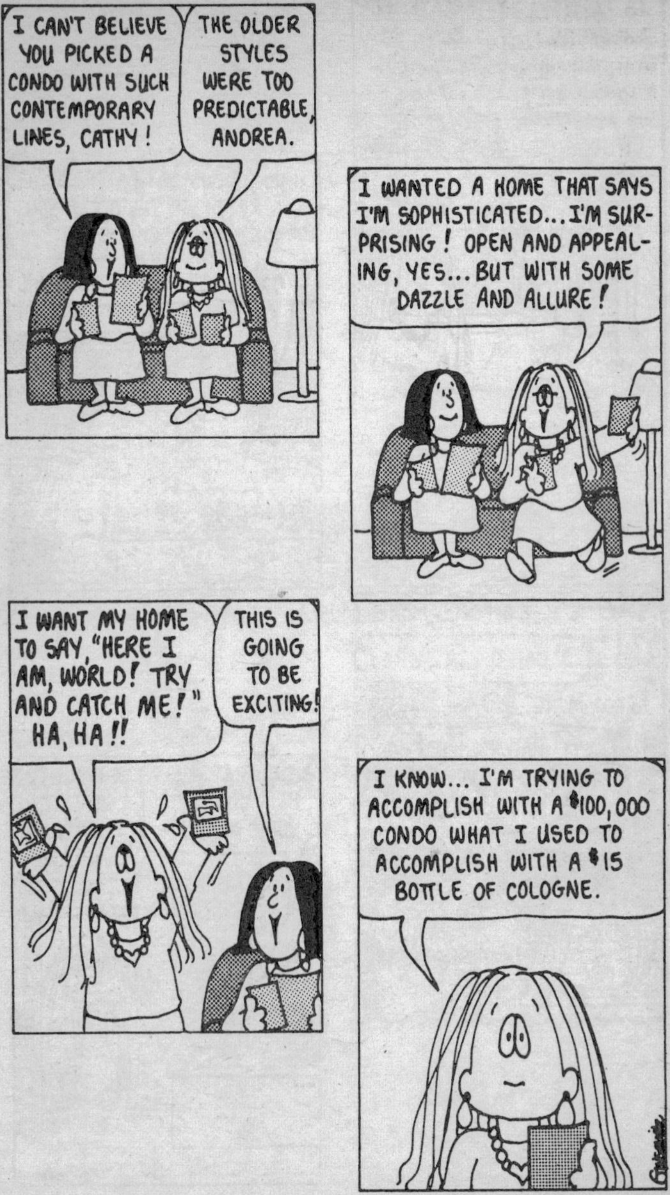
I CAN'T BELIEVE YOU PICKED A CONDO WITH SUCH CONTEMPORARY LINES, CATHY!
THE OLDER STYLES WERE TOO PREDICTABLE, ANDREA.
I WANTED A HOME THAT SAYS I'M SOPHISTICATED... I'M SURPRISING! OPEN AND APPEALING, YES... BUT WITH SOME DAZZLE AND ALLURE!
I WANT MY HOME TO SAY, "HERE I AM, WORLD! TRY AND CATCH ME!" HA, HA!!
THIS IS GOING TO BE EXCITING!
I KNOW... I'M TRYING TO ACCOMPLISH WITH A $100,000 CONDO WHAT I USED TO ACCOMPLISH WITH A $15 BOTTLE OF COLOGNE.
Guisewite

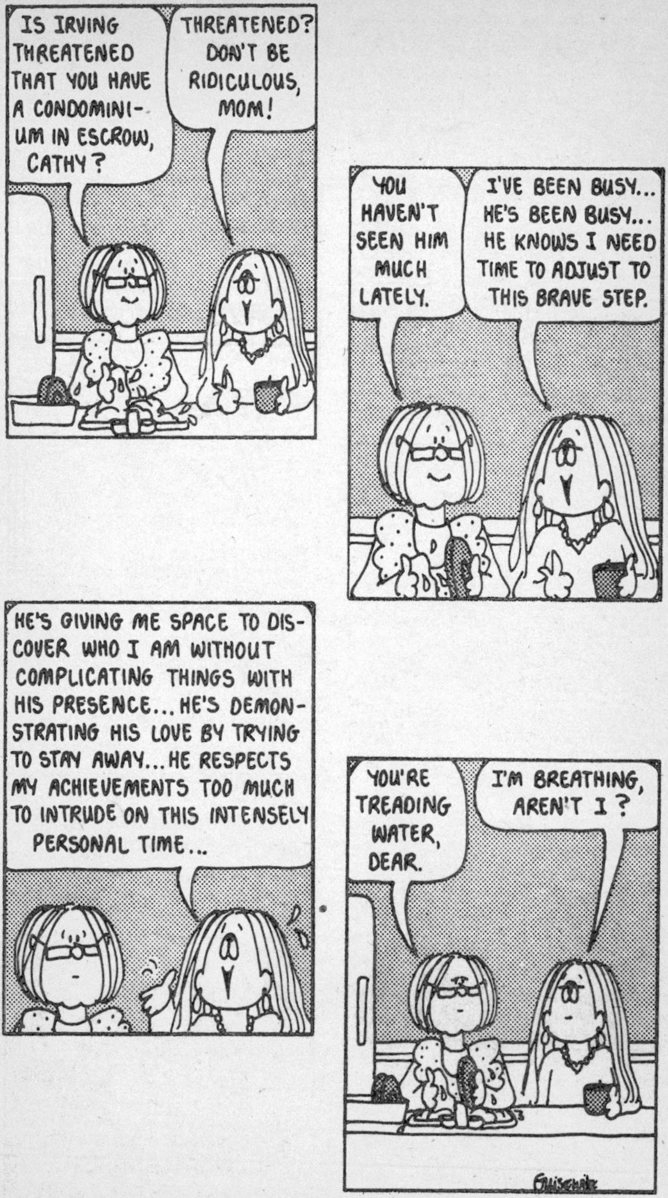
IS IRVING THREATENED THAT YOU HAVE A CONDOMINIUM IN ESCROW, CATHY?
THREATENED? DON'T BE RIDICULOUS, MOM!
YOU HAVEN'T SEEN HIM MUCH LATELY.
I'VE BEEN BUSY... HE'S BEEN BUSY... HE KNOWS I NEED TIME TO ADJUST TO THIS BRAVE STEP.
HE'S GIVING ME SPACE TO DISCOVER WHO I AM WITHOUT COMPLICATING THINGS WITH HIS PRESENCE... HE'S DEMONSTRATING HIS LOVE BY TRYING TO STAY AWAY... HE RESPECTS MY ACHIEVEMENTS TOO MUCH TO INTRUDE ON THIS INTENSELY PERSONAL TIME...
YOU'RE TREADING WATER, DEAR.
I'M BREATHING, AREN'T I?

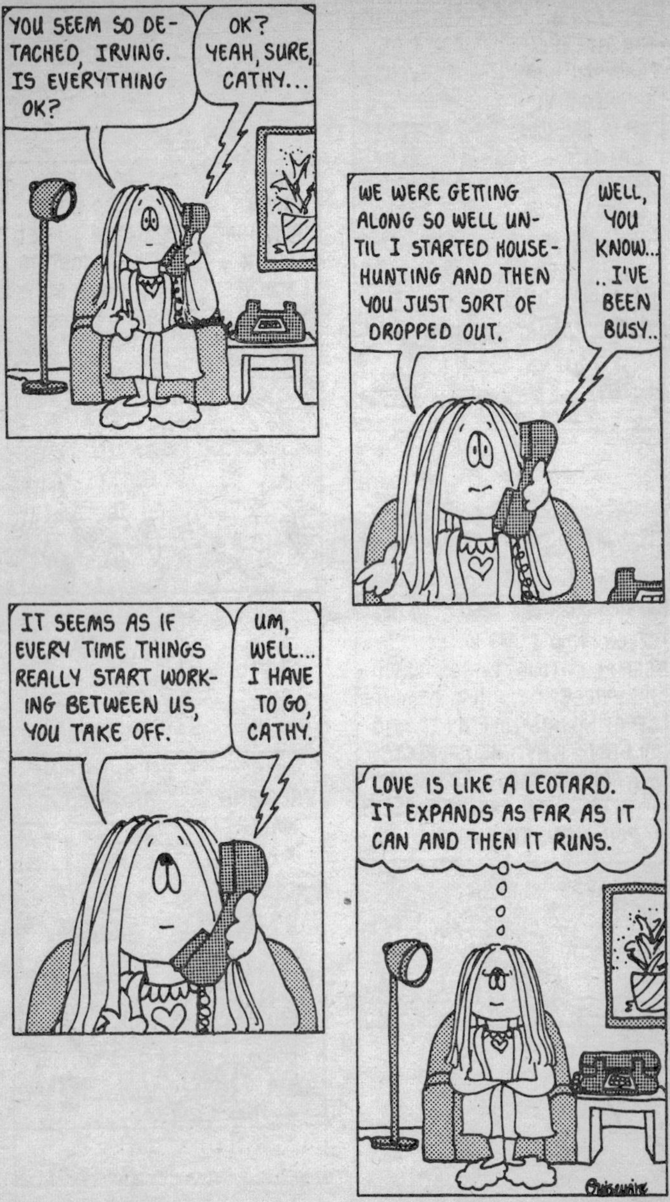
YOU SEEM SO DE-TACHED, IRVING. IS EVERYTHING OK?
OK? YEAH, SURE, CATHY...
WE WERE GETTING ALONG SO WELL UN-TIL I STARTED HOUSE-HUNTING AND THEN YOU JUST SORT OF DROPPED OUT.
WELL, YOU KNOW... ..I'VE BEEN BUSY..
IT SEEMS AS IF EVERY TIME THINGS REALLY START WORK-ING BETWEEN US, YOU TAKE OFF.
UM, WELL... I HAVE TO GO, CATHY.
LOVE IS LIKE A LEOTARD. IT EXPANDS AS FAR AS IT CAN AND THEN IT RUNS.
Guisewaite

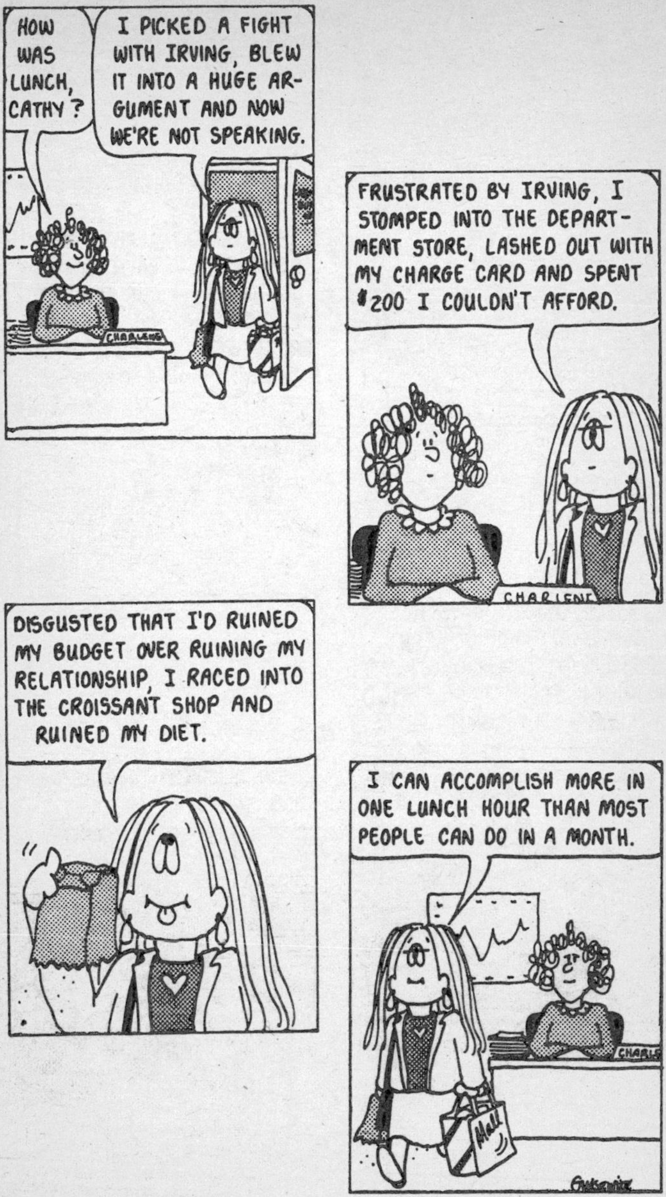

HOW WAS LUNCH, CATHY?
I PICKED A FIGHT WITH IRVING, BLEW IT INTO A HUGE ARGUMENT AND NOW WE'RE NOT SPEAKING.
FRUSTRATED BY IRVING, I STOMPED INTO THE DEPARTMENT STORE, LASHED OUT WITH MY CHARGE CARD AND SPENT $200 I COULDN'T AFFORD.
DISGUSTED THAT I'D RUINED MY BUDGET OVER RUINING MY RELATIONSHIP, I RACED INTO THE CROISSANT SHOP AND RUINED MY DIET.
I CAN ACCOMPLISH MORE IN ONE LUNCH HOUR THAN MOST PEOPLE CAN DO IN A MONTH.
Mall

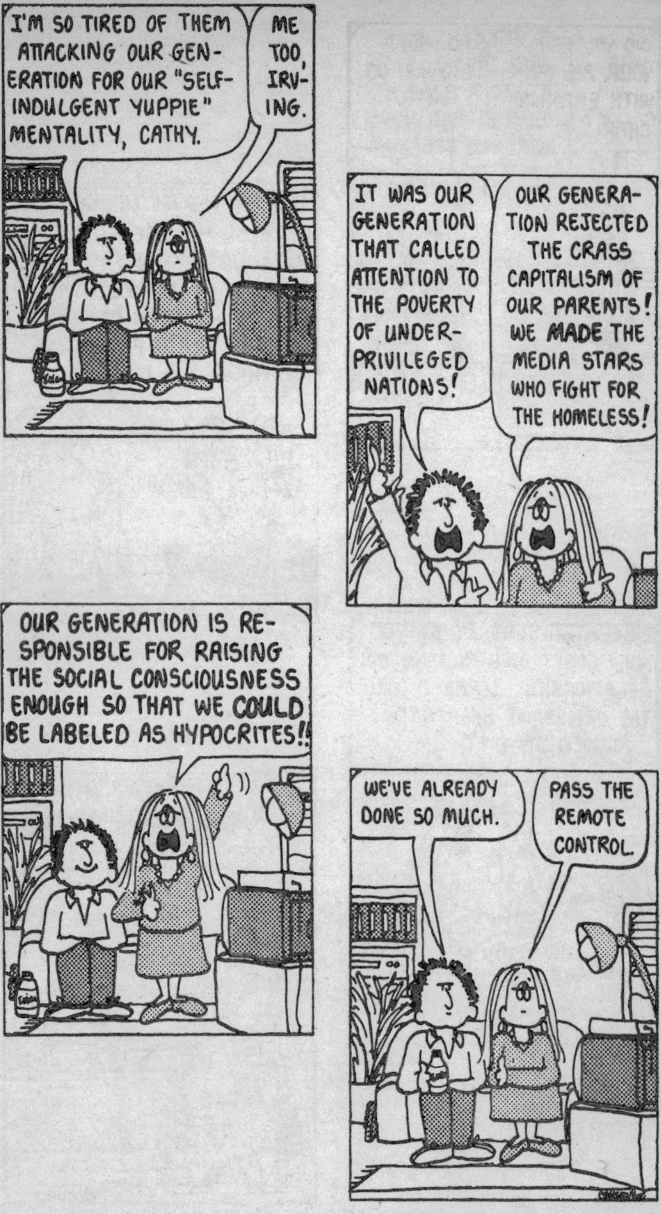
I'M SO TIRED OF THEM ATTACKING OUR GENERATION FOR OUR "SELF-INDULGENT YUPPIE" MENTALITY, CATHY.
ME TOO, IRVING.
IT WAS OUR GENERATION THAT CALLED ATTENTION TO THE POVERTY OF UNDER-PRIVILEGED NATIONS!
OUR GENERATION REJECTED THE CRASS CAPITALISM OF OUR PARENTS! WE MADE THE MEDIA STARS WHO FIGHT FOR THE HOMELESS!
OUR GENERATION IS RESPONSIBLE FOR RAISING THE SOCIAL CONSCIOUSNESS ENOUGH SO THAT WE COULD BE LABELED AS HYPOCRITES!!
WE'VE ALREADY DONE SO MUCH.
PASS THE REMOTE CONTROL.

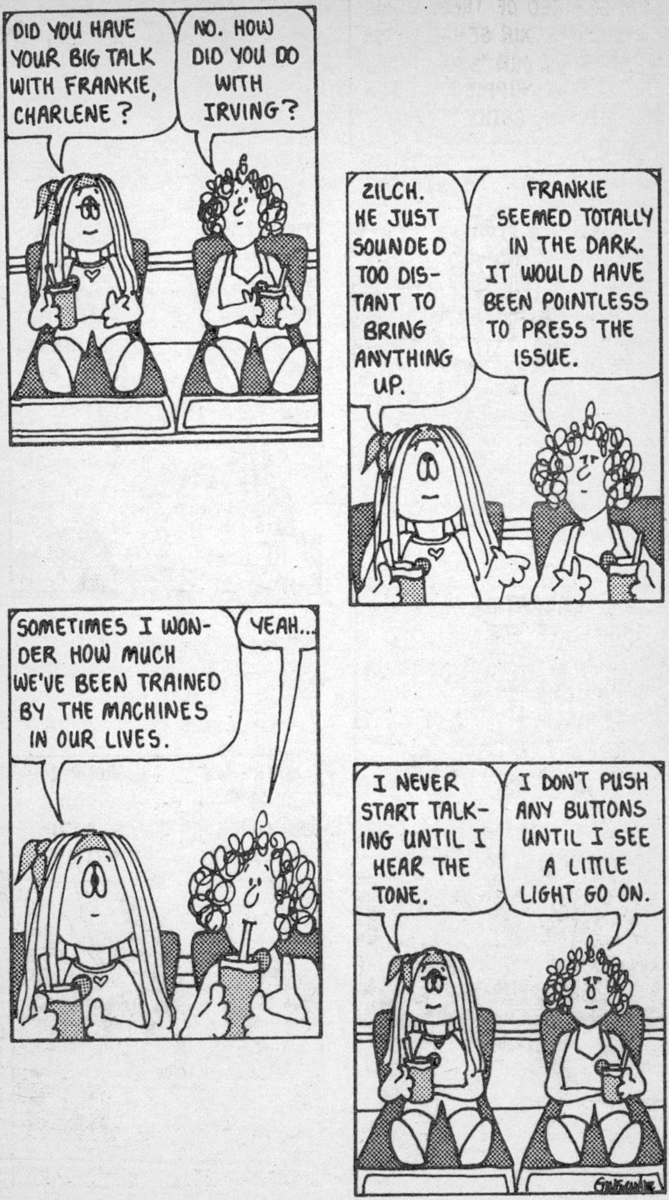
DID YOU HAVE YOUR BIG TALK WITH FRANKIE, CHARLENE?
NO. HOW DID YOU DO WITH IRVING?
ZILCH. HE JUST SOUNDED TOO DIS-TANT TO BRING ANYTHING UP.
FRANKIE SEEMED TOTALLY IN THE DARK. IT WOULD HAVE BEEN POINTLESS TO PRESS THE ISSUE.
SOMETIMES I WON-DER HOW MUCH WE'VE BEEN TRAINED BY THE MACHINES IN OUR LIVES.
YEAH...
I NEVER START TALK-ING UNTIL I HEAR THE TONE.
I DON'T PUSH ANY BUTTONS UNTIL I SEE A LITTLE LIGHT GO ON.

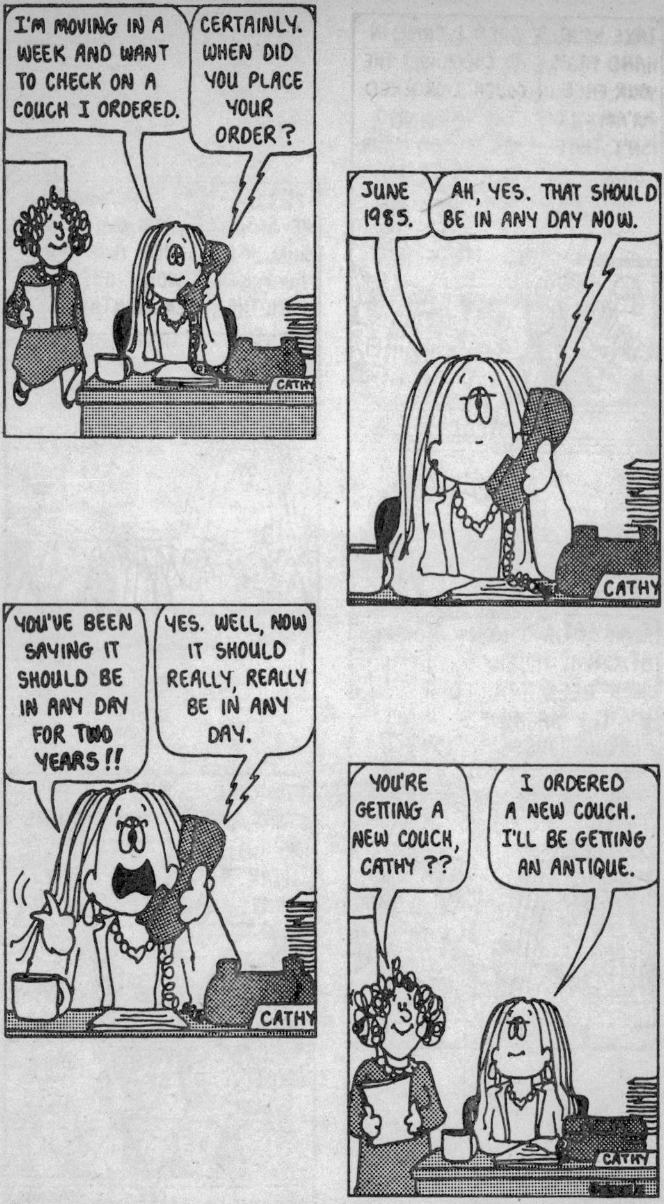
I'M MOVING IN A WEEK AND WANT TO CHECK ON A COUCH I ORDERED.
CERTAINLY. WHEN DID YOU PLACE YOUR ORDER?
CATHY
JUNE 1985.
AH, YES. THAT SHOULD BE IN ANY DAY NOW.
CATHY
YOU'VE BEEN SAYING IT SHOULD BE IN ANY DAY FOR TWO YEARS!!
YES. WELL, NOW IT SHOULD REALLY, REALLY BE IN ANY DAY.
CATHY
YOU'RE GETTING A NEW COUCH, CATHY??
I ORDERED A NEW COUCH. I'LL BE GETTING AN ANTIQUE.
CATHY

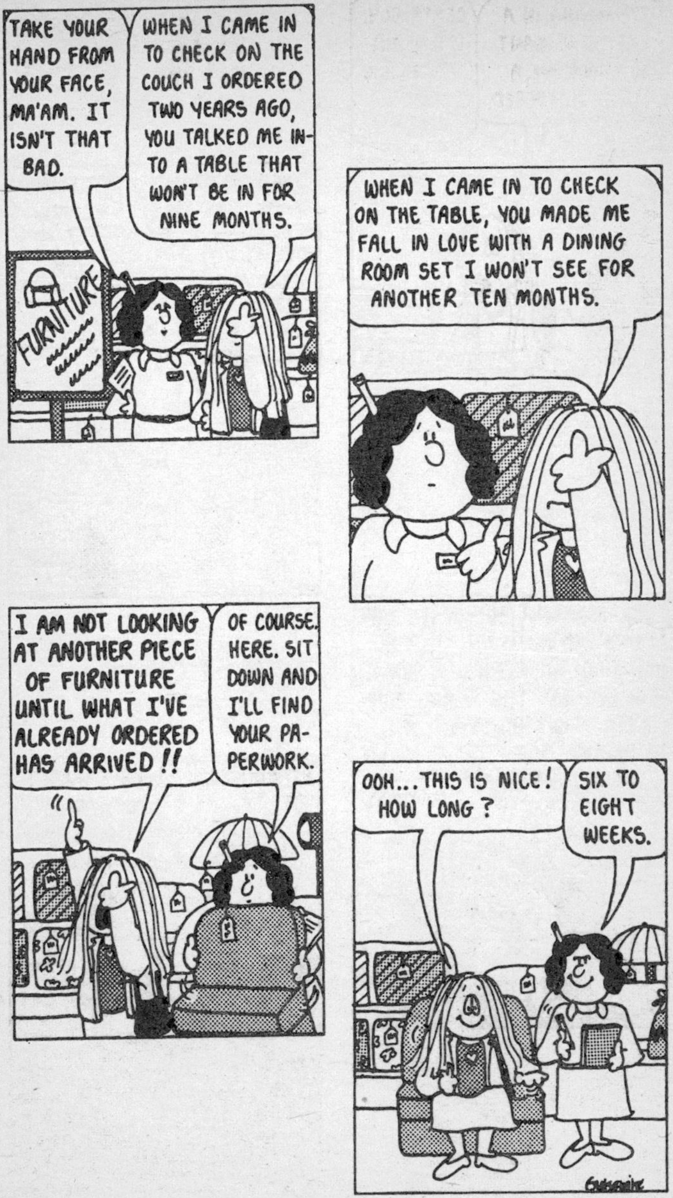
TAKE YOUR HAND FROM YOUR FACE, MA'AM. IT ISN'T THAT BAD.
WHEN I CAME IN TO CHECK ON THE COUCH I ORDERED TWO YEARS AGO, YOU TALKED ME INTO A TABLE THAT WON'T BE IN FOR NINE MONTHS.
FURNITURE
WHEN I CAME IN TO CHECK ON THE TABLE, YOU MADE ME FALL IN LOVE WITH A DINING ROOM SET I WON'T SEE FOR ANOTHER TEN MONTHS.
I AM NOT LOOKING AT ANOTHER PIECE OF FURNITURE UNTIL WHAT I'VE ALREADY ORDERED HAS ARRIVED!!
OF COURSE. HERE. SIT DOWN AND I'LL FIND YOUR PAPERWORK.
OOH... THIS IS NICE! HOW LONG?
SIX TO EIGHT WEEKS.

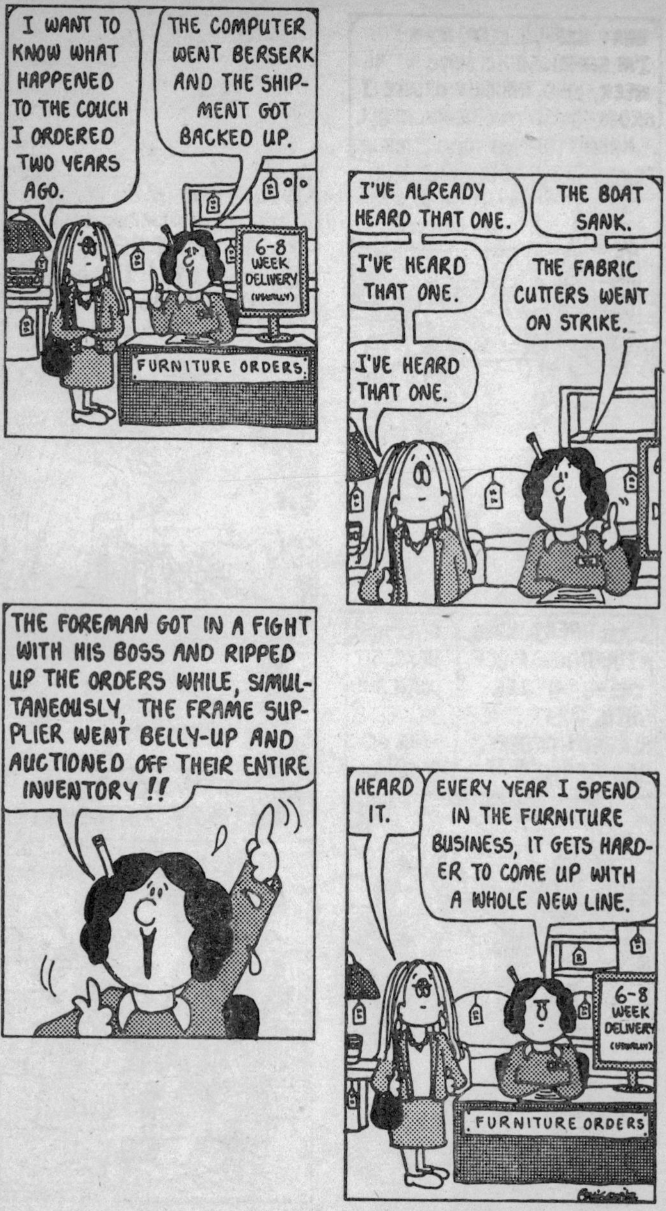
I WANT TO KNOW WHAT HAPPENED TO THE COUCH I ORDERED TWO YEARS AGO.
THE COMPUTER WENT BERSERK AND THE SHIPMENT GOT BACKED UP.
6-8 WEEK DELIVERY
FURNITURE ORDERS
I'VE ALREADY HEARD THAT ONE.
THE BOAT SANK.
I'VE HEARD THAT ONE.
THE FABRIC CUTTERS WENT ON STRIKE.
I'VE HEARD THAT ONE.
THE FOREMAN GOT IN A FIGHT WITH HIS BOSS AND RIPPED UP THE ORDERS WHILE, SIMULTANEOUSLY, THE FRAME SUPPLIER WENT BELLY-UP AND AUCTIONED OFF THEIR ENTIRE INVENTORY !!
HEARD IT.
EVERY YEAR I SPEND IN THE FURNITURE BUSINESS, IT GETS HARDER TO COME UP WITH A WHOLE NEW LINE.
6-8 WEEK DELIVERY
FURNITURE ORDERS

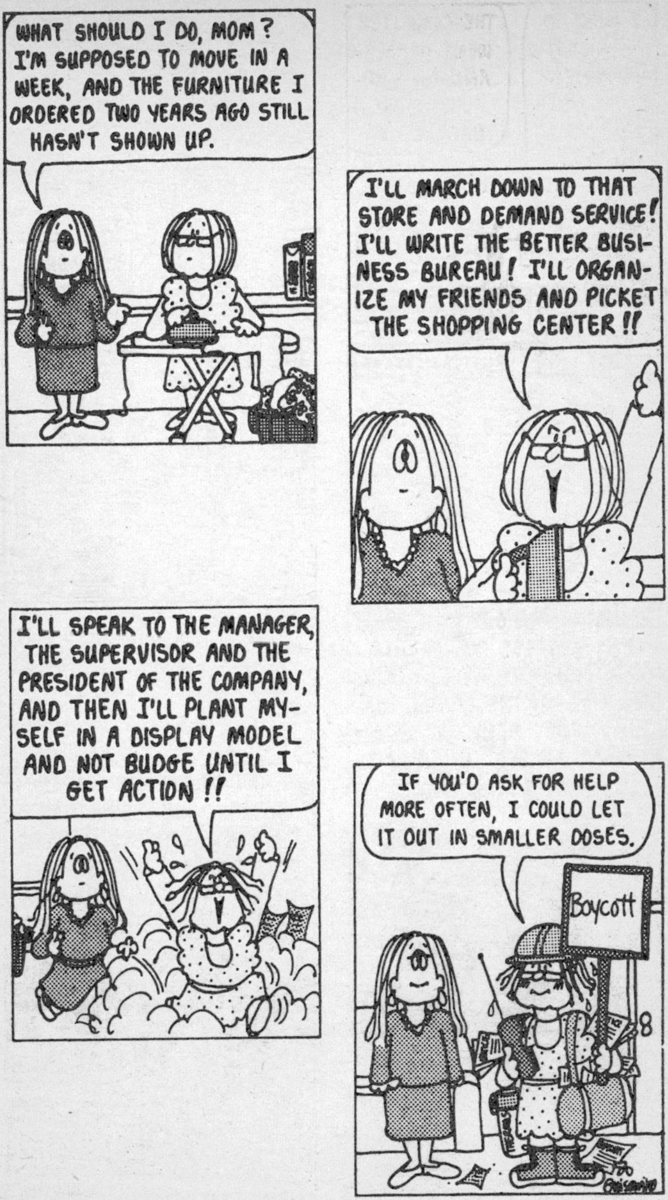

WHAT SHOULD I DO, MOM? I'M SUPPOSED TO MOVE IN A WEEK, AND THE FURNITURE I ORDERED TWO YEARS AGO STILL HASN'T SHOWN UP.
I'LL MARCH DOWN TO THAT STORE AND DEMAND SERVICE! I'LL WRITE THE BETTER BUSINESS BUREAU! I'LL ORGANIZE MY FRIENDS AND PICKET THE SHOPPING CENTER!!
I'LL SPEAK TO THE MANAGER, THE SUPERVISOR AND THE PRESIDENT OF THE COMPANY, AND THEN I'LL PLANT MYSELF IN A DISPLAY MODEL AND NOT BUDGE UNTIL I GET ACTION!!
IF YOU'D ASK FOR HELP MORE OFTEN, I COULD LET IT OUT IN SMALLER DOSES.
Boycott

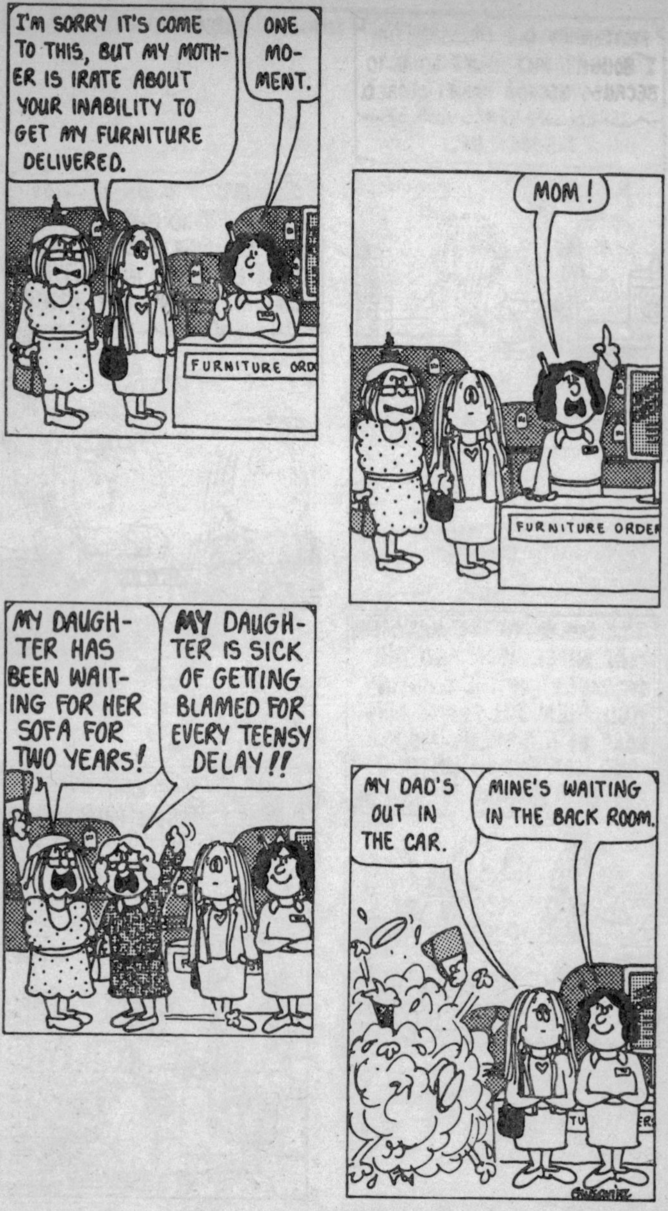

I'M SORRY IT'S COME TO THIS, BUT MY MOTHER IS IRATE ABOUT YOUR INABILITY TO GET MY FURNITURE DELIVERED.
ONE MOMENT.
FURNITURE ORD
MOM!
FURNITURE ORDER
MY DAUGHTER HAS BEEN WAITING FOR HER SOFA FOR TWO YEARS!
MY DAUGHTER IS SICK OF GETTING BLAMED FOR EVERY TEENSY DELAY!!
MY DAD'S OUT IN THE CAR.
MINE'S WAITING IN THE BACK ROOM.

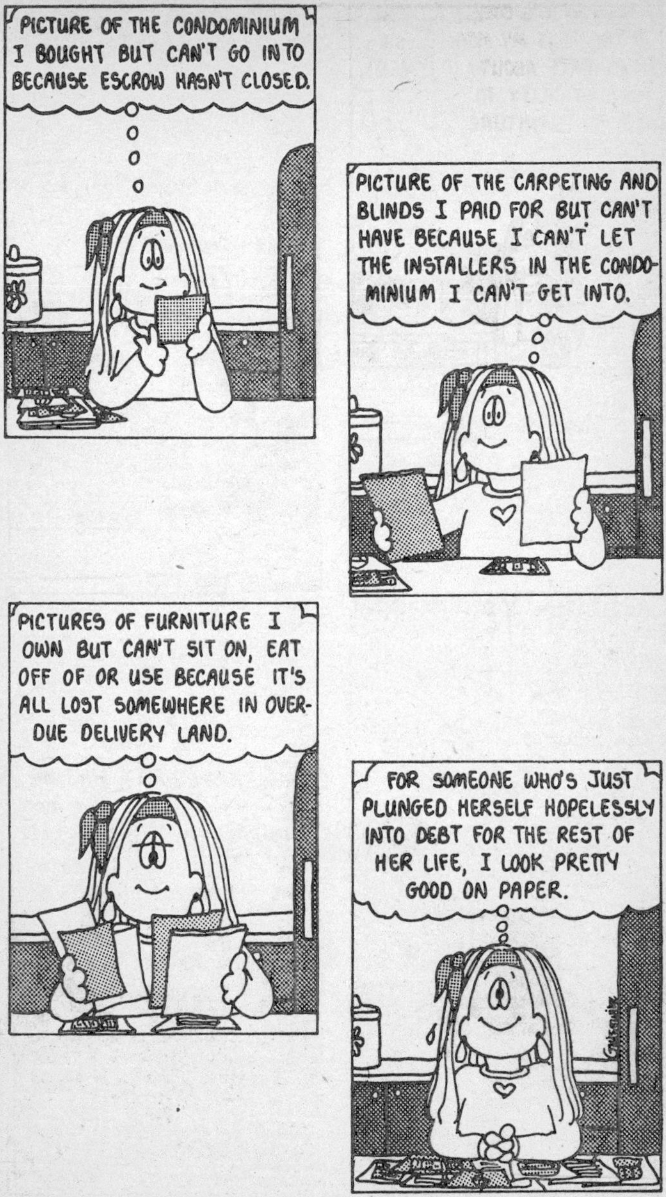
PICTURE OF THE CONDOMINIUM I BOUGHT BUT CAN'T GO INTO BECAUSE ESCROW HASN'T CLOSED.
PICTURE OF THE CARPETING AND BLINDS I PAID FOR BUT CAN'T HAVE BECAUSE I CAN'T LET THE INSTALLERS IN THE CONDOMINIUM I CAN'T GET INTO.
PICTURES OF FURNITURE I OWN BUT CAN'T SIT ON, EAT OFF OF OR USE BECAUSE IT'S ALL LOST SOMEWHERE IN OVERDUE DELIVERY LAND.
FOR SOMEONE WHO'S JUST PLUNGED HERSELF HOPELESSLY INTO DEBT FOR THE REST OF HER LIFE, I LOOK PRETTY GOOD ON PAPER.

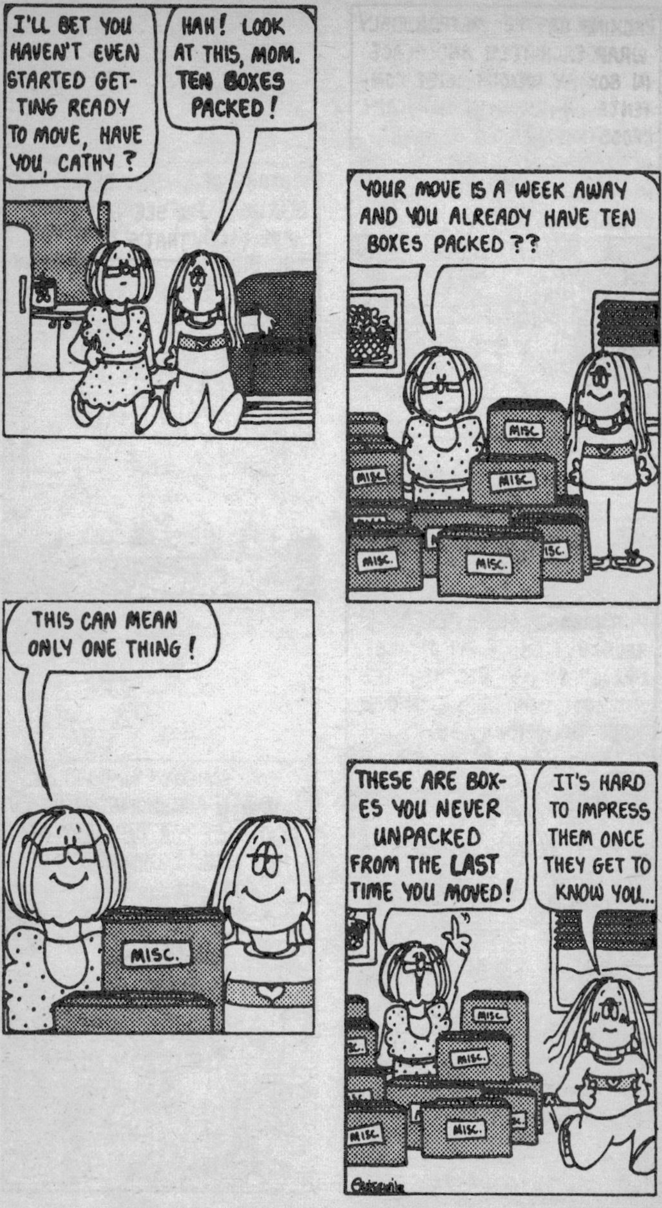
I'LL BET YOU HAVEN'T EVEN STARTED GETTING READY TO MOVE, HAVE YOU, CATHY?
HAH! LOOK AT THIS, MOM. TEN BOXES PACKED!
YOUR MOVE IS A WEEK AWAY AND YOU ALREADY HAVE TEN BOXES PACKED??
MISC.
THIS CAN MEAN ONLY ONE THING!
MISC.
THESE ARE BOXES YOU NEVER UNPACKED FROM THE LAST TIME YOU MOVED!
IT'S HARD TO IMPRESS THEM ONCE THEY GET TO KNOW YOU...
MISC.

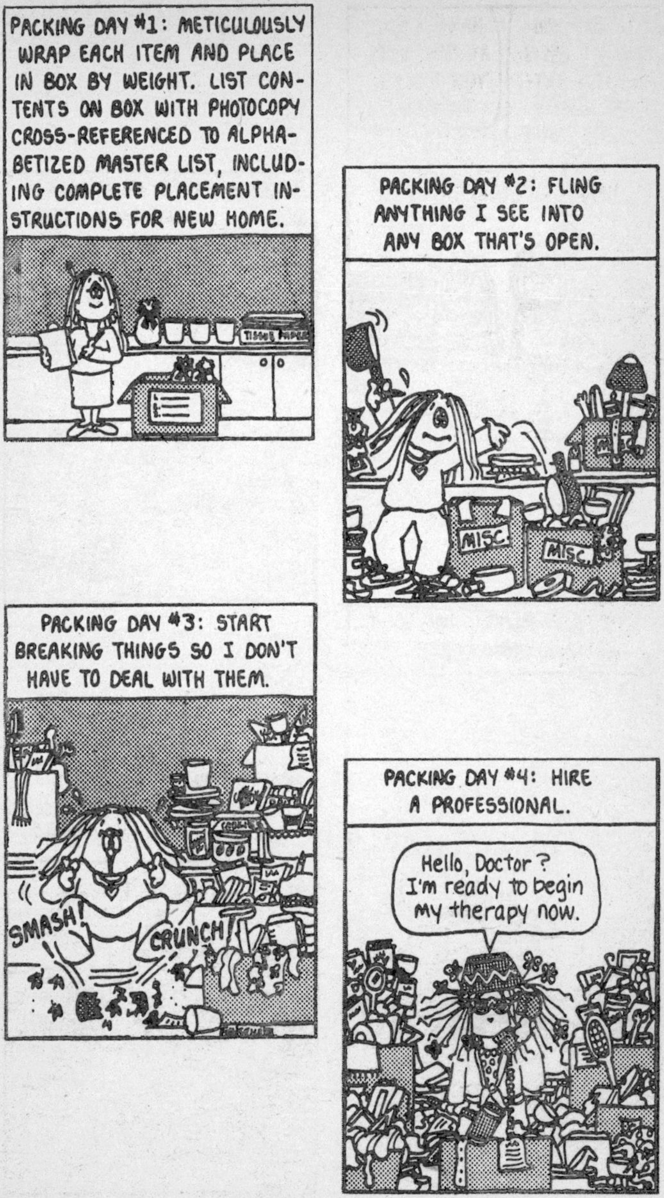
PACKING DAY #1: METICULOUSLY WRAP EACH ITEM AND PLACE IN BOX BY WEIGHT. LIST CONTENTS ON BOX WITH PHOTOCOPY CROSS-REFERENCED TO ALPHABETIZED MASTER LIST, INCLUDING COMPLETE PLACEMENT INSTRUCTIONS FOR NEW HOME.
PACKING DAY #2: FLING ANYTHING I SEE INTO ANY BOX THAT'S OPEN.
MISC.
MISC.
PACKING DAY #3: START BREAKING THINGS SO I DON'T HAVE TO DEAL WITH THEM.
SMASH!
CRUNCH!
PACKING DAY #4: HIRE A PROFESSIONAL.
Hello, Doctor? I'm ready to begin my therapy now.

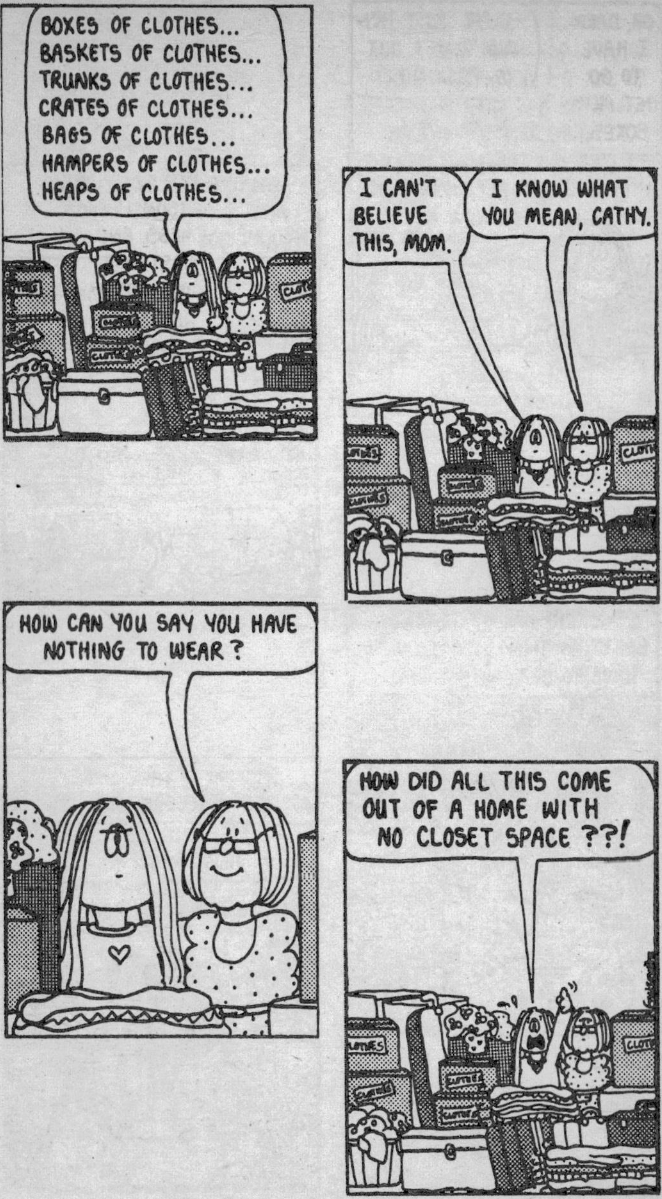
BOXES OF CLOTHES...
BASKETS OF CLOTHES...
TRUNKS OF CLOTHES...
CRATES OF CLOTHES...
BAGS OF CLOTHES...
HAMPERS OF CLOTHES...
HEAPS OF CLOTHES...
I CAN'T BELIEVE THIS, MOM.
I KNOW WHAT YOU MEAN, CATHY.
HOW CAN YOU SAY YOU HAVE NOTHING TO WEAR?
HOW DID ALL THIS COME OUT OF A HOME WITH NO CLOSET SPACE??!

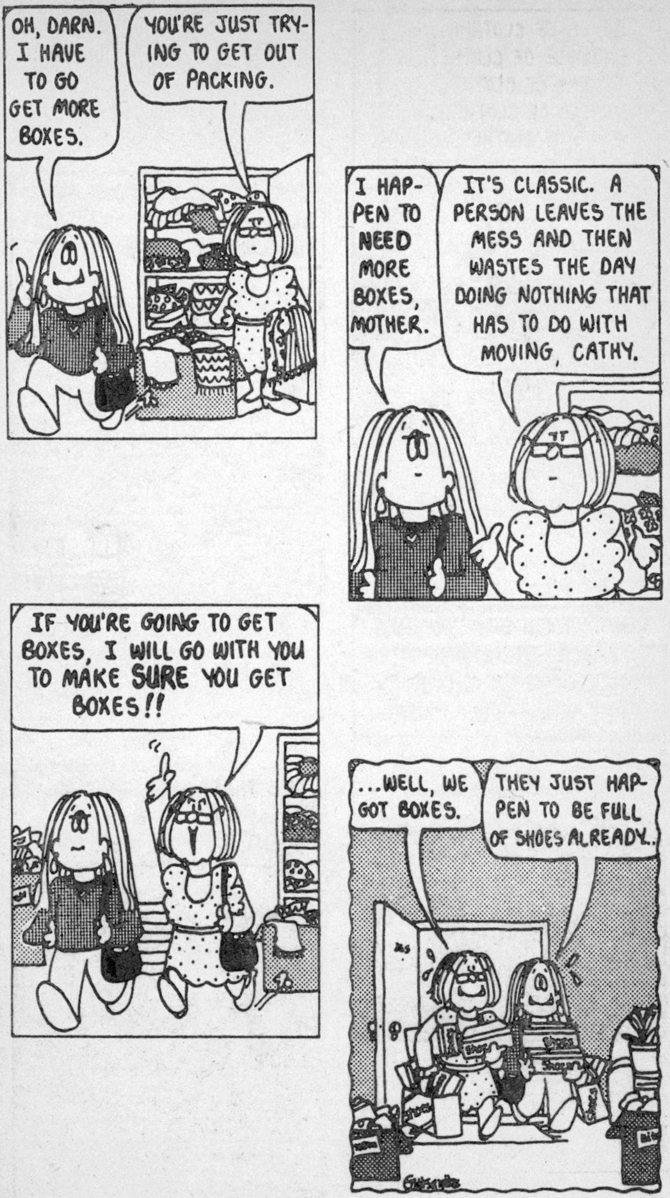

OH, DARN. I HAVE TO GO GET MORE BOXES.
YOU'RE JUST TRY-ING TO GET OUT OF PACKING.
I HAP-PEN TO NEED MORE BOXES, MOTHER.
IT'S CLASSIC. A PERSON LEAVES THE MESS AND THEN WASTES THE DAY DOING NOTHING THAT HAS TO DO WITH MOVING, CATHY.
IF YOU'RE GOING TO GET BOXES, I WILL GO WITH YOU TO MAKE SURE YOU GET BOXES!!
...WELL, WE GOT BOXES.
THEY JUST HAP-PEN TO BE FULL OF SHOES ALREADY..

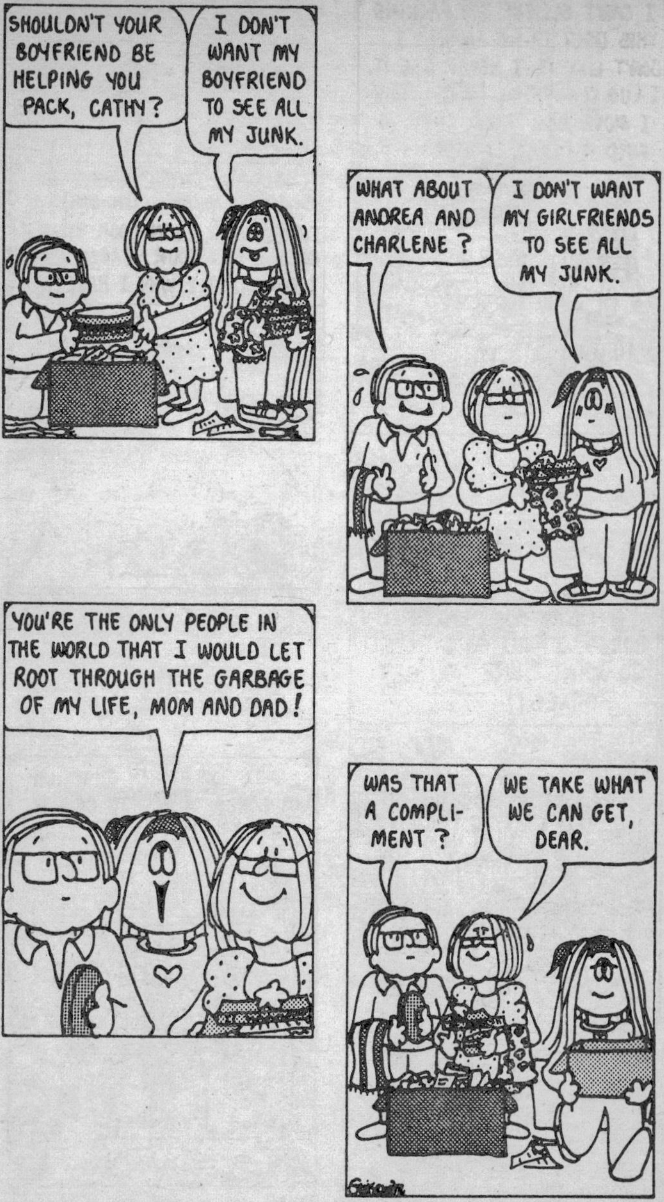
SHOULDN'T YOUR BOYFRIEND BE HELPING YOU PACK, CATHY?
I DON'T WANT MY BOYFRIEND TO SEE ALL MY JUNK.
WHAT ABOUT ANDREA AND CHARLENE?
I DON'T WANT MY GIRLFRIENDS TO SEE ALL MY JUNK.
YOU'RE THE ONLY PEOPLE IN THE WORLD THAT I WOULD LET ROOT THROUGH THE GARBAGE OF MY LIFE, MOM AND DAD!
WAS THAT A COMPLIMENT?
WE TAKE WHAT WE CAN GET, DEAR.

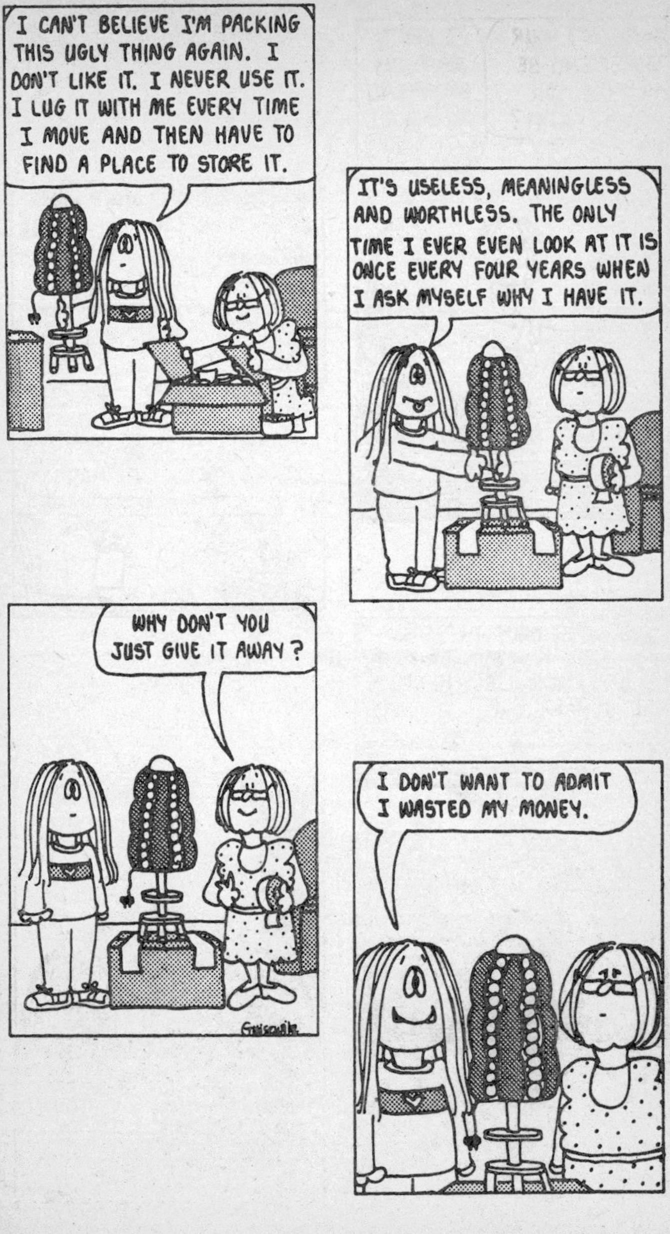
I CAN'T BELIEVE I'M PACKING THIS UGLY THING AGAIN. I DON'T LIKE IT. I NEVER USE IT. I LUG IT WITH ME EVERY TIME I MOVE AND THEN HAVE TO FIND A PLACE TO STORE IT.
IT'S USELESS, MEANINGLESS AND WORTHLESS. THE ONLY TIME I EVER EVEN LOOK AT IT IS ONCE EVERY FOUR YEARS WHEN I ASK MYSELF WHY I HAVE IT.
WHY DON'T YOU JUST GIVE IT AWAY?
I DON'T WANT TO ADMIT I WASTED MY MONEY.

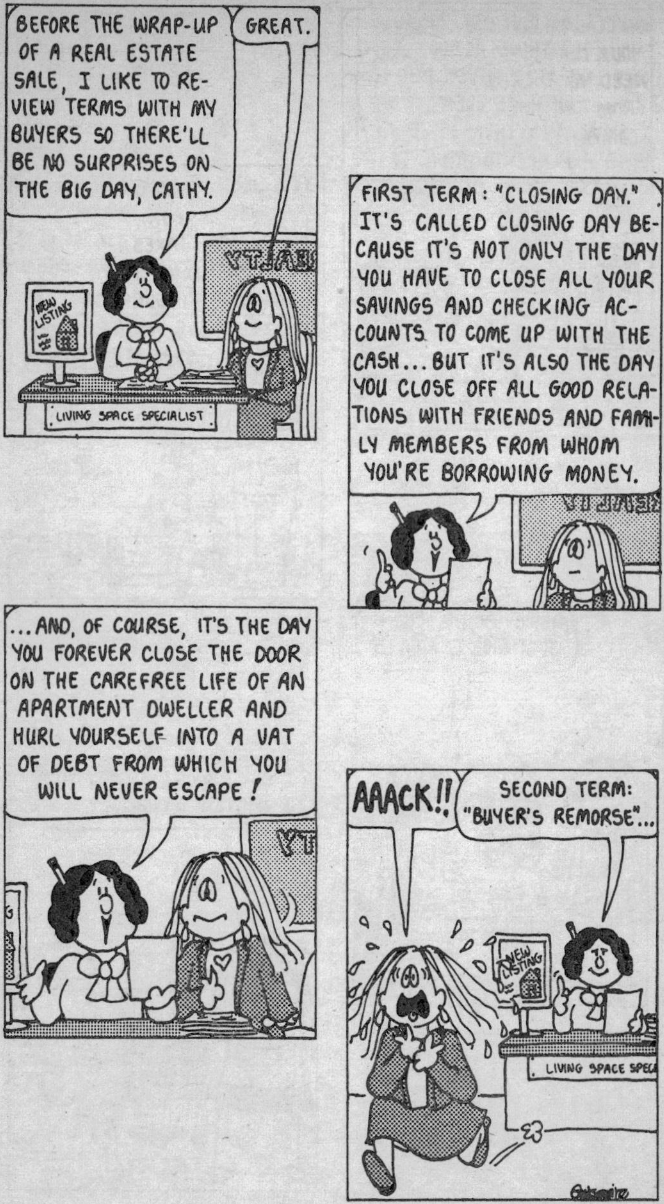
BEFORE THE WRAP-UP OF A REAL ESTATE SALE, I LIKE TO REVIEW TERMS WITH MY BUYERS SO THERE'LL BE NO SURPRISES ON THE BIG DAY, CATHY.
GREAT.
NEW LISTING
LIVING SPACE SPECIALIST
FIRST TERM: "CLOSING DAY." IT'S CALLED CLOSING DAY BECAUSE IT'S NOT ONLY THE DAY YOU HAVE TO CLOSE ALL YOUR SAVINGS AND CHECKING ACCOUNTS TO COME UP WITH THE CASH... BUT IT'S ALSO THE DAY YOU CLOSE OFF ALL GOOD RELATIONS WITH FRIENDS AND FAMILY MEMBERS FROM WHOM YOU'RE BORROWING MONEY.
...AND, OF COURSE, IT'S THE DAY YOU FOREVER CLOSE THE DOOR ON THE CAREFREE LIFE OF AN APARTMENT DWELLER AND HURL YOURSELF INTO A VAT OF DEBT FROM WHICH YOU WILL NEVER ESCAPE!
AAACK!!
SECOND TERM: "BUYER'S REMORSE"...
NEW LISTING
LIVING SPACE SPEC

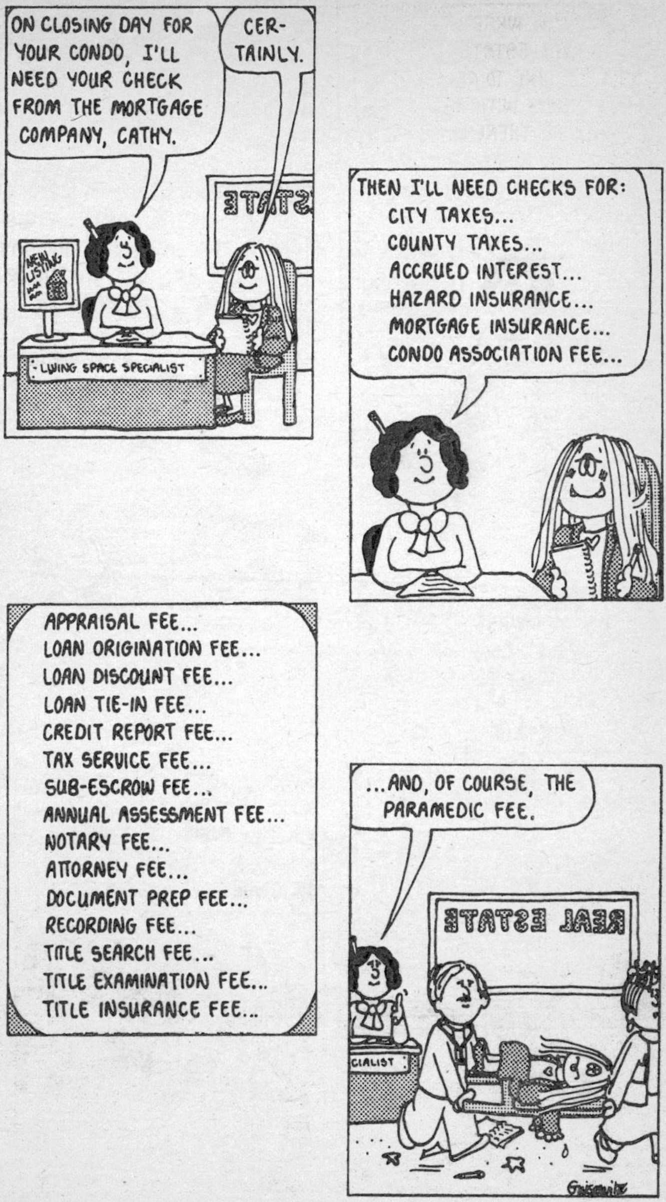
ON CLOSING DAY FOR YOUR CONDO, I'LL NEED YOUR CHECK FROM THE MORTGAGE COMPANY, CATHY.
CER-TAINLY.
NEW LISTING
LIVING SPACE SPECIALIST
THEN I'LL NEED CHECKS FOR:
CITY TAXES...
COUNTY TAXES...
ACCRUED INTEREST...
HAZARD INSURANCE...
MORTGAGE INSURANCE...
CONDO ASSOCIATION FEE...
APPRAISAL FEE...
LOAN ORIGINATION FEE...
LOAN DISCOUNT FEE...
LOAN TIE-IN FEE...
CREDIT REPORT FEE...
TAX SERVICE FEE...
SUB-ESCROW FEE...
ANNUAL ASSESSMENT FEE...
NOTARY FEE...
ATTORNEY FEE...
DOCUMENT PREP FEE...
RECORDING FEE...
TITLE SEARCH FEE...
TITLE EXAMINATION FEE...
TITLE INSURANCE FEE...
...AND, OF COURSE, THE PARAMEDIC FEE.
CIALIST
Guisewite

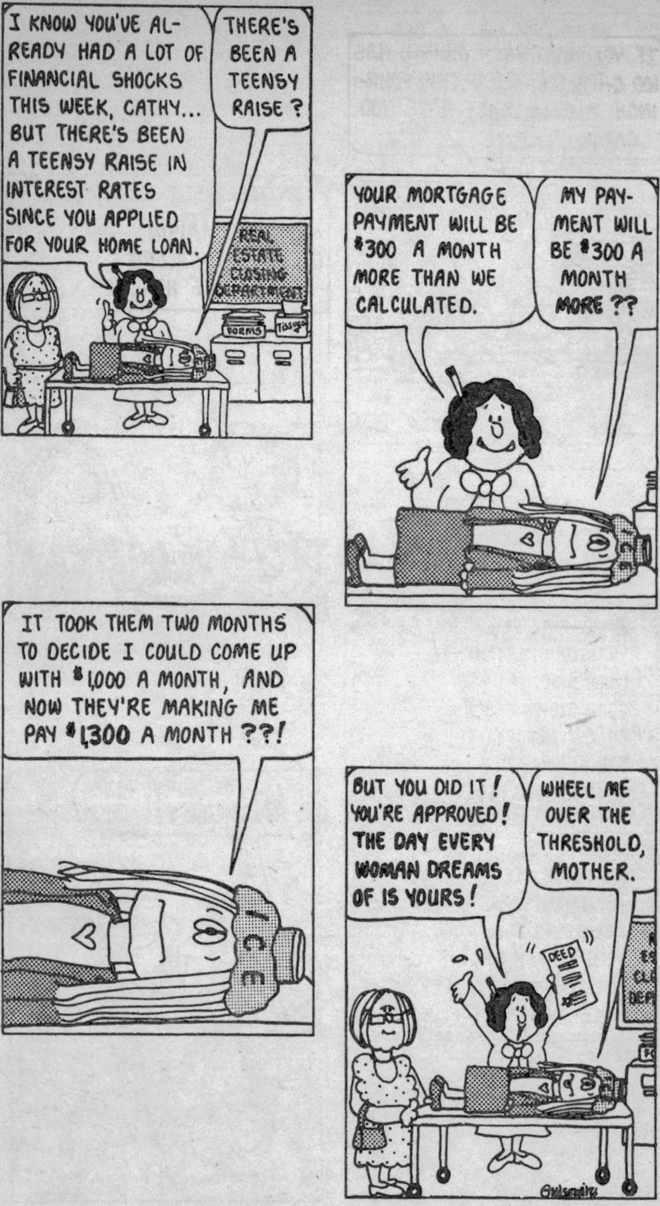
I KNOW YOU'VE ALREADY HAD A LOT OF FINANCIAL SHOCKS THIS WEEK, CATHY... BUT THERE'S BEEN A TEENSY RAISE IN INTEREST RATES SINCE YOU APPLIED FOR YOUR HOME LOAN.
THERE'S BEEN A TEENSY RAISE ?
REAL ESTATE CLOSING DEPARTMENT
FORMS
Tissues
YOUR MORTGAGE PAYMENT WILL BE $300 A MONTH MORE THAN WE CALCULATED.
MY PAYMENT WILL BE $300 A MONTH MORE ??
IT TOOK THEM TWO MONTHS TO DECIDE I COULD COME UP WITH $1,000 A MONTH, AND NOW THEY'RE MAKING ME PAY $1,300 A MONTH ??!
BUT YOU DID IT! YOU'RE APPROVED! THE DAY EVERY WOMAN DREAMS OF IS YOURS!
WHEEL ME OVER THE THRESHOLD, MOTHER.
DEED
Guisewite

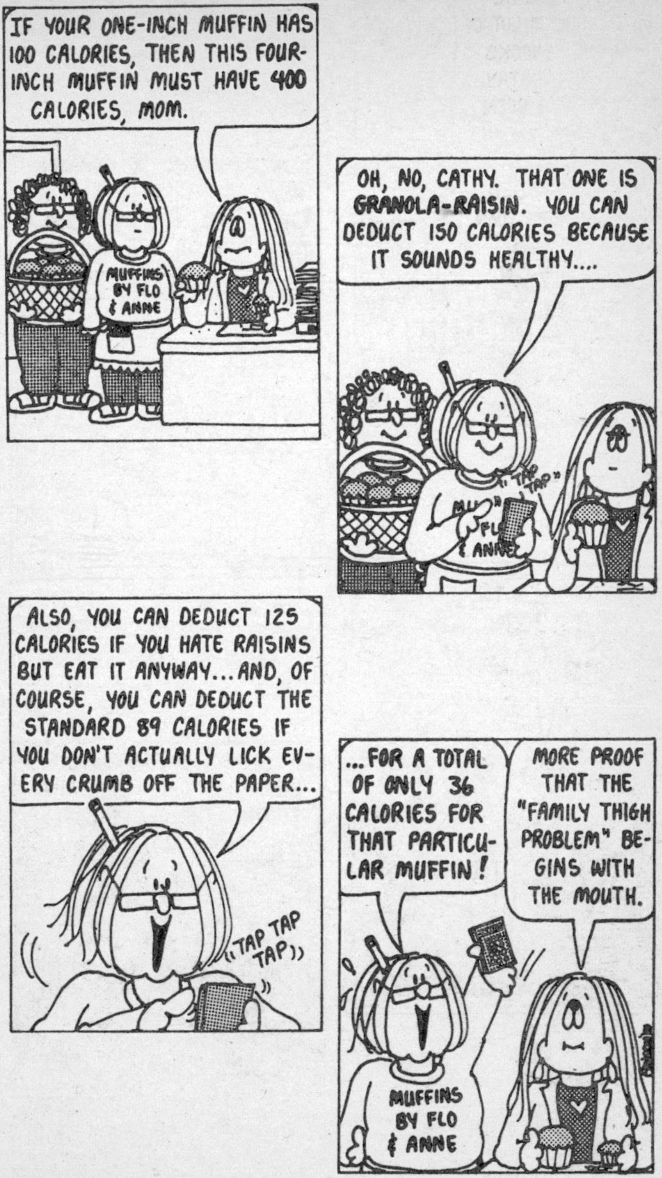

IF YOUR ONE-INCH MUFFIN HAS 100 CALORIES, THEN THIS FOUR-INCH MUFFIN MUST HAVE 400 CALORIES, MOM.
MUFFINS BY FLO & ANNE
OH, NO, CATHY. THAT ONE IS GRANOLA-RAISIN. YOU CAN DEDUCT 150 CALORIES BECAUSE IT SOUNDS HEALTHY....
"TAP TAP"
ALSO, YOU CAN DEDUCT 125 CALORIES IF YOU HATE RAISINS BUT EAT IT ANYWAY...AND, OF COURSE, YOU CAN DEDUCT THE STANDARD 89 CALORIES IF YOU DON'T ACTUALLY LICK EVERY CRUMB OFF THE PAPER...
"TAP TAP TAP"
...FOR A TOTAL OF ONLY 36 CALORIES FOR THAT PARTICULAR MUFFIN!
MORE PROOF THAT THE "FAMILY THIGH PROBLEM" BEGINS WITH THE MOUTH.
MUFFINS BY FLO & ANNE

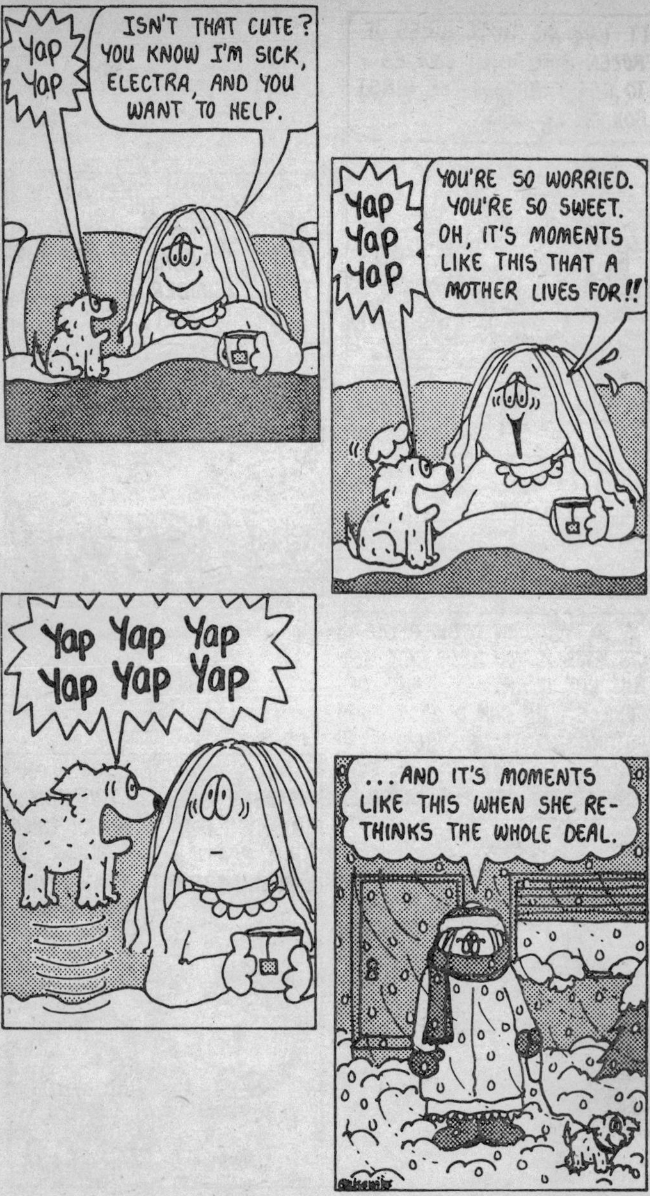
Yap Yap
ISN'T THAT CUTE? YOU KNOW I'M SICK, ELECTRA, AND YOU WANT TO HELP.
Yap Yap Yap
YOU'RE SO WORRIED. YOU'RE SO SWEET. OH, IT'S MOMENTS LIKE THIS THAT A MOTHER LIVES FOR!!
Yap Yap Yap Yap Yap Yap
...AND IT'S MOMENTS LIKE THIS WHEN SHE RE-THINKS THE WHOLE DEAL.

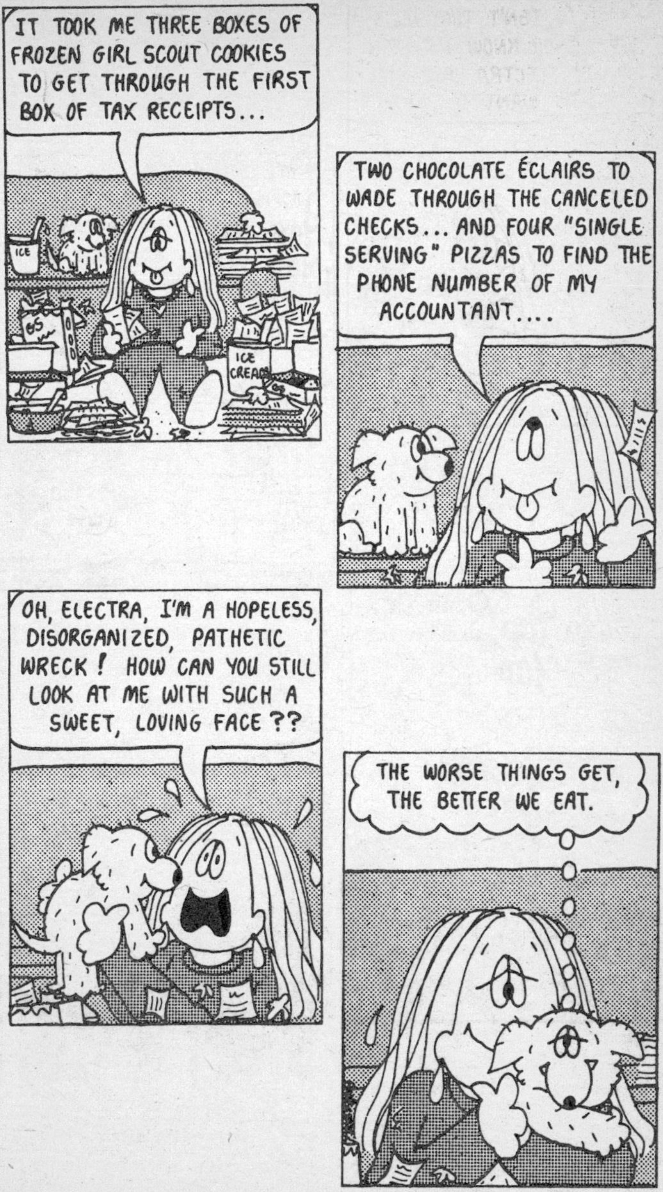
IT TOOK ME THREE BOXES OF FROZEN GIRL SCOUT COOKIES TO GET THROUGH THE FIRST BOX OF TAX RECEIPTS...
ICE
TWO CHOCOLATE ÉCLAIRS TO WADE THROUGH THE CANCELED CHECKS... AND FOUR "SINGLE SERVING" PIZZAS TO FIND THE PHONE NUMBER OF MY ACCOUNTANT....
OH, ELECTRA, I'M A HOPELESS, DISORGANIZED, PATHETIC WRECK! HOW CAN YOU STILL LOOK AT ME WITH SUCH A SWEET, LOVING FACE??
THE WORSE THINGS GET, THE BETTER WE EAT.

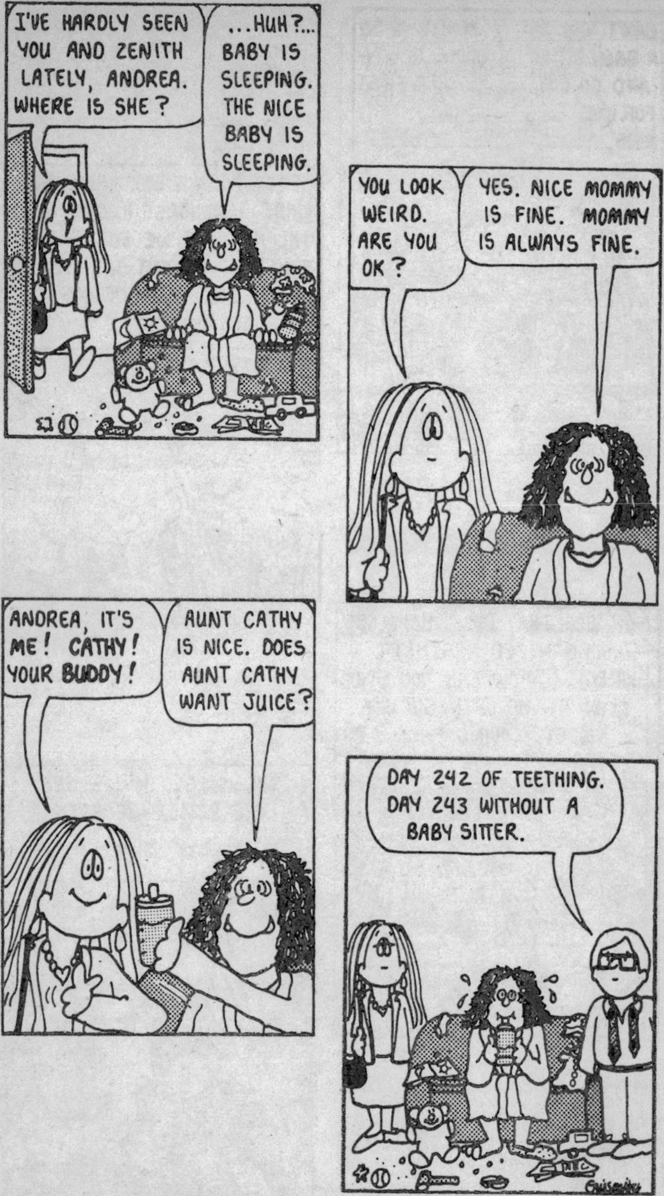

I'VE HARDLY SEEN YOU AND ZENITH LATELY, ANDREA. WHERE IS SHE?
...HUH?... BABY IS SLEEPING. THE NICE BABY IS SLEEPING.
YOU LOOK WEIRD. ARE YOU OK?
YES. NICE MOMMY IS FINE. MOMMY IS ALWAYS FINE.
ANDREA, IT'S ME! CATHY! YOUR BUDDY!
AUNT CATHY IS NICE. DOES AUNT CATHY WANT JUICE?
DAY 242 OF TEETHING. DAY 243 WITHOUT A BABY SITTER.

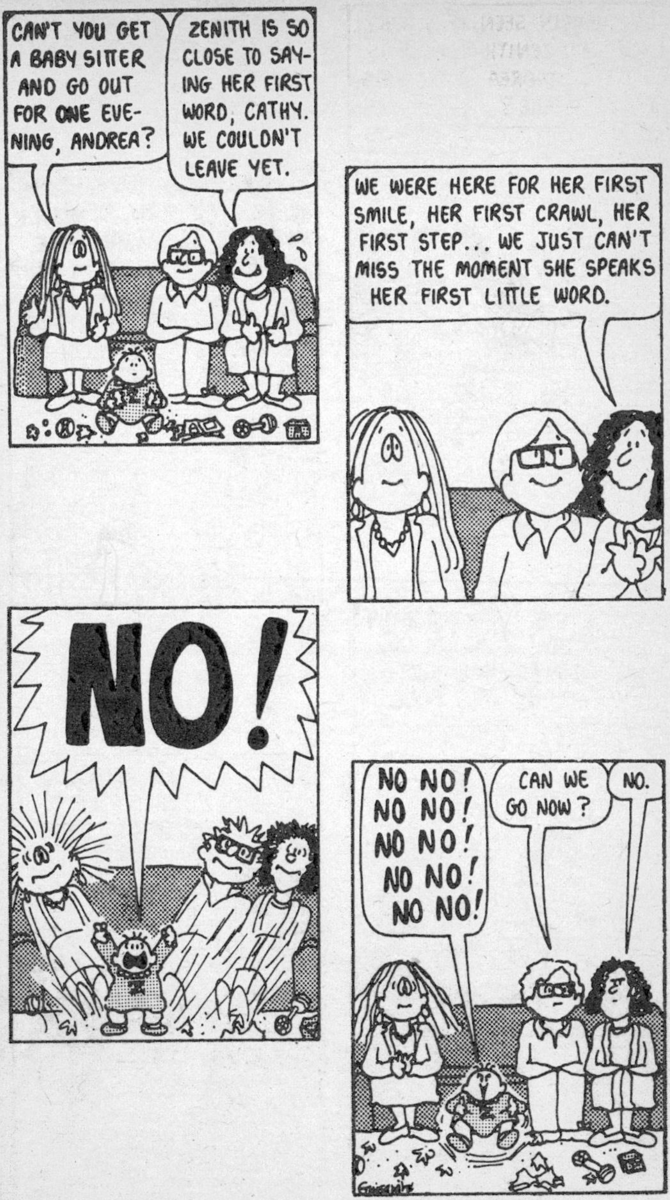
CAN'T YOU GET A BABY SITTER AND GO OUT FOR ONE EVENING, ANDREA?
ZENITH IS SO CLOSE TO SAYING HER FIRST WORD, CATHY. WE COULDN'T LEAVE YET.
WE WERE HERE FOR HER FIRST SMILE, HER FIRST CRAWL, HER FIRST STEP... WE JUST CAN'T MISS THE MOMENT SHE SPEAKS HER FIRST LITTLE WORD.
NO!
NO NO! NO NO! NO NO! NO NO! NO NO!
CAN WE GO NOW?
NO.

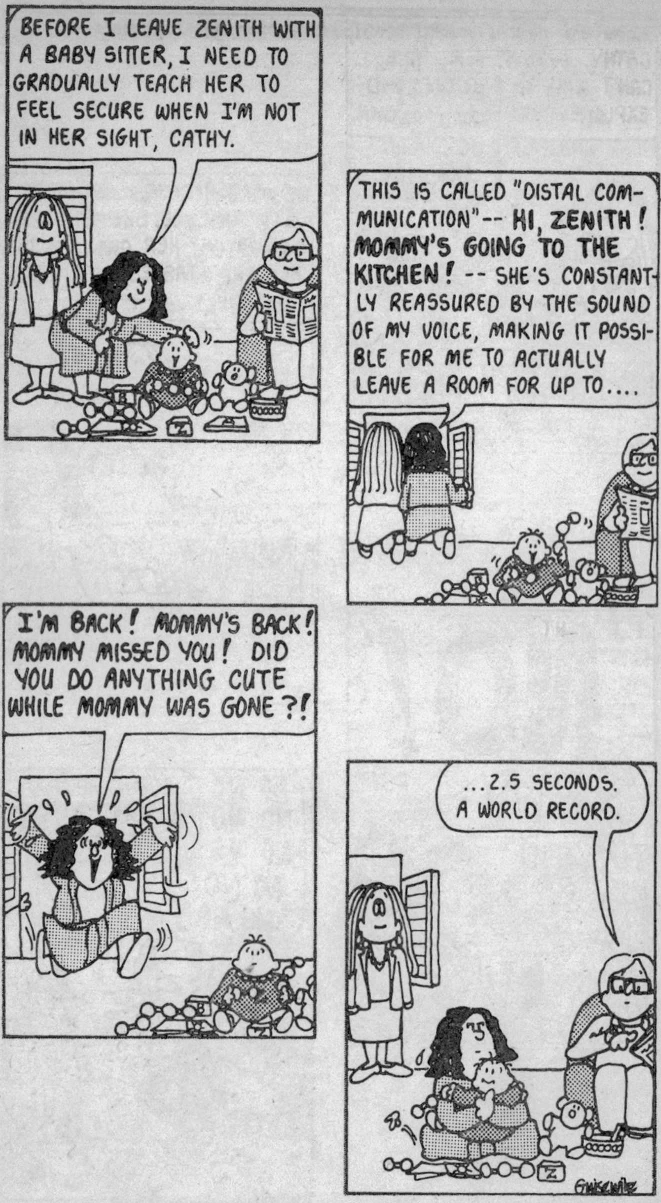
BEFORE I LEAVE ZENITH WITH A BABY SITTER, I NEED TO GRADUALLY TEACH HER TO FEEL SECURE WHEN I'M NOT IN HER SIGHT, CATHY.
THIS IS CALLED "DISTAL COMMUNICATION"-- HI, ZENITH! MOMMY'S GOING TO THE KITCHEN! -- SHE'S CONSTANTLY REASSURED BY THE SOUND OF MY VOICE, MAKING IT POSSIBLE FOR ME TO ACTUALLY LEAVE A ROOM FOR UP TO....
I'M BACK! MOMMY'S BACK! MOMMY MISSED YOU! DID YOU DO ANYTHING CUTE WHILE MOMMY WAS GONE?!
...2.5 SECONDS. A WORLD RECORD.
GUISEWITE

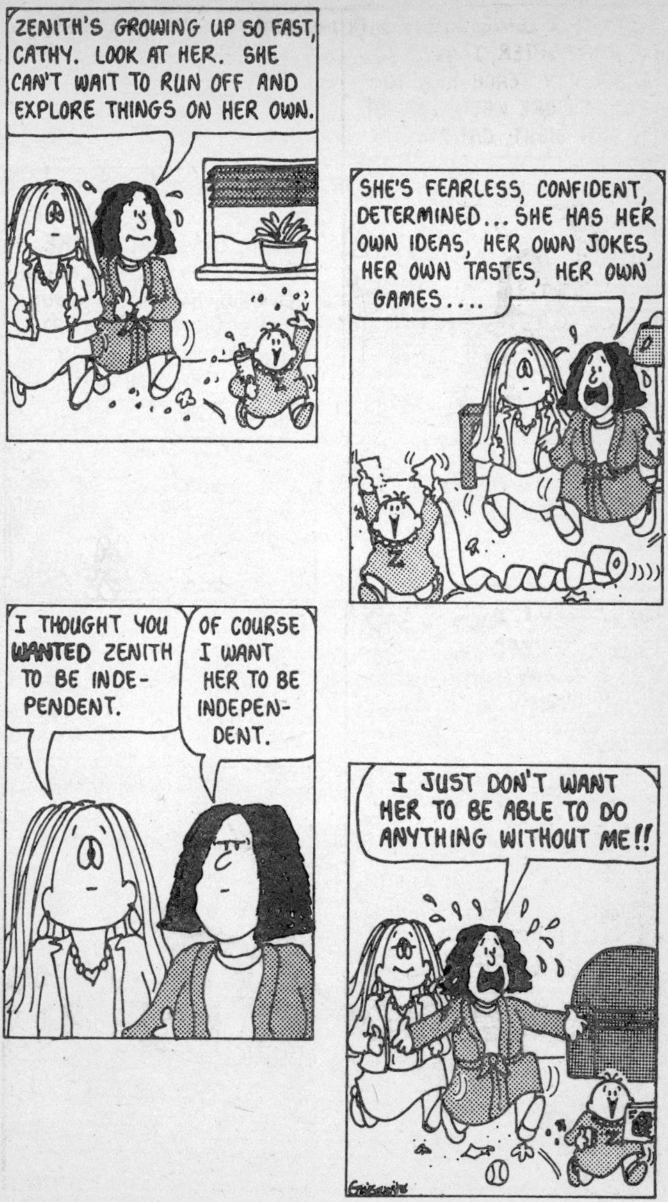
ZENITH'S GROWING UP SO FAST, CATHY. LOOK AT HER. SHE CAN'T WAIT TO RUN OFF AND EXPLORE THINGS ON HER OWN.
SHE'S FEARLESS, CONFIDENT, DETERMINED... SHE HAS HER OWN IDEAS, HER OWN JOKES, HER OWN TASTES, HER OWN GAMES....
I THOUGHT YOU WANTED ZENITH TO BE INDE-PENDENT.
OF COURSE I WANT HER TO BE INDEPEN-DENT.
I JUST DON'T WANT HER TO BE ABLE TO DO ANYTHING WITHOUT ME!!

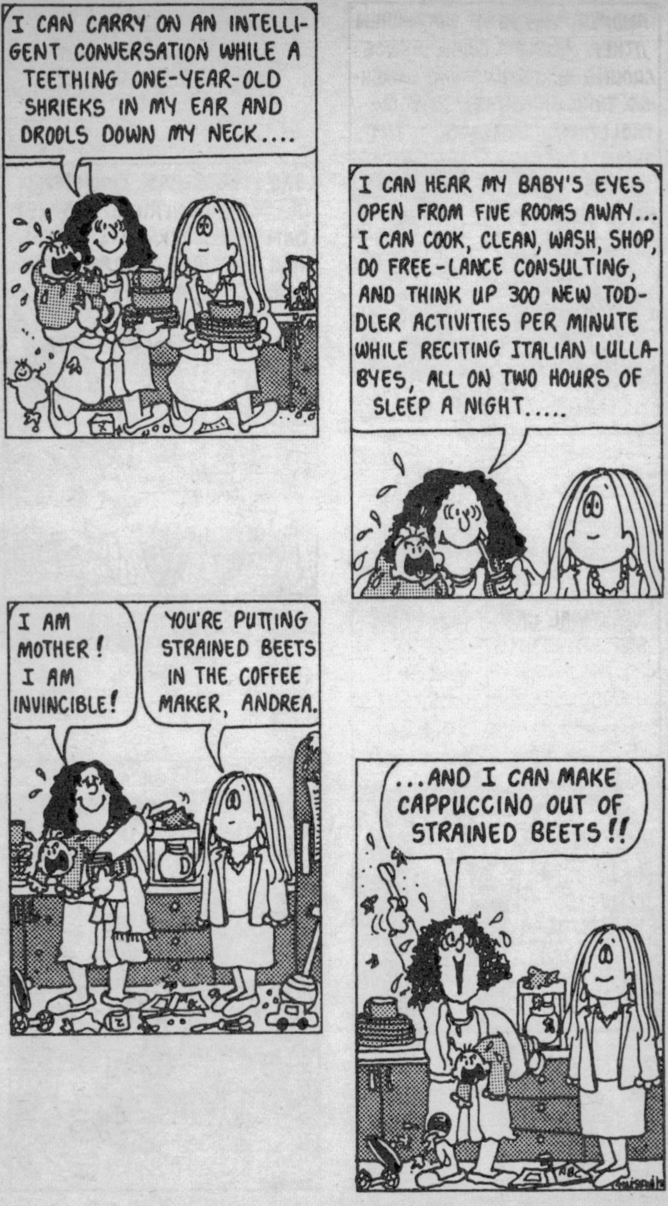
I CAN CARRY ON AN INTELLIGENT CONVERSATION WHILE A TEETHING ONE-YEAR-OLD SHRIEKS IN MY EAR AND DROOLS DOWN MY NECK....
I CAN HEAR MY BABY'S EYES OPEN FROM FIVE ROOMS AWAY... I CAN COOK, CLEAN, WASH, SHOP, DO FREE-LANCE CONSULTING, AND THINK UP 300 NEW TODDLER ACTIVITIES PER MINUTE WHILE RECITING ITALIAN LULLABYES, ALL ON TWO HOURS OF SLEEP A NIGHT.....
I AM MOTHER! I AM INVINCIBLE!
YOU'RE PUTTING STRAINED BEETS IN THE COFFEE MAKER, ANDREA.
...AND I CAN MAKE CAPPUCCINO OUT OF STRAINED BEETS!!

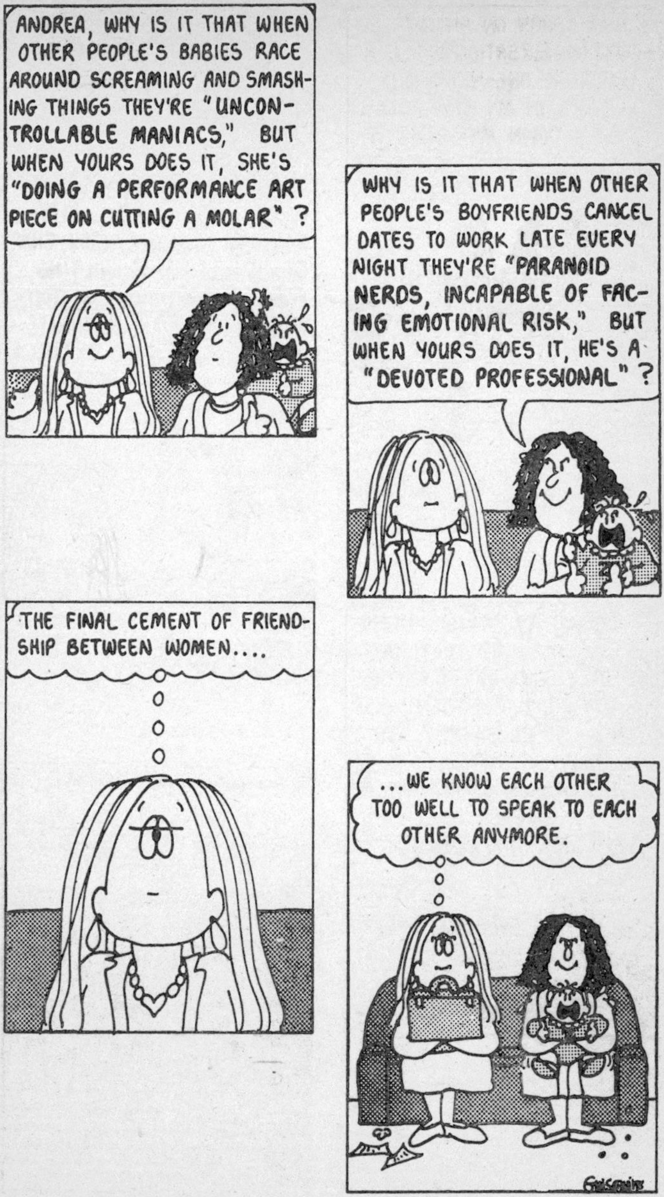
ANDREA, WHY IS IT THAT WHEN OTHER PEOPLE'S BABIES RACE AROUND SCREAMING AND SMASHING THINGS THEY'RE "UNCONTROLLABLE MANIACS," BUT WHEN YOURS DOES IT, SHE'S "DOING A PERFORMANCE ART PIECE ON CUTTING A MOLAR"?
WHY IS IT THAT WHEN OTHER PEOPLE'S BOYFRIENDS CANCEL DATES TO WORK LATE EVERY NIGHT THEY'RE "PARANOID NERDS, INCAPABLE OF FACING EMOTIONAL RISK," BUT WHEN YOURS DOES IT, HE'S A "DEVOTED PROFESSIONAL"?
THE FINAL CEMENT OF FRIENDSHIP BETWEEN WOMEN....
...WE KNOW EACH OTHER TOO WELL TO SPEAK TO EACH OTHER ANYMORE.

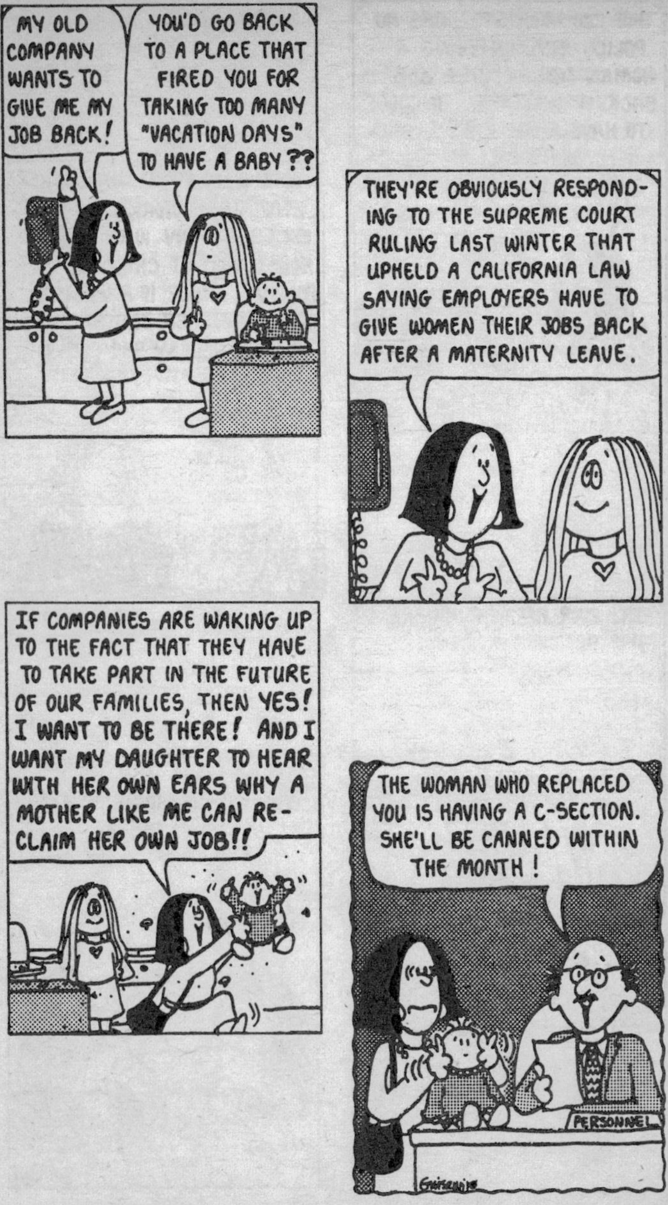
MY OLD COMPANY WANTS TO GIVE ME MY JOB BACK!
YOU'D GO BACK TO A PLACE THAT FIRED YOU FOR TAKING TOO MANY "VACATION DAYS" TO HAVE A BABY??
THEY'RE OBVIOUSLY RESPONDING TO THE SUPREME COURT RULING LAST WINTER THAT UPHELD A CALIFORNIA LAW SAYING EMPLOYERS HAVE TO GIVE WOMEN THEIR JOBS BACK AFTER A MATERNITY LEAVE.
IF COMPANIES ARE WAKING UP TO THE FACT THAT THEY HAVE TO TAKE PART IN THE FUTURE OF OUR FAMILIES, THEN YES! I WANT TO BE THERE! AND I WANT MY DAUGHTER TO HEAR WITH HER OWN EARS WHY A MOTHER LIKE ME CAN RECLAIM HER OWN JOB!!
THE WOMAN WHO REPLACED YOU IS HAVING A C-SECTION. SHE'LL BE CANNED WITHIN THE MONTH!
PERSONNEL

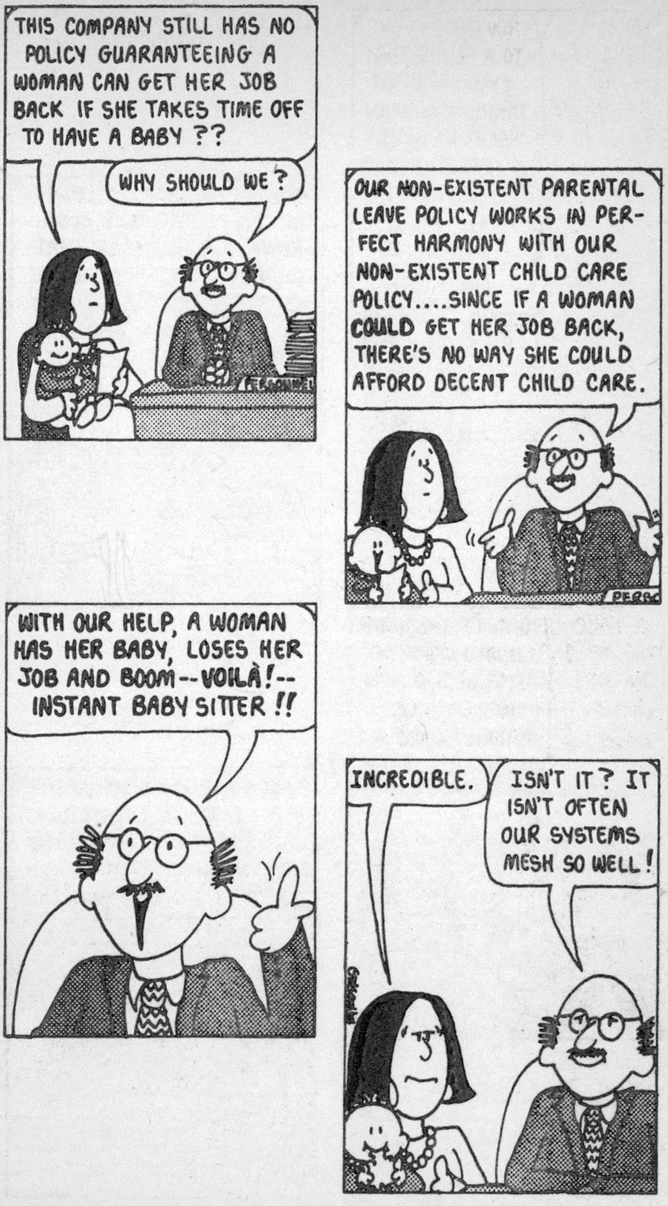
THIS COMPANY STILL HAS NO POLICY GUARANTEEING A WOMAN CAN GET HER JOB BACK IF SHE TAKES TIME OFF TO HAVE A BABY ??
WHY SHOULD WE ?
OUR NON-EXISTENT PARENTAL LEAVE POLICY WORKS IN PER-FECT HARMONY WITH OUR NON-EXISTENT CHILD CARE POLICY....SINCE IF A WOMAN COULD GET HER JOB BACK, THERE'S NO WAY SHE COULD AFFORD DECENT CHILD CARE.
WITH OUR HELP, A WOMAN HAS HER BABY, LOSES HER JOB AND BOOM--VOILÀ!-- INSTANT BABY SITTER !!
INCREDIBLE.
ISN'T IT ? IT ISN'T OFTEN OUR SYSTEMS MESH SO WELL !

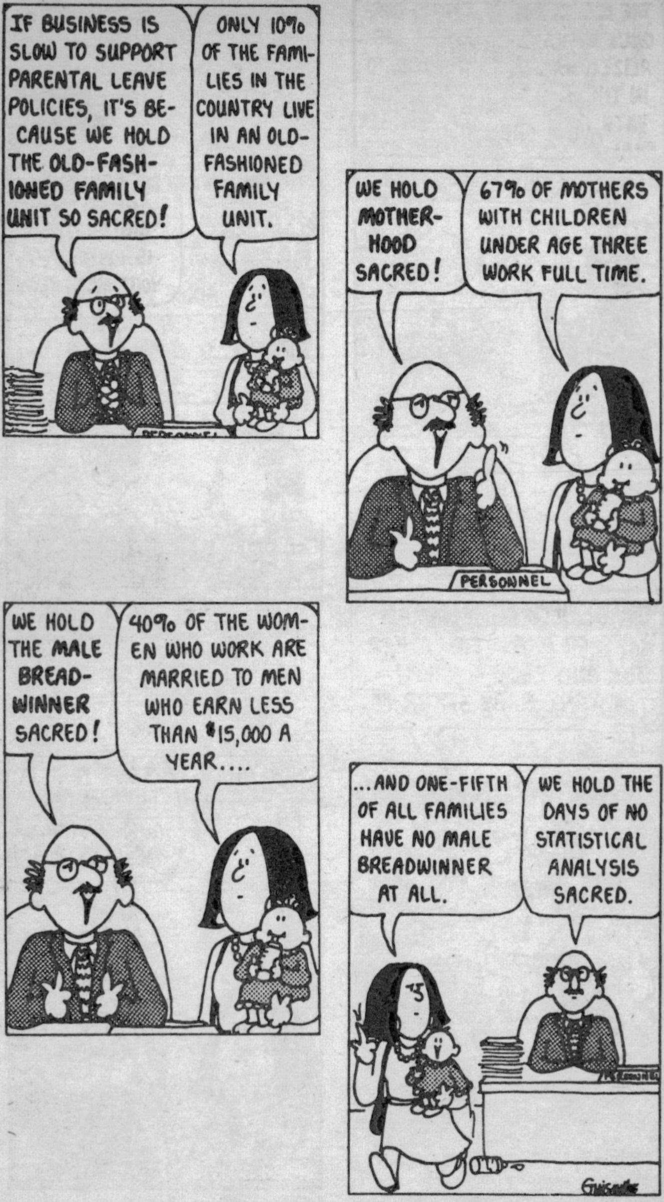
IF BUSINESS IS SLOW TO SUPPORT PARENTAL LEAVE POLICIES, IT'S BECAUSE WE HOLD THE OLD-FASHIONED FAMILY UNIT SO SACRED!
ONLY 10% OF THE FAMILIES IN THE COUNTRY LIVE IN AN OLD-FASHIONED FAMILY UNIT.
WE HOLD MOTHERHOOD SACRED!
67% OF MOTHERS WITH CHILDREN UNDER AGE THREE WORK FULL TIME.
PERSONNEL
WE HOLD THE MALE BREADWINNER SACRED!
40% OF THE WOMEN WHO WORK ARE MARRIED TO MEN WHO EARN LESS THAN $15,000 A YEAR....
...AND ONE-FIFTH OF ALL FAMILIES HAVE NO MALE BREADWINNER AT ALL.
WE HOLD THE DAYS OF NO STATISTICAL ANALYSIS SACRED.

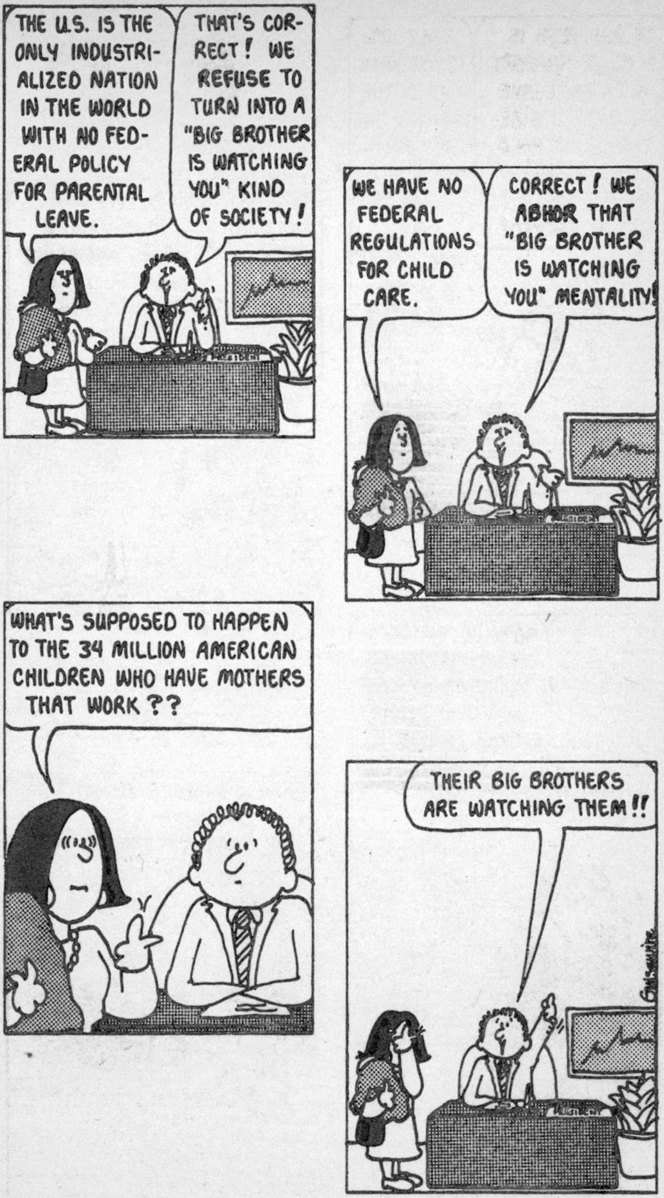
THE U.S. IS THE ONLY INDUSTRIALIZED NATION IN THE WORLD WITH NO FEDERAL POLICY FOR PARENTAL LEAVE.
THAT'S CORRECT! WE REFUSE TO TURN INTO A "BIG BROTHER IS WATCHING YOU" KIND OF SOCIETY!
WE HAVE NO FEDERAL REGULATIONS FOR CHILD CARE.
CORRECT! WE ABHOR THAT "BIG BROTHER IS WATCHING YOU" MENTALITY!
WHAT'S SUPPOSED TO HAPPEN TO THE 34 MILLION AMERICAN CHILDREN WHO HAVE MOTHERS THAT WORK??
THEIR BIG BROTHERS ARE WATCHING THEM!!

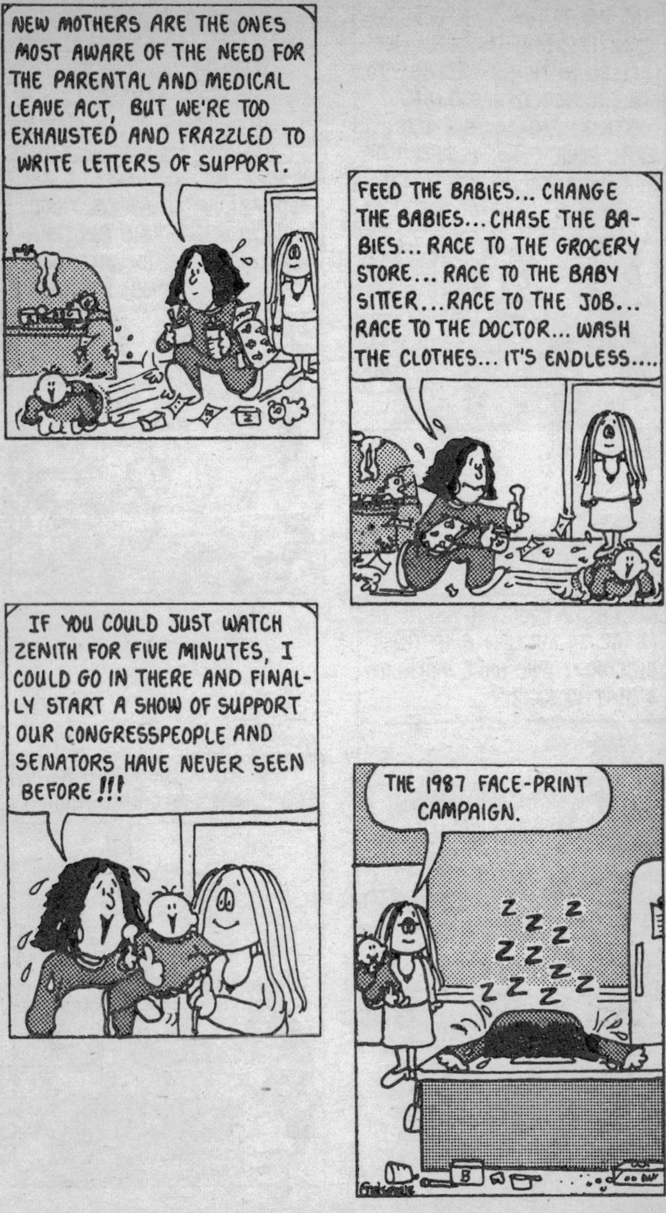
NEW MOTHERS ARE THE ONES MOST AWARE OF THE NEED FOR THE PARENTAL AND MEDICAL LEAVE ACT, BUT WE'RE TOO EXHAUSTED AND FRAZZLED TO WRITE LETTERS OF SUPPORT.
FEED THE BABIES... CHANGE THE BABIES... CHASE THE BABIES... RACE TO THE GROCERY STORE... RACE TO THE BABY SITTER... RACE TO THE JOB... RACE TO THE DOCTOR... WASH THE CLOTHES... IT'S ENDLESS....
IF YOU COULD JUST WATCH ZENITH FOR FIVE MINUTES, I COULD GO IN THERE AND FINALLY START A SHOW OF SUPPORT OUR CONGRESSPEOPLE AND SENATORS HAVE NEVER SEEN BEFORE!!!
THE 1987 FACE-PRINT CAMPAIGN.
Z Z Z Z Z Z Z Z Z Z Z Z

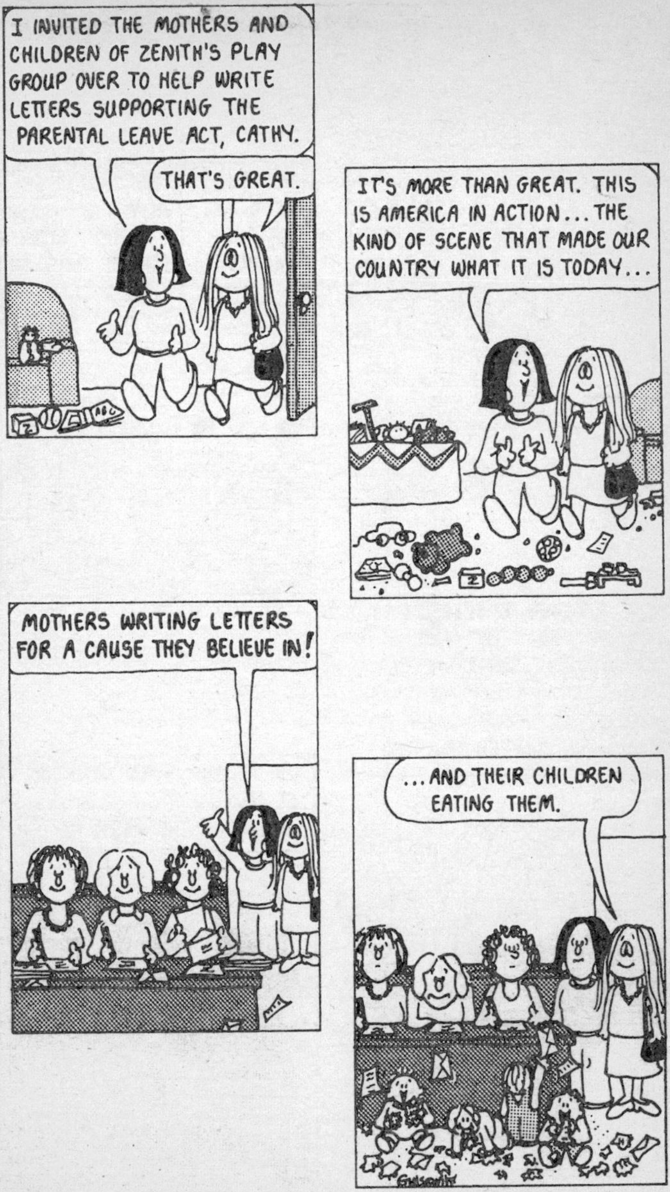
I INVITED THE MOTHERS AND CHILDREN OF ZENITH'S PLAY GROUP OVER TO HELP WRITE LETTERS SUPPORTING THE PARENTAL LEAVE ACT, CATHY.
THAT'S GREAT.
IT'S MORE THAN GREAT. THIS IS AMERICA IN ACTION... THE KIND OF SCENE THAT MADE OUR COUNTRY WHAT IT IS TODAY...
MOTHERS WRITING LETTERS FOR A CAUSE THEY BELIEVE IN!
...AND THEIR CHILDREN EATING THEM.

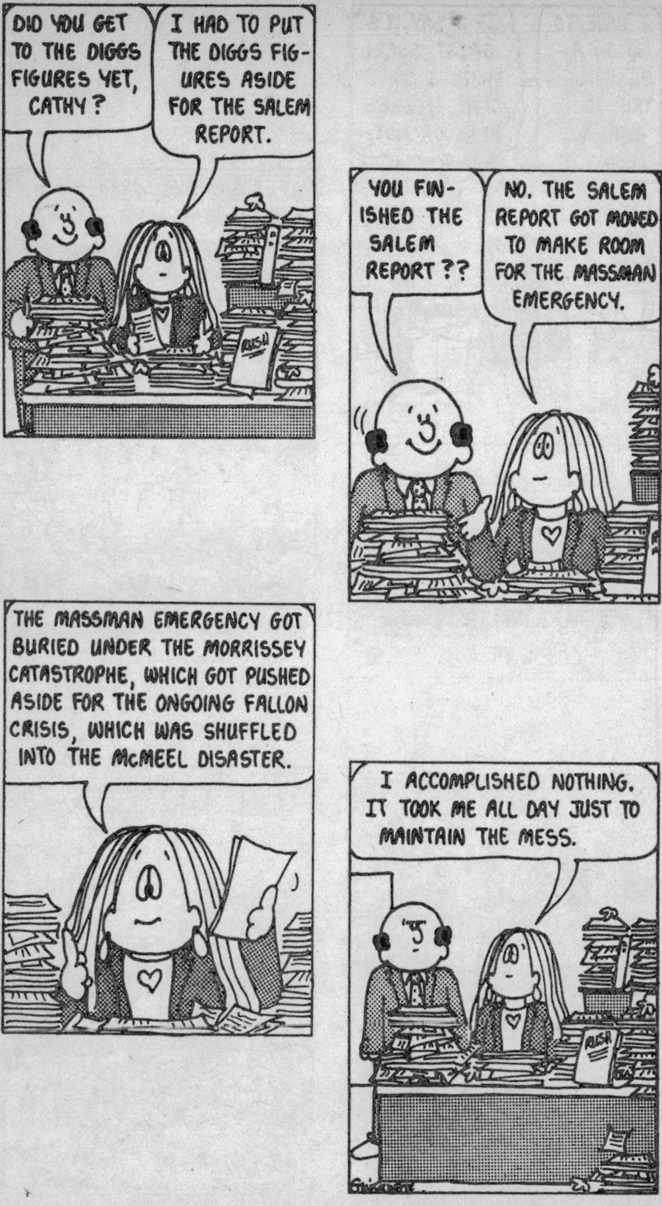
DID YOU GET TO THE DIGGS FIGURES YET, CATHY?
I HAD TO PUT THE DIGGS FIGURES ASIDE FOR THE SALEM REPORT.
RUSH
YOU FINISHED THE SALEM REPORT??
NO. THE SALEM REPORT GOT MOVED TO MAKE ROOM FOR THE MASSMAN EMERGENCY.
THE MASSMAN EMERGENCY GOT BURIED UNDER THE MORRISSEY CATASTROPHE, WHICH GOT PUSHED ASIDE FOR THE ONGOING FALLON CRISIS, WHICH WAS SHUFFLED INTO THE McMEEL DISASTER.
I ACCOMPLISHED NOTHING. IT TOOK ME ALL DAY JUST TO MAINTAIN THE MESS.
RUSH

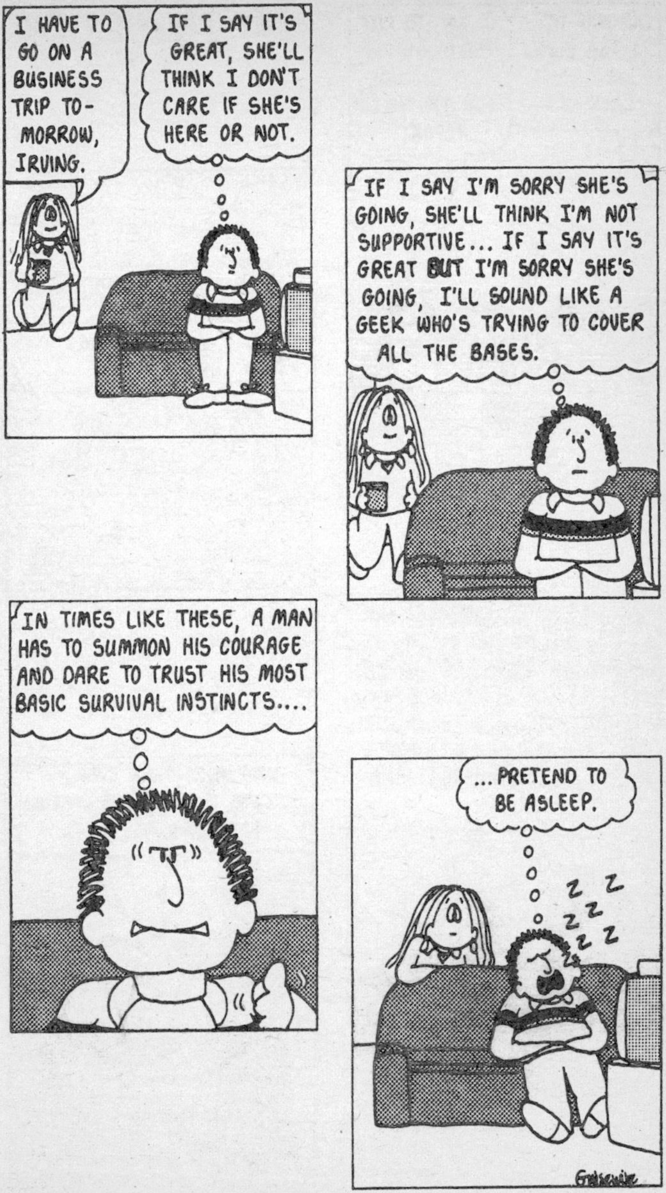
I HAVE TO GO ON A BUSINESS TRIP TOMORROW, IRVING.
IF I SAY IT'S GREAT, SHE'LL THINK I DON'T CARE IF SHE'S HERE OR NOT.
IF I SAY I'M SORRY SHE'S GOING, SHE'LL THINK I'M NOT SUPPORTIVE... IF I SAY IT'S GREAT BUT I'M SORRY SHE'S GOING, I'LL SOUND LIKE A GEEK WHO'S TRYING TO COVER ALL THE BASES.
IN TIMES LIKE THESE, A MAN HAS TO SUMMON HIS COURAGE AND DARE TO TRUST HIS MOST BASIC SURVIVAL INSTINCTS....
...PRETEND TO BE ASLEEP.
Z Z Z Z Z Z

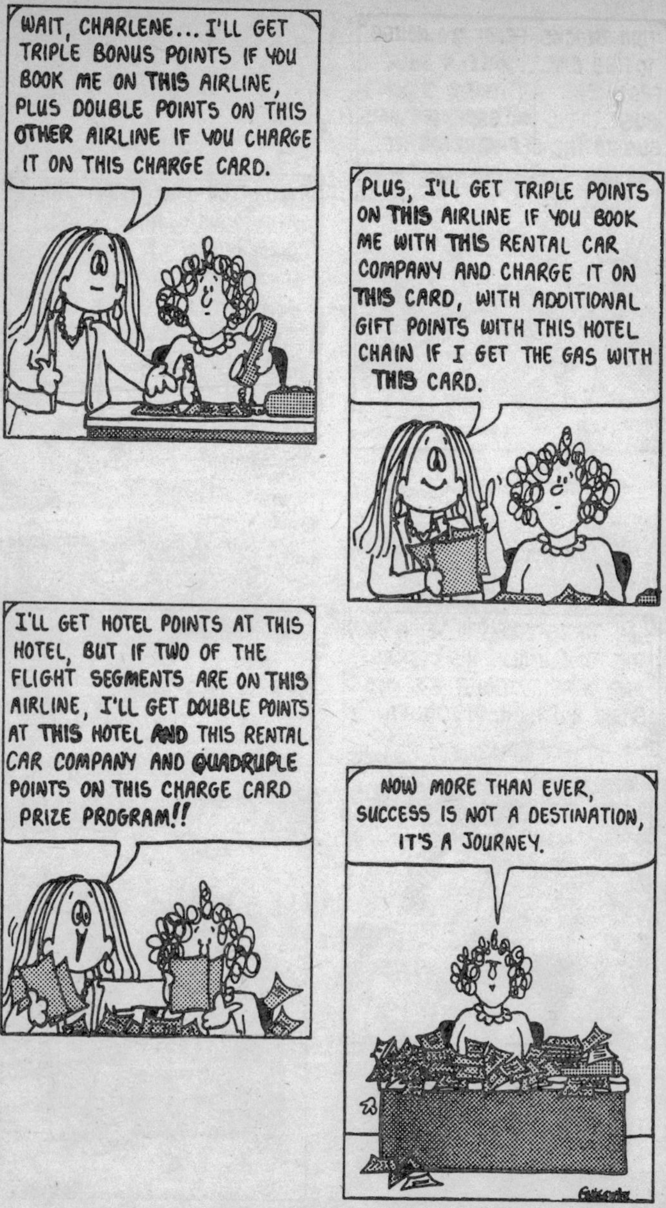
WAIT, CHARLENE... I'LL GET TRIPLE BONUS POINTS IF YOU BOOK ME ON THIS AIRLINE, PLUS DOUBLE POINTS ON THIS OTHER AIRLINE IF YOU CHARGE IT ON THIS CHARGE CARD.
PLUS, I'LL GET TRIPLE POINTS ON THIS AIRLINE IF YOU BOOK ME WITH THIS RENTAL CAR COMPANY AND CHARGE IT ON THIS CARD, WITH ADDITIONAL GIFT POINTS WITH THIS HOTEL CHAIN IF I GET THE GAS WITH THIS CARD.
I'LL GET HOTEL POINTS AT THIS HOTEL, BUT IF TWO OF THE FLIGHT SEGMENTS ARE ON THIS AIRLINE, I'LL GET DOUBLE POINTS AT THIS HOTEL AND THIS RENTAL CAR COMPANY AND QUADRUPLE POINTS ON THIS CHARGE CARD PRIZE PROGRAM!!
NOW MORE THAN EVER, SUCCESS IS NOT A DESTINATION, IT'S A JOURNEY.

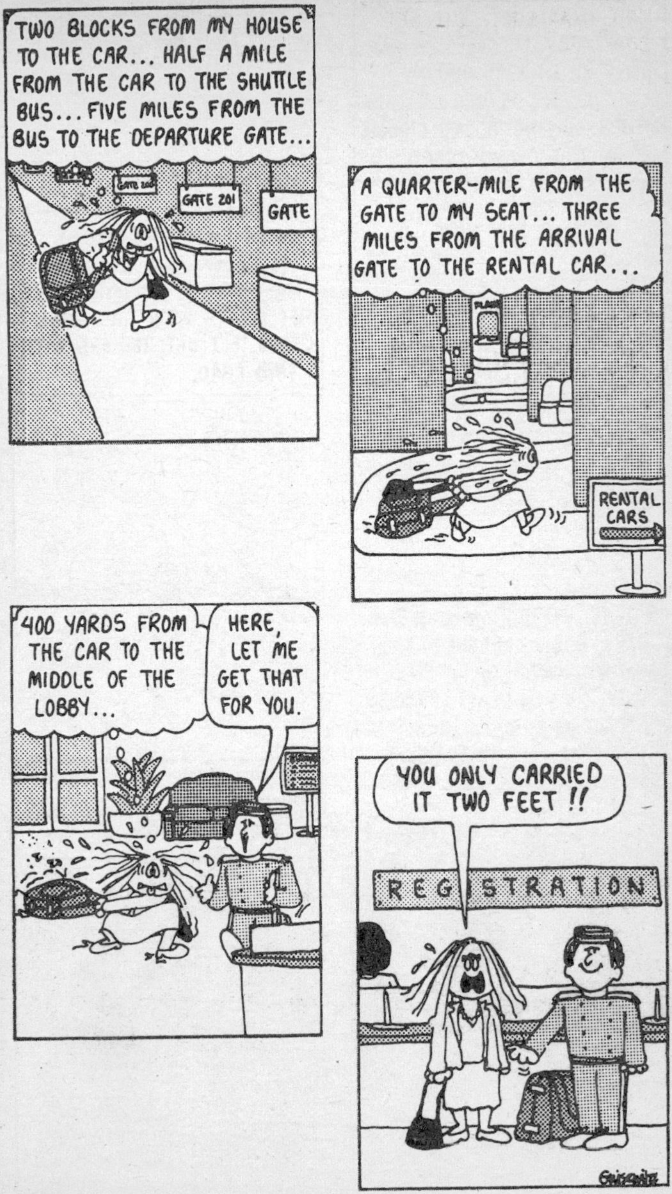

TWO BLOCKS FROM MY HOUSE TO THE CAR... HALF A MILE FROM THE CAR TO THE SHUTTLE BUS... FIVE MILES FROM THE BUS TO THE DEPARTURE GATE...
GATE 201
GATE
A QUARTER-MILE FROM THE GATE TO MY SEAT... THREE MILES FROM THE ARRIVAL GATE TO THE RENTAL CAR...
RENTAL CARS
400 YARDS FROM THE CAR TO THE MIDDLE OF THE LOBBY...
HERE, LET ME GET THAT FOR YOU.
YOU ONLY CARRIED IT TWO FEET !!
REG STRATION

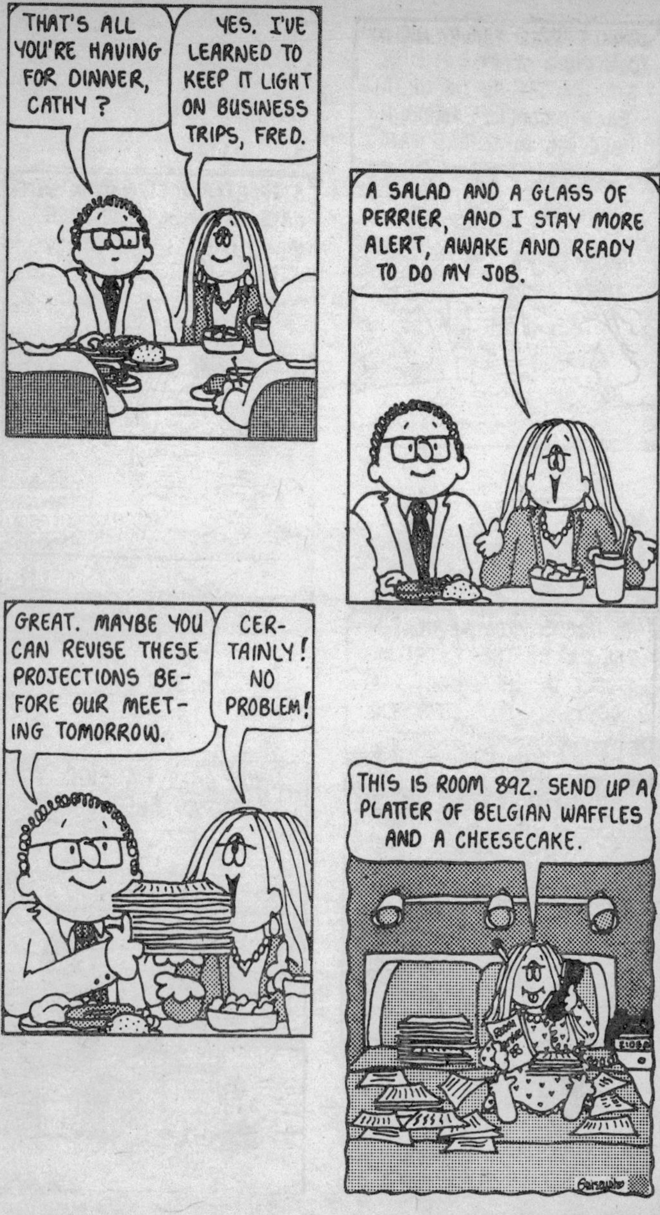
THAT'S ALL YOU'RE HAVING FOR DINNER, CATHY ?
YES. I'VE LEARNED TO KEEP IT LIGHT ON BUSINESS TRIPS, FRED.
A SALAD AND A GLASS OF PERRIER, AND I STAY MORE ALERT, AWAKE AND READY TO DO MY JOB.
GREAT. MAYBE YOU CAN REVISE THESE PROJECTIONS BEFORE OUR MEETING TOMORROW.
CERTAINLY! NO PROBLEM!
THIS IS ROOM 892. SEND UP A PLATTER OF BELGIAN WAFFLES AND A CHEESECAKE.

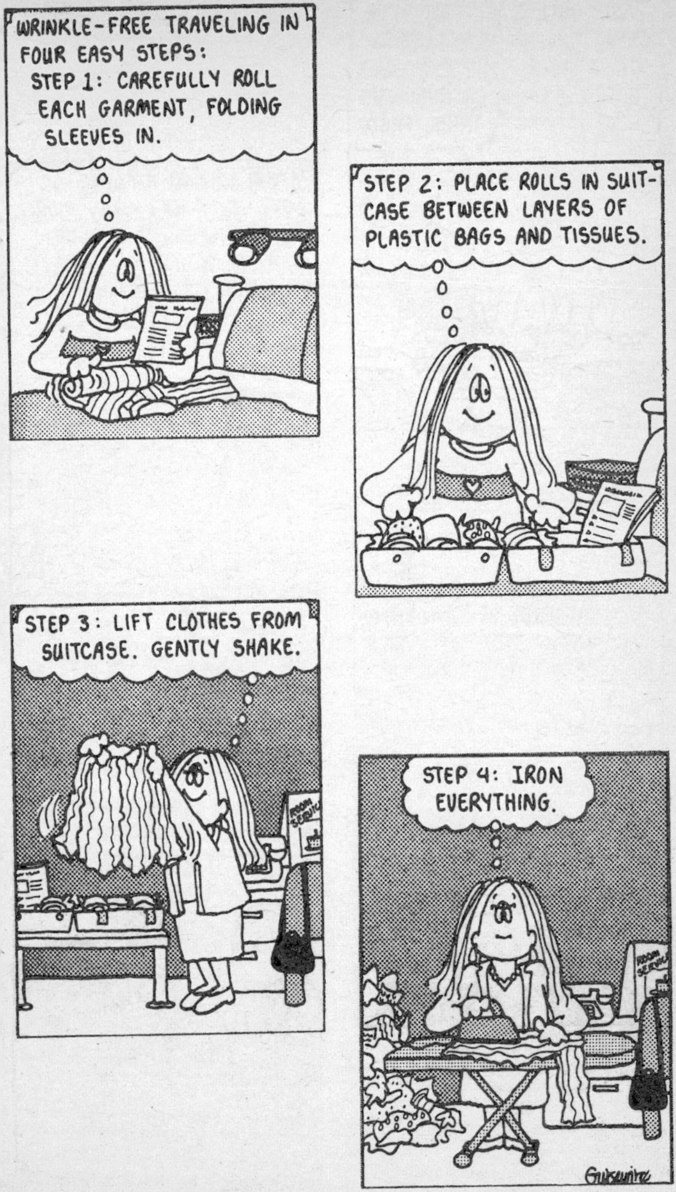
WRINKLE-FREE TRAVELING IN FOUR EASY STEPS:
STEP 1: CAREFULLY ROLL EACH GARMENT, FOLDING SLEEVES IN.
STEP 2: PLACE ROLLS IN SUITCASE BETWEEN LAYERS OF PLASTIC BAGS AND TISSUES.
STEP 3: LIFT CLOTHES FROM SUITCASE. GENTLY SHAKE.
STEP 4: IRON EVERYTHING.
Guisewite

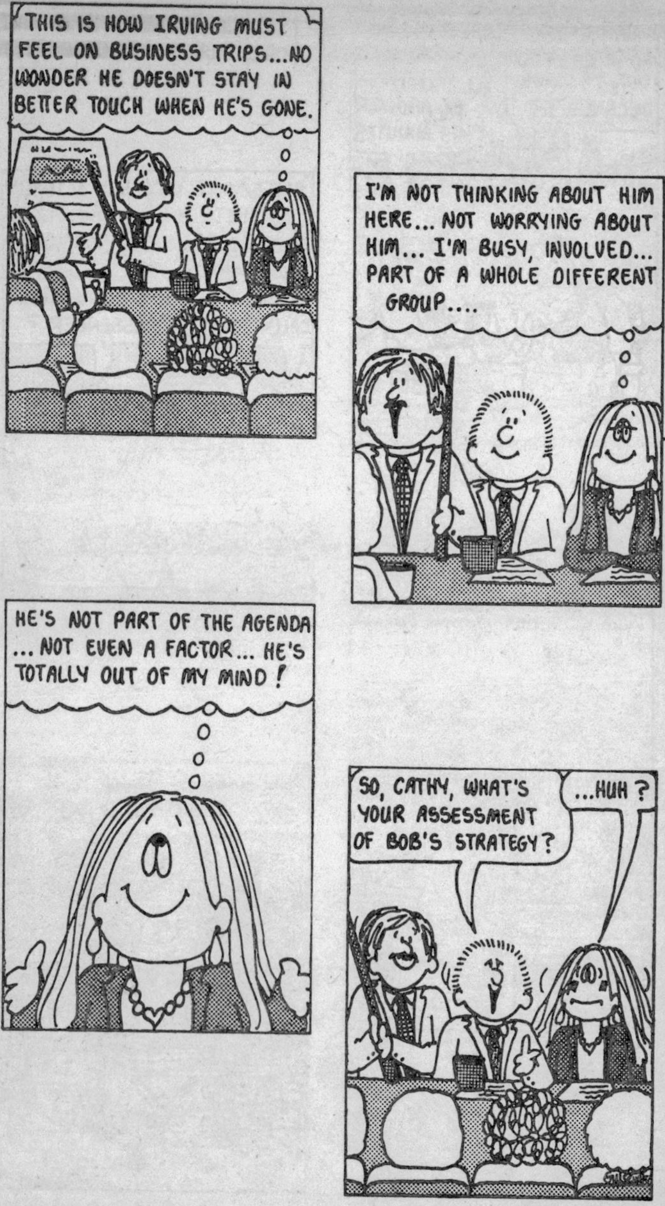
THIS IS HOW IRVING MUST FEEL ON BUSINESS TRIPS...NO WONDER HE DOESN'T STAY IN BETTER TOUCH WHEN HE'S GONE.
I'M NOT THINKING ABOUT HIM HERE... NOT WORRYING ABOUT HIM... I'M BUSY, INVOLVED... PART OF A WHOLE DIFFERENT GROUP....
HE'S NOT PART OF THE AGENDA ... NOT EVEN A FACTOR... HE'S TOTALLY OUT OF MY MIND!
SO, CATHY, WHAT'S YOUR ASSESSMENT OF BOB'S STRATEGY?
...HUH?

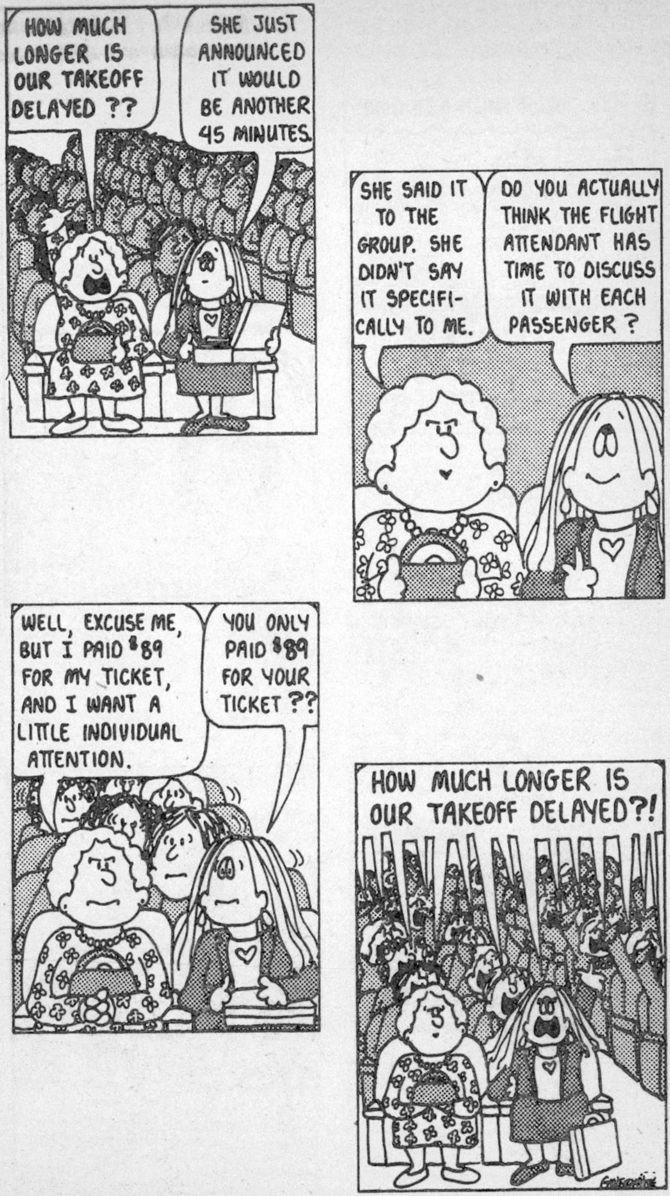
HOW MUCH LONGER IS OUR TAKEOFF DELAYED ??
SHE JUST ANNOUNCED IT WOULD BE ANOTHER 45 MINUTES.
SHE SAID IT TO THE GROUP. SHE DIDN'T SAY IT SPECIFI- CALLY TO ME.
DO YOU ACTUALLY THINK THE FLIGHT ATTENDANT HAS TIME TO DISCUSS IT WITH EACH PASSENGER ?
WELL, EXCUSE ME, BUT I PAID $89 FOR MY TICKET, AND I WANT A LITTLE INDIVIDUAL ATTENTION.
YOU ONLY PAID $89 FOR YOUR TICKET ??
HOW MUCH LONGER IS OUR TAKEOFF DELAYED?!

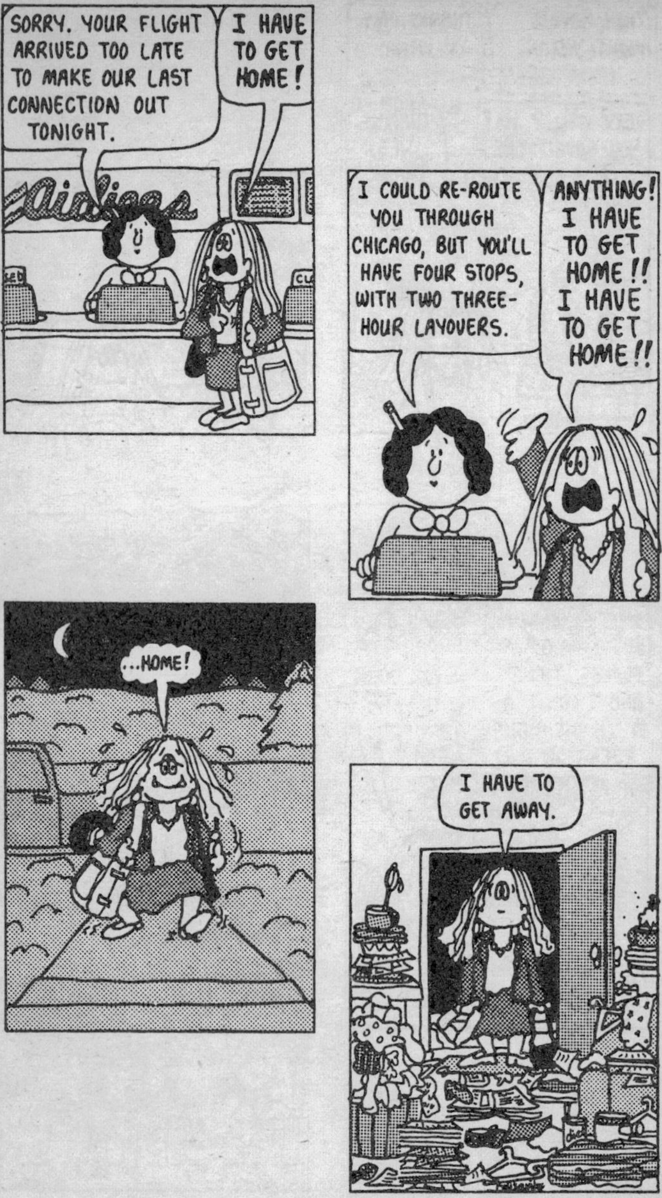
SORRY. YOUR FLIGHT ARRIVED TOO LATE TO MAKE OUR LAST CONNECTION OUT TONIGHT.
I HAVE TO GET HOME!
I COULD RE-ROUTE YOU THROUGH CHICAGO, BUT YOU'LL HAVE FOUR STOPS, WITH TWO THREE-HOUR LAYOVERS.
ANYTHING! I HAVE TO GET HOME!! I HAVE TO GET HOME!!
...HOME!
I HAVE TO GET AWAY.

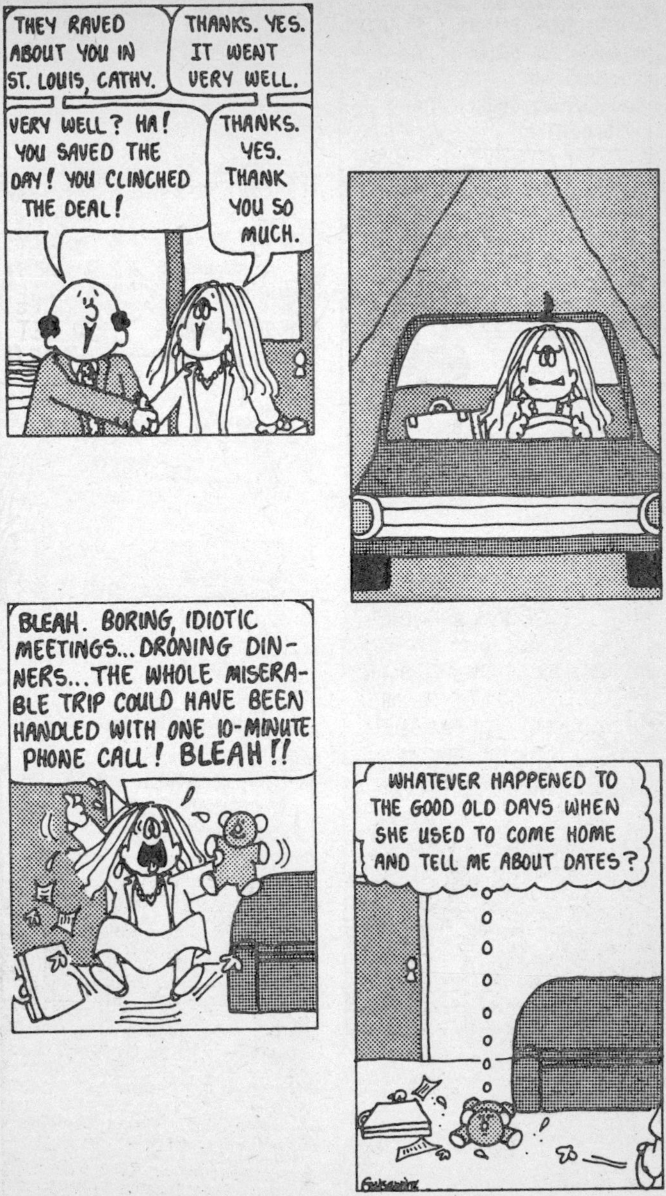
THEY RAVED ABOUT YOU IN ST. LOUIS, CATHY.
THANKS. YES. IT WENT VERY WELL.
VERY WELL? HA! YOU SAVED THE DAY! YOU CLINCHED THE DEAL!
THANKS. YES. THANK YOU SO MUCH.
BLEAH. BORING, IDIOTIC MEETINGS... DRONING DINNERS... THE WHOLE MISERABLE TRIP COULD HAVE BEEN HANDLED WITH ONE 10-MINUTE PHONE CALL! BLEAH!!
WHATEVER HAPPENED TO THE GOOD OLD DAYS WHEN SHE USED TO COME HOME AND TELL ME ABOUT DATES?

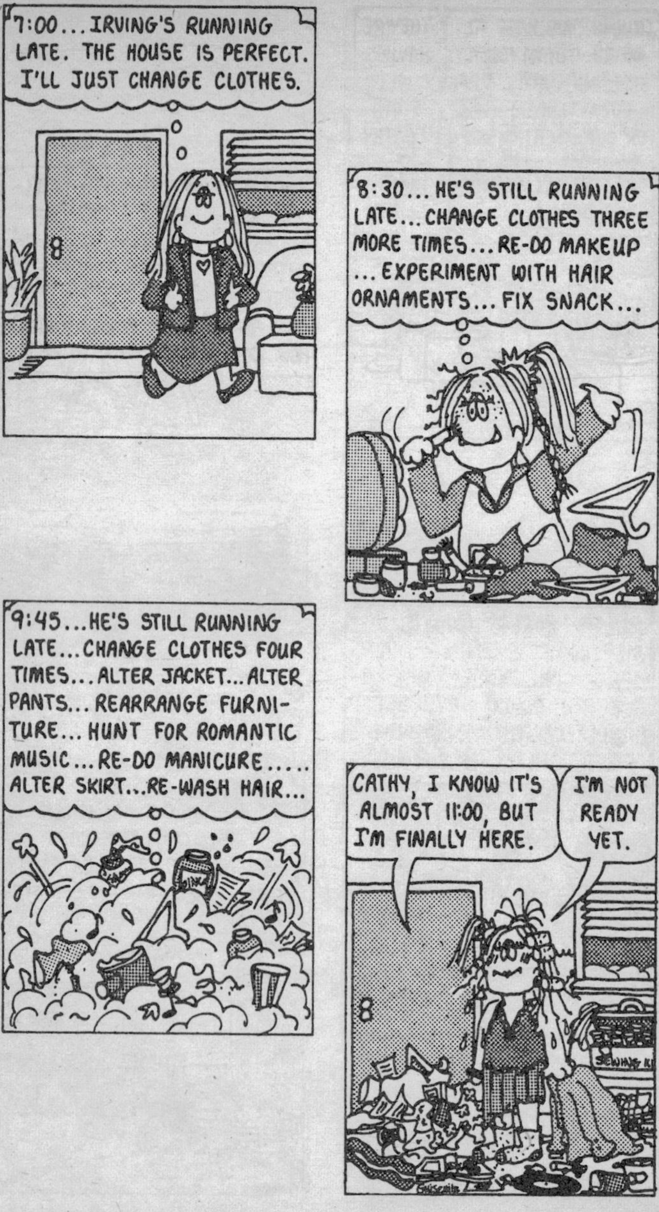
7:00... IRVING'S RUNNING LATE. THE HOUSE IS PERFECT. I'LL JUST CHANGE CLOTHES.
8:30... HE'S STILL RUNNING LATE... CHANGE CLOTHES THREE MORE TIMES... RE-DO MAKEUP ... EXPERIMENT WITH HAIR ORNAMENTS... FIX SNACK...
9:45... HE'S STILL RUNNING LATE... CHANGE CLOTHES FOUR TIMES... ALTER JACKET... ALTER PANTS... REARRANGE FURNITURE... HUNT FOR ROMANTIC MUSIC.... RE-DO MANICURE..... ALTER SKIRT... RE-WASH HAIR...
CATHY, I KNOW IT'S ALMOST 11:00, BUT I'M FINALLY HERE.
I'M NOT READY YET.

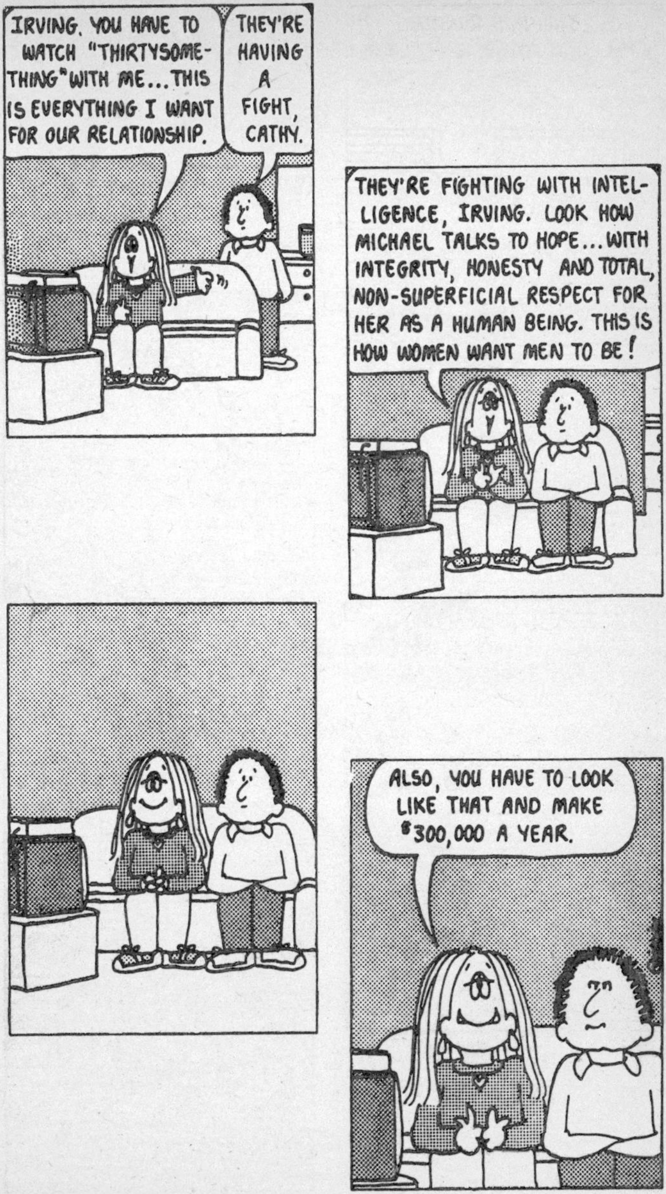
IRVING, YOU HAVE TO WATCH "THIRTYSOMETHING" WITH ME... THIS IS EVERYTHING I WANT FOR OUR RELATIONSHIP.
THEY'RE HAVING A FIGHT, CATHY.
THEY'RE FIGHTING WITH INTELLIGENCE, IRVING. LOOK HOW MICHAEL TALKS TO HOPE... WITH INTEGRITY, HONESTY AND TOTAL, NON-SUPERFICIAL RESPECT FOR HER AS A HUMAN BEING. THIS IS HOW WOMEN WANT MEN TO BE!
ALSO, YOU HAVE TO LOOK LIKE THAT AND MAKE $300,000 A YEAR.

A WHOLE MONTH UNTIL TAXES ARE DUE... 11 WEEKS UNTIL I HAVE TO BE SEEN IN A BATHING SUIT... AND 47 DAYS UNTIL INVITATIONS START ARRIVING FOR THE SUMMER WEDDINGS OF THE ONLY DECENT REMAINING SINGLE MEN IN TOWN.

FOR A FEW INCREDIBLE WEEKS, THE CONCEPTS OF FINANCIAL SECURITY, PHYSICAL PERFECTION AND ROMANTIC BLISS ARE ALL STILL WITHIN MY GRASP!

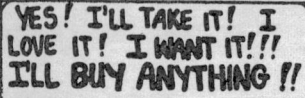

YES! I'LL TAKE IT! I LOVE IT! I WANT IT!!! I'LL BUY ANYTHING !!

THOSE WHO DREAM OF APRIL IN PARIS HAVE NEVER SEEN MARCH AT THE MALL.

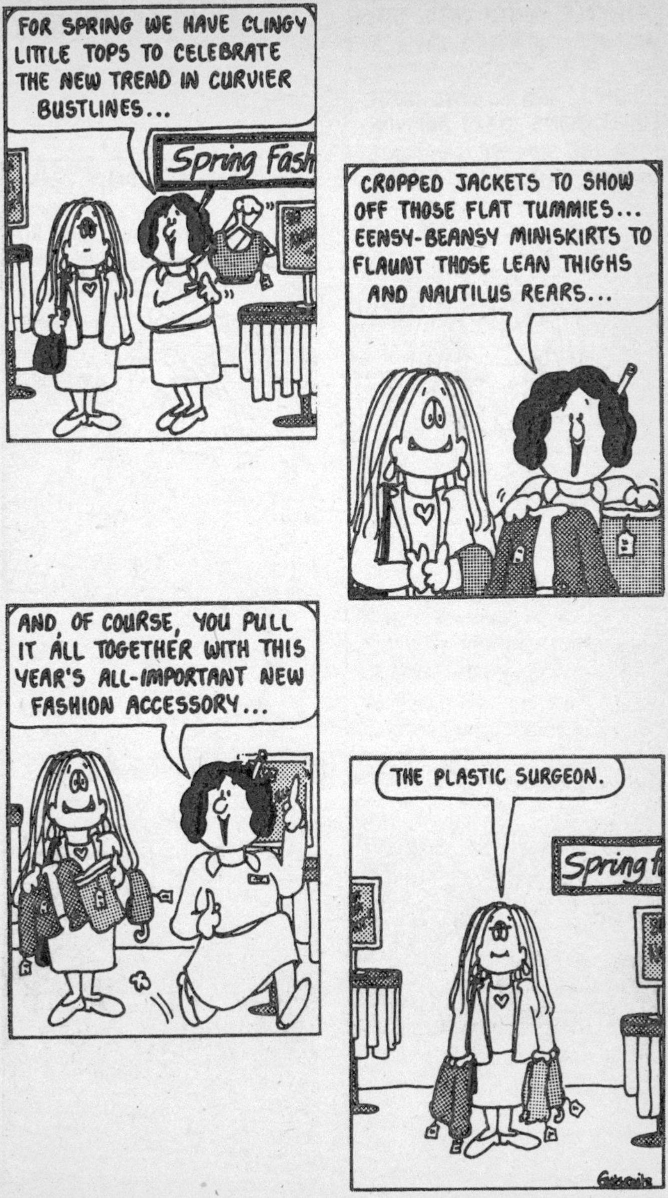
FOR SPRING WE HAVE CLINGY LITTLE TOPS TO CELEBRATE THE NEW TREND IN CURVIER BUSTLINES...
Spring Fash
CROPPED JACKETS TO SHOW OFF THOSE FLAT TUMMIES... EENSY-BEANSY MINISKIRTS TO FLAUNT THOSE LEAN THIGHS AND NAUTILUS REARS...
AND, OF COURSE, YOU PULL IT ALL TOGETHER WITH THIS YEAR'S ALL-IMPORTANT NEW FASHION ACCESSORY...
THE PLASTIC SURGEON.
Spring

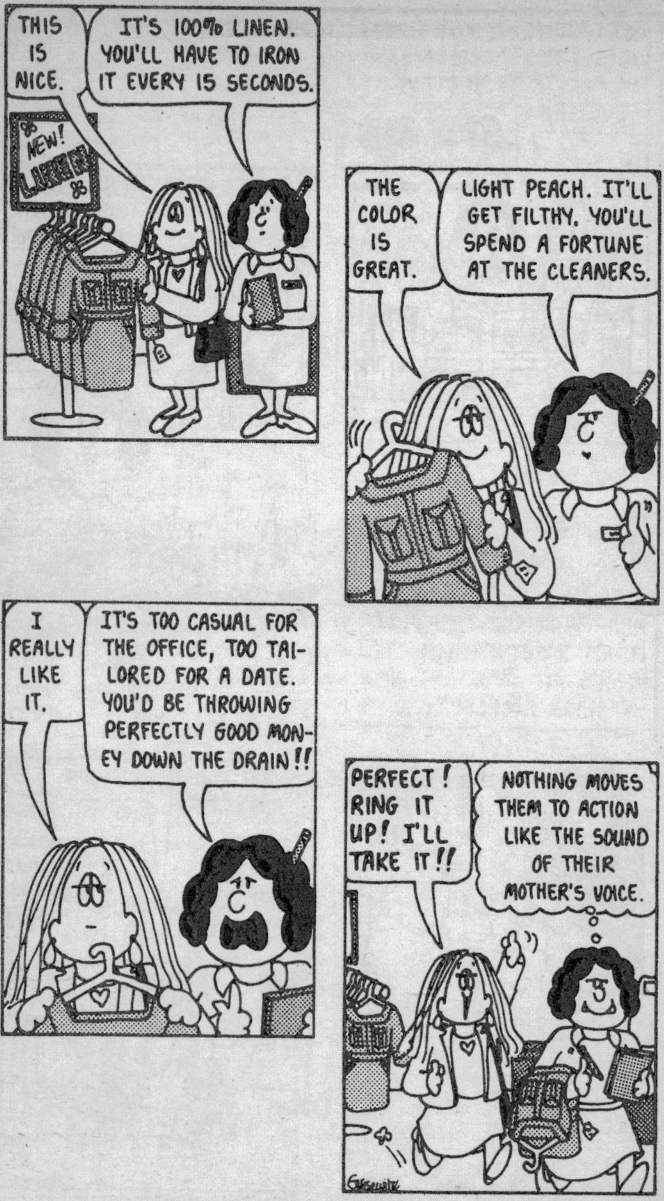
NEW!
THIS IS NICE.
IT'S 100% LINEN. YOU'LL HAVE TO IRON IT EVERY 15 SECONDS.
THE COLOR IS GREAT.
LIGHT PEACH. IT'LL GET FILTHY. YOU'LL SPEND A FORTUNE AT THE CLEANERS.
I REALLY LIKE IT.
IT'S TOO CASUAL FOR THE OFFICE, TOO TAILORED FOR A DATE. YOU'D BE THROWING PERFECTLY GOOD MONEY DOWN THE DRAIN!!
PERFECT! RING IT UP! I'LL TAKE IT!!
NOTHING MOVES THEM TO ACTION LIKE THE SOUND OF THEIR MOTHER'S VOICE.

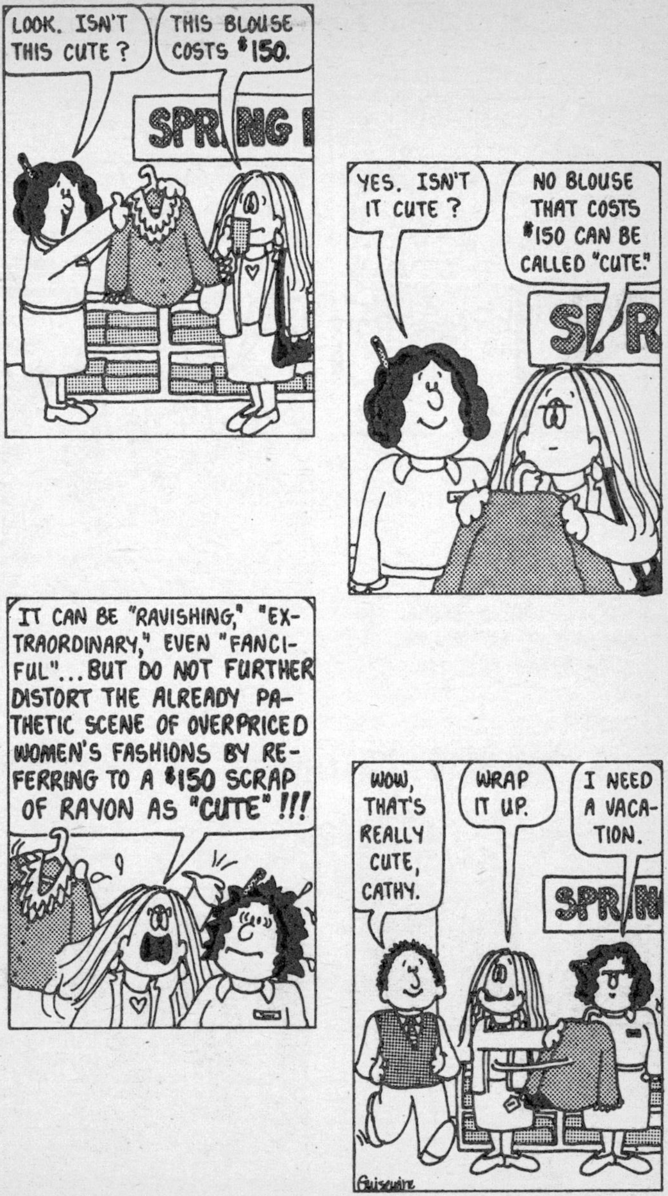

LOOK. ISN'T THIS CUTE?
THIS BLOUSE COSTS $150.
SPRING
YES. ISN'T IT CUTE?
NO BLOUSE THAT COSTS $150 CAN BE CALLED "CUTE."
IT CAN BE "RAVISHING," "EXTRAORDINARY," EVEN "FANCIFUL"... BUT DO NOT FURTHER DISTORT THE ALREADY PATHETIC SCENE OF OVERPRICED WOMEN'S FASHIONS BY REFERRING TO A $150 SCRAP OF RAYON AS "CUTE"!!!
WOW, THAT'S REALLY CUTE, CATHY.
WRAP IT UP.
I NEED A VACATION.
Guisewite

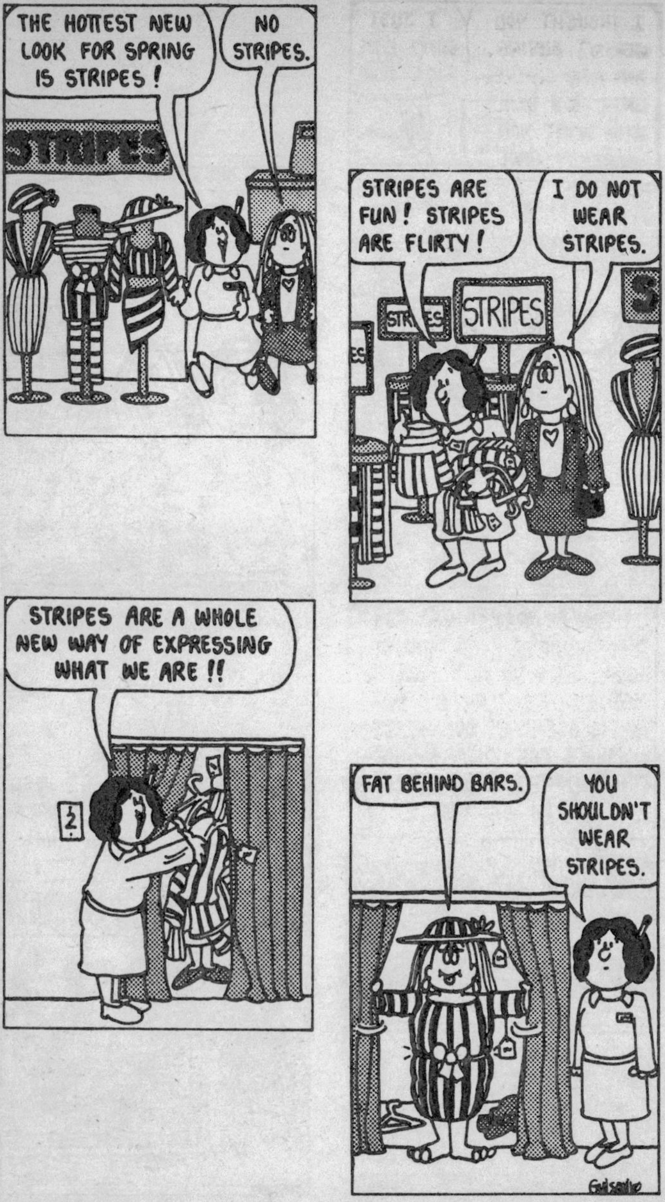
THE HOTTEST NEW LOOK FOR SPRING IS STRIPES!
NO STRIPES.
STRIPES
STRIPES ARE FUN! STRIPES ARE FLIRTY!
I DO NOT WEAR STRIPES.
STRIPES
STRIPES ARE A WHOLE NEW WAY OF EXPRESSING WHAT WE ARE!!
FAT BEHIND BARS.
YOU SHOULDN'T WEAR STRIPES.

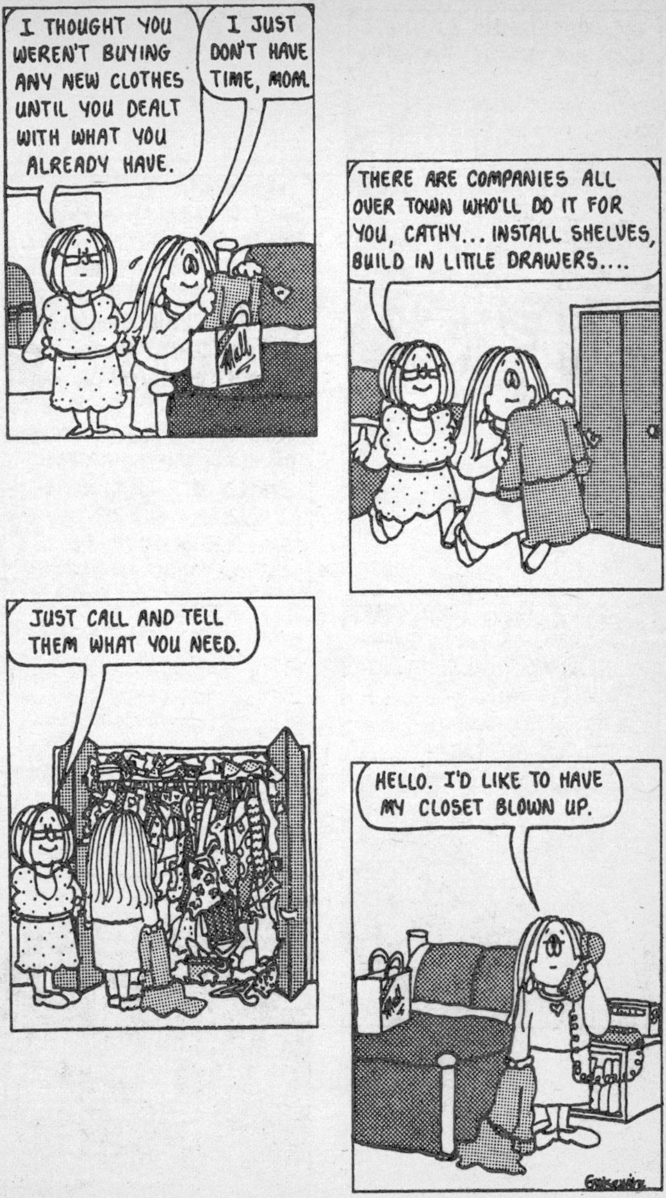
I THOUGHT YOU WEREN'T BUYING ANY NEW CLOTHES UNTIL YOU DEALT WITH WHAT YOU ALREADY HAVE.
I JUST DON'T HAVE TIME, MOM.
THERE ARE COMPANIES ALL OVER TOWN WHO'LL DO IT FOR YOU, CATHY... INSTALL SHELVES, BUILD IN LITTLE DRAWERS....
JUST CALL AND TELL THEM WHAT YOU NEED.
HELLO. I'D LIKE TO HAVE MY CLOSET BLOWN UP.

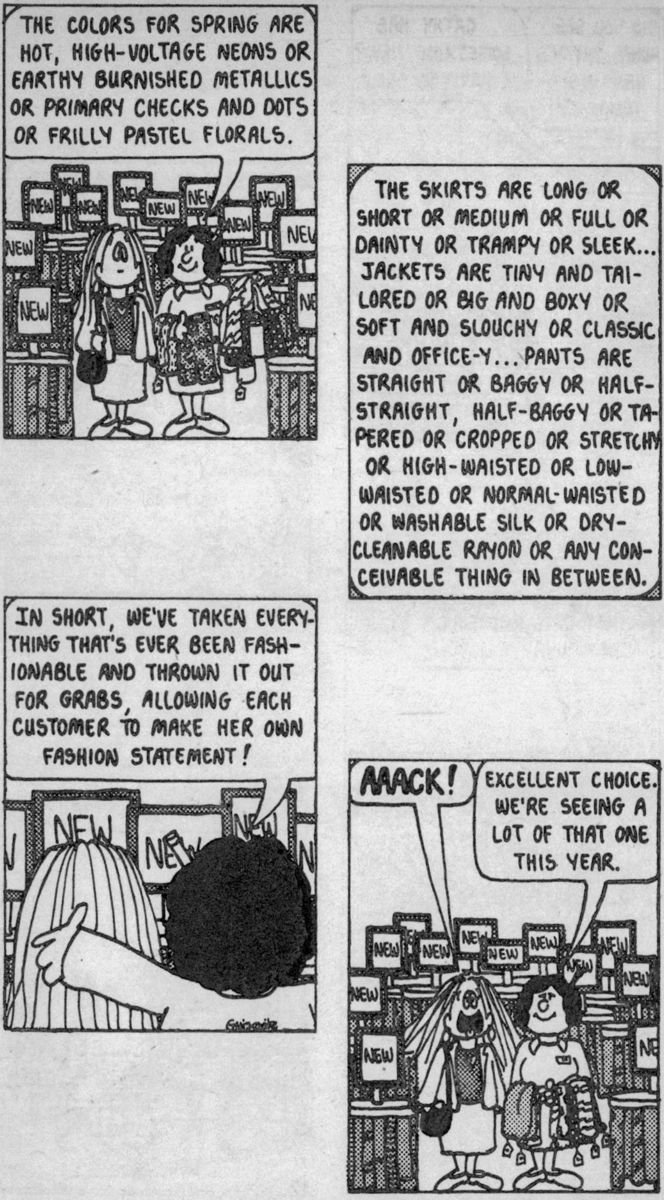
THE COLORS FOR SPRING ARE HOT, HIGH-VOLTAGE NEONS OR EARTHY BURNISHED METALLICS OR PRIMARY CHECKS AND DOTS OR FRILLY PASTEL FLORALS.
NEW
THE SKIRTS ARE LONG OR SHORT OR MEDIUM OR FULL OR DAINTY OR TRAMPY OR SLEEK... JACKETS ARE TINY AND TAILORED OR BIG AND BOXY OR SOFT AND SLOUCHY OR CLASSIC AND OFFICE-Y... PANTS ARE STRAIGHT OR BAGGY OR HALF-STRAIGHT, HALF-BAGGY OR TAPERED OR CROPPED OR STRETCHY OR HIGH-WAISTED OR LOW-WAISTED OR NORMAL-WAISTED OR WASHABLE SILK OR DRY-CLEANABLE RAYON OR ANY CONCEIVABLE THING IN BETWEEN.
IN SHORT, WE'VE TAKEN EVERYTHING THAT'S EVER BEEN FASHIONABLE AND THROWN IT OUT FOR GRABS, ALLOWING EACH CUSTOMER TO MAKE HER OWN FASHION STATEMENT!
AAACK!
EXCELLENT CHOICE. WE'RE SEEING A LOT OF THAT ONE THIS YEAR.

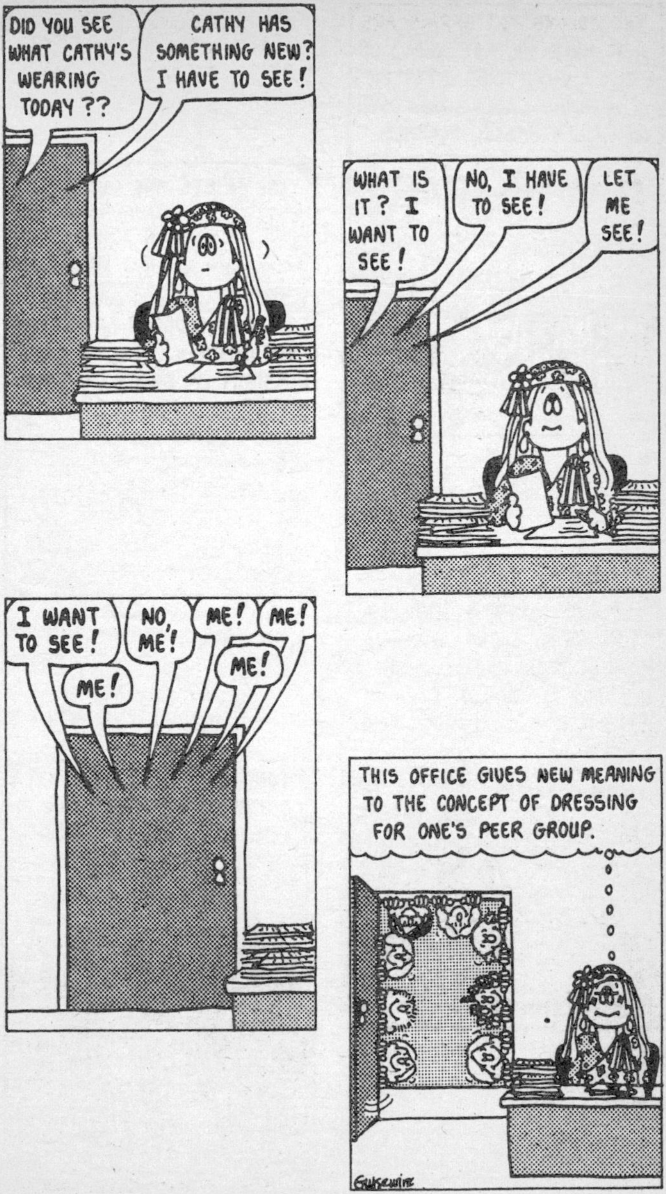
DID YOU SEE WHAT CATHY'S WEARING TODAY??
CATHY HAS SOMETHING NEW? I HAVE TO SEE!
WHAT IS IT? I WANT TO SEE!
NO, I HAVE TO SEE!
LET ME SEE!
I WANT TO SEE!
ME!
NO, ME!
ME!
ME!
ME!
THIS OFFICE GIVES NEW MEANING TO THE CONCEPT OF DRESSING FOR ONE'S PEER GROUP.

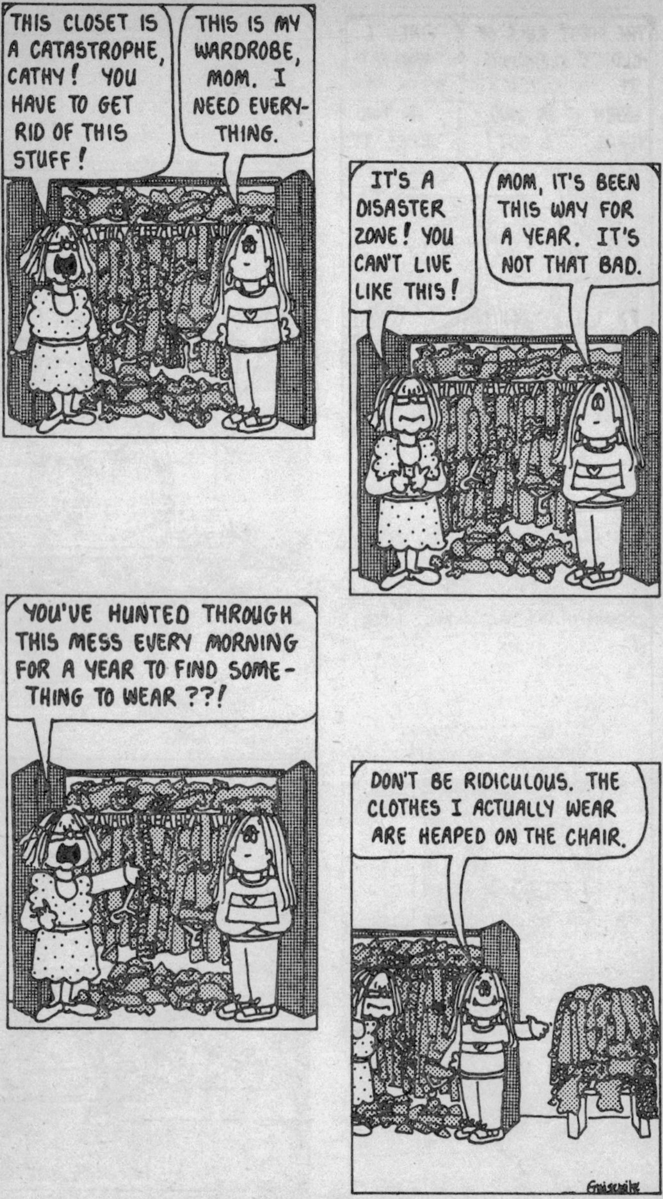
THIS CLOSET IS A CATASTROPHE, CATHY! YOU HAVE TO GET RID OF THIS STUFF!
THIS IS MY WARDROBE, MOM. I NEED EVERYTHING.
IT'S A DISASTER ZONE! YOU CAN'T LIVE LIKE THIS!
MOM, IT'S BEEN THIS WAY FOR A YEAR. IT'S NOT THAT BAD.
YOU'VE HUNTED THROUGH THIS MESS EVERY MORNING FOR A YEAR TO FIND SOMETHING TO WEAR??!
DON'T BE RIDICULOUS. THE CLOTHES I ACTUALLY WEAR ARE HEAPED ON THE CHAIR.
Guisewite

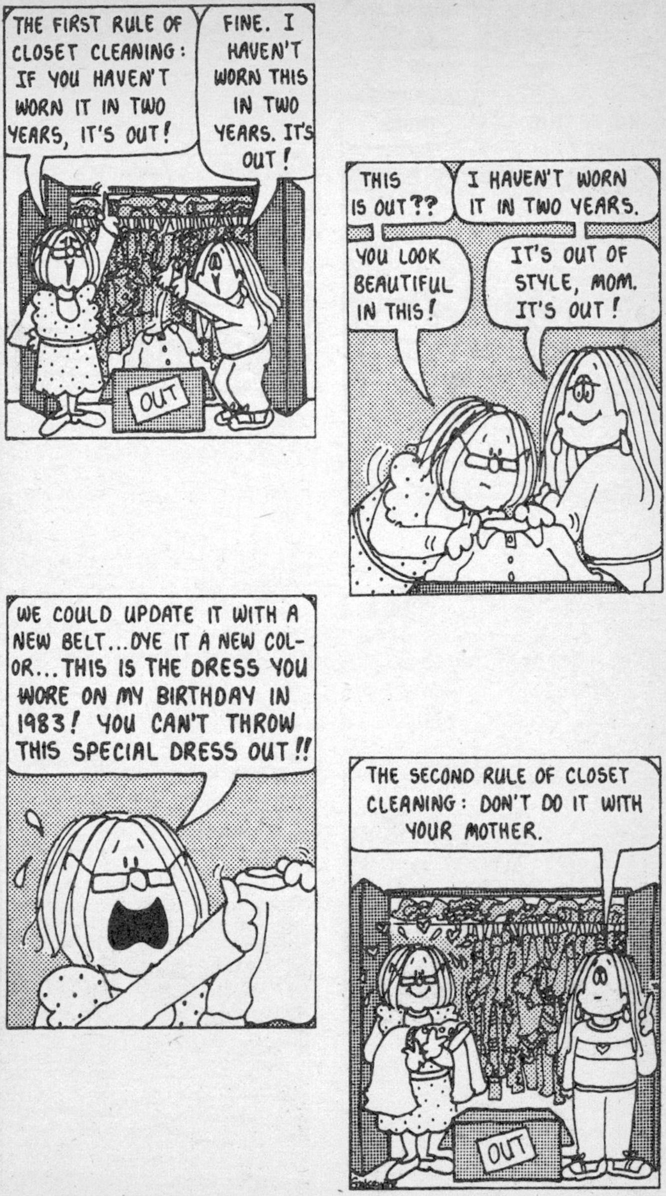
THE FIRST RULE OF CLOSET CLEANING: IF YOU HAVEN'T WORN IT IN TWO YEARS, IT'S OUT!
FINE. I HAVEN'T WORN THIS IN TWO YEARS. IT'S OUT!
OUT
THIS IS OUT??
I HAVEN'T WORN IT IN TWO YEARS.
YOU LOOK BEAUTIFUL IN THIS!
IT'S OUT OF STYLE, MOM. IT'S OUT!
WE COULD UPDATE IT WITH A NEW BELT...DYE IT A NEW COLOR...THIS IS THE DRESS YOU WORE ON MY BIRTHDAY IN 1983! YOU CAN'T THROW THIS SPECIAL DRESS OUT!!
THE SECOND RULE OF CLOSET CLEANING: DON'T DO IT WITH YOUR MOTHER.
OUT

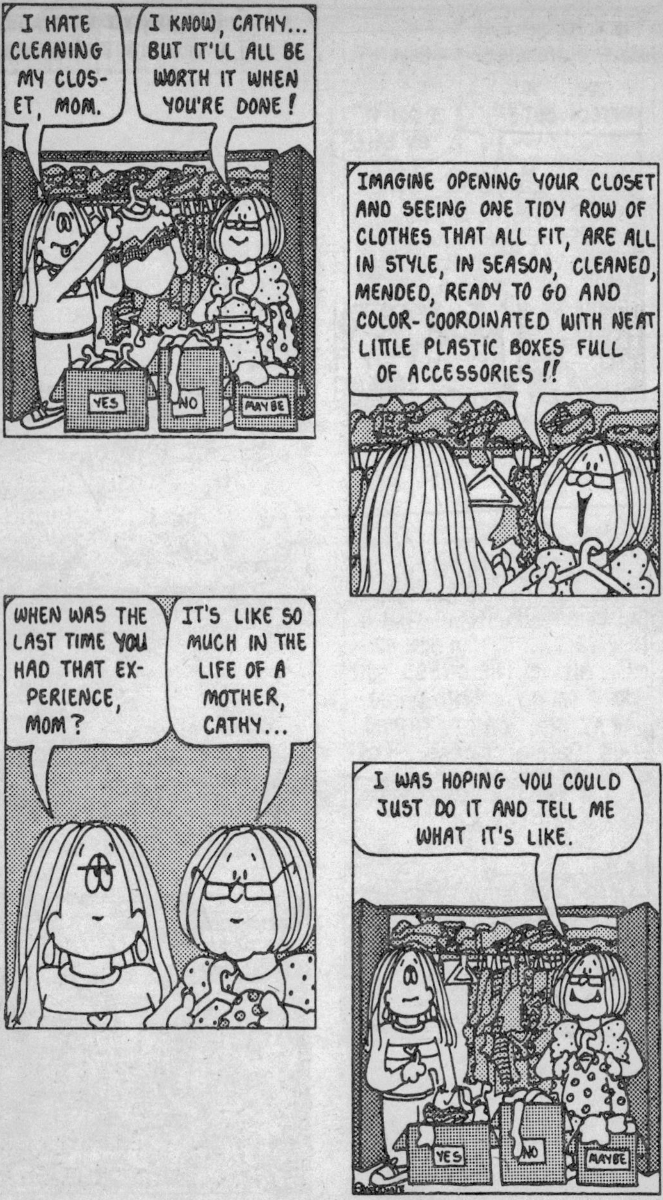
I HATE CLEANING MY CLOSET, MOM.
I KNOW, CATHY... BUT IT'LL ALL BE WORTH IT WHEN YOU'RE DONE!
YES
NO
MAYBE
IMAGINE OPENING YOUR CLOSET AND SEEING ONE TIDY ROW OF CLOTHES THAT ALL FIT, ARE ALL IN STYLE, IN SEASON, CLEANED, MENDED, READY TO GO AND COLOR-COORDINATED WITH NEAT LITTLE PLASTIC BOXES FULL OF ACCESSORIES!!
WHEN WAS THE LAST TIME YOU HAD THAT EXPERIENCE, MOM?
IT'S LIKE SO MUCH IN THE LIFE OF A MOTHER, CATHY...
I WAS HOPING YOU COULD JUST DO IT AND TELL ME WHAT IT'S LIKE.
YES
NO
MAYBE

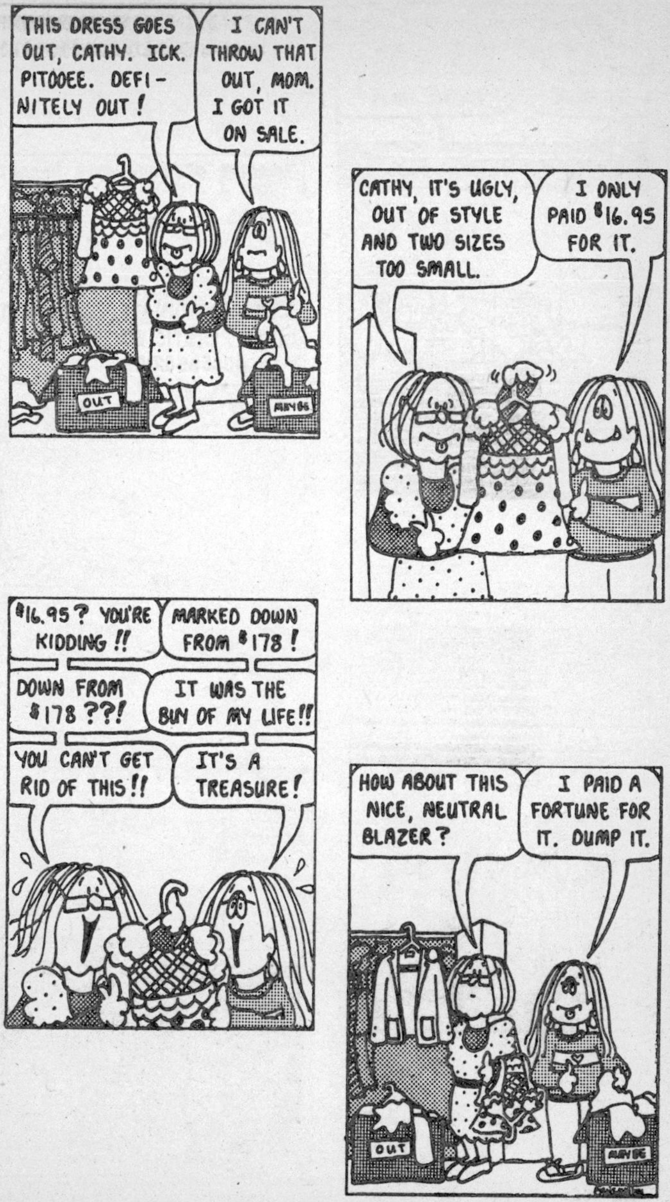
THIS DRESS GOES OUT, CATHY. ICK. PITOOEE. DEFI- NITELY OUT!
I CAN'T THROW THAT OUT, MOM. I GOT IT ON SALE.
OUT
MAYBE
CATHY, IT'S UGLY, OUT OF STYLE AND TWO SIZES TOO SMALL.
I ONLY PAID $16.95 FOR IT.
$16.95? YOU'RE KIDDING!!
MARKED DOWN FROM $178!
DOWN FROM $178??!
IT WAS THE BUY OF MY LIFE!!
YOU CAN'T GET RID OF THIS!!
IT'S A TREASURE!
HOW ABOUT THIS NICE, NEUTRAL BLAZER?
I PAID A FORTUNE FOR IT. DUMP IT.
OUT
MAYBE

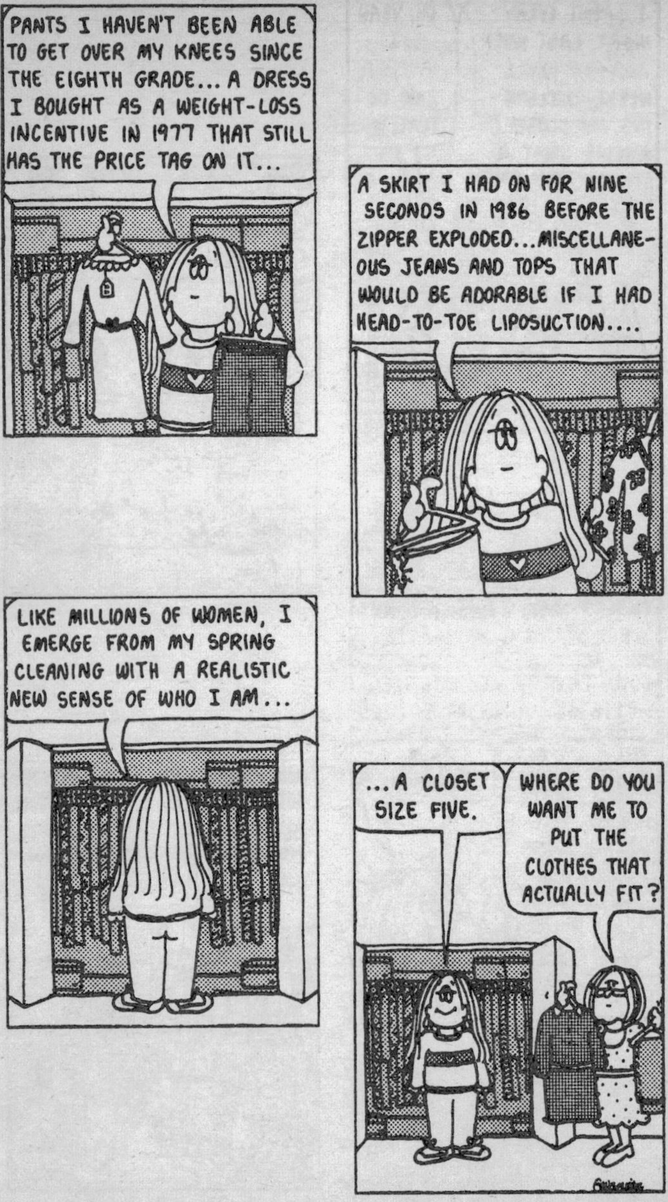
PANTS I HAVEN'T BEEN ABLE TO GET OVER MY KNEES SINCE THE EIGHTH GRADE... A DRESS I BOUGHT AS A WEIGHT-LOSS INCENTIVE IN 1977 THAT STILL HAS THE PRICE TAG ON IT...
A SKIRT I HAD ON FOR NINE SECONDS IN 1986 BEFORE THE ZIPPER EXPLODED...MISCELLANEOUS JEANS AND TOPS THAT WOULD BE ADORABLE IF I HAD HEAD-TO-TOE LIPOSUCTION....
LIKE MILLIONS OF WOMEN, I EMERGE FROM MY SPRING CLEANING WITH A REALISTIC NEW SENSE OF WHO I AM...
...A CLOSET SIZE FIVE.
WHERE DO YOU WANT ME TO PUT THE CLOTHES THAT ACTUALLY FIT?

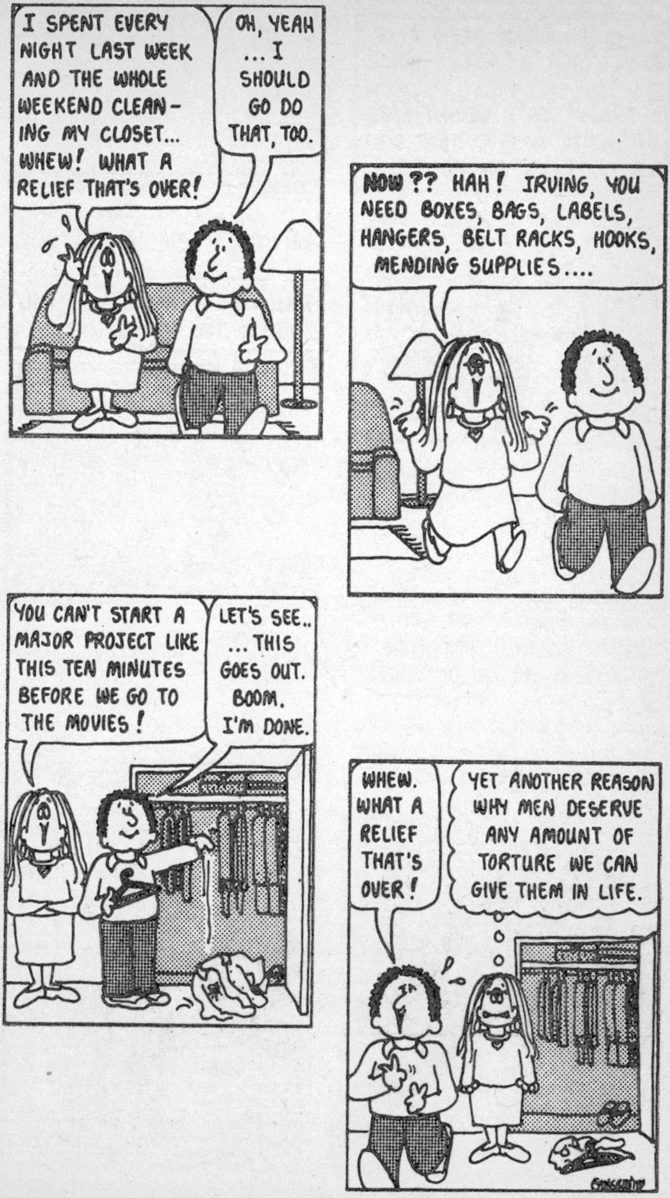

I SPENT EVERY NIGHT LAST WEEK AND THE WHOLE WEEKEND CLEANING MY CLOSET... WHEW! WHAT A RELIEF THAT'S OVER!
OH, YEAH ... I SHOULD GO DO THAT, TOO.
NOW?? HAH! IRVING, YOU NEED BOXES, BAGS, LABELS, HANGERS, BELT RACKS, HOOKS, MENDING SUPPLIES....
YOU CAN'T START A MAJOR PROJECT LIKE THIS TEN MINUTES BEFORE WE GO TO THE MOVIES!
LET'S SEE.. ...THIS GOES OUT. BOOM. I'M DONE.
WHEW. WHAT A RELIEF THAT'S OVER!
YET ANOTHER REASON WHY MEN DESERVE ANY AMOUNT OF TORTURE WE CAN GIVE THEM IN LIFE.

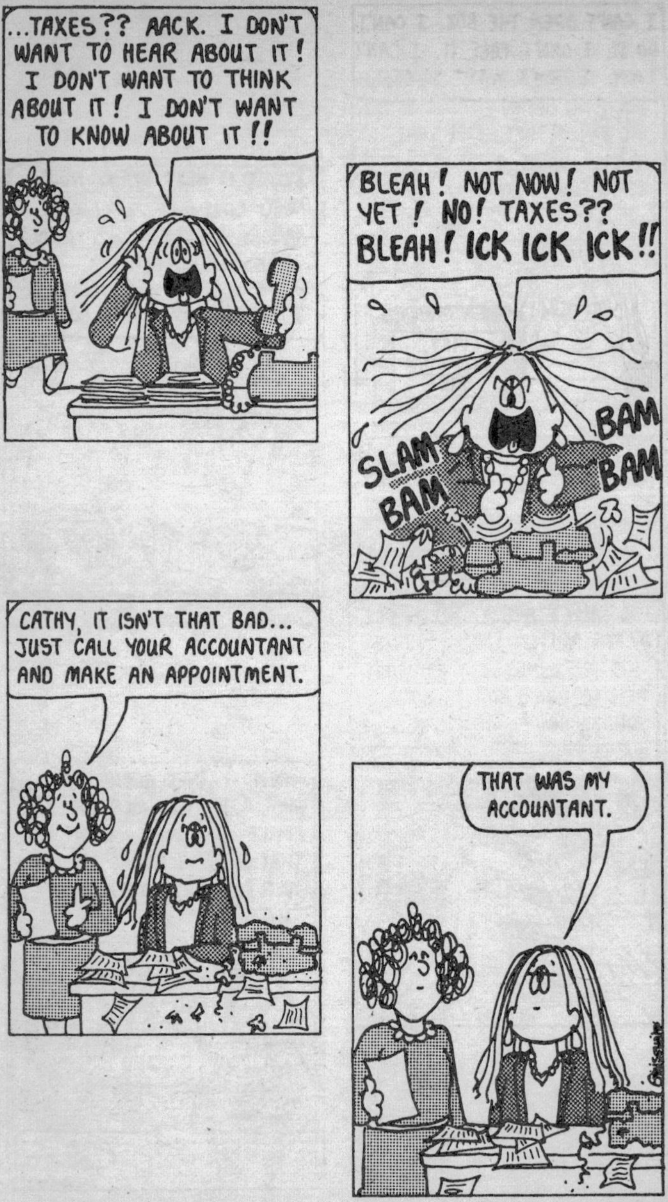
...TAXES?? AACK. I DON'T WANT TO HEAR ABOUT IT! I DON'T WANT TO THINK ABOUT IT! I DON'T WANT TO KNOW ABOUT IT!!
BLEAH! NOT NOW! NOT YET! NO! TAXES?? BLEAH! ICK ICK ICK!!
SLAM BAM
BAM BAM
CATHY, IT ISN'T THAT BAD... JUST CALL YOUR ACCOUNTANT AND MAKE AN APPOINTMENT.
THAT WAS MY ACCOUNTANT.

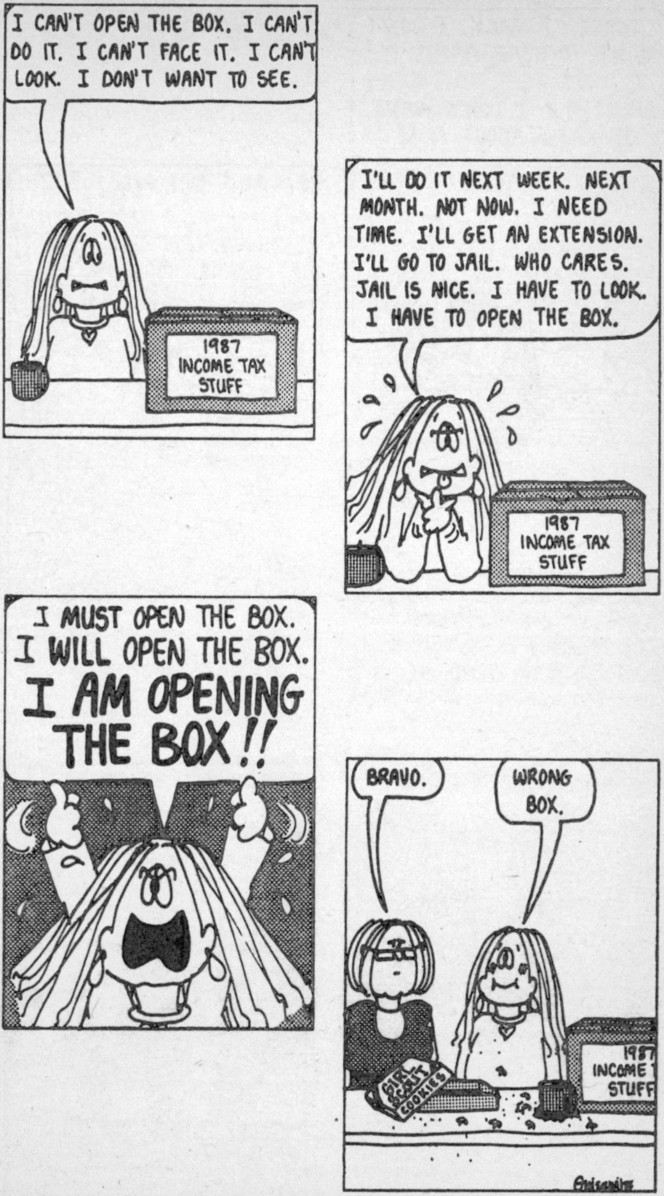
I CAN'T OPEN THE BOX. I CAN'T DO IT. I CAN'T FACE IT. I CAN'T LOOK. I DON'T WANT TO SEE.
1987 INCOME TAX STUFF
I'LL DO IT NEXT WEEK. NEXT MONTH. NOT NOW. I NEED TIME. I'LL GET AN EXTENSION. I'LL GO TO JAIL. WHO CARES. JAIL IS NICE. I HAVE TO LOOK. I HAVE TO OPEN THE BOX.
1987 INCOME TAX STUFF
I MUST OPEN THE BOX. I WILL OPEN THE BOX. I AM OPENING THE BOX!!
BRAVO.
WRONG BOX.
GIRL SCOUT COOKIES
STUFF

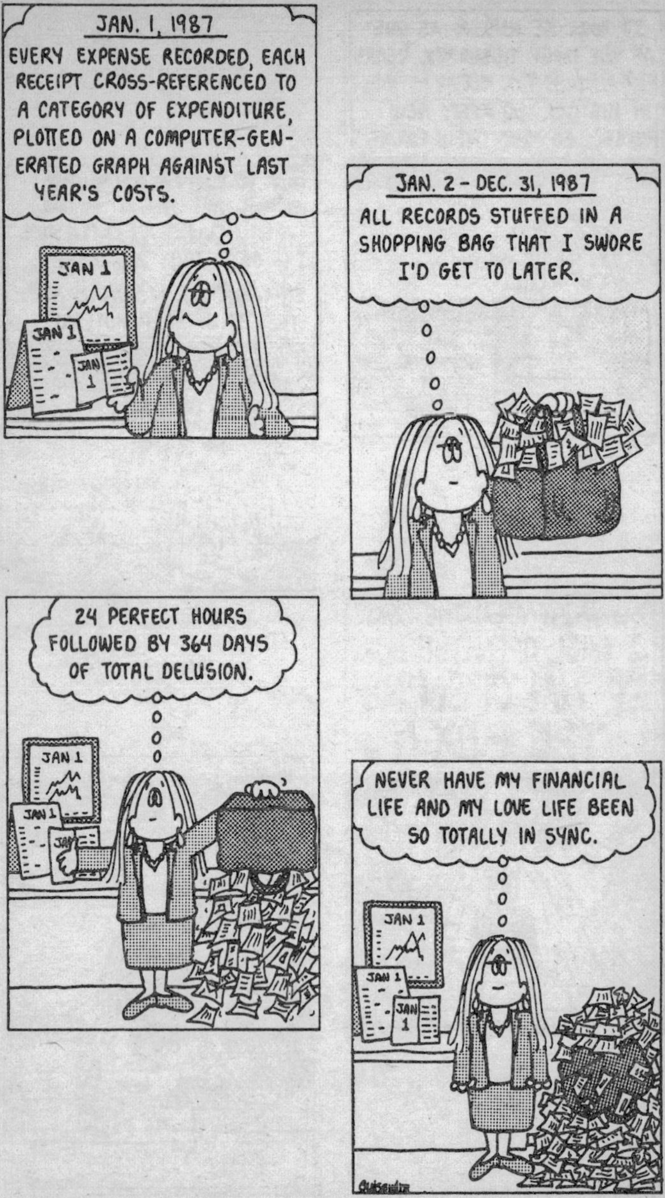
JAN. 1, 1987
EVERY EXPENSE RECORDED, EACH RECEIPT CROSS-REFERENCED TO A CATEGORY OF EXPENDITURE, PLOTTED ON A COMPUTER-GENERATED GRAPH AGAINST LAST YEAR'S COSTS.
JAN. 2 - DEC. 31, 1987
ALL RECORDS STUFFED IN A SHOPPING BAG THAT I SWORE I'D GET TO LATER.
24 PERFECT HOURS FOLLOWED BY 364 DAYS OF TOTAL DELUSION.
NEVER HAVE MY FINANCIAL LIFE AND MY LOVE LIFE BEEN SO TOTALLY IN SYNC.

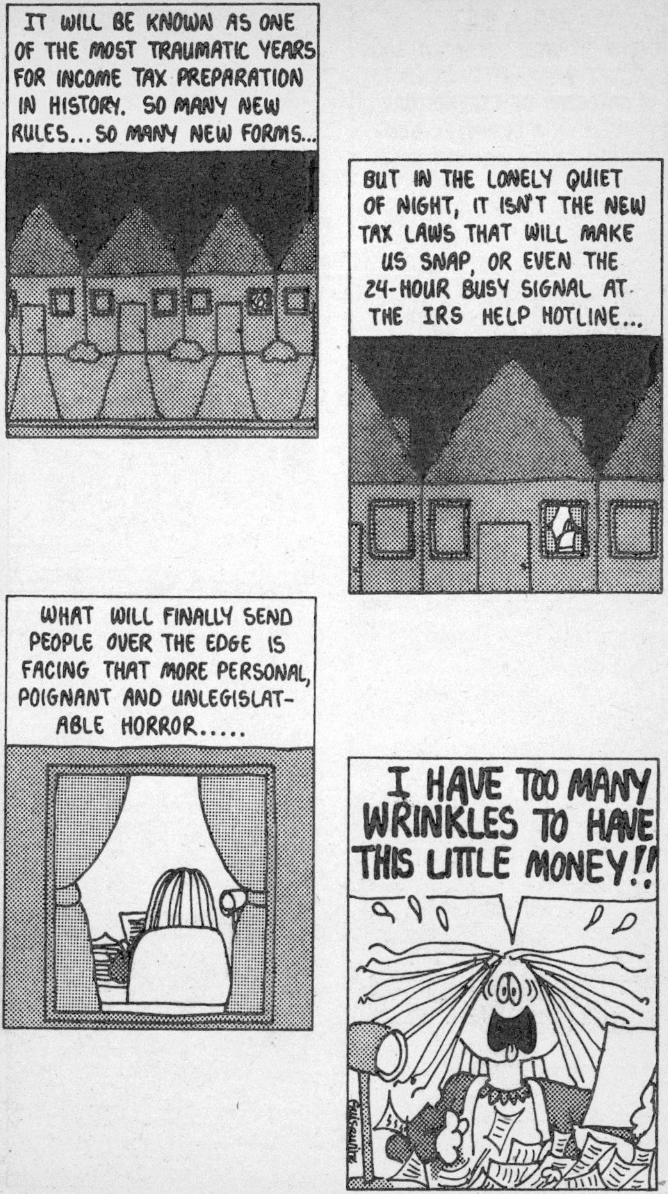
IT WILL BE KNOWN AS ONE OF THE MOST TRAUMATIC YEARS FOR INCOME TAX PREPARATION IN HISTORY. SO MANY NEW RULES... SO MANY NEW FORMS...
BUT IN THE LONELY QUIET OF NIGHT, IT ISN'T THE NEW TAX LAWS THAT WILL MAKE US SNAP, OR EVEN THE 24-HOUR BUSY SIGNAL AT THE IRS HELP HOTLINE...
WHAT WILL FINALLY SEND PEOPLE OVER THE EDGE IS FACING THAT MORE PERSONAL, POIGNANT AND UNLEGISLATABLE HORROR.....
I HAVE TOO MANY WRINKLES TO HAVE THIS LITTLE MONEY!!

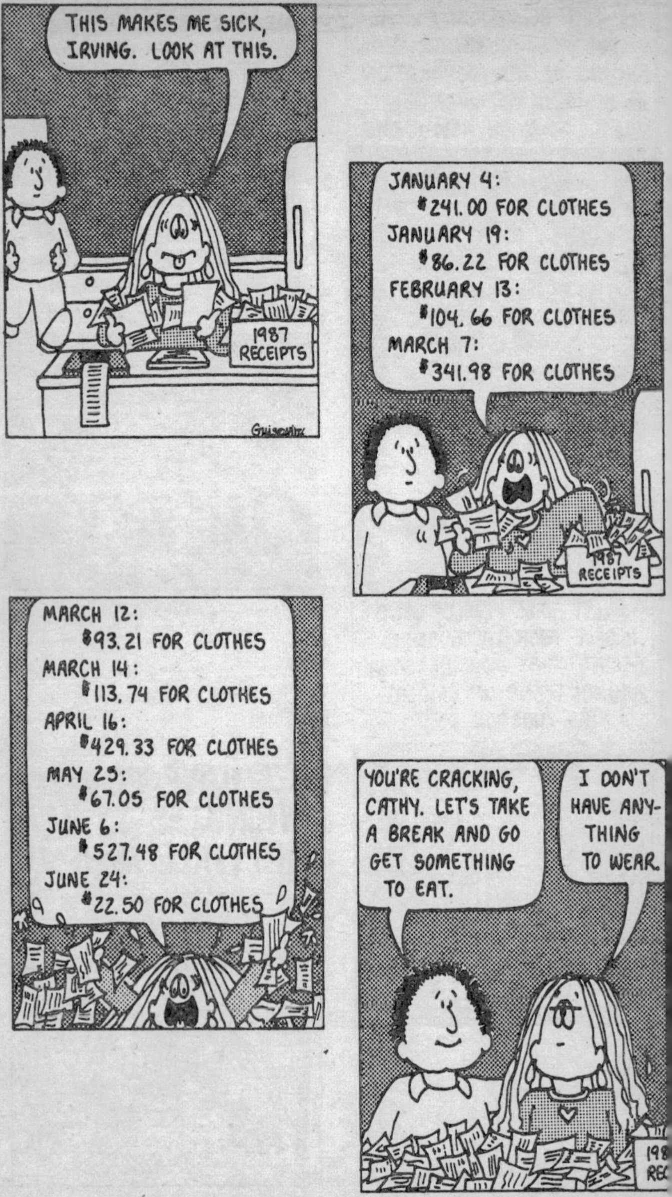
THIS MAKES ME SICK, IRVING. LOOK AT THIS.
1987 RECEIPTS
JANUARY 4: $241.00 FOR CLOTHES JANUARY 19: $86.22 FOR CLOTHES FEBRUARY 13: $104.66 FOR CLOTHES MARCH 7: $341.98 FOR CLOTHES
1987 RECEIPTS
MARCH 12: $93.21 FOR CLOTHES MARCH 14: $113.74 FOR CLOTHES APRIL 16: $429.33 FOR CLOTHES MAY 25: $67.05 FOR CLOTHES JUNE 6: $527.48 FOR CLOTHES JUNE 24: $22.50 FOR CLOTHES
YOU'RE CRACKING, CATHY. LET'S TAKE A BREAK AND GO GET SOMETHING TO EAT.
I DON'T HAVE ANYTHING TO WEAR.

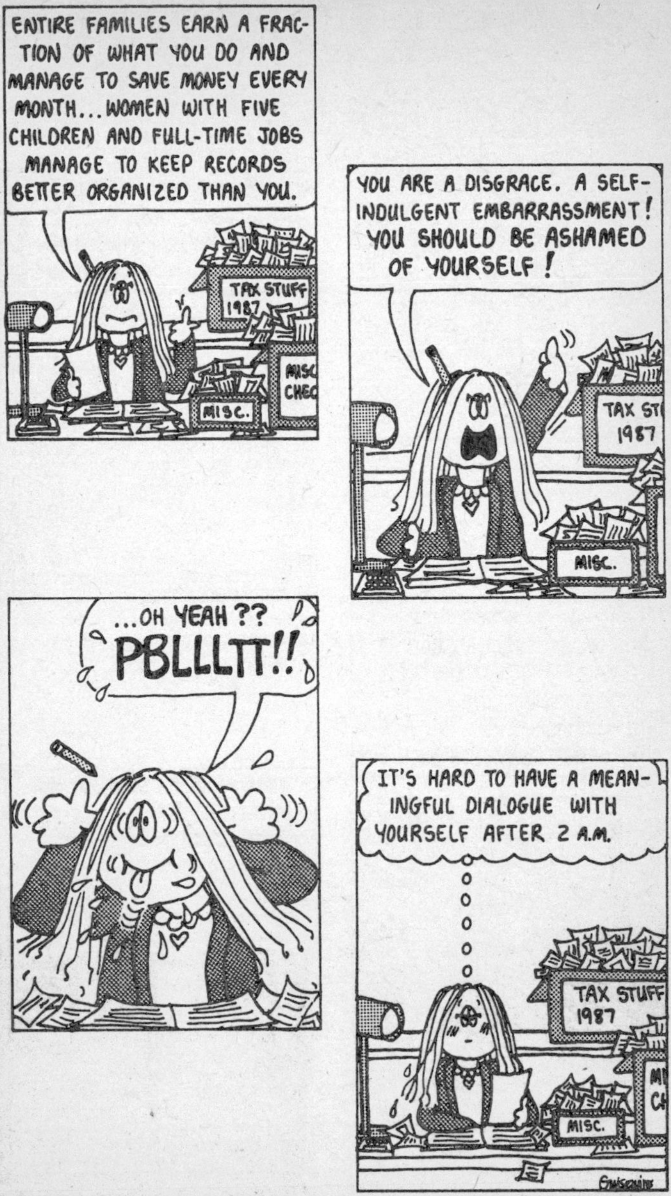
ENTIRE FAMILIES EARN A FRACTION OF WHAT YOU DO AND MANAGE TO SAVE MONEY EVERY MONTH... WOMEN WITH FIVE CHILDREN AND FULL-TIME JOBS MANAGE TO KEEP RECORDS BETTER ORGANIZED THAN YOU.
TAX STUFF 1987
MISC.
YOU ARE A DISGRACE. A SELF-INDULGENT EMBARRASSMENT! YOU SHOULD BE ASHAMED OF YOURSELF!
...OH YEAH?? PBLLLTT!!
IT'S HARD TO HAVE A MEANINGFUL DIALOGUE WITH YOURSELF AFTER 2 A.M.
TAX STUFF 1987
MISC.

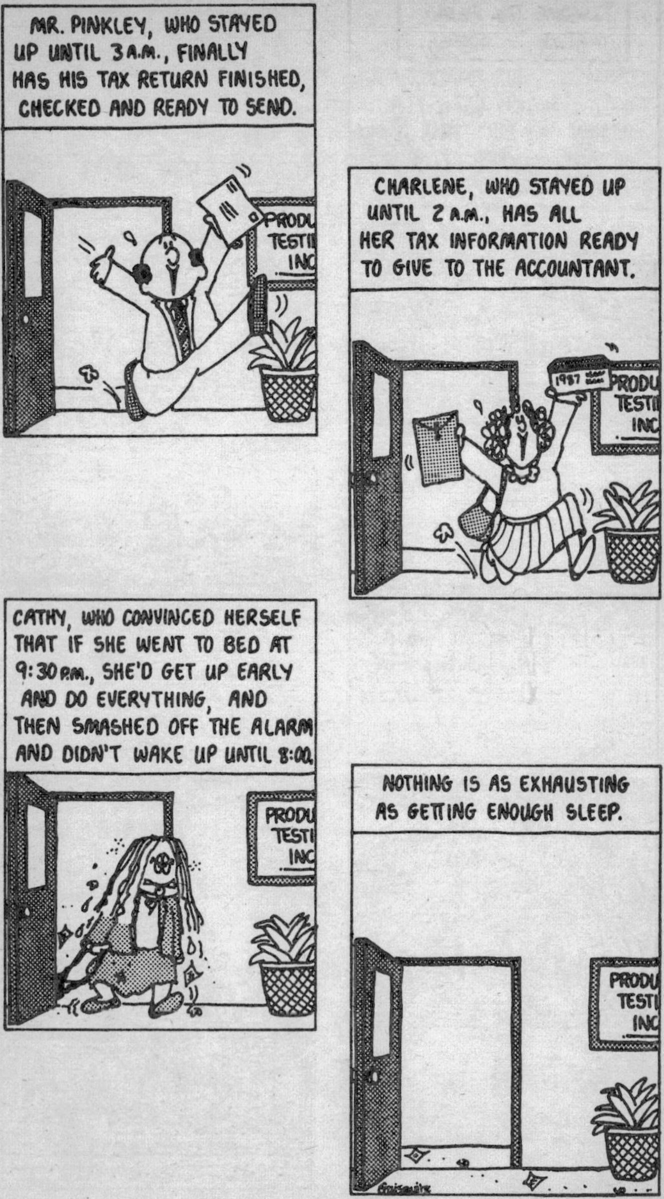
MR. PINKLEY, WHO STAYED UP UNTIL 3 A.M., FINALLY HAS HIS TAX RETURN FINISHED, CHECKED AND READY TO SEND.
CHARLENE, WHO STAYED UP UNTIL 2 A.M., HAS ALL HER TAX INFORMATION READY TO GIVE TO THE ACCOUNTANT.
CATHY, WHO CONVINCED HERSELF THAT IF SHE WENT TO BED AT 9:30 P.M., SHE'D GET UP EARLY AND DO EVERYTHING, AND THEN SMASHED OFF THE ALARM AND DIDN'T WAKE UP UNTIL 8:00,
NOTHING IS AS EXHAUSTING AS GETTING ENOUGH SLEEP.

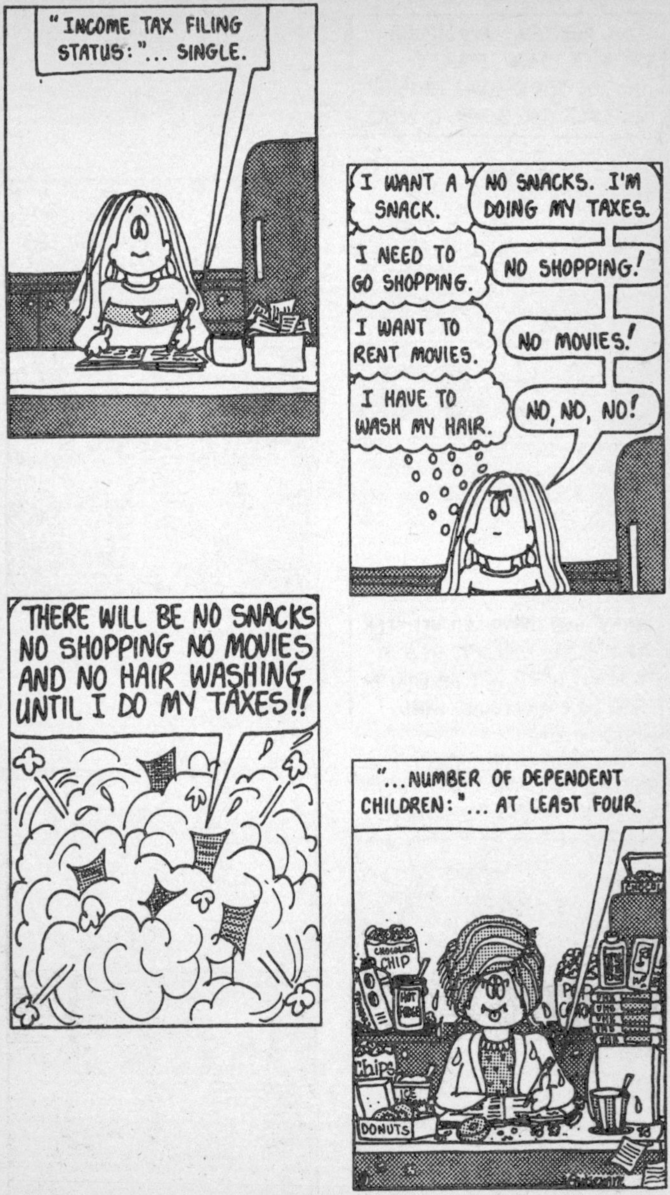
"INCOME TAX FILING STATUS:"... SINGLE.
I WANT A SNACK.
NO SNACKS. I'M DOING MY TAXES.
I NEED TO GO SHOPPING.
NO SHOPPING!
I WANT TO RENT MOVIES.
NO MOVIES!
I HAVE TO WASH MY HAIR.
NO, NO, NO!
THERE WILL BE NO SNACKS NO SHOPPING NO MOVIES AND NO HAIR WASHING UNTIL I DO MY TAXES!!
"...NUMBER OF DEPENDENT CHILDREN:"... AT LEAST FOUR.
CHIP
Chips
DONUTS

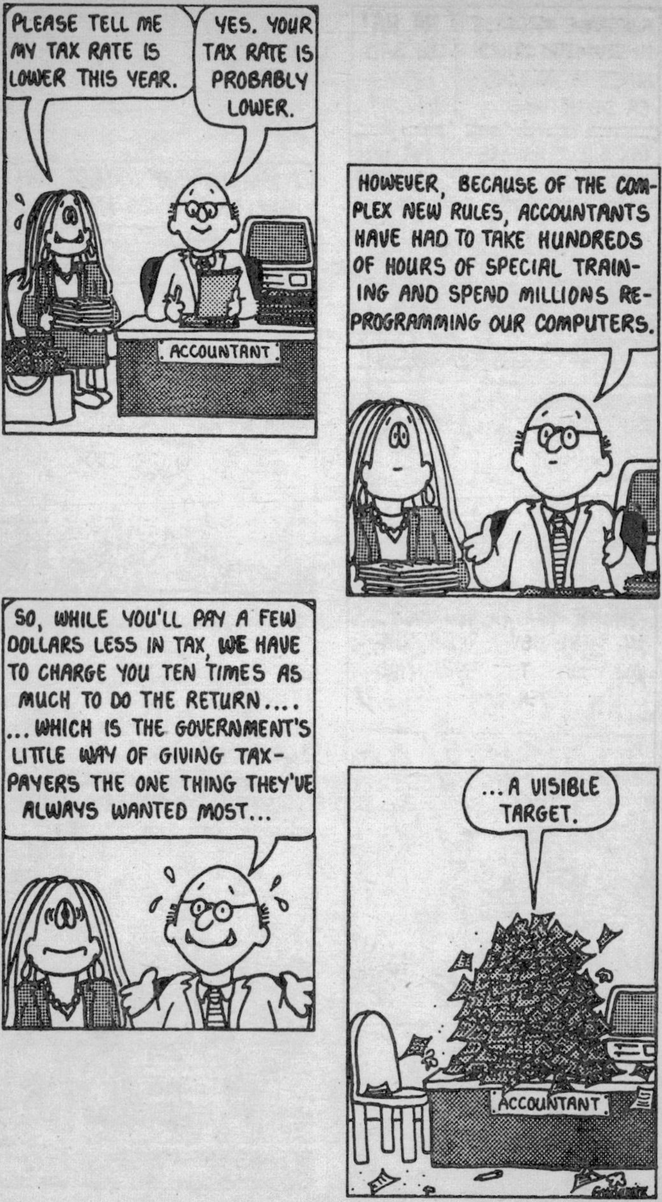
PLEASE TELL ME MY TAX RATE IS LOWER THIS YEAR.
YES. YOUR TAX RATE IS PROBABLY LOWER.
ACCOUNTANT
HOWEVER, BECAUSE OF THE COMPLEX NEW RULES, ACCOUNTANTS HAVE HAD TO TAKE HUNDREDS OF HOURS OF SPECIAL TRAINING AND SPEND MILLIONS REPROGRAMMING OUR COMPUTERS.
SO, WHILE YOU'LL PAY A FEW DOLLARS LESS IN TAX, WE HAVE TO CHARGE YOU TEN TIMES AS MUCH TO DO THE RETURN.... ...WHICH IS THE GOVERNMENT'S LITTLE WAY OF GIVING TAXPAYERS THE ONE THING THEY'VE ALWAYS WANTED MOST...
...A VISIBLE TARGET.
ACCOUNTANT

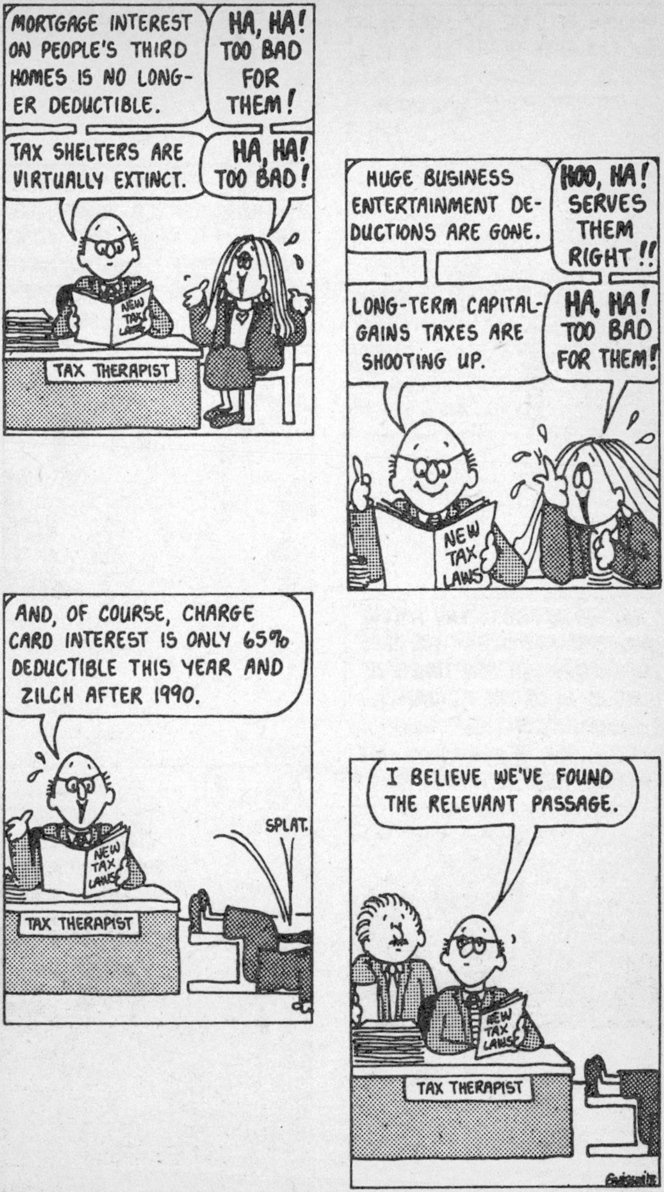
MORTGAGE INTEREST ON PEOPLE'S THIRD HOMES IS NO LONGER DEDUCTIBLE.
HA, HA! TOO BAD FOR THEM!
TAX SHELTERS ARE VIRTUALLY EXTINCT.
HA, HA! TOO BAD!
NEW TAX LAWS
TAX THERAPIST
HUGE BUSINESS ENTERTAINMENT DEDUCTIONS ARE GONE.
HOO, HA! SERVES THEM RIGHT!!
LONG-TERM CAPITAL-GAINS TAXES ARE SHOOTING UP.
HA, HA! TOO BAD FOR THEM!
NEW TAX LAWS
AND, OF COURSE, CHARGE CARD INTEREST IS ONLY 65% DEDUCTIBLE THIS YEAR AND ZILCH AFTER 1990.
NEW TAX LAWS
SPLAT.
TAX THERAPIST
I BELIEVE WE'VE FOUND THE RELEVANT PASSAGE.
NEW TAX LAWS
TAX THERAPIST

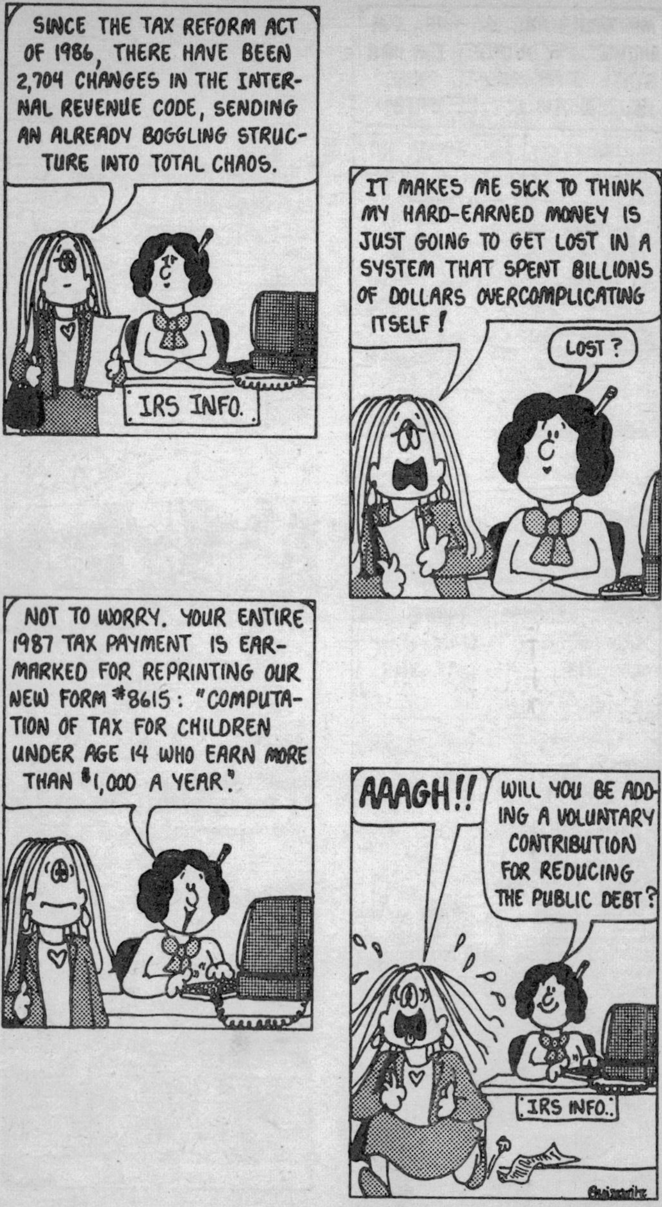
SINCE THE TAX REFORM ACT OF 1986, THERE HAVE BEEN 2,704 CHANGES IN THE INTERNAL REVENUE CODE, SENDING AN ALREADY BOGGLING STRUCTURE INTO TOTAL CHAOS.
IRS INFO.
IT MAKES ME SICK TO THINK MY HARD-EARNED MONEY IS JUST GOING TO GET LOST IN A SYSTEM THAT SPENT BILLIONS OF DOLLARS OVERCOMPLICATING ITSELF!
LOST?
NOT TO WORRY. YOUR ENTIRE 1987 TAX PAYMENT IS EARMARKED FOR REPRINTING OUR NEW FORM #8615: "COMPUTATION OF TAX FOR CHILDREN UNDER AGE 14 WHO EARN MORE THAN $1,000 A YEAR."
AAAGH!!
WILL YOU BE ADDING A VOLUNTARY CONTRIBUTION FOR REDUCING THE PUBLIC DEBT?
IRS INFO.

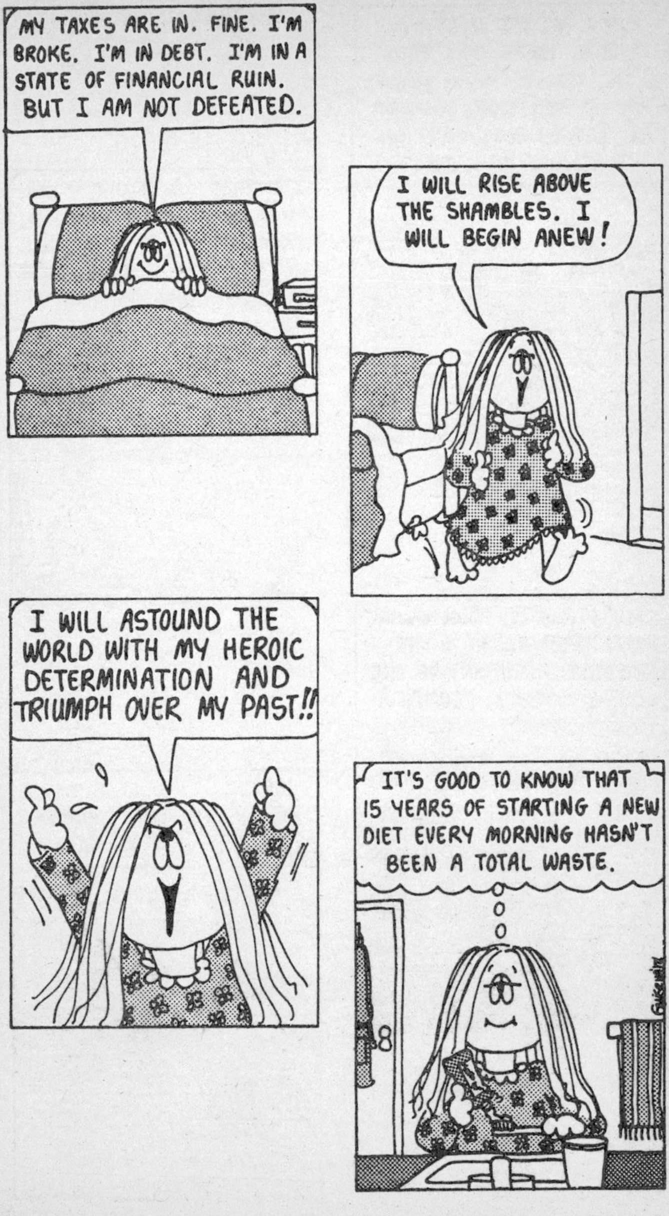
MY TAXES ARE IN. FINE. I'M BROKE. I'M IN DEBT. I'M IN A STATE OF FINANCIAL RUIN. BUT I AM NOT DEFEATED.
I WILL RISE ABOVE THE SHAMBLES. I WILL BEGIN ANEW!
I WILL ASTOUND THE WORLD WITH MY HEROIC DETERMINATION AND TRIUMPH OVER MY PAST!!
IT'S GOOD TO KNOW THAT 15 YEARS OF STARTING A NEW DIET EVERY MORNING HASN'T BEEN A TOTAL WASTE.

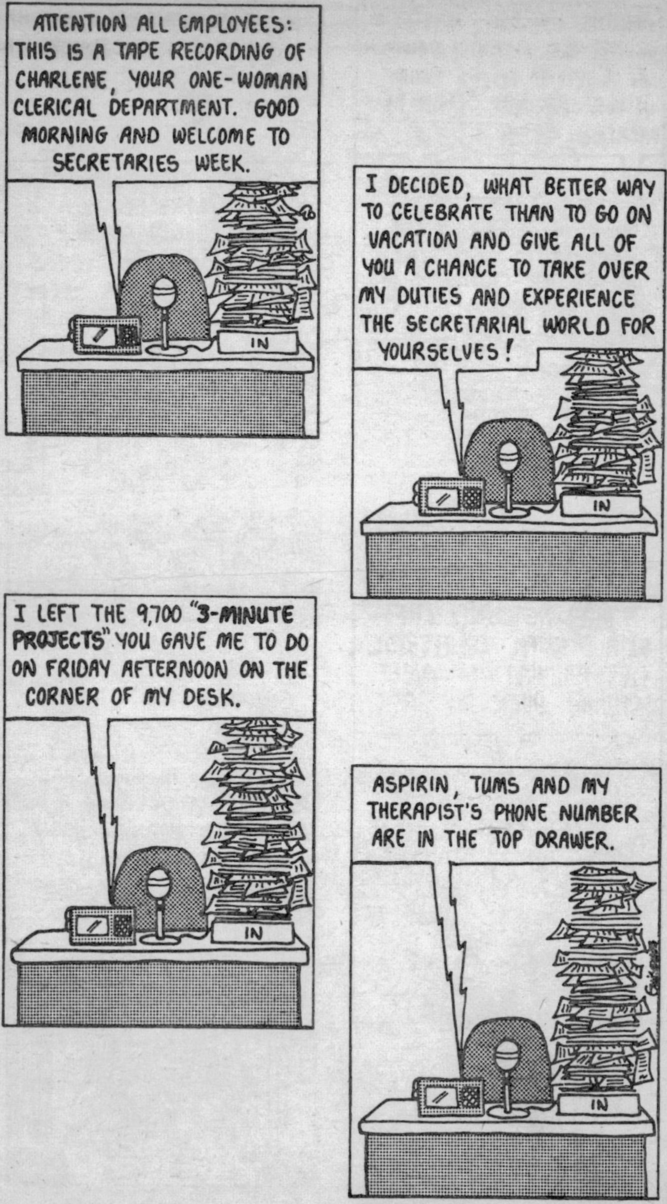
ATTENTION ALL EMPLOYEES: THIS IS A TAPE RECORDING OF CHARLENE, YOUR ONE-WOMAN CLERICAL DEPARTMENT. GOOD MORNING AND WELCOME TO SECRETARIES WEEK.
IN
I DECIDED, WHAT BETTER WAY TO CELEBRATE THAN TO GO ON VACATION AND GIVE ALL OF YOU A CHANCE TO TAKE OVER MY DUTIES AND EXPERIENCE THE SECRETARIAL WORLD FOR YOURSELVES!
IN
I LEFT THE 9,700 "3-MINUTE PROJECTS" YOU GAVE ME TO DO ON FRIDAY AFTERNOON ON THE CORNER OF MY DESK.
IN
ASPIRIN, TUMS AND MY THERAPIST'S PHONE NUMBER ARE IN THE TOP DRAWER.
IN

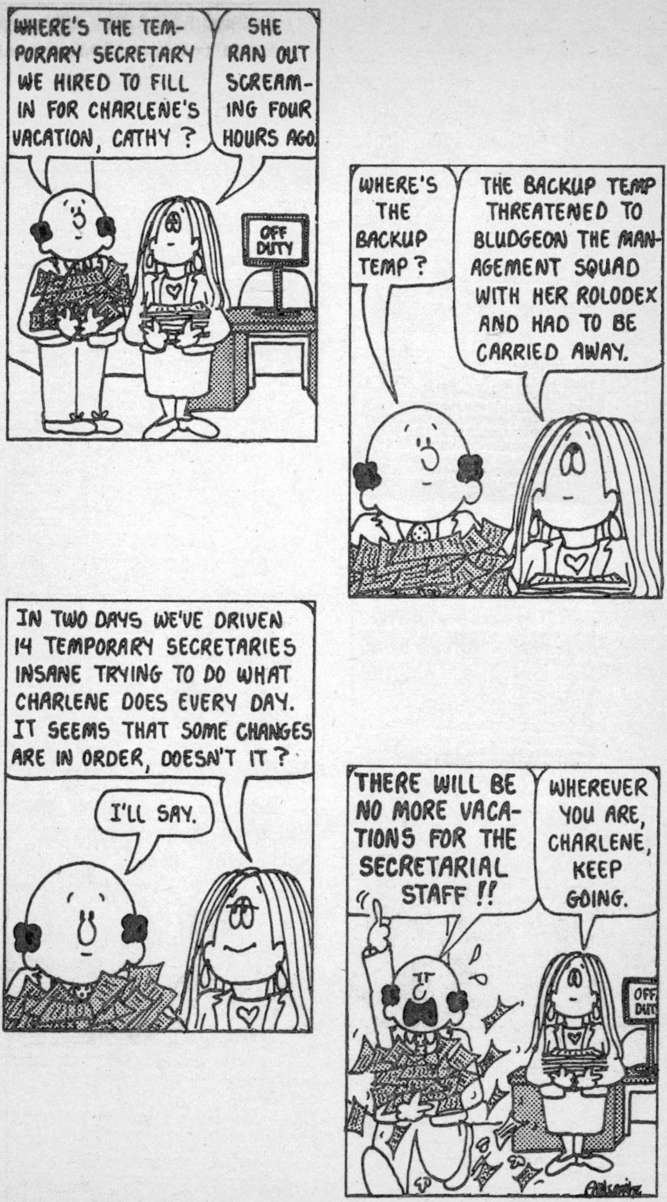

WHERE'S THE TEMPORARY SECRETARY WE HIRED TO FILL IN FOR CHARLENE'S VACATION, CATHY ?
SHE RAN OUT SCREAMING FOUR HOURS AGO.
OFF DUTY
WHERE'S THE BACKUP TEMP ?
THE BACKUP TEMP THREATENED TO BLUDGEON THE MANAGEMENT SQUAD WITH HER ROLODEX AND HAD TO BE CARRIED AWAY.
IN TWO DAYS WE'VE DRIVEN 14 TEMPORARY SECRETARIES INSANE TRYING TO DO WHAT CHARLENE DOES EVERY DAY. IT SEEMS THAT SOME CHANGES ARE IN ORDER, DOESN'T IT ?
I'LL SAY.
THERE WILL BE NO MORE VACATIONS FOR THE SECRETARIAL STAFF !!
WHEREVER YOU ARE, CHARLENE, KEEP GOING.

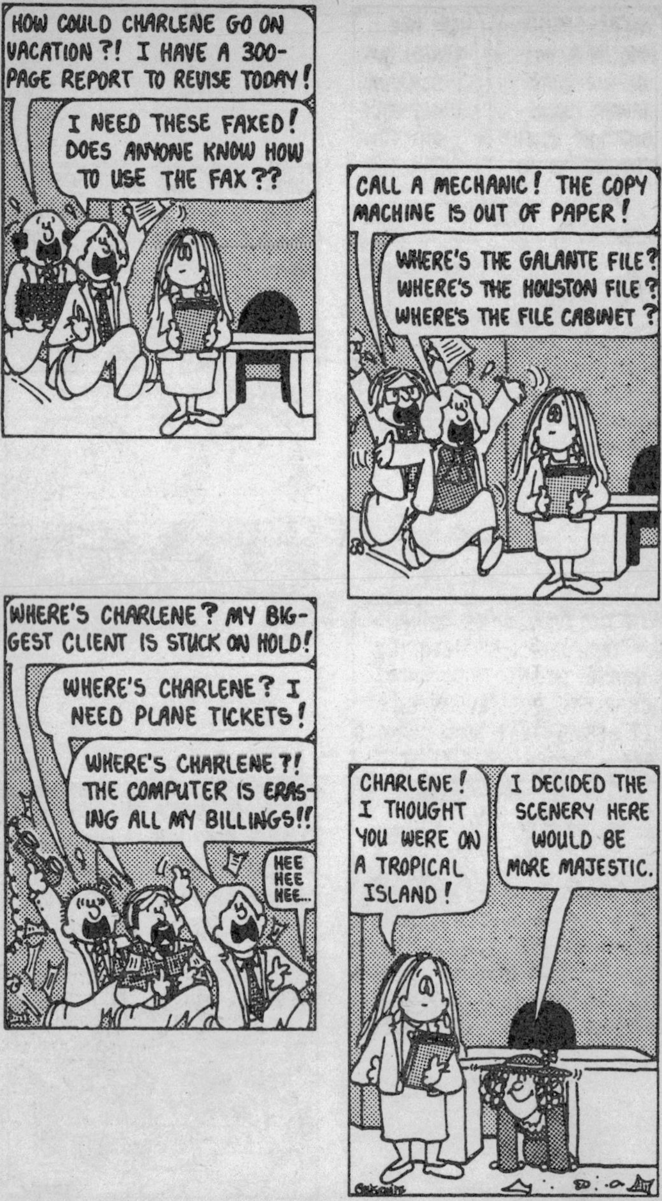
HOW COULD CHARLENE GO ON VACATION ?! I HAVE A 300-PAGE REPORT TO REVISE TODAY!
I NEED THESE FAXED! DOES ANYONE KNOW HOW TO USE THE FAX??
CALL A MECHANIC! THE COPY MACHINE IS OUT OF PAPER!
WHERE'S THE GALANTE FILE? WHERE'S THE HOUSTON FILE? WHERE'S THE FILE CABINET?
WHERE'S CHARLENE? MY BIGGEST CLIENT IS STUCK ON HOLD!
WHERE'S CHARLENE? I NEED PLANE TICKETS!
WHERE'S CHARLENE?! THE COMPUTER IS ERASING ALL MY BILLINGS!!
HEE HEE HEE...
CHARLENE! I THOUGHT YOU WERE ON A TROPICAL ISLAND!
I DECIDED THE SCENERY HERE WOULD BE MORE MAJESTIC.

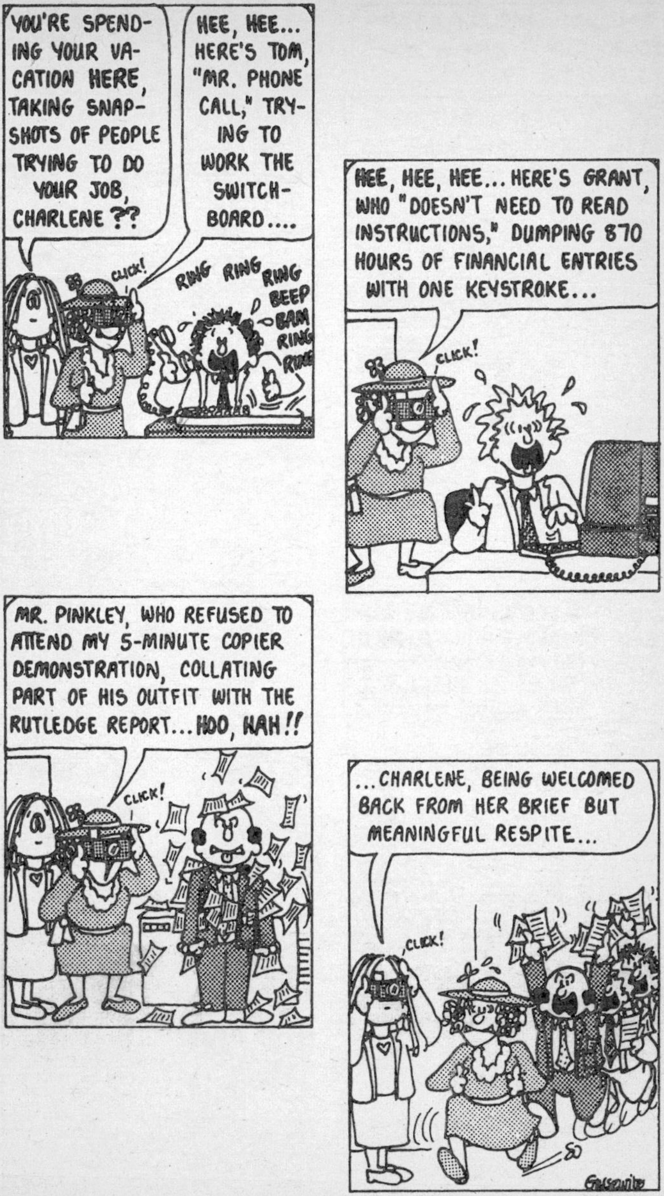
YOU'RE SPENDING YOUR VACATION HERE, TAKING SNAPSHOTS OF PEOPLE TRYING TO DO YOUR JOB, CHARLENE ??
HEE, HEE... HERE'S TOM, "MR. PHONE CALL," TRYING TO WORK THE SWITCHBOARD....
CLICK!
RING RING RING
BEEP
BAM
RING
HEE, HEE, HEE... HERE'S GRANT, WHO "DOESN'T NEED TO READ INSTRUCTIONS," DUMPING 870 HOURS OF FINANCIAL ENTRIES WITH ONE KEYSTROKE...
CLICK!
MR. PINKLEY, WHO REFUSED TO ATTEND MY 5-MINUTE COPIER DEMONSTRATION, COLLATING PART OF HIS OUTFIT WITH THE RUTLEDGE REPORT... HOO, HAH!!
CLICK!
...CHARLENE, BEING WELCOMED BACK FROM HER BRIEF BUT MEANINGFUL RESPITE...
CLICK!

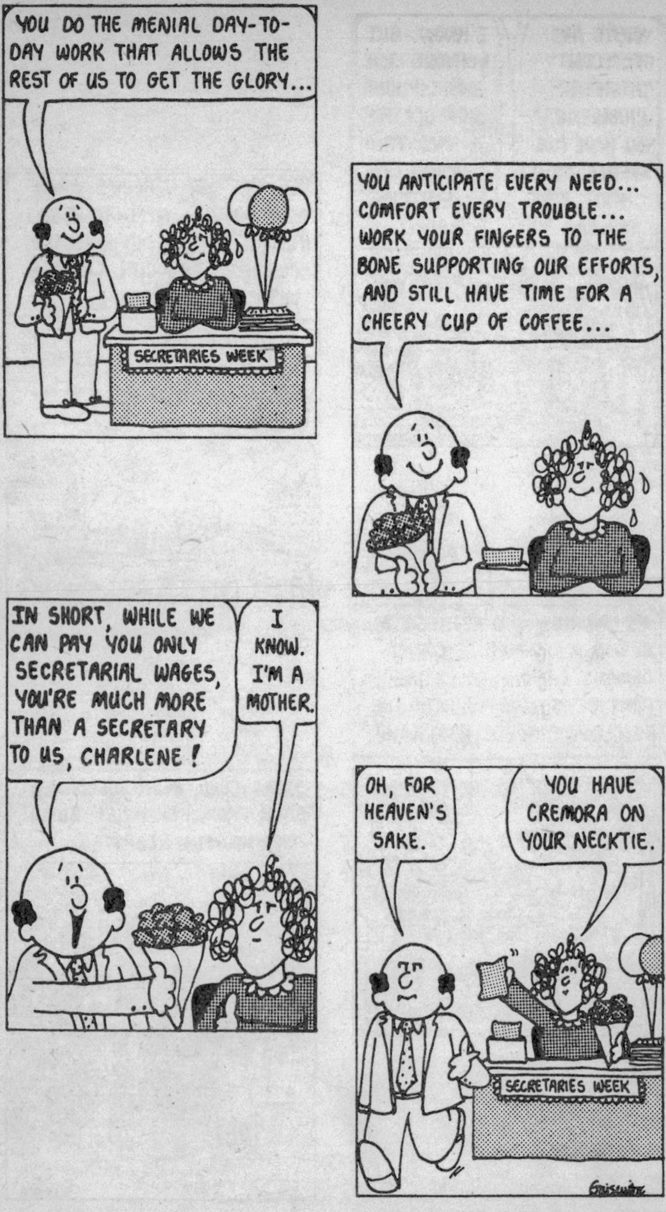
YOU DO THE MENIAL DAY-TO-DAY WORK THAT ALLOWS THE REST OF US TO GET THE GLORY...
SECRETARIES WEEK
YOU ANTICIPATE EVERY NEED... COMFORT EVERY TROUBLE... WORK YOUR FINGERS TO THE BONE SUPPORTING OUR EFFORTS, AND STILL HAVE TIME FOR A CHEERY CUP OF COFFEE...
IN SHORT, WHILE WE CAN PAY YOU ONLY SECRETARIAL WAGES, YOU'RE MUCH MORE THAN A SECRETARY TO US, CHARLENE!
I KNOW. I'M A MOTHER.
OH, FOR HEAVEN'S SAKE.
YOU HAVE CREMORA ON YOUR NECKTIE.
SECRETARIES WEEK
Guisewite

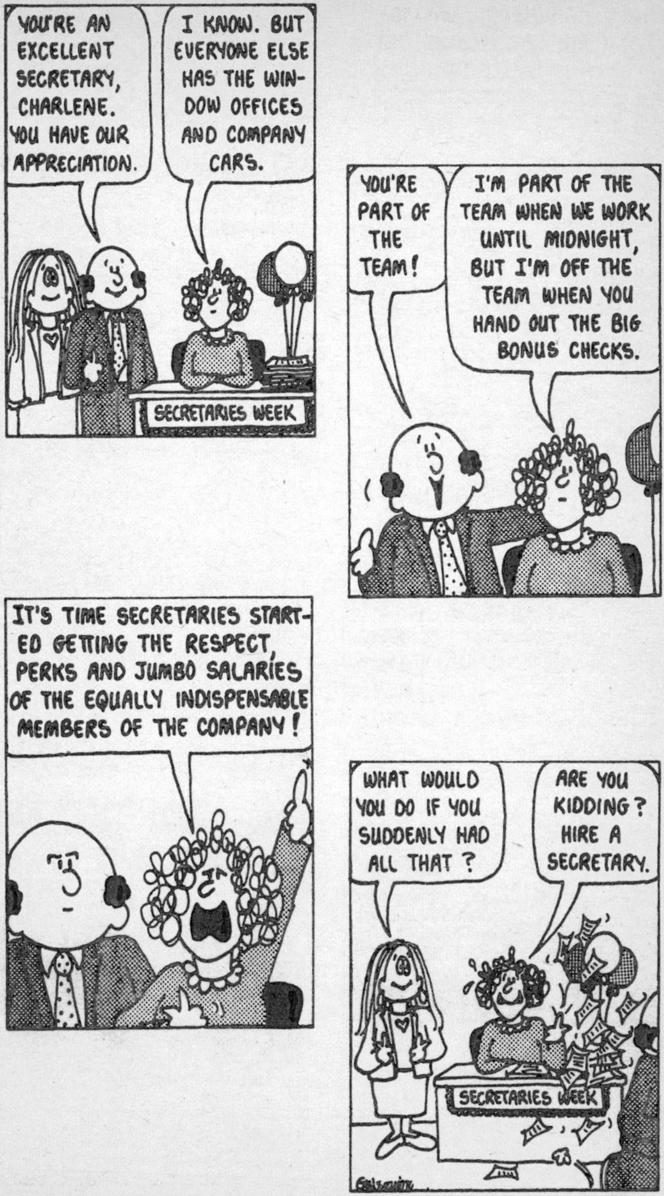
YOU'RE AN EXCELLENT SECRETARY, CHARLENE. YOU HAVE OUR APPRECIATION.
I KNOW. BUT EVERYONE ELSE HAS THE WINDOW OFFICES AND COMPANY CARS.
SECRETARIES WEEK
YOU'RE PART OF THE TEAM!
I'M PART OF THE TEAM WHEN WE WORK UNTIL MIDNIGHT, BUT I'M OFF THE TEAM WHEN YOU HAND OUT THE BIG BONUS CHECKS.
IT'S TIME SECRETARIES STARTED GETTING THE RESPECT, PERKS AND JUMBO SALARIES OF THE EQUALLY INDISPENSABLE MEMBERS OF THE COMPANY!
WHAT WOULD YOU DO IF YOU SUDDENLY HAD ALL THAT?
ARE YOU KIDDING? HIRE A SECRETARY.
SECRETARIES WEEK

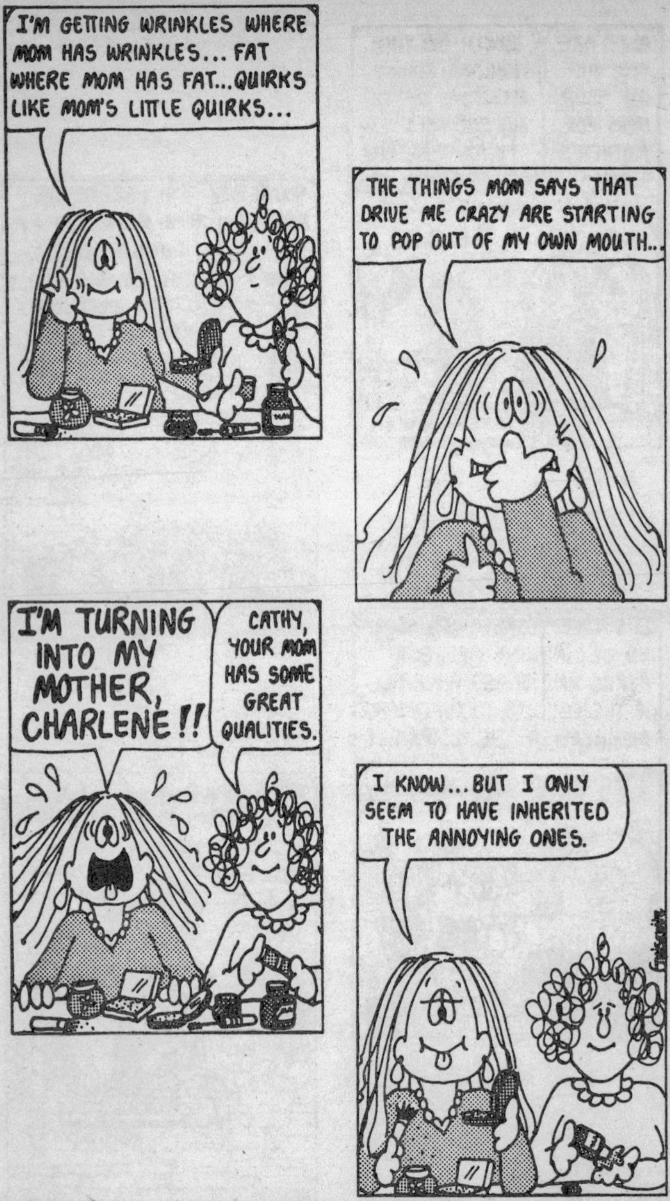
I'M GETTING WRINKLES WHERE MOM HAS WRINKLES... FAT WHERE MOM HAS FAT...QUIRKS LIKE MOM'S LITTLE QUIRKS...
THE THINGS MOM SAYS THAT DRIVE ME CRAZY ARE STARTING TO POP OUT OF MY OWN MOUTH...
I'M TURNING INTO MY MOTHER, CHARLENE!!
CATHY, YOUR MOM HAS SOME GREAT QUALITIES.
I KNOW...BUT I ONLY SEEM TO HAVE INHERITED THE ANNOYING ONES.

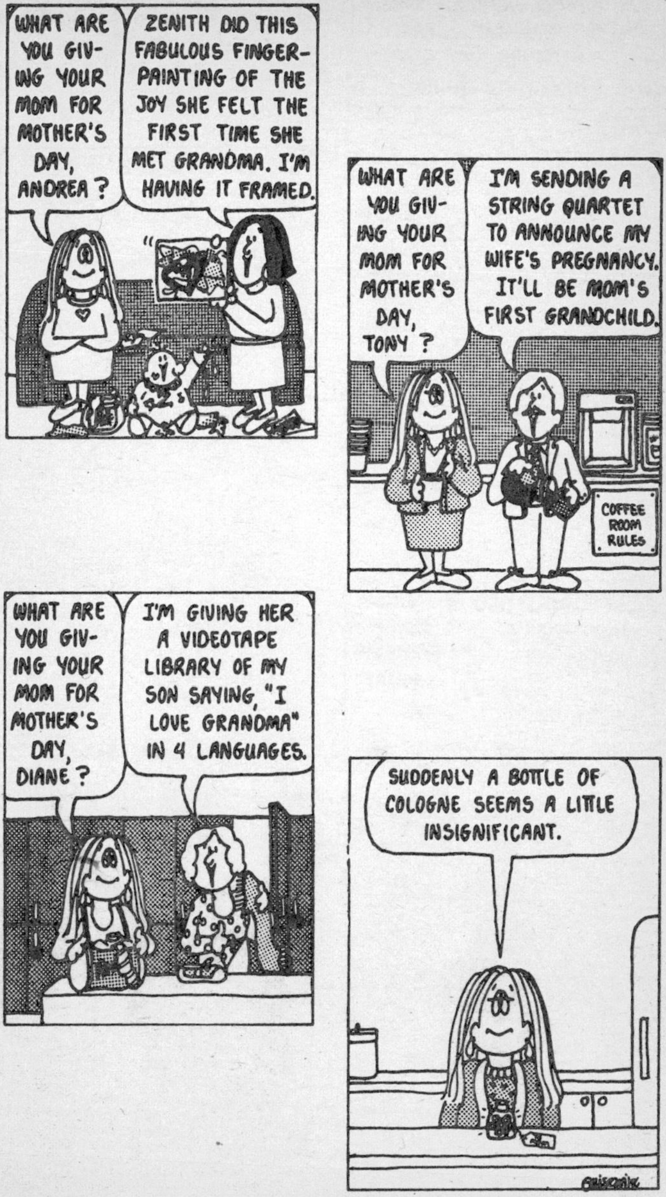
WHAT ARE YOU GIVING YOUR MOM FOR MOTHER'S DAY, ANDREA?
ZENITH DID THIS FABULOUS FINGER-PAINTING OF THE JOY SHE FELT THE FIRST TIME SHE MET GRANDMA. I'M HAVING IT FRAMED.
WHAT ARE YOU GIVING YOUR MOM FOR MOTHER'S DAY, TONY?
I'M SENDING A STRING QUARTET TO ANNOUNCE MY WIFE'S PREGNANCY. IT'LL BE MOM'S FIRST GRANDCHILD.
COFFEE ROOM RULES
WHAT ARE YOU GIVING YOUR MOM FOR MOTHER'S DAY, DIANE?
I'M GIVING HER A VIDEOTAPE LIBRARY OF MY SON SAYING, "I LOVE GRANDMA" IN 4 LANGUAGES.
SUDDENLY A BOTTLE OF COLOGNE SEEMS A LITTLE INSIGNIFICANT.

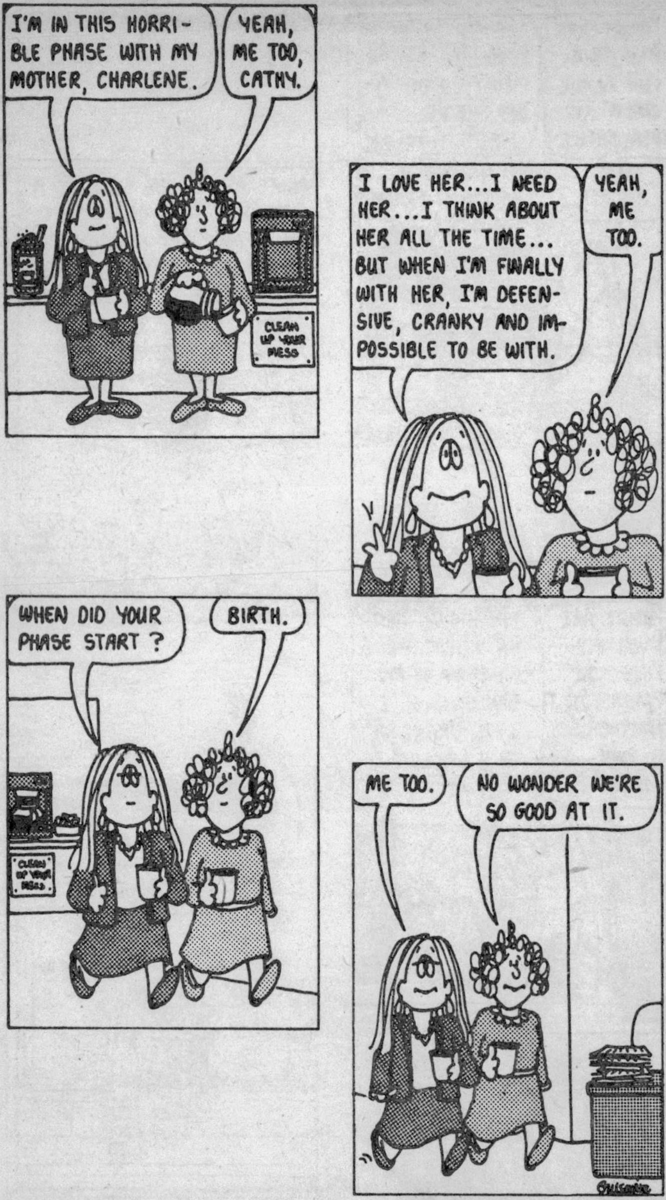

I'M IN THIS HORRIBLE PHASE WITH MY MOTHER, CHARLENE.
YEAH, ME TOO, CATHY.
CLEAN UP YOUR MESS
I LOVE HER...I NEED HER...I THINK ABOUT HER ALL THE TIME... BUT WHEN I'M FINALLY WITH HER, I'M DEFENSIVE, CRANKY AND IMPOSSIBLE TO BE WITH.
YEAH, ME TOO.
WHEN DID YOUR PHASE START ?
BIRTH.
ME TOO.
NO WONDER WE'RE SO GOOD AT IT.

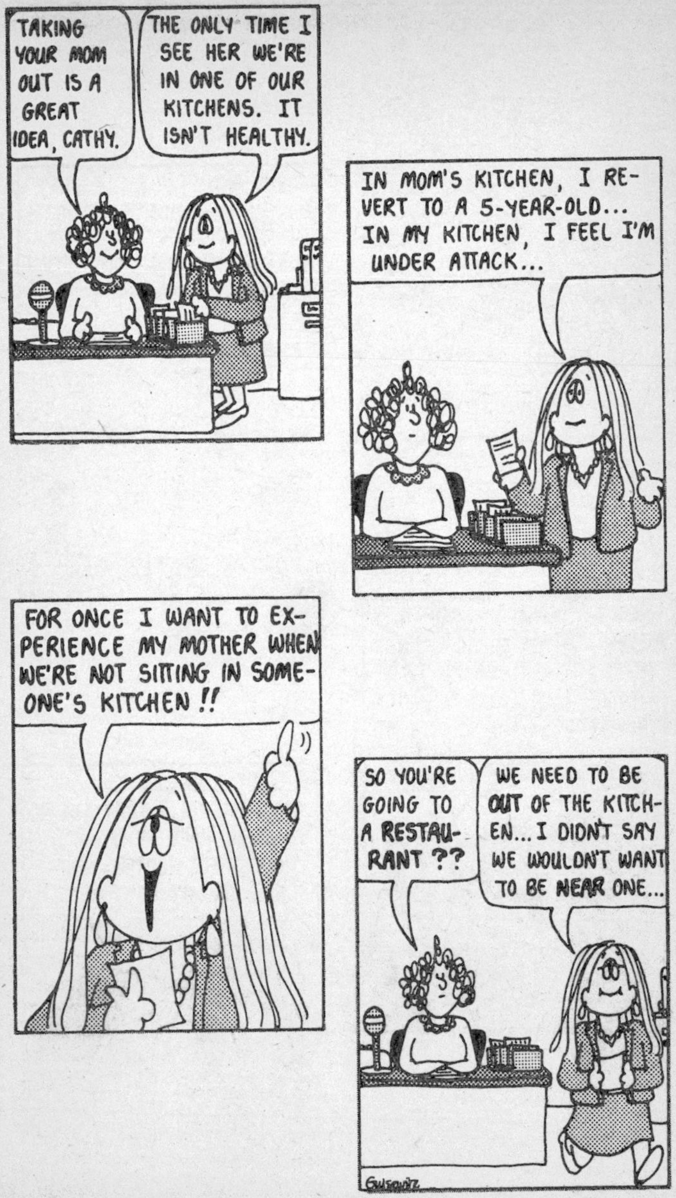
TAKING YOUR MOM OUT IS A GREAT IDEA, CATHY.
THE ONLY TIME I SEE HER WE'RE IN ONE OF OUR KITCHENS. IT ISN'T HEALTHY.
IN MOM'S KITCHEN, I RE-VERT TO A 5-YEAR-OLD... IN MY KITCHEN, I FEEL I'M UNDER ATTACK...
FOR ONCE I WANT TO EX-PERIENCE MY MOTHER WHEN WE'RE NOT SITTING IN SOME-ONE'S KITCHEN !!
SO YOU'RE GOING TO A RESTAU-RANT ??
WE NEED TO BE OUT OF THE KITCH-EN... I DIDN'T SAY WE WOULDN'T WANT TO BE NEAR ONE...
GUISEWITE

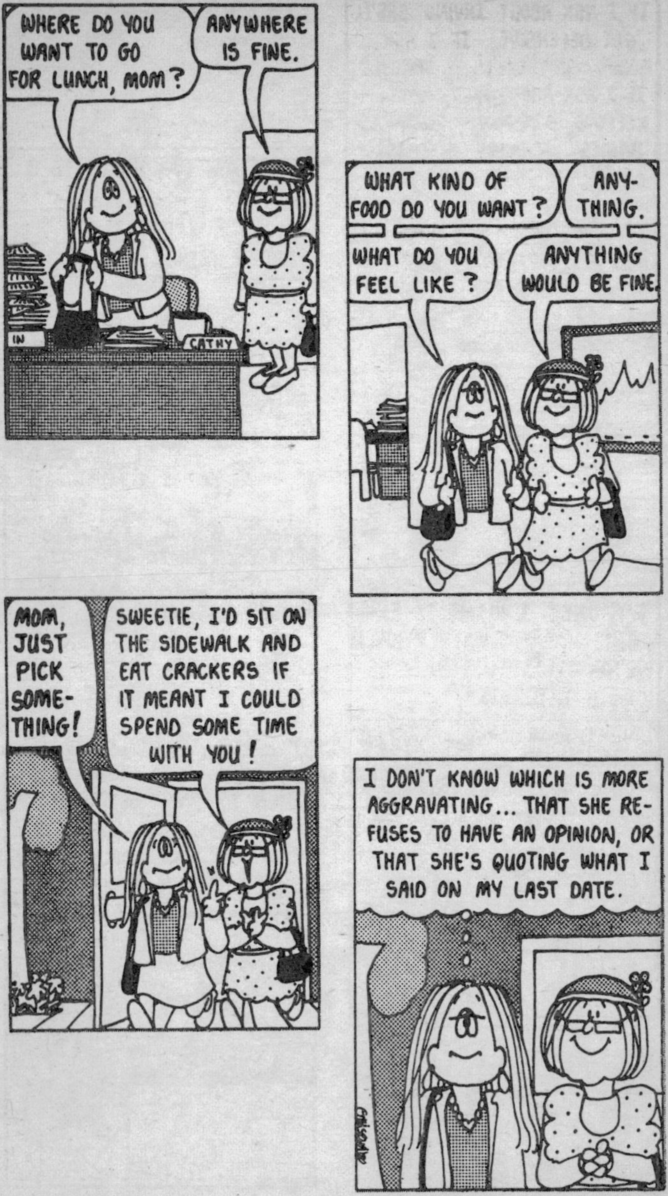

WHERE DO YOU WANT TO GO FOR LUNCH, MOM?
ANYWHERE IS FINE.
IN
CATHY
WHAT KIND OF FOOD DO YOU WANT?
ANY-THING.
WHAT DO YOU FEEL LIKE?
ANYTHING WOULD BE FINE.
MOM, JUST PICK SOME-THING!
SWEETIE, I'D SIT ON THE SIDEWALK AND EAT CRACKERS IF IT MEANT I COULD SPEND SOME TIME WITH YOU!
I DON'T KNOW WHICH IS MORE AGGRAVATING... THAT SHE RE-FUSES TO HAVE AN OPINION, OR THAT SHE'S QUOTING WHAT I SAID ON MY LAST DATE.

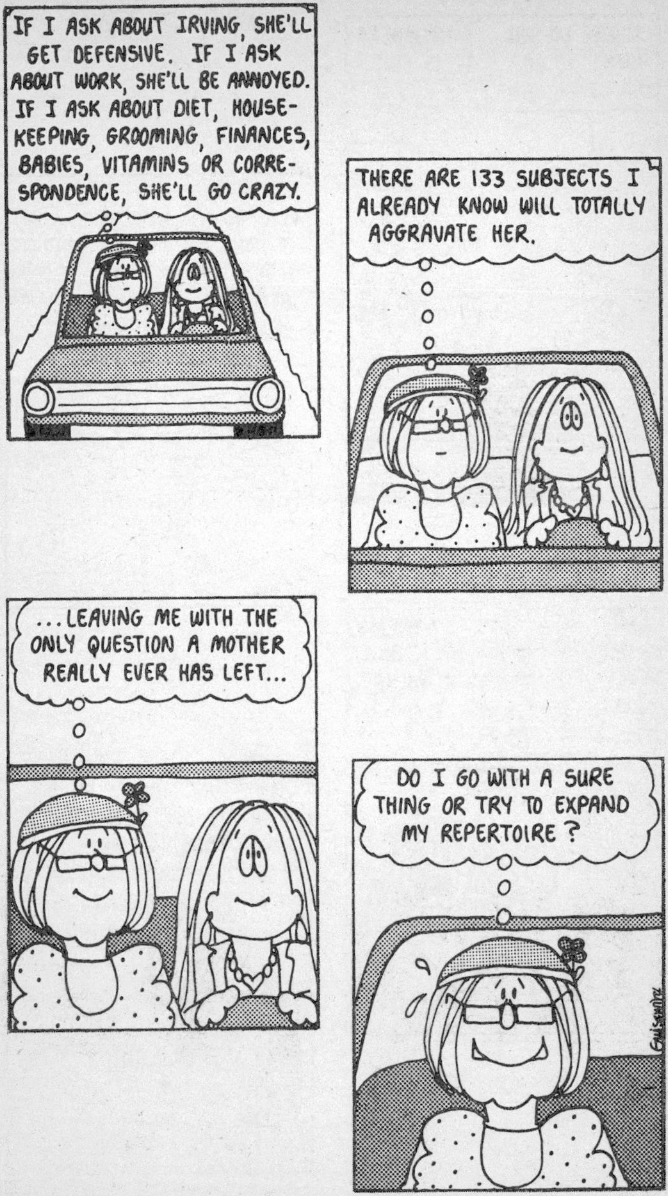
IF I ASK ABOUT IRVING, SHE'LL GET DEFENSIVE. IF I ASK ABOUT WORK, SHE'LL BE ANNOYED. IF I ASK ABOUT DIET, HOUSE-KEEPING, GROOMING, FINANCES, BABIES, VITAMINS OR CORRE-SPONDENCE, SHE'LL GO CRAZY.
THERE ARE 133 SUBJECTS I ALREADY KNOW WILL TOTALLY AGGRAVATE HER.
...LEAVING ME WITH THE ONLY QUESTION A MOTHER REALLY EVER HAS LEFT...
DO I GO WITH A SURE THING OR TRY TO EXPAND MY REPERTOIRE?

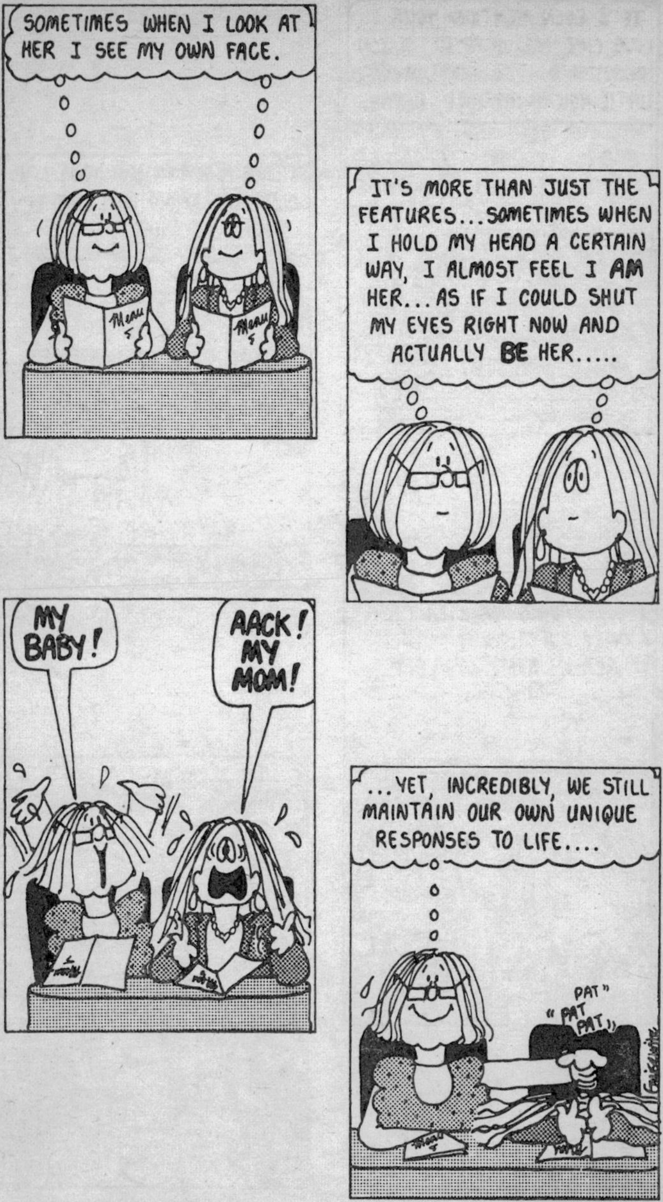
SOMETIMES WHEN I LOOK AT HER I SEE MY OWN FACE.
IT'S MORE THAN JUST THE FEATURES...SOMETIMES WHEN I HOLD MY HEAD A CERTAIN WAY, I ALMOST FEEL I AM HER...AS IF I COULD SHUT MY EYES RIGHT NOW AND ACTUALLY BE HER.....
MY BABY!
AACK! MY MOM!
...YET, INCREDIBLY, WE STILL MAINTAIN OUR OWN UNIQUE RESPONSES TO LIFE....
"PAT PAT PAT"

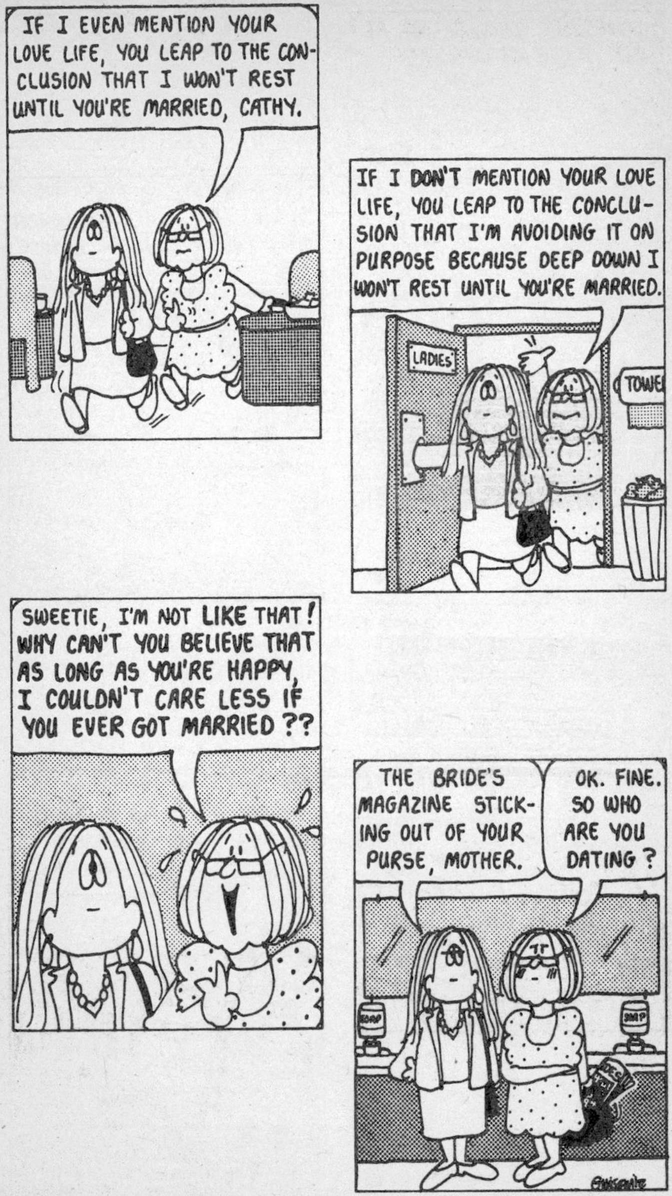

IF I EVEN MENTION YOUR LOVE LIFE, YOU LEAP TO THE CONCLUSION THAT I WON'T REST UNTIL YOU'RE MARRIED, CATHY.
IF I DON'T MENTION YOUR LOVE LIFE, YOU LEAP TO THE CONCLUSION THAT I'M AVOIDING IT ON PURPOSE BECAUSE DEEP DOWN I WON'T REST UNTIL YOU'RE MARRIED.
LADIES
SWEETIE, I'M NOT LIKE THAT! WHY CAN'T YOU BELIEVE THAT AS LONG AS YOU'RE HAPPY, I COULDN'T CARE LESS IF YOU EVER GOT MARRIED??
THE BRIDE'S MAGAZINE STICKING OUT OF YOUR PURSE, MOTHER.
OK. FINE. SO WHO ARE YOU DATING?

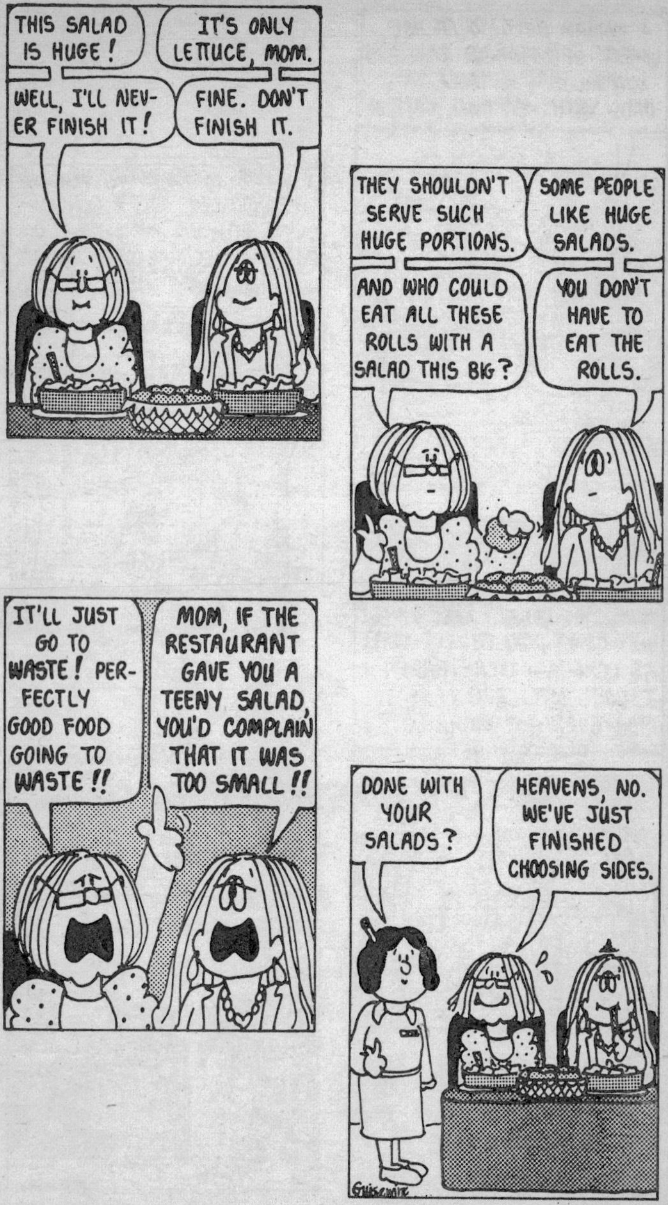
THIS SALAD IS HUGE!
IT'S ONLY LETTUCE, MOM.
WELL, I'LL NEVER FINISH IT!
FINE. DON'T FINISH IT.
THEY SHOULDN'T SERVE SUCH HUGE PORTIONS.
SOME PEOPLE LIKE HUGE SALADS.
AND WHO COULD EAT ALL THESE ROLLS WITH A SALAD THIS BIG?
YOU DON'T HAVE TO EAT THE ROLLS.
IT'LL JUST GO TO WASTE! PERFECTLY GOOD FOOD GOING TO WASTE!!
MOM, IF THE RESTAURANT GAVE YOU A TEENY SALAD, YOU'D COMPLAIN THAT IT WAS TOO SMALL!!
DONE WITH YOUR SALADS?
HEAVENS, NO. WE'VE JUST FINISHED CHOOSING SIDES.

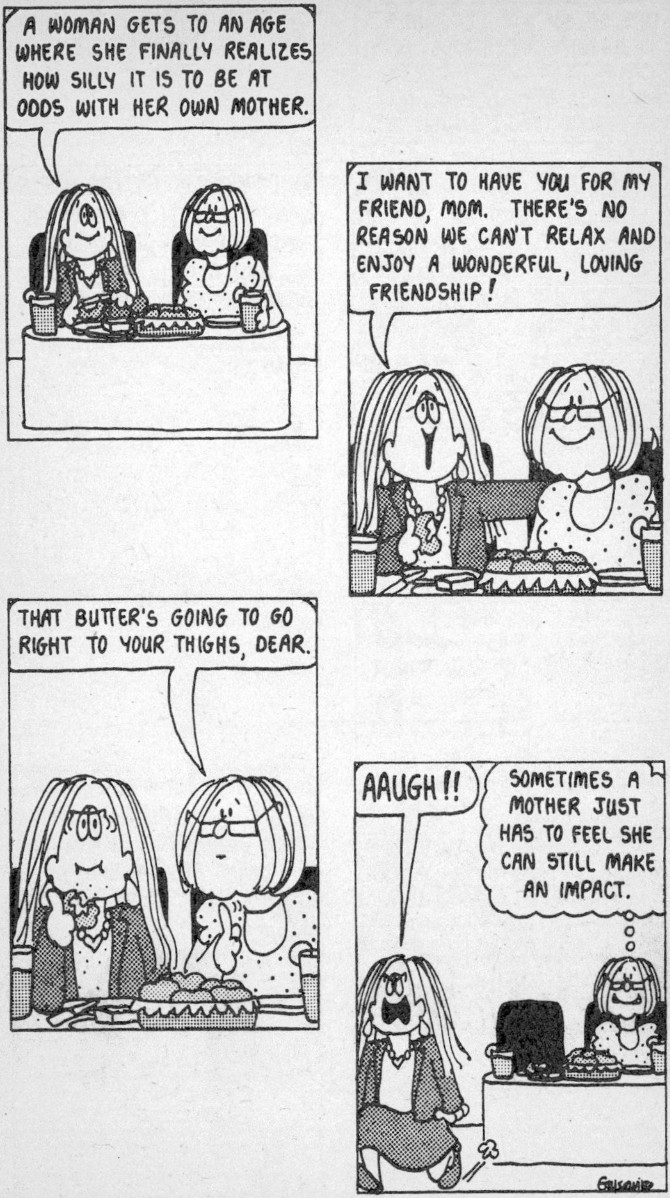
A WOMAN GETS TO AN AGE WHERE SHE FINALLY REALIZES HOW SILLY IT IS TO BE AT ODDS WITH HER OWN MOTHER.
I WANT TO HAVE YOU FOR MY FRIEND, MOM. THERE'S NO REASON WE CAN'T RELAX AND ENJOY A WONDERFUL, LOVING FRIENDSHIP!
THAT BUTTER'S GOING TO GO RIGHT TO YOUR THIGHS, DEAR.
AAUGH!!
SOMETIMES A MOTHER JUST HAS TO FEEL SHE CAN STILL MAKE AN IMPACT.

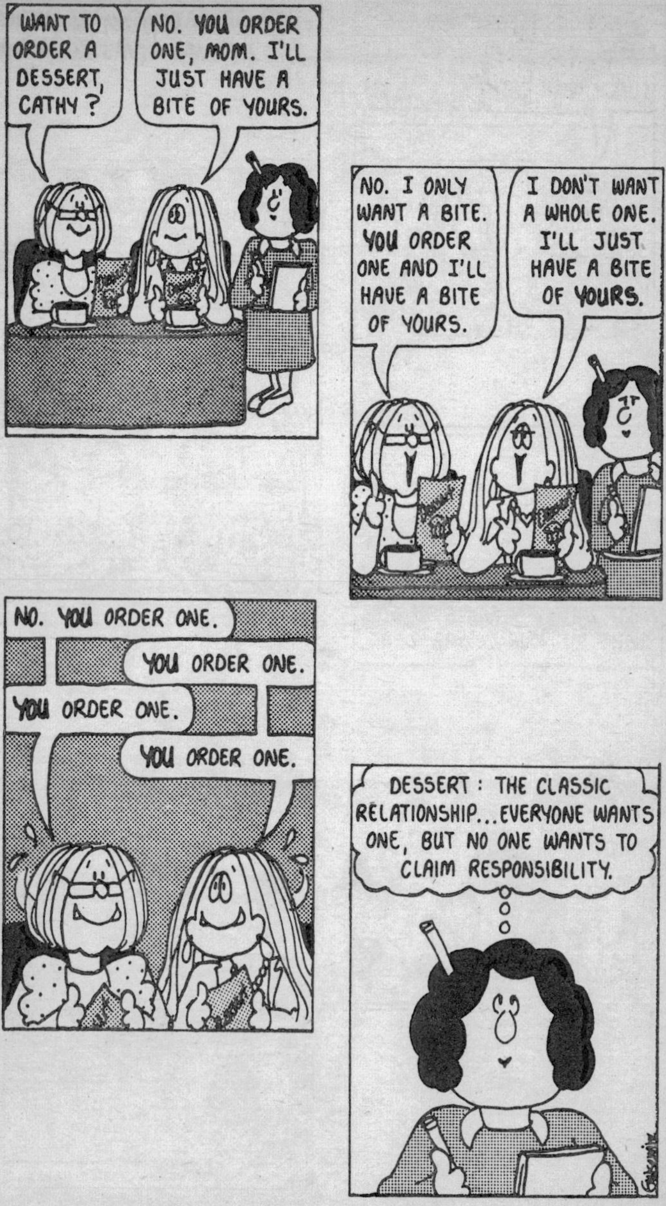
WANT TO ORDER A DESSERT, CATHY?
NO. YOU ORDER ONE, MOM. I'LL JUST HAVE A BITE OF YOURS.
NO. I ONLY WANT A BITE. YOU ORDER ONE AND I'LL HAVE A BITE OF YOURS.
I DON'T WANT A WHOLE ONE. I'LL JUST HAVE A BITE OF YOURS.
NO. YOU ORDER ONE.
YOU ORDER ONE.
YOU ORDER ONE.
YOU ORDER ONE.
DESSERT: THE CLASSIC RELATIONSHIP...EVERYONE WANTS ONE, BUT NO ONE WANTS TO CLAIM RESPONSIBILITY.

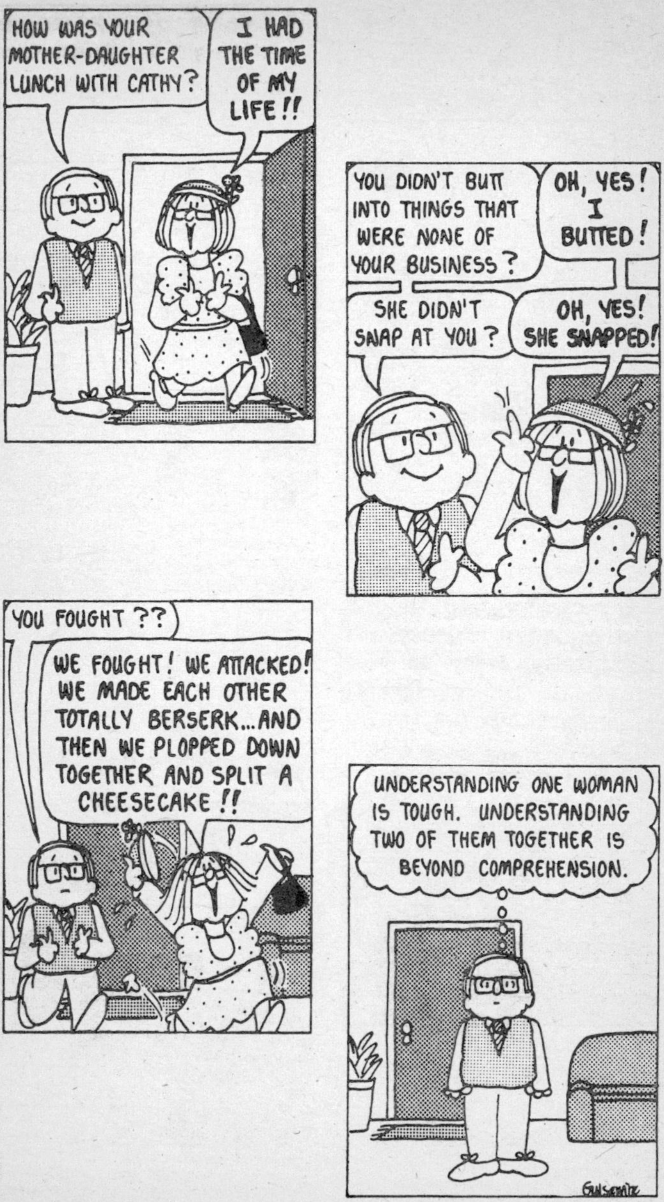

HOW WAS YOUR MOTHER-DAUGHTER LUNCH WITH CATHY?
I HAD THE TIME OF MY LIFE!!
YOU DIDN'T BUTT INTO THINGS THAT WERE NONE OF YOUR BUSINESS?
OH, YES! I BUTTED!
SHE DIDN'T SNAP AT YOU?
OH, YES! SHE SNAPPED!
YOU FOUGHT??
WE FOUGHT! WE ATTACKED! WE MADE EACH OTHER TOTALLY BERSERK...AND THEN WE PLOPPED DOWN TOGETHER AND SPLIT A CHEESECAKE!!
UNDERSTANDING ONE WOMAN IS TOUGH. UNDERSTANDING TWO OF THEM TOGETHER IS BEYOND COMPREHENSION.
GUISEWITE

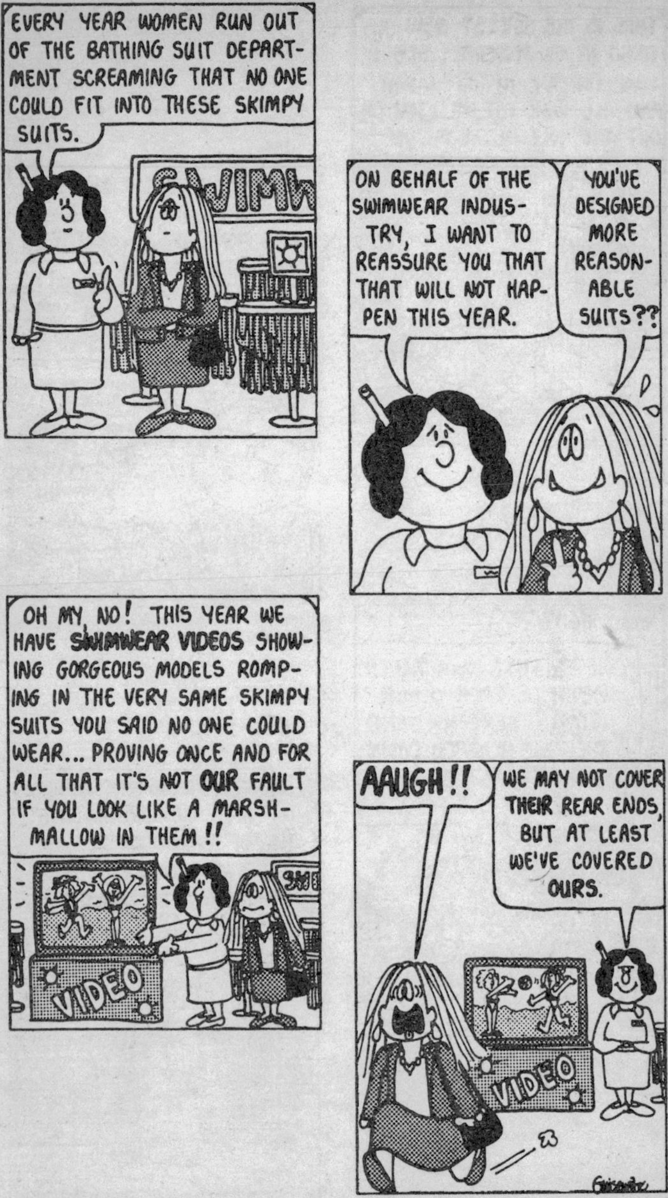
EVERY YEAR WOMEN RUN OUT OF THE BATHING SUIT DEPARTMENT SCREAMING THAT NO ONE COULD FIT INTO THESE SKIMPY SUITS.
ON BEHALF OF THE SWIMWEAR INDUSTRY, I WANT TO REASSURE YOU THAT THAT WILL NOT HAPPEN THIS YEAR.
YOU'VE DESIGNED MORE REASONABLE SUITS??
OH MY, NO! THIS YEAR WE HAVE SWIMWEAR VIDEOS SHOWING GORGEOUS MODELS ROMPING IN THE VERY SAME SKIMPY SUITS YOU SAID NO ONE COULD WEAR... PROVING ONCE AND FOR ALL THAT IT'S NOT OUR FAULT IF YOU LOOK LIKE A MARSHMALLOW IN THEM!!
VIDEO
AAUGH!!
WE MAY NOT COVER THEIR REAR ENDS, BUT AT LEAST WE'VE COVERED OURS.
VIDEO

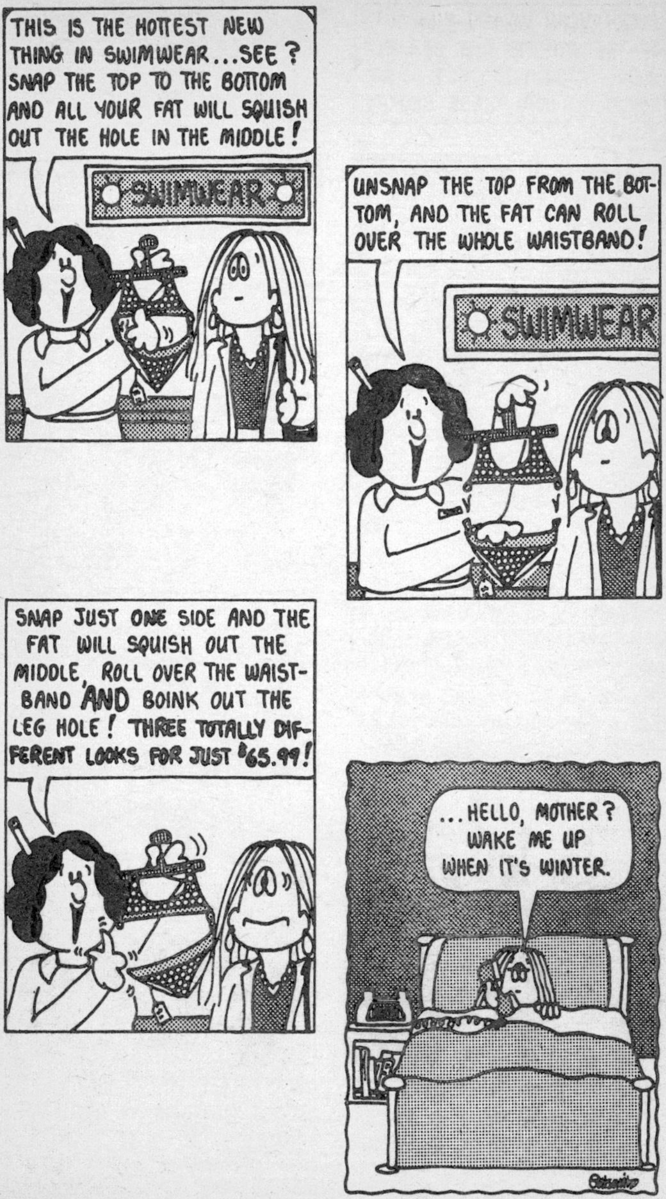
THIS IS THE HOTTEST NEW THING IN SWIMWEAR...SEE? SNAP THE TOP TO THE BOTTOM AND ALL YOUR FAT WILL SQUISH OUT THE HOLE IN THE MIDDLE!
SWIMWEAR
UNSNAP THE TOP FROM THE BOTTOM, AND THE FAT CAN ROLL OVER THE WHOLE WAISTBAND!
SWIMWEAR
SNAP JUST ONE SIDE AND THE FAT WILL SQUISH OUT THE MIDDLE, ROLL OVER THE WAISTBAND AND BOINK OUT THE LEG HOLE! THREE TOTALLY DIFFERENT LOOKS FOR JUST $65.99!
...HELLO, MOTHER? WAKE ME UP WHEN IT'S WINTER.

AREN'T THE NEW SWIMSUITS FABULOUS? THEY SAY, "I'M FUN!"... "I'M FLIRTY!"... "I'M CONFIDENT!"... "I'M HIP!"... "I'M SPORTY!"... "I'M WILD!"...
MORE THAN EVER BEFORE, A SWIMSUIT REALLY SAYS SOMETHING ABOUT THE WOMAN WHO WEARS IT!!
SHE HASN'T BEEN TO HER HEALTH CLUB IN 18 MONTHS!!..

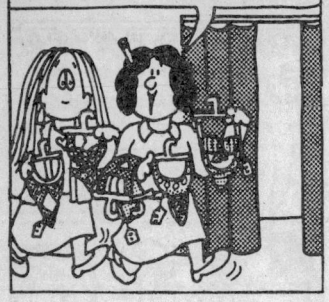

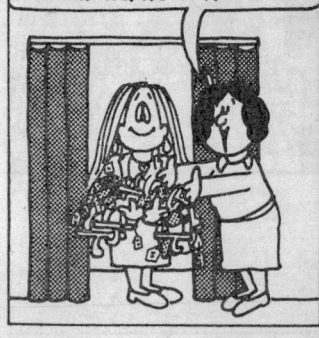

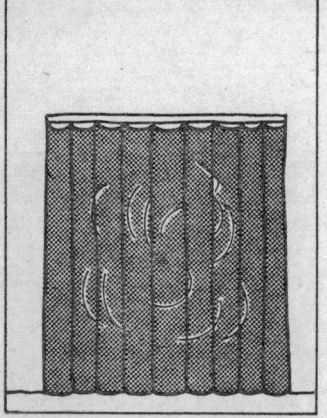

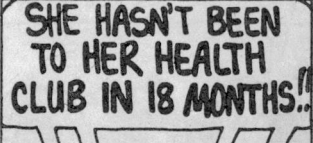

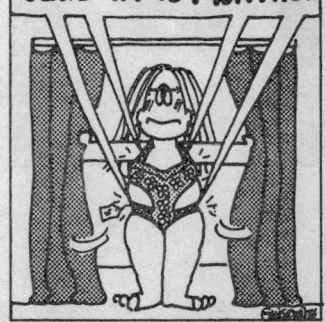

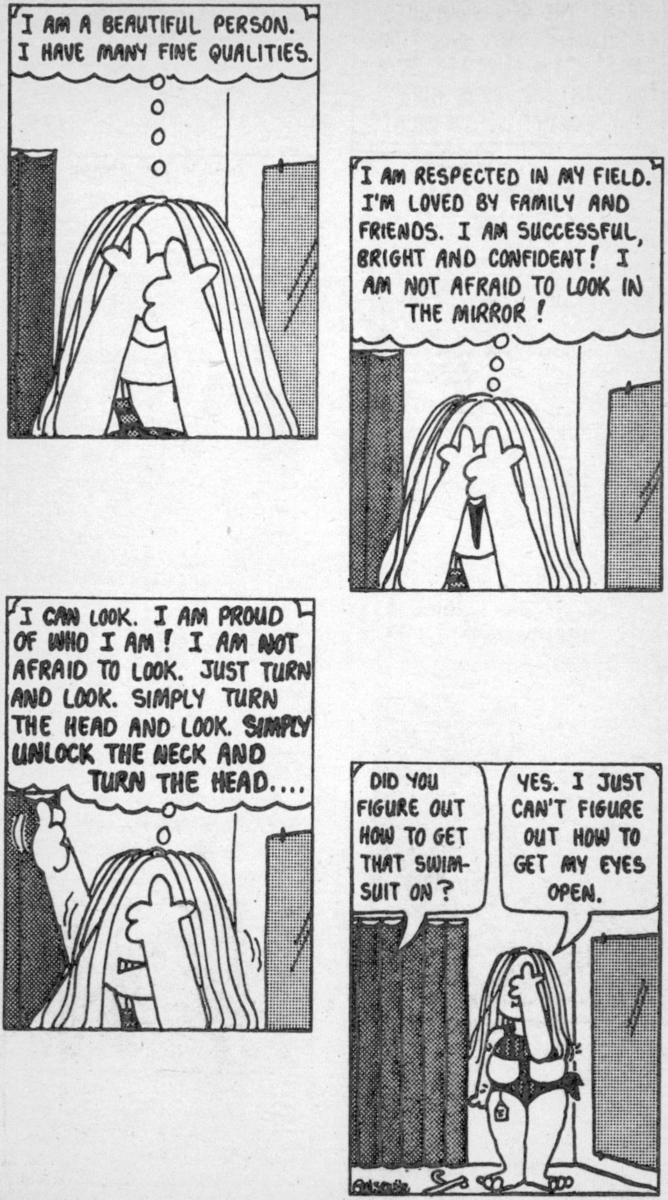
I AM A BEAUTIFUL PERSON. I HAVE MANY FINE QUALITIES.
I AM RESPECTED IN MY FIELD. I'M LOVED BY FAMILY AND FRIENDS. I AM SUCCESSFUL, BRIGHT AND CONFIDENT! I AM NOT AFRAID TO LOOK IN THE MIRROR!
I CAN LOOK. I AM PROUD OF WHO I AM! I AM NOT AFRAID TO LOOK. JUST TURN AND LOOK. SIMPLY TURN THE HEAD AND LOOK. SIMPLY UNLOCK THE NECK AND TURN THE HEAD....
DID YOU FIGURE OUT HOW TO GET THAT SWIM-SUIT ON?
YES. I JUST CAN'T FIGURE OUT HOW TO GET MY EYES OPEN.
Guisewite

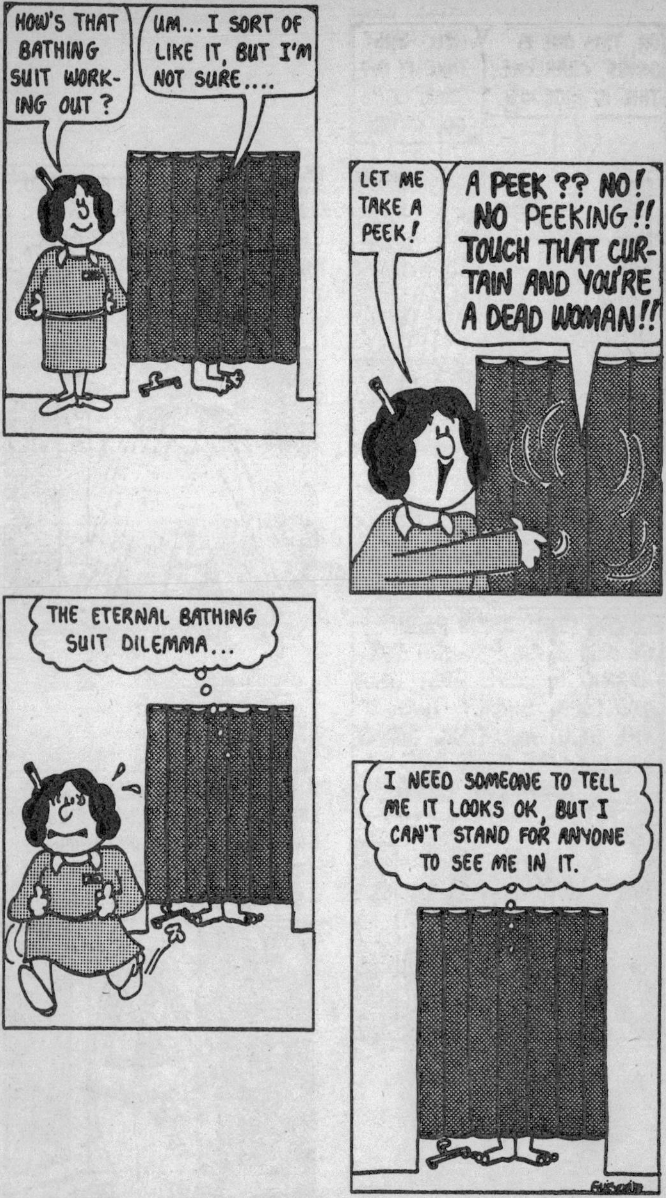
HOW'S THAT BATHING SUIT WORKING OUT ?
UM... I SORT OF LIKE IT, BUT I'M NOT SURE....
LET ME TAKE A PEEK!
A PEEK ?? NO! NO PEEKING !! TOUCH THAT CURTAIN AND YOU'RE A DEAD WOMAN!!
THE ETERNAL BATHING SUIT DILEMMA...
I NEED SOMEONE TO TELL ME IT LOOKS OK, BUT I CAN'T STAND FOR ANYONE TO SEE ME IN IT.

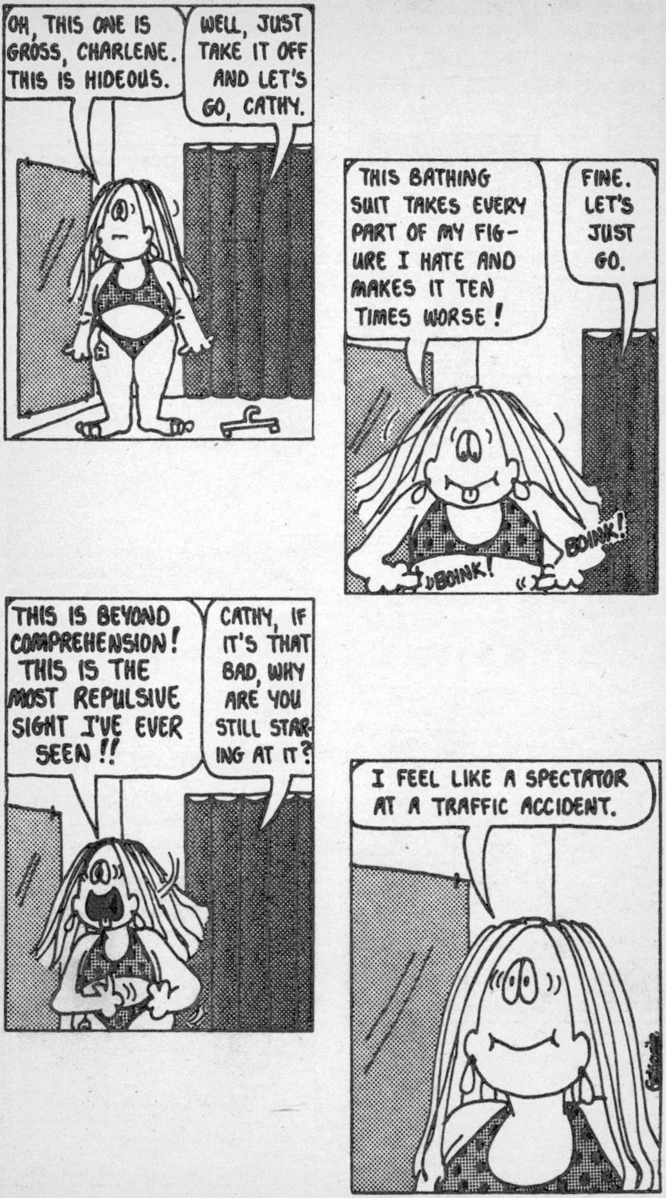
OH, THIS ONE IS GROSS, CHARLENE. THIS IS HIDEOUS.
WELL, JUST TAKE IT OFF AND LET'S GO, CATHY.
THIS BATHING SUIT TAKES EVERY PART OF MY FIG-URE I HATE AND MAKES IT TEN TIMES WORSE!
FINE. LET'S JUST GO.
BOINK!
BOINK!
THIS IS BEYOND COMPREHENSION! THIS IS THE MOST REPULSIVE SIGHT I'VE EVER SEEN!!
CATHY, IF IT'S THAT BAD, WHY ARE YOU STILL STAR-ING AT IT?
I FEEL LIKE A SPECTATOR AT A TRAFFIC ACCIDENT.

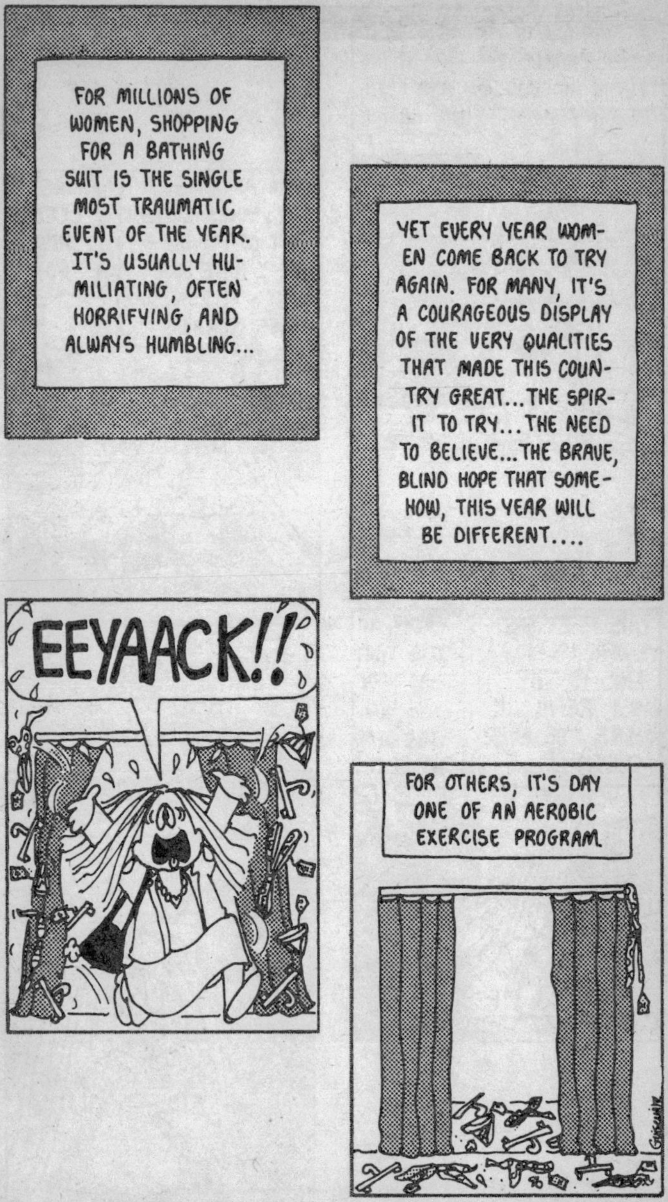
FOR MILLIONS OF WOMEN, SHOPPING FOR A BATHING SUIT IS THE SINGLE MOST TRAUMATIC EVENT OF THE YEAR. IT'S USUALLY HUMILIATING, OFTEN HORRIFYING, AND ALWAYS HUMBLING...
YET EVERY YEAR WOMEN COME BACK TO TRY AGAIN. FOR MANY, IT'S A COURAGEOUS DISPLAY OF THE VERY QUALITIES THAT MADE THIS COUNTRY GREAT...THE SPIRIT TO TRY...THE NEED TO BELIEVE...THE BRAVE, BLIND HOPE THAT SOMEHOW, THIS YEAR WILL BE DIFFERENT....
EEYAACK!!
FOR OTHERS, IT'S DAY ONE OF AN AEROBIC EXERCISE PROGRAM

MAYBE IF I STUFF THE SHOULDER PADS FROM MY BLOUSE IN THE TOP OF THIS BATHING SUIT IT WOULD LOOK BETTER...
HEE, HEE... SHOULDER PADS IN THE TOP AND I'LL WEAR SUPPORT PANTYHOSE UNDER THE BOTTOM OF THE SUIT... HEE, HEE... WITH HIGH HEELS!... TA, DA! HA, HA!... TA.......
WARNING: THIS DRESSING ROOM IS MONITORED BY STORE PERSONNEL.
DID YOU NEED A DIFFERENT SIZE?
GO AWAY.

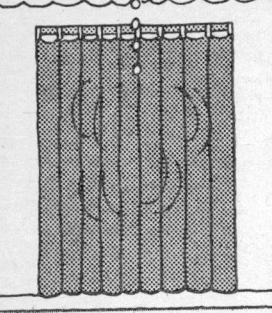

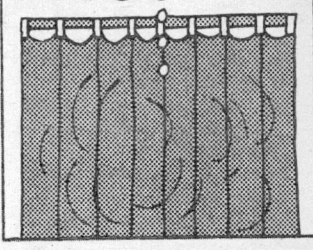

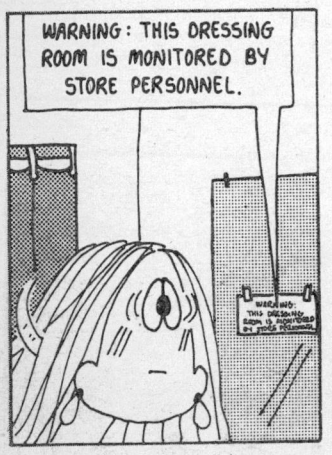

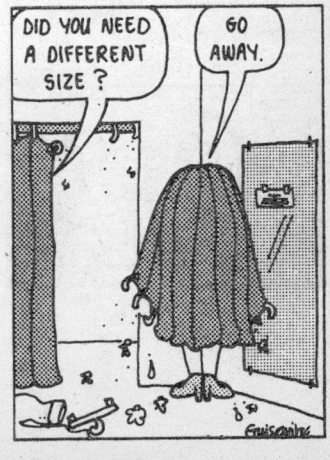

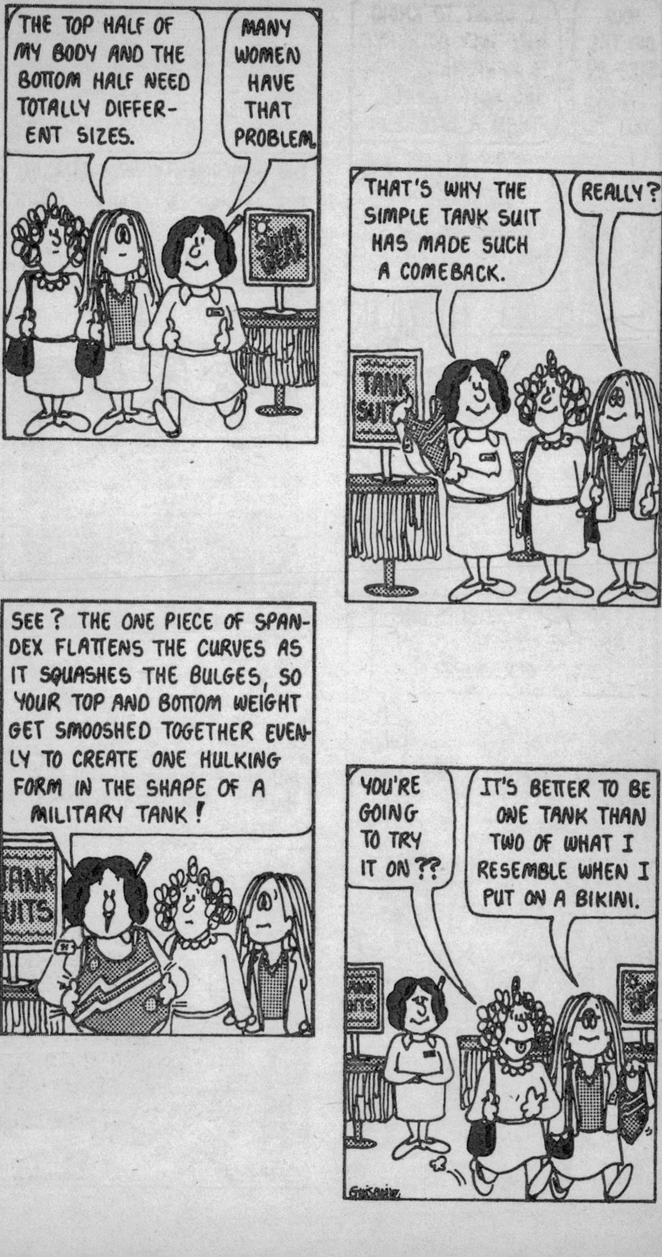
THE TOP HALF OF MY BODY AND THE BOTTOM HALF NEED TOTALLY DIFFERENT SIZES.
MANY WOMEN HAVE THAT PROBLEM.
THAT'S WHY THE SIMPLE TANK SUIT HAS MADE SUCH A COMEBACK.
REALLY?
TANK SUIT
SEE? THE ONE PIECE OF SPANDEX FLATTENS THE CURVES AS IT SQUASHES THE BULGES, SO YOUR TOP AND BOTTOM WEIGHT GET SMOOSHED TOGETHER EVENLY TO CREATE ONE HULKING FORM IN THE SHAPE OF A MILITARY TANK!
YOU'RE GOING TO TRY IT ON??
IT'S BETTER TO BE ONE TANK THAN TWO OF WHAT I RESEMBLE WHEN I PUT ON A BIKINI.

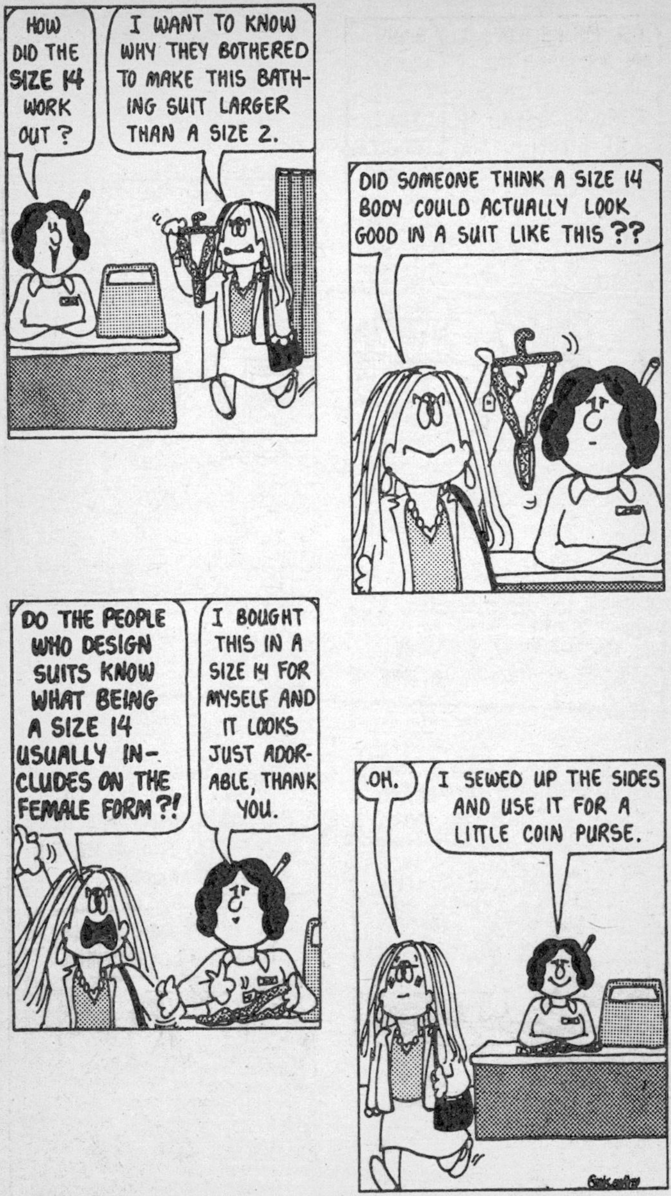
HOW DID THE SIZE 14 WORK OUT ?
I WANT TO KNOW WHY THEY BOTHERED TO MAKE THIS BATHING SUIT LARGER THAN A SIZE 2.
DID SOMEONE THINK A SIZE 14 BODY COULD ACTUALLY LOOK GOOD IN A SUIT LIKE THIS ??
DO THE PEOPLE WHO DESIGN SUITS KNOW WHAT BEING A SIZE 14 USUALLY INCLUDES ON THE FEMALE FORM ?!
I BOUGHT THIS IN A SIZE 14 FOR MYSELF AND IT LOOKS JUST ADORABLE, THANK YOU.
OH.
I SEWED UP THE SIDES AND USE IT FOR A LITTLE COIN PURSE.

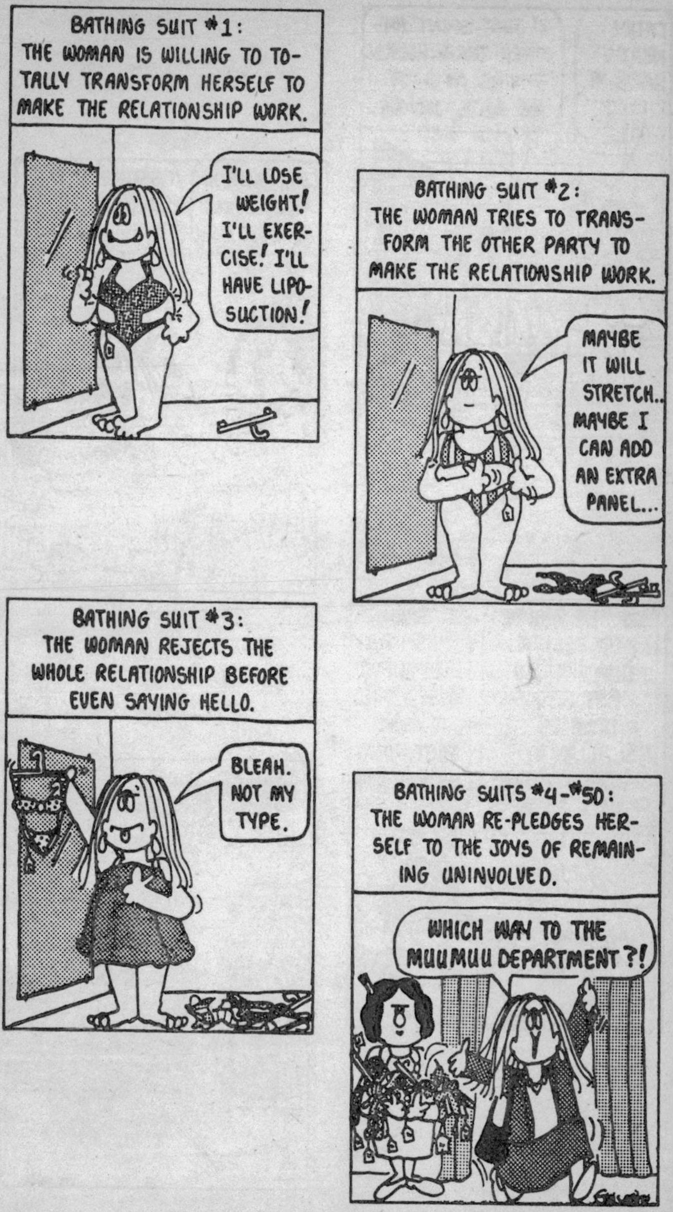
BATHING SUIT #1:
THE WOMAN IS WILLING TO TOTALLY TRANSFORM HERSELF TO MAKE THE RELATIONSHIP WORK.
I'LL LOSE WEIGHT! I'LL EXERCISE! I'LL HAVE LIPOSUCTION!
BATHING SUIT #2:
THE WOMAN TRIES TO TRANSFORM THE OTHER PARTY TO MAKE THE RELATIONSHIP WORK.
MAYBE IT WILL STRETCH.. MAYBE I CAN ADD AN EXTRA PANEL...
BATHING SUIT #3:
THE WOMAN REJECTS THE WHOLE RELATIONSHIP BEFORE EVEN SAYING HELLO.
BLEAH. NOT MY TYPE.
BATHING SUITS #4-#50:
THE WOMAN RE-PLEDGES HERSELF TO THE JOYS OF REMAINING UNINVOLVED.
WHICH WAY TO THE MUUMUU DEPARTMENT?!

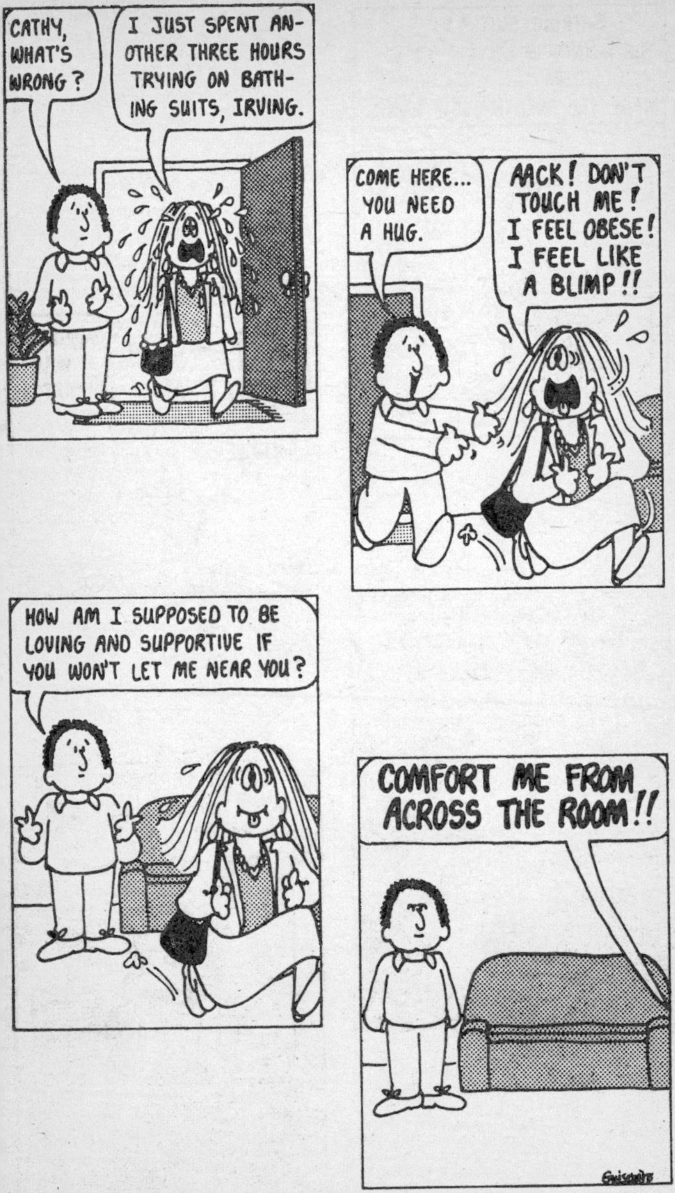
CATHY, WHAT'S WRONG?
I JUST SPENT ANOTHER THREE HOURS TRYING ON BATHING SUITS, IRVING.
COME HERE... YOU NEED A HUG.
AACK! DON'T TOUCH ME! I FEEL OBESE! I FEEL LIKE A BLIMP!!
HOW AM I SUPPOSED TO BE LOVING AND SUPPORTIVE IF YOU WON'T LET ME NEAR YOU?
COMFORT ME FROM ACROSS THE ROOM!!

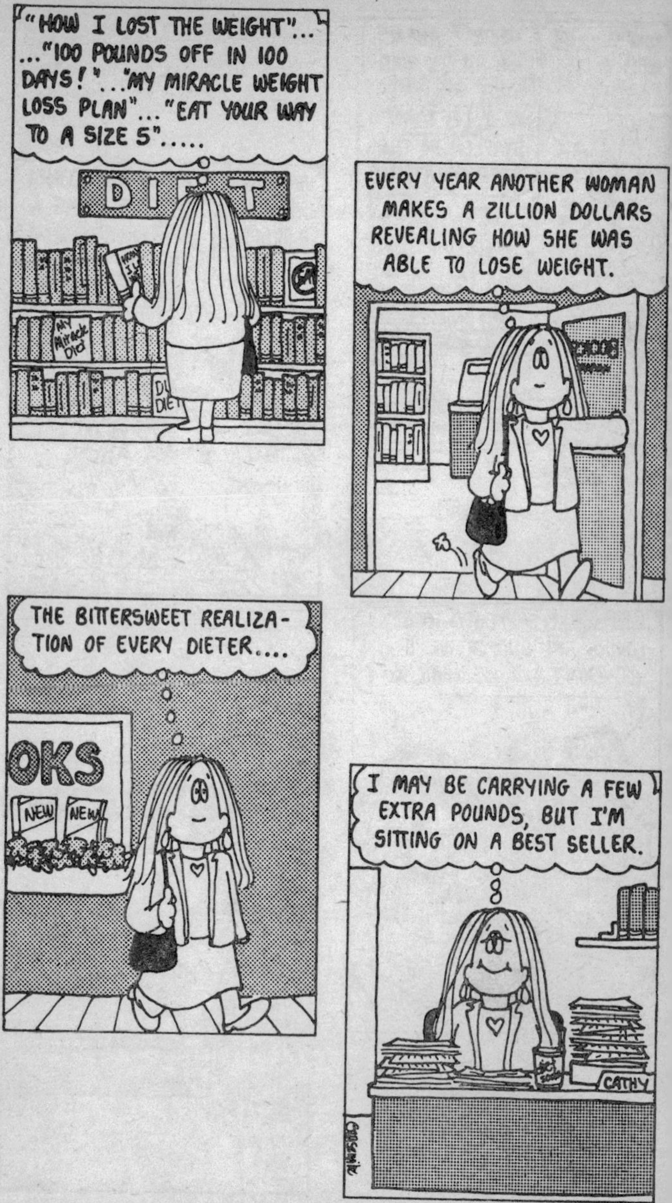
"HOW I LOST THE WEIGHT"... ..."100 POUNDS OFF IN 100 DAYS!"..."MY MIRACLE WEIGHT LOSS PLAN"..."EAT YOUR WAY TO A SIZE 5".....
EVERY YEAR ANOTHER WOMAN MAKES A ZILLION DOLLARS REVEALING HOW SHE WAS ABLE TO LOSE WEIGHT.
THE BITTERSWEET REALIZATION OF EVERY DIETER....
NEW
NEW
I MAY BE CARRYING A FEW EXTRA POUNDS, BUT I'M SITTING ON A BEST SELLER.
CATHY

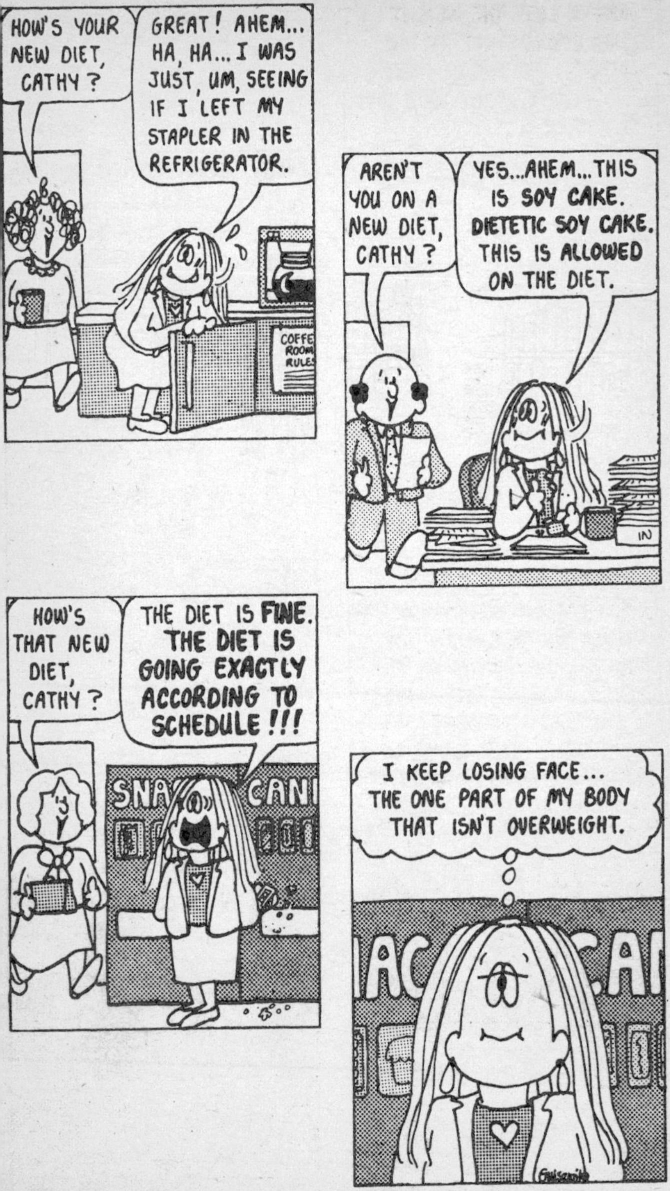
HOW'S YOUR NEW DIET, CATHY?
GREAT! AHEM... HA, HA... I WAS JUST, UM, SEEING IF I LEFT MY STAPLER IN THE REFRIGERATOR.
COFFEE ROOM RULES
AREN'T YOU ON A NEW DIET, CATHY?
YES... AHEM... THIS IS SOY CAKE. DIETETIC SOY CAKE. THIS IS ALLOWED ON THE DIET.
IN
HOW'S THAT NEW DIET, CATHY?
THE DIET IS FINE. THE DIET IS GOING EXACTLY ACCORDING TO SCHEDULE!!!
I KEEP LOSING FACE... THE ONE PART OF MY BODY THAT ISN'T OVERWEIGHT.
Guisewite

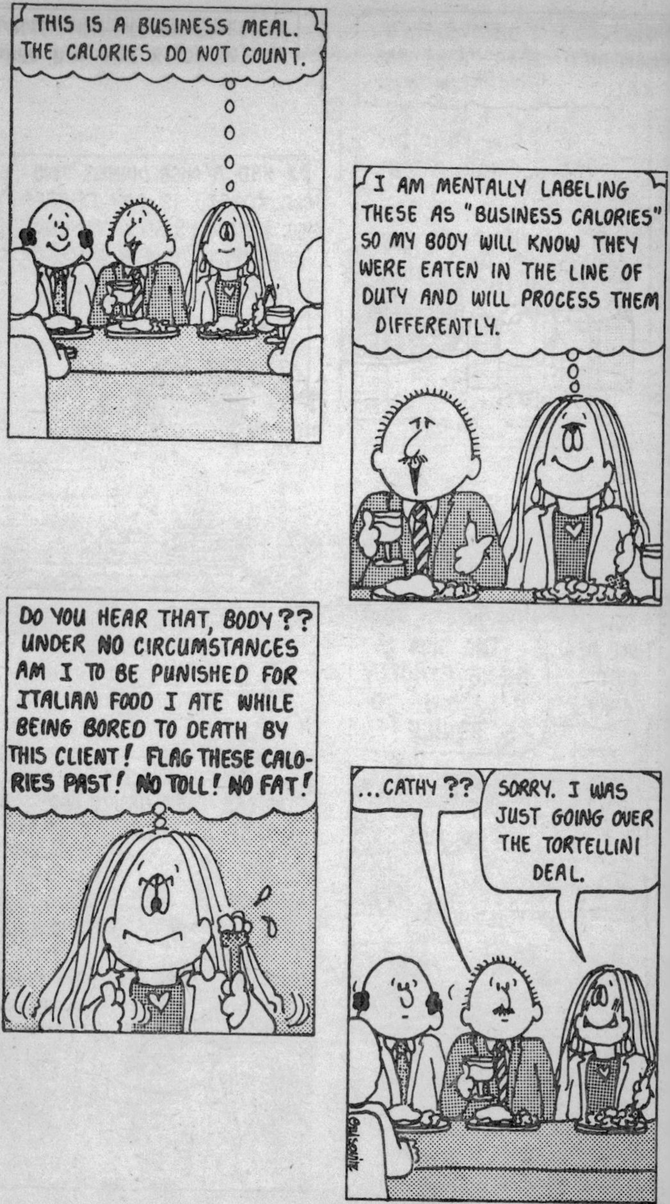
THIS IS A BUSINESS MEAL. THE CALORIES DO NOT COUNT.
I AM MENTALLY LABELING THESE AS "BUSINESS CALORIES" SO MY BODY WILL KNOW THEY WERE EATEN IN THE LINE OF DUTY AND WILL PROCESS THEM DIFFERENTLY.
DO YOU HEAR THAT, BODY?? UNDER NO CIRCUMSTANCES AM I TO BE PUNISHED FOR ITALIAN FOOD I ATE WHILE BEING BORED TO DEATH BY THIS CLIENT! FLAG THESE CALORIES PAST! NO TOLL! NO FAT!
...CATHY??
SORRY. I WAS JUST GOING OVER THE TORTELLINI DEAL.
©Guisewite

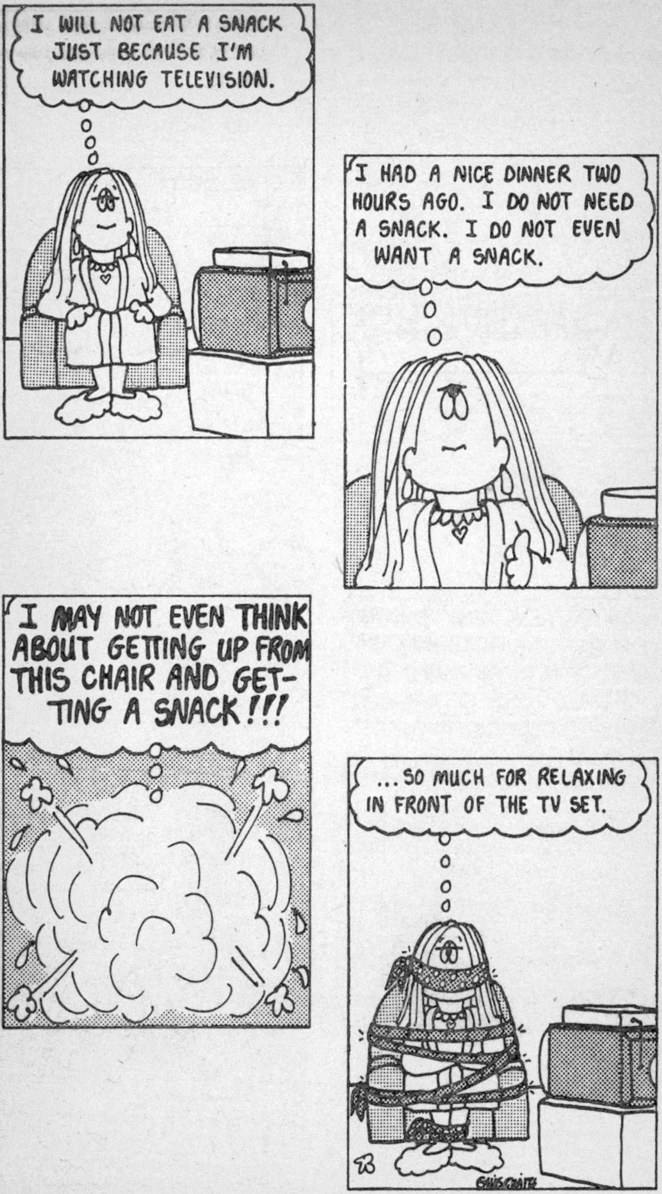
I WILL NOT EAT A SNACK JUST BECAUSE I'M WATCHING TELEVISION.
I HAD A NICE DINNER TWO HOURS AGO. I DO NOT NEED A SNACK. I DO NOT EVEN WANT A SNACK.
I MAY NOT EVEN THINK ABOUT GETTING UP FROM THIS CHAIR AND GETTING A SNACK!!!
...SO MUCH FOR RELAXING IN FRONT OF THE TV SET.

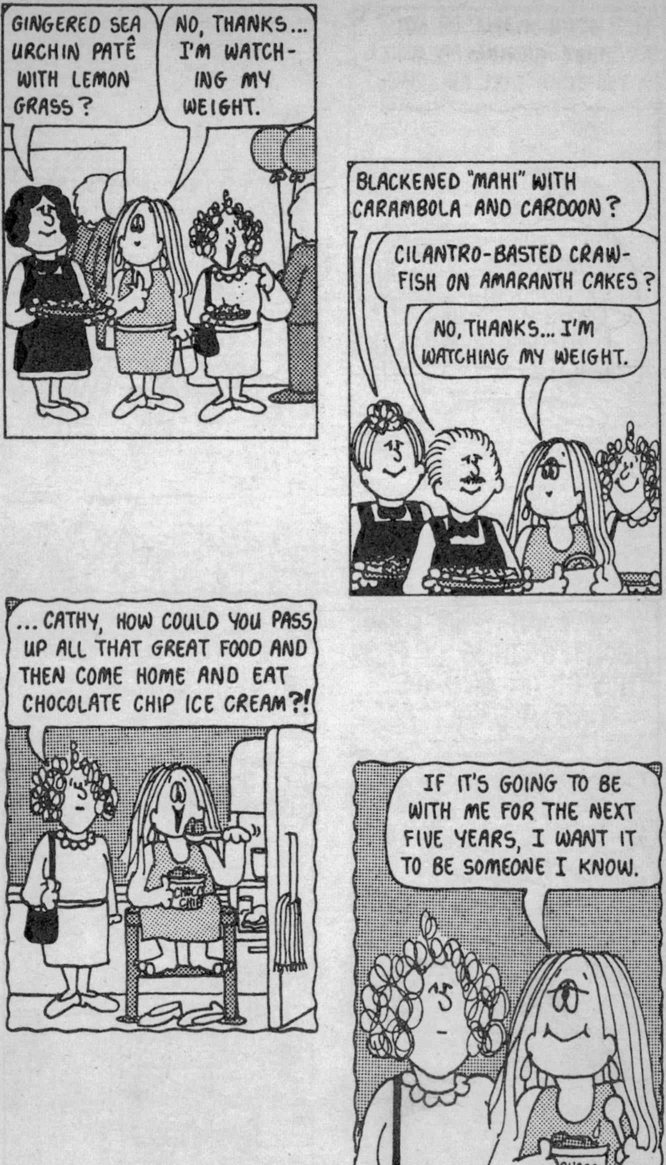
GINGERED SEA URCHIN PATÊ WITH LEMON GRASS?
NO, THANKS... I'M WATCHING MY WEIGHT.
BLACKENED "MAHI" WITH CARAMBOLA AND CARDOON?
CILANTRO-BASTED CRAWFISH ON AMARANTH CAKES?
NO, THANKS... I'M WATCHING MY WEIGHT.
...CATHY, HOW COULD YOU PASS UP ALL THAT GREAT FOOD AND THEN COME HOME AND EAT CHOCOLATE CHIP ICE CREAM?!
CHOC CHIP
IF IT'S GOING TO BE WITH ME FOR THE NEXT FIVE YEARS, I WANT IT TO BE SOMEONE I KNOW.
CHOCOL CHIP

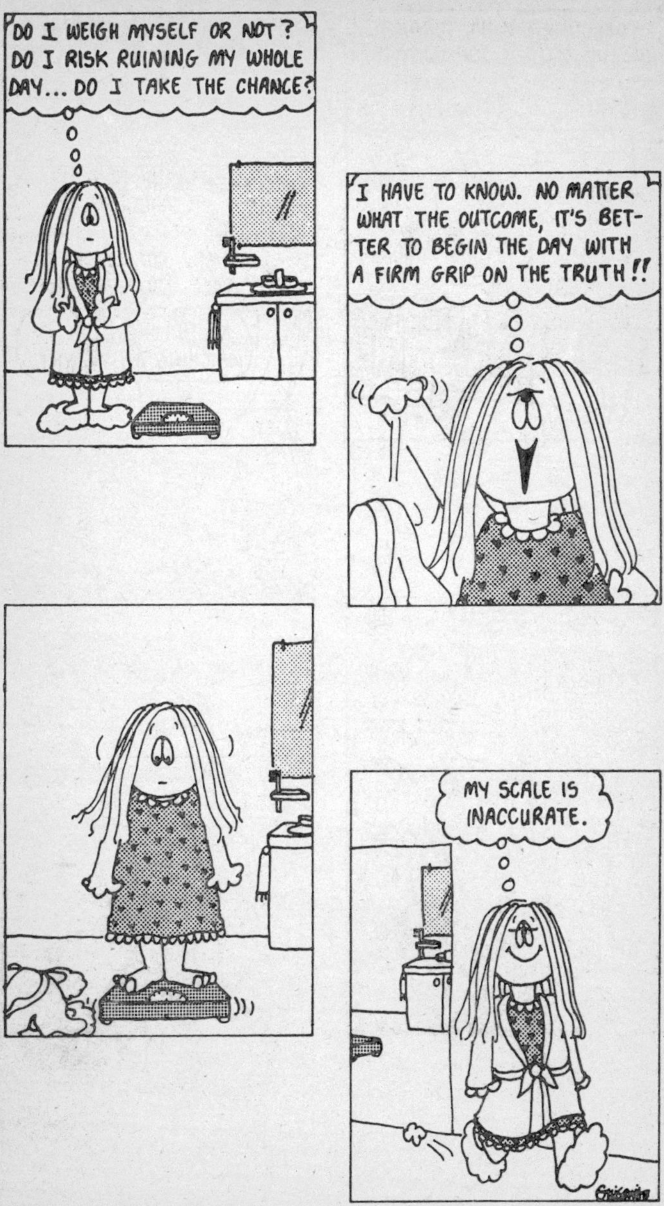
DO I WEIGH MYSELF OR NOT? DO I RISK RUINING MY WHOLE DAY... DO I TAKE THE CHANCE?
I HAVE TO KNOW. NO MATTER WHAT THE OUTCOME, IT'S BETTER TO BEGIN THE DAY WITH A FIRM GRIP ON THE TRUTH!!
MY SCALE IS INACCURATE.

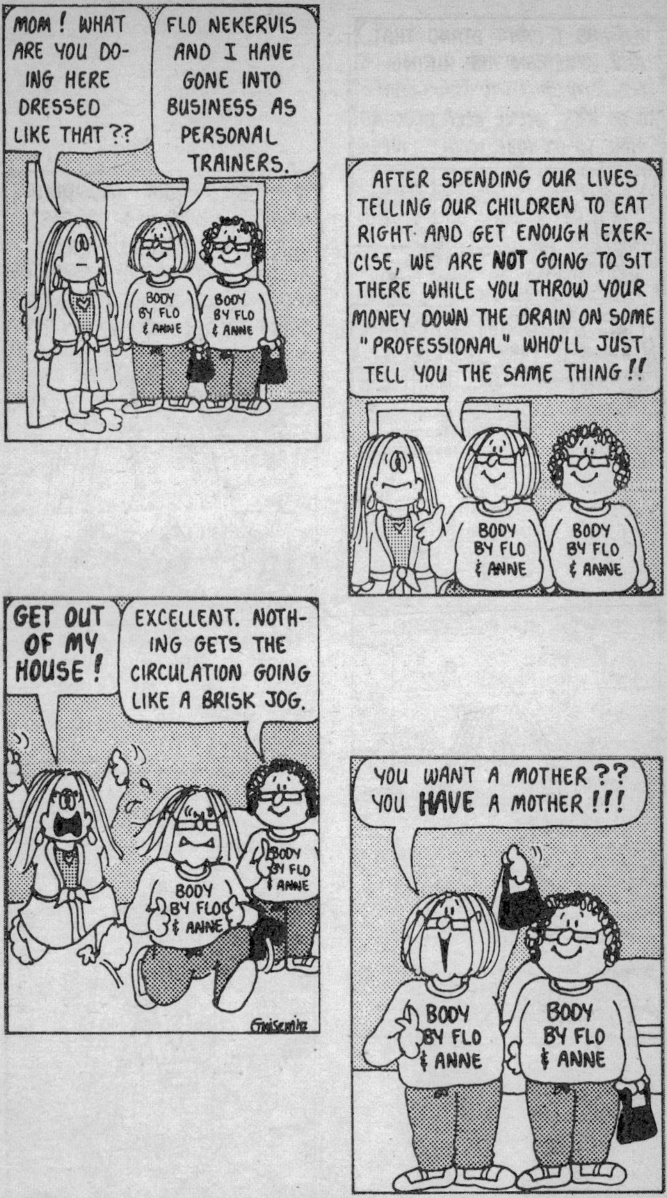
MOM! WHAT ARE YOU DOING HERE DRESSED LIKE THAT??
FLO NEKERVIS AND I HAVE GONE INTO BUSINESS AS PERSONAL TRAINERS.
BODY BY FLO & ANNE
AFTER SPENDING OUR LIVES TELLING OUR CHILDREN TO EAT RIGHT AND GET ENOUGH EXERCISE, WE ARE **NOT** GOING TO SIT THERE WHILE YOU THROW YOUR MONEY DOWN THE DRAIN ON SOME "PROFESSIONAL" WHO'LL JUST TELL YOU THE SAME THING!!
GET OUT OF MY HOUSE!
EXCELLENT. NOTHING GETS THE CIRCULATION GOING LIKE A BRISK JOG.
Guisewite
YOU WANT A MOTHER?? YOU **HAVE** A MOTHER!!!

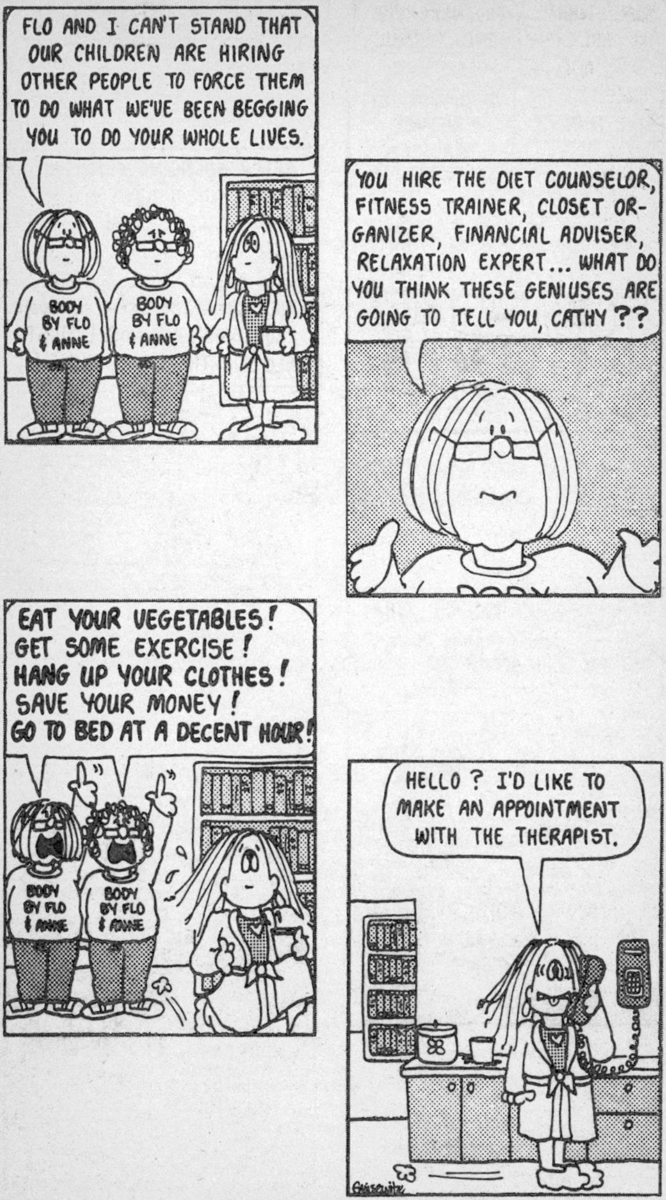
FLO AND I CAN'T STAND THAT OUR CHILDREN ARE HIRING OTHER PEOPLE TO FORCE THEM TO DO WHAT WE'VE BEEN BEGGING YOU TO DO YOUR WHOLE LIVES.
BODY BY FLO & ANNE
BODY BY FLO & ANNE
YOU HIRE THE DIET COUNSELOR, FITNESS TRAINER, CLOSET ORGANIZER, FINANCIAL ADVISER, RELAXATION EXPERT... WHAT DO YOU THINK THESE GENIUSES ARE GOING TO TELL YOU, CATHY??
EAT YOUR VEGETABLES! GET SOME EXERCISE! HANG UP YOUR CLOTHES! SAVE YOUR MONEY! GO TO BED AT A DECENT HOUR!
BODY BY FLO & ANNE
BODY BY FLO & ANNE
HELLO? I'D LIKE TO MAKE AN APPOINTMENT WITH THE THERAPIST.

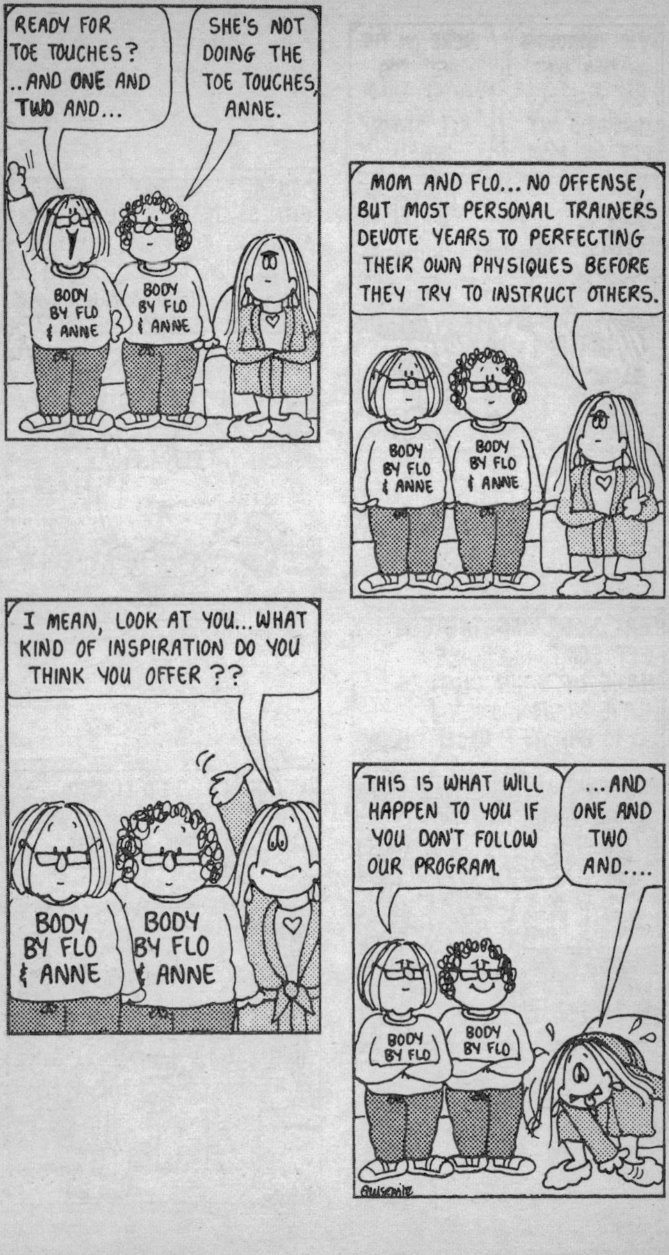

READY FOR TOE TOUCHES? ..AND ONE AND TWO AND...
SHE'S NOT DOING THE TOE TOUCHES, ANNE.
MOM AND FLO... NO OFFENSE, BUT MOST PERSONAL TRAINERS DEVOTE YEARS TO PERFECTING THEIR OWN PHYSIQUES BEFORE THEY TRY TO INSTRUCT OTHERS.
BODY BY FLO & ANNE
I MEAN, LOOK AT YOU...WHAT KIND OF INSPIRATION DO YOU THINK YOU OFFER??
THIS IS WHAT WILL HAPPEN TO YOU IF YOU DON'T FOLLOW OUR PROGRAM.
...AND ONE AND TWO AND....
BODY BY FLO

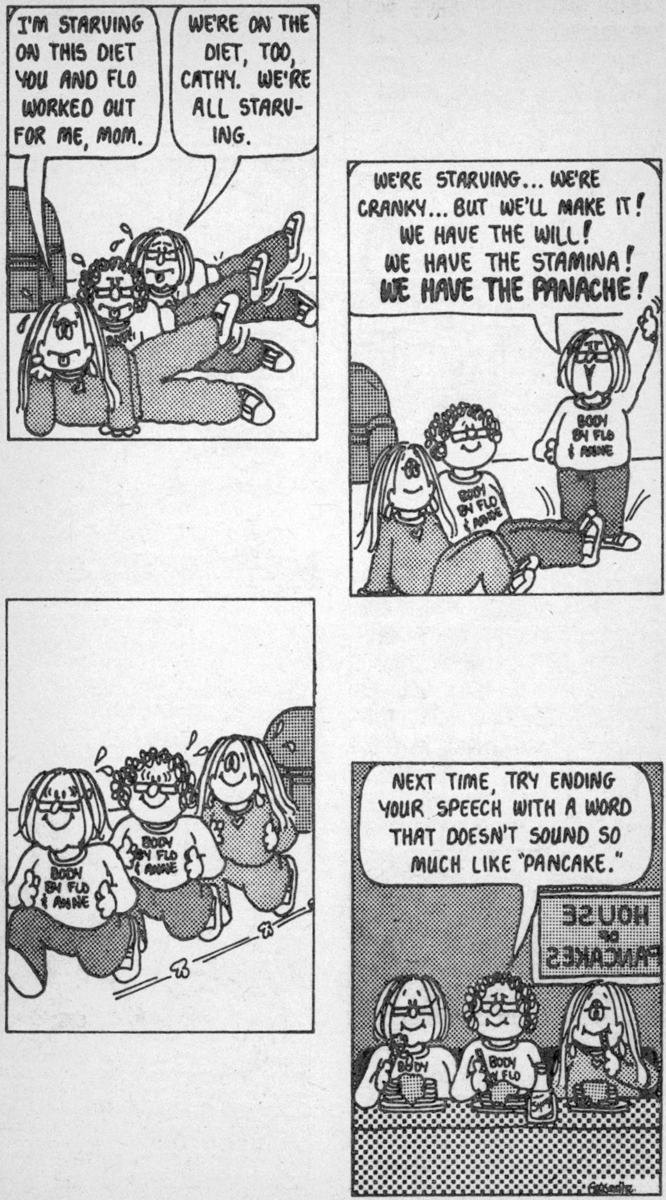
I'M STARVING ON THIS DIET YOU AND FLO WORKED OUT FOR ME, MOM.
WE'RE ON THE DIET, TOO, CATHY. WE'RE ALL STARVING.
WE'RE STARVING... WE'RE CRANKY... BUT WE'LL MAKE IT! WE HAVE THE WILL! WE HAVE THE STAMINA! WE HAVE THE PANACHE!
BODY BY FLO & ANNE
NEXT TIME, TRY ENDING YOUR SPEECH WITH A WORD THAT DOESN'T SOUND SO MUCH LIKE "PANCAKE."

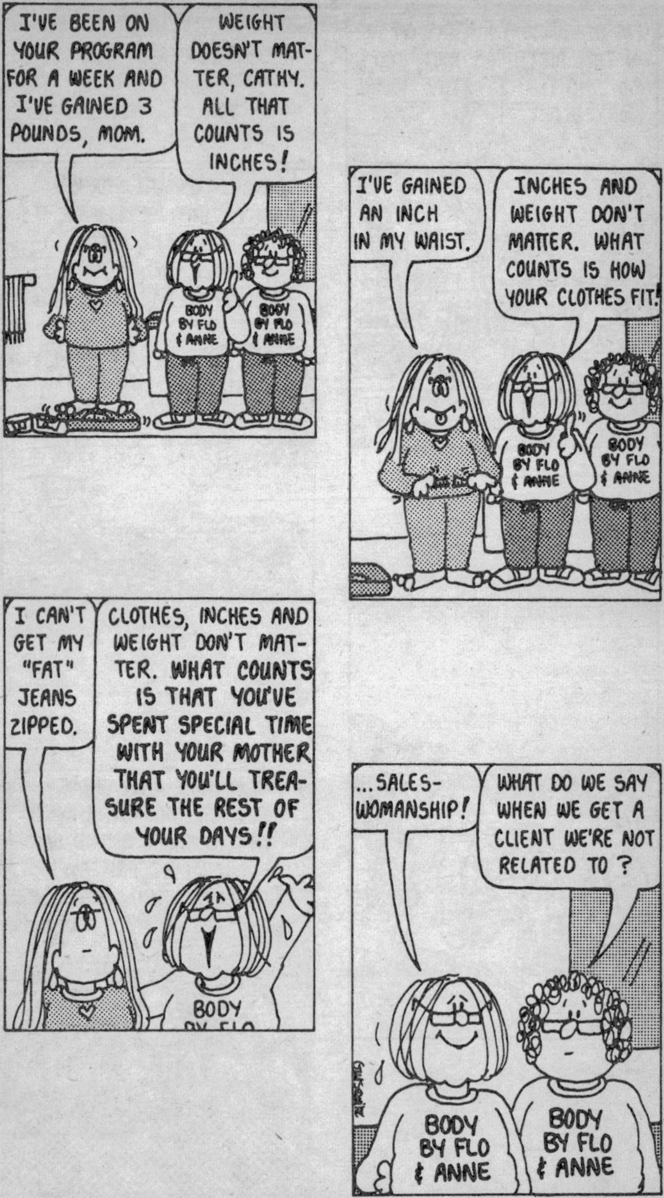
I'VE BEEN ON YOUR PROGRAM FOR A WEEK AND I'VE GAINED 3 POUNDS, MOM.
WEIGHT DOESN'T MATTER, CATHY. ALL THAT COUNTS IS INCHES!
BODY BY FLO & ANNE
I'VE GAINED AN INCH IN MY WAIST.
INCHES AND WEIGHT DON'T MATTER. WHAT COUNTS IS HOW YOUR CLOTHES FIT!
BODY BY FLO & ANNE
I CAN'T GET MY "FAT" JEANS ZIPPED.
CLOTHES, INCHES AND WEIGHT DON'T MATTER. WHAT COUNTS IS THAT YOU'VE SPENT SPECIAL TIME WITH YOUR MOTHER THAT YOU'LL TREASURE THE REST OF YOUR DAYS!!
WHAT DO WE SAY WHEN WE GET A CLIENT WE'RE NOT RELATED TO?
...SALES-WOMANSHIP!
BODY BY FLO & ANNE
BODY BY FLO & ANNE

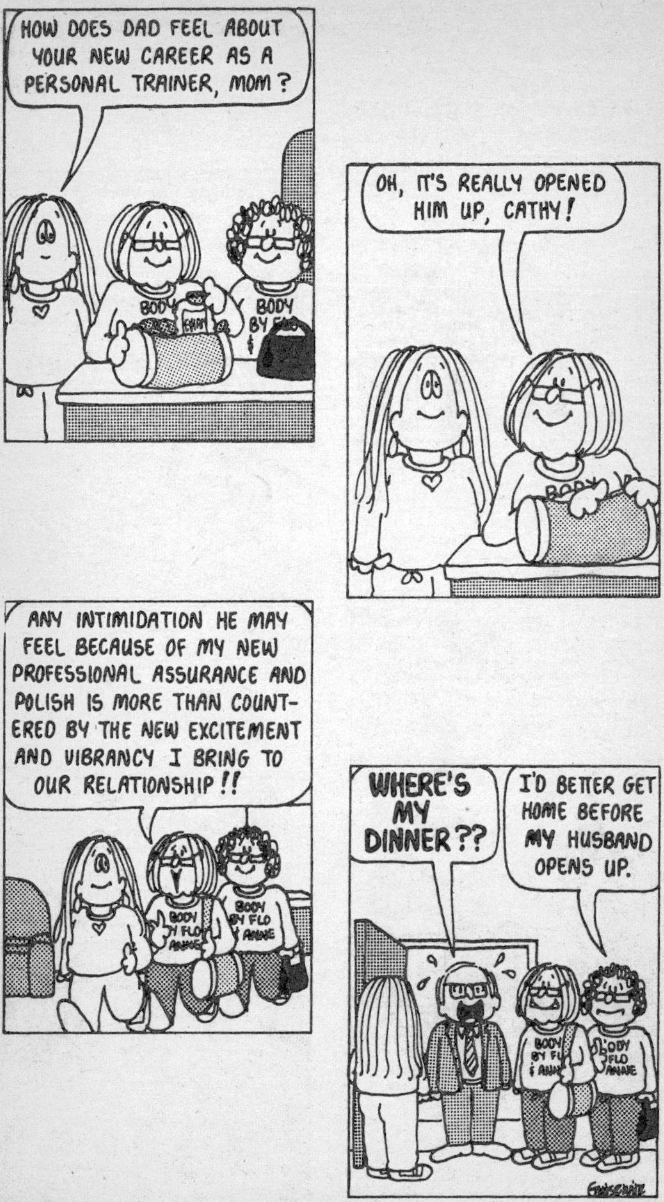
HOW DOES DAD FEEL ABOUT YOUR NEW CAREER AS A PERSONAL TRAINER, MOM?
OH, IT'S REALLY OPENED HIM UP, CATHY!
ANY INTIMIDATION HE MAY FEEL BECAUSE OF MY NEW PROFESSIONAL ASSURANCE AND POLISH IS MORE THAN COUNTERED BY THE NEW EXCITEMENT AND VIBRANCY I BRING TO OUR RELATIONSHIP!!
WHERE'S MY DINNER??
I'D BETTER GET HOME BEFORE MY HUSBAND OPENS UP.

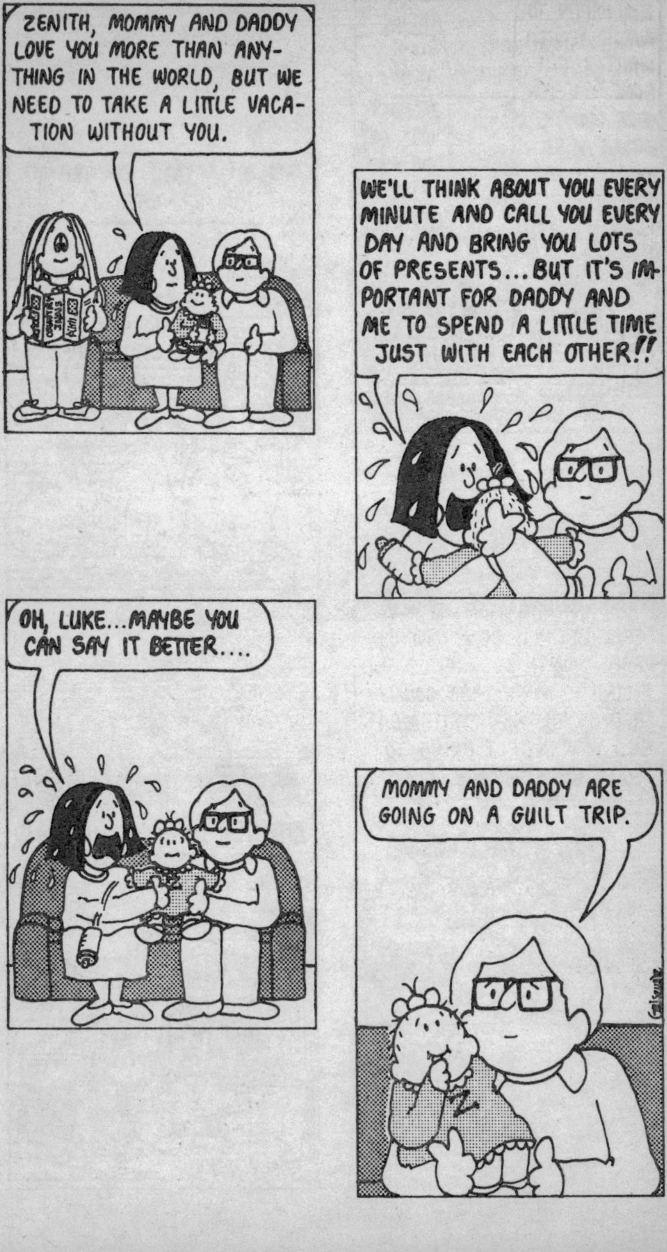
ZENITH, MOMMY AND DADDY LOVE YOU MORE THAN ANYTHING IN THE WORLD, BUT WE NEED TO TAKE A LITTLE VACATION WITHOUT YOU.
WE'LL THINK ABOUT YOU EVERY MINUTE AND CALL YOU EVERY DAY AND BRING YOU LOTS OF PRESENTS... BUT IT'S IMPORTANT FOR DADDY AND ME TO SPEND A LITTLE TIME JUST WITH EACH OTHER!!
OH, LUKE...MAYBE YOU CAN SAY IT BETTER....
MOMMY AND DADDY ARE GOING ON A GUILT TRIP.

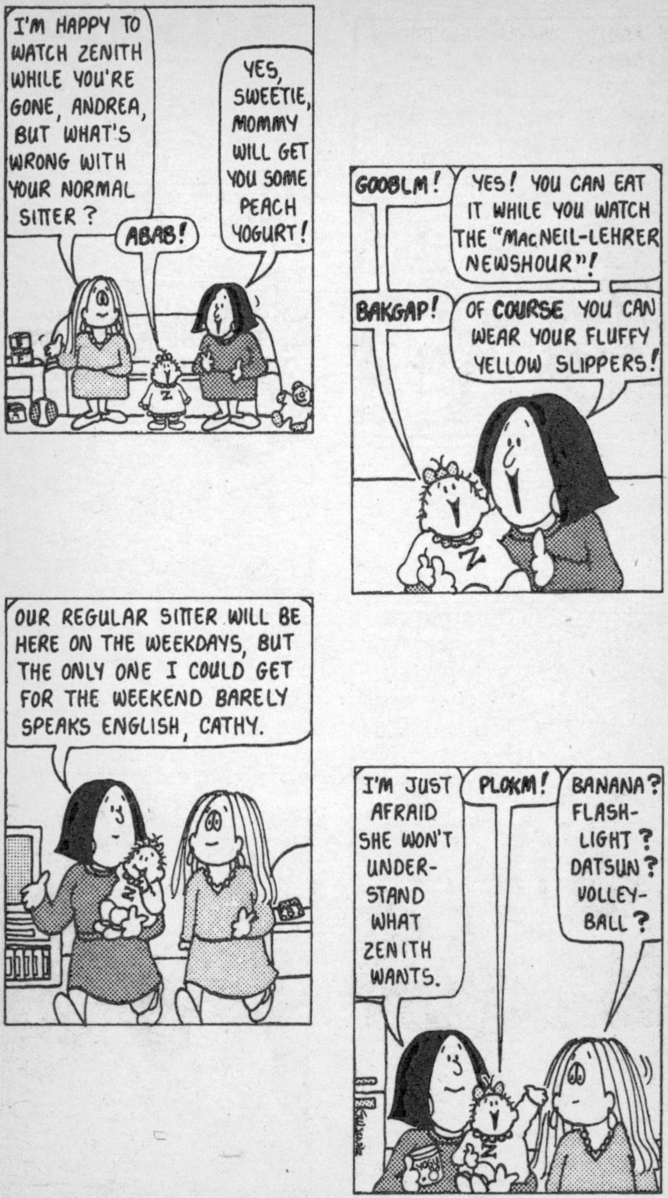
I'M HAPPY TO WATCH ZENITH WHILE YOU'RE GONE, ANDREA, BUT WHAT'S WRONG WITH YOUR NORMAL SITTER?
ABAB!
YES, SWEETIE, MOMMY WILL GET YOU SOME PEACH YOGURT!
GOOBLM!
YES! YOU CAN EAT IT WHILE YOU WATCH THE "MACNEIL-LEHRER NEWSHOUR"!
BAKGAP!
OF COURSE YOU CAN WEAR YOUR FLUFFY YELLOW SLIPPERS!
OUR REGULAR SITTER WILL BE HERE ON THE WEEKDAYS, BUT THE ONLY ONE I COULD GET FOR THE WEEKEND BARELY SPEAKS ENGLISH, CATHY.
I'M JUST AFRAID SHE WON'T UNDERSTAND WHAT ZENITH WANTS.
PLOKM!
BANANA? FLASHLIGHT? DATSUN? VOLLEYBALL?

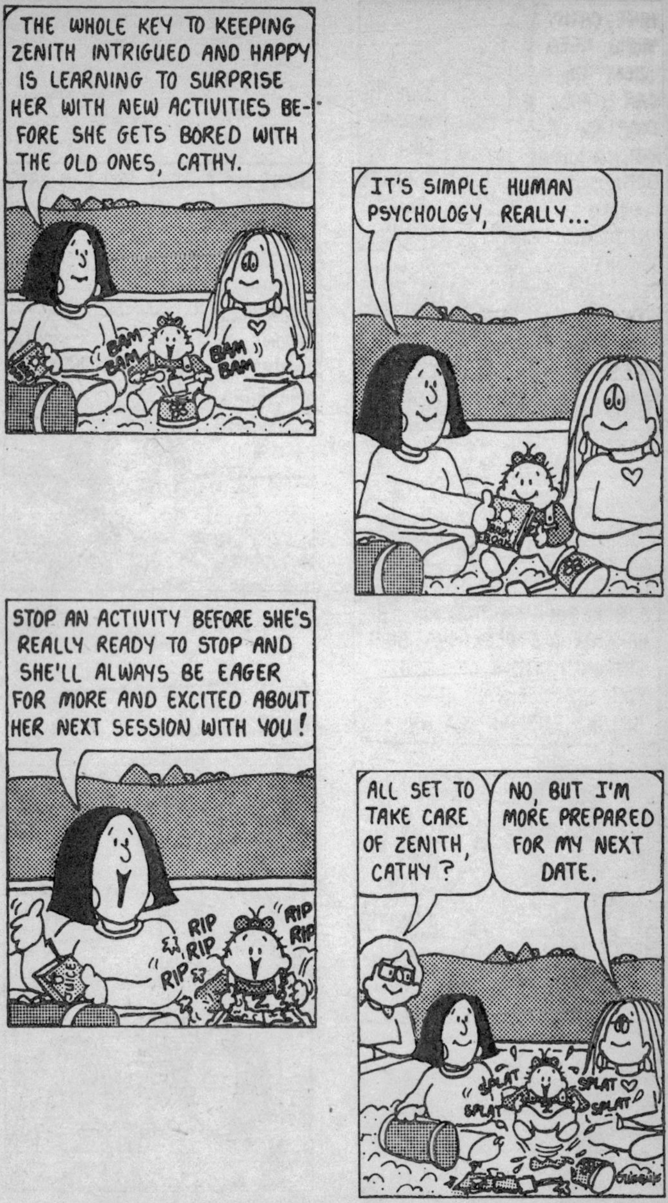
THE WHOLE KEY TO KEEPING ZENITH INTRIGUED AND HAPPY IS LEARNING TO SURPRISE HER WITH NEW ACTIVITIES BEFORE SHE GETS BORED WITH THE OLD ONES, CATHY.
BAM BAM
BAM BAM
IT'S SIMPLE HUMAN PSYCHOLOGY, REALLY...
BABY BOOK
STOP AN ACTIVITY BEFORE SHE'S REALLY READY TO STOP AND SHE'LL ALWAYS BE EAGER FOR MORE AND EXCITED ABOUT HER NEXT SESSION WITH YOU!
RIP RIP RIP
RIP RIP
JUICE
ALL SET TO TAKE CARE OF ZENITH, CATHY?
NO, BUT I'M MORE PREPARED FOR MY NEXT DATE.
SPLAT
SPLAT
SPLAT
SPLAT

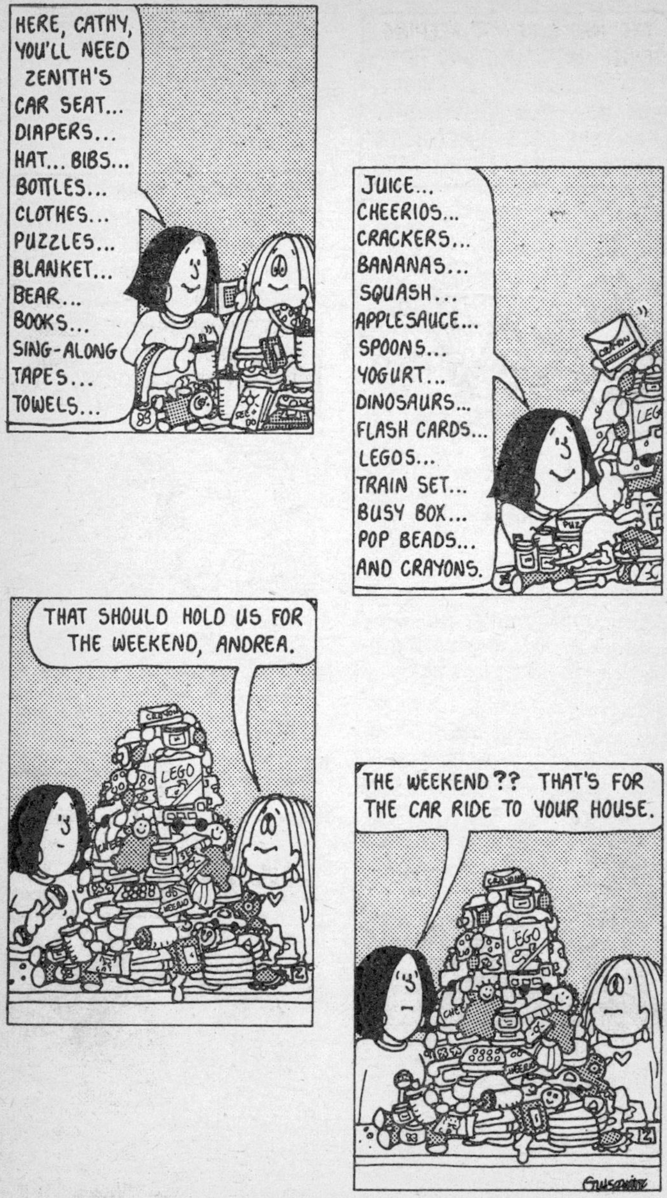
HERE, CATHY, YOU'LL NEED ZENITH'S CAR SEAT... DIAPERS... HAT... BIBS... BOTTLES... CLOTHES... PUZZLES... BLANKET... BEAR... BOOKS... SING-ALONG TAPES... TOWELS...
JUICE... CHEERIOS... CRACKERS... BANANAS... SQUASH... APPLESAUCE... SPOONS... YOGURT... DINOSAURS... FLASH CARDS... LEGOS... TRAIN SET... BUSY BOX... POP BEADS... AND CRAYONS.
THAT SHOULD HOLD US FOR THE WEEKEND, ANDREA.
THE WEEKEND?? THAT'S FOR THE CAR RIDE TO YOUR HOUSE.

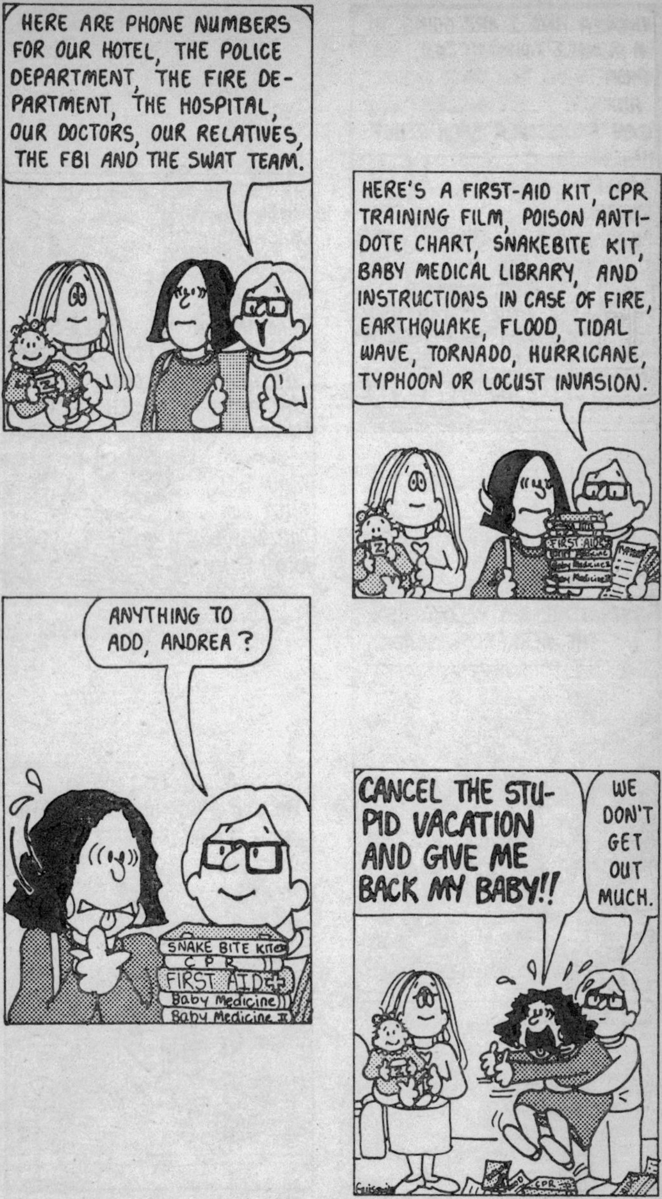
HERE ARE PHONE NUMBERS FOR OUR HOTEL, THE POLICE DEPARTMENT, THE FIRE DEPARTMENT, THE HOSPITAL, OUR DOCTORS, OUR RELATIVES, THE FBI AND THE SWAT TEAM.
HERE'S A FIRST-AID KIT, CPR TRAINING FILM, POISON ANTIDOTE CHART, SNAKEBITE KIT, BABY MEDICAL LIBRARY, AND INSTRUCTIONS IN CASE OF FIRE, EARTHQUAKE, FLOOD, TIDAL WAVE, TORNADO, HURRICANE, TYPHOON OR LOCUST INVASION.
ANYTHING TO ADD, ANDREA?
SNAKE BITE KIT
CPR
FIRST AID
Baby Medicine
Baby Medicine II
CANCEL THE STUPID VACATION AND GIVE ME BACK MY BABY!!
WE DON'T GET OUT MUCH.

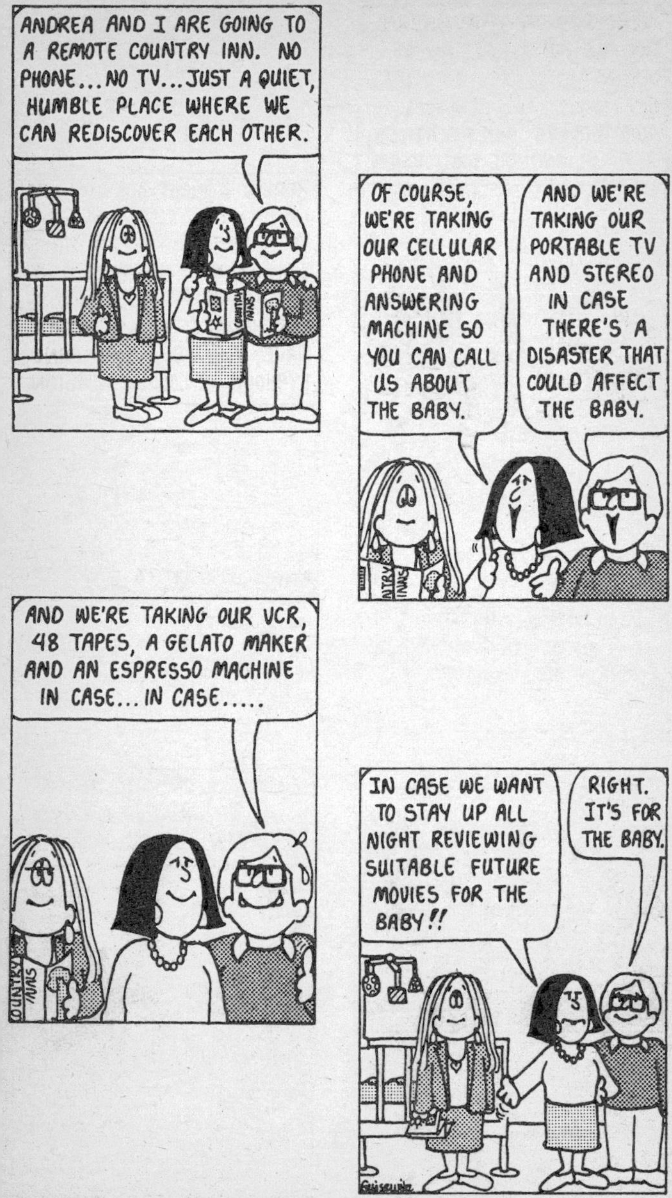
ANDREA AND I ARE GOING TO A REMOTE COUNTRY INN. NO PHONE... NO TV... JUST A QUIET, HUMBLE PLACE WHERE WE CAN REDISCOVER EACH OTHER.
OF COURSE, WE'RE TAKING OUR CELLULAR PHONE AND ANSWERING MACHINE SO YOU CAN CALL US ABOUT THE BABY.
AND WE'RE TAKING OUR PORTABLE TV AND STEREO IN CASE THERE'S A DISASTER THAT COULD AFFECT THE BABY.
AND WE'RE TAKING OUR VCR, 48 TAPES, A GELATO MAKER AND AN ESPRESSO MACHINE IN CASE... IN CASE.....
IN CASE WE WANT TO STAY UP ALL NIGHT REVIEWING SUITABLE FUTURE MOVIES FOR THE BABY!!
RIGHT. IT'S FOR THE BABY.

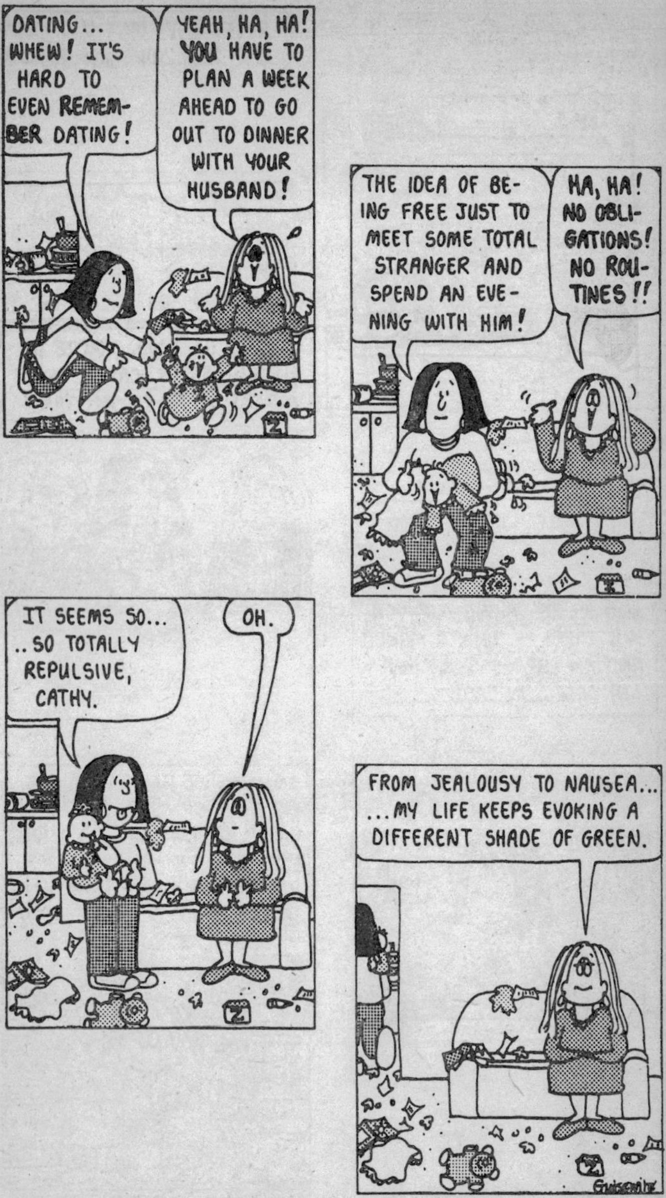
DATING... WHEW! IT'S HARD TO EVEN REMEMBER DATING!
YEAH, HA, HA! YOU HAVE TO PLAN A WEEK AHEAD TO GO OUT TO DINNER WITH YOUR HUSBAND!
THE IDEA OF BEING FREE JUST TO MEET SOME TOTAL STRANGER AND SPEND AN EVENING WITH HIM!
HA, HA! NO OBLIGATIONS! NO ROUTINES!!
IT SEEMS SO... ..SO TOTALLY REPULSIVE, CATHY.
OH.
FROM JEALOUSY TO NAUSEA... ...MY LIFE KEEPS EVOKING A DIFFERENT SHADE OF GREEN.

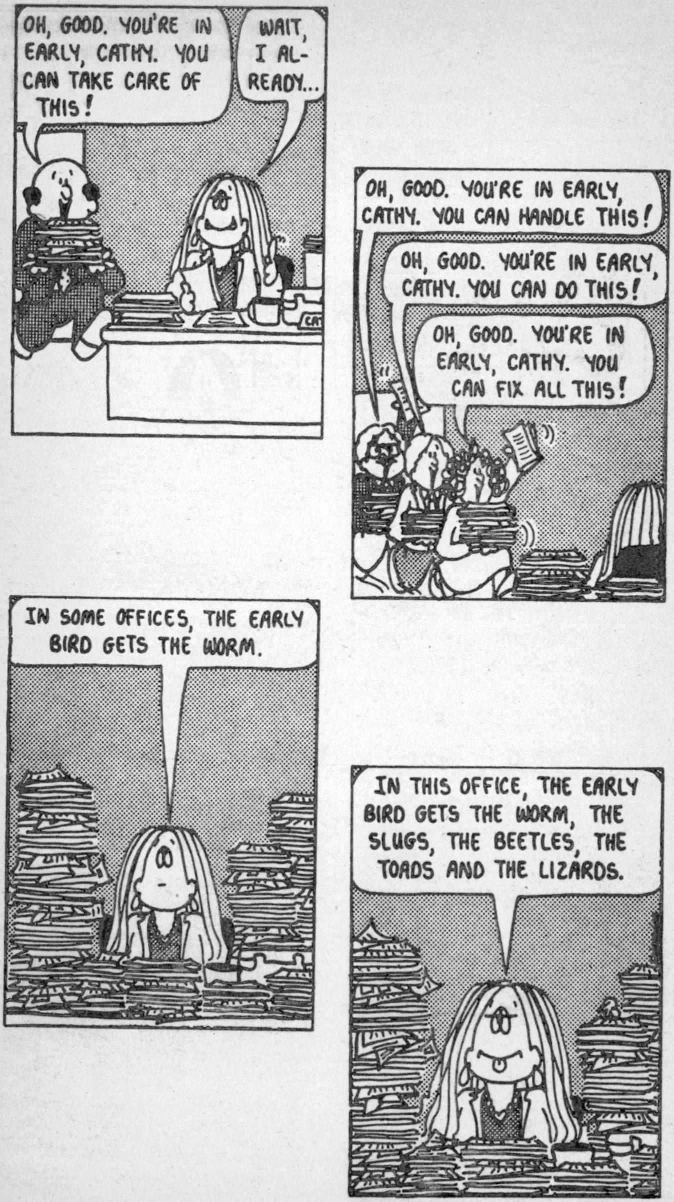

OH, GOOD. YOU'RE IN EARLY, CATHY. YOU CAN TAKE CARE OF THIS!
WAIT, I AL-READY...
OH, GOOD. YOU'RE IN EARLY, CATHY. YOU CAN HANDLE THIS!
OH, GOOD. YOU'RE IN EARLY, CATHY. YOU CAN DO THIS!
OH, GOOD. YOU'RE IN EARLY, CATHY. YOU CAN FIX ALL THIS!
IN SOME OFFICES, THE EARLY BIRD GETS THE WORM.
IN THIS OFFICE, THE EARLY BIRD GETS THE WORM, THE SLUGS, THE BEETLES, THE TOADS AND THE LIZARDS.

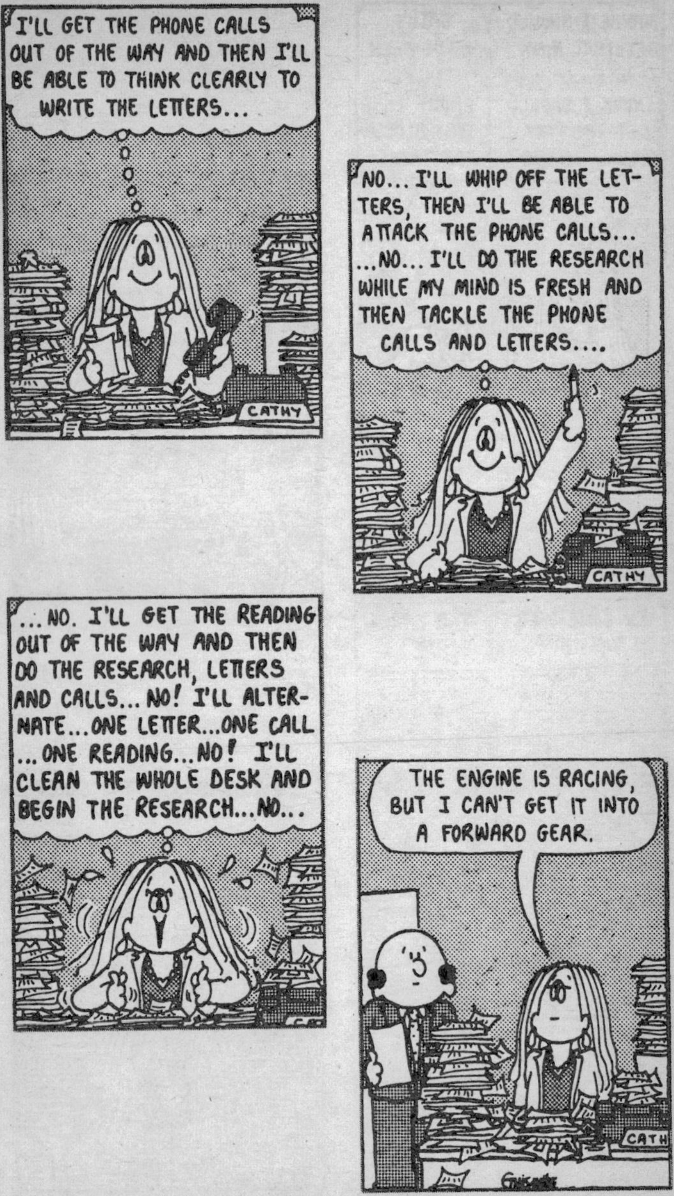
I'LL GET THE PHONE CALLS OUT OF THE WAY AND THEN I'LL BE ABLE TO THINK CLEARLY TO WRITE THE LETTERS...
CATHY
NO... I'LL WHIP OFF THE LETTERS, THEN I'LL BE ABLE TO ATTACK THE PHONE CALLS... ...NO... I'LL DO THE RESEARCH WHILE MY MIND IS FRESH AND THEN TACKLE THE PHONE CALLS AND LETTERS....
CATHY
...NO. I'LL GET THE READING OUT OF THE WAY AND THEN DO THE RESEARCH, LETTERS AND CALLS... NO! I'LL ALTERNATE...ONE LETTER...ONE CALL ...ONE READING...NO! I'LL CLEAN THE WHOLE DESK AND BEGIN THE RESEARCH...NO...
THE ENGINE IS RACING, BUT I CAN'T GET IT INTO A FORWARD GEAR.

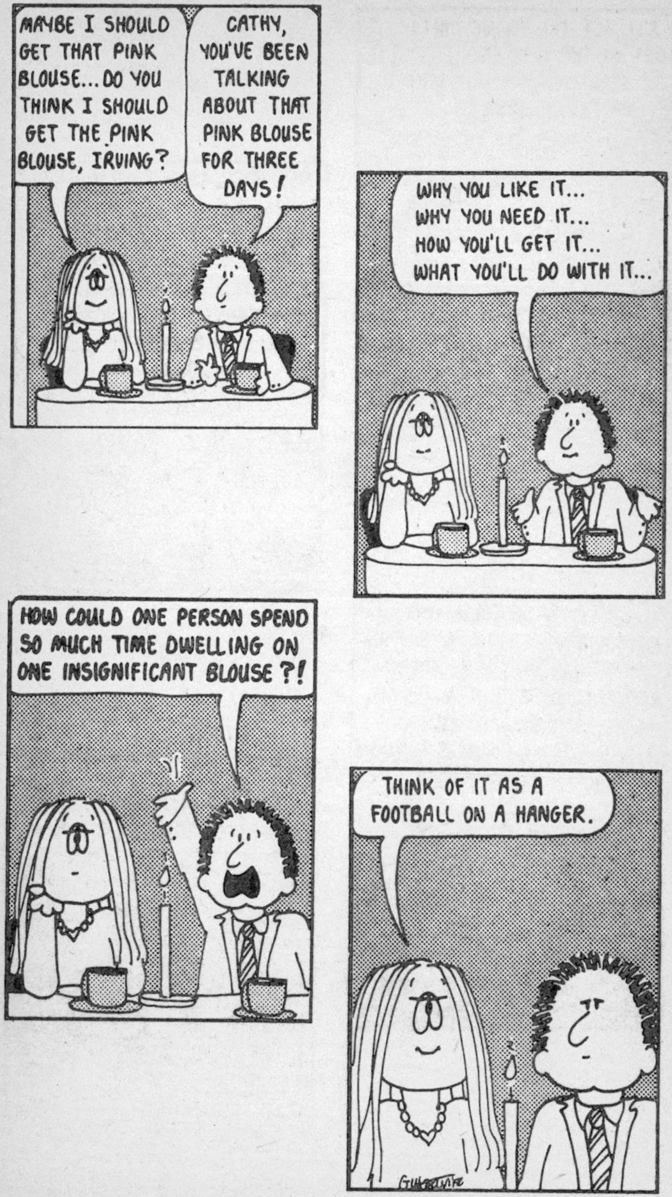

MAYBE I SHOULD GET THAT PINK BLOUSE... DO YOU THINK I SHOULD GET THE PINK BLOUSE, IRVING?
CATHY, YOU'VE BEEN TALKING ABOUT THAT PINK BLOUSE FOR THREE DAYS!
WHY YOU LIKE IT... WHY YOU NEED IT... HOW YOU'LL GET IT... WHAT YOU'LL DO WITH IT...
HOW COULD ONE PERSON SPEND SO MUCH TIME DWELLING ON ONE INSIGNIFICANT BLOUSE?!
THINK OF IT AS A FOOTBALL ON A HANGER.

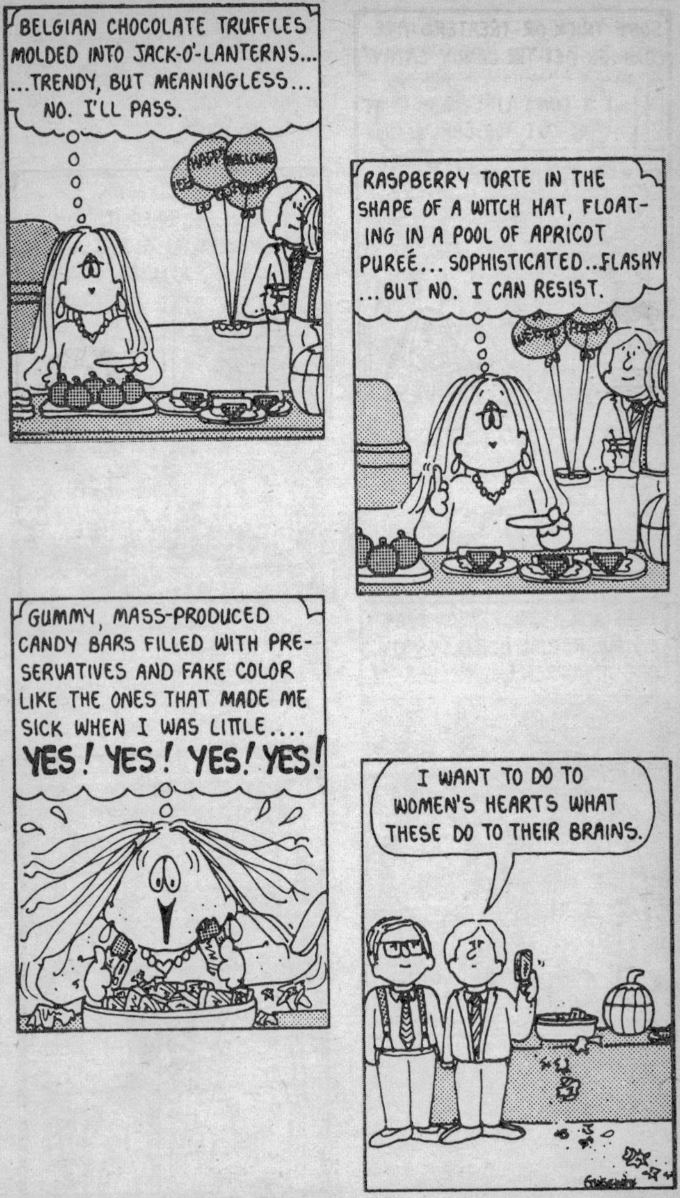
BELGIAN CHOCOLATE TRUFFLES MOLDED INTO JACK-O'-LANTERNS... ...TRENDY, BUT MEANINGLESS... NO. I'LL PASS.
RASPBERRY TORTE IN THE SHAPE OF A WITCH HAT, FLOATING IN A POOL OF APRICOT PUREÉ... SOPHISTICATED...FLASHY ...BUT NO. I CAN RESIST.
GUMMY, MASS-PRODUCED CANDY BARS FILLED WITH PRESERVATIVES AND FAKE COLOR LIKE THE ONES THAT MADE ME SICK WHEN I WAS LITTLE.... YES! YES! YES! YES!
I WANT TO DO TO WOMEN'S HEARTS WHAT THESE DO TO THEIR BRAINS.

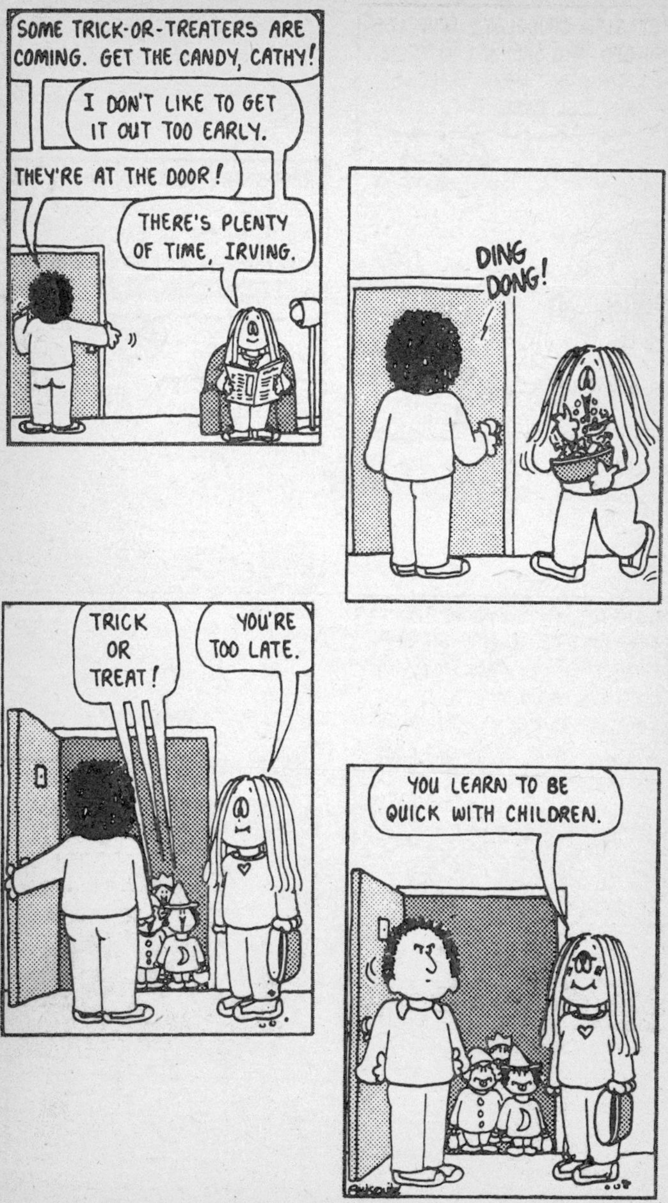
SOME TRICK-OR-TREATERS ARE COMING. GET THE CANDY, CATHY!
I DON'T LIKE TO GET IT OUT TOO EARLY.
THEY'RE AT THE DOOR!
THERE'S PLENTY OF TIME, IRVING.
DING DONG!
TRICK OR TREAT!
YOU'RE TOO LATE.
YOU LEARN TO BE QUICK WITH CHILDREN.

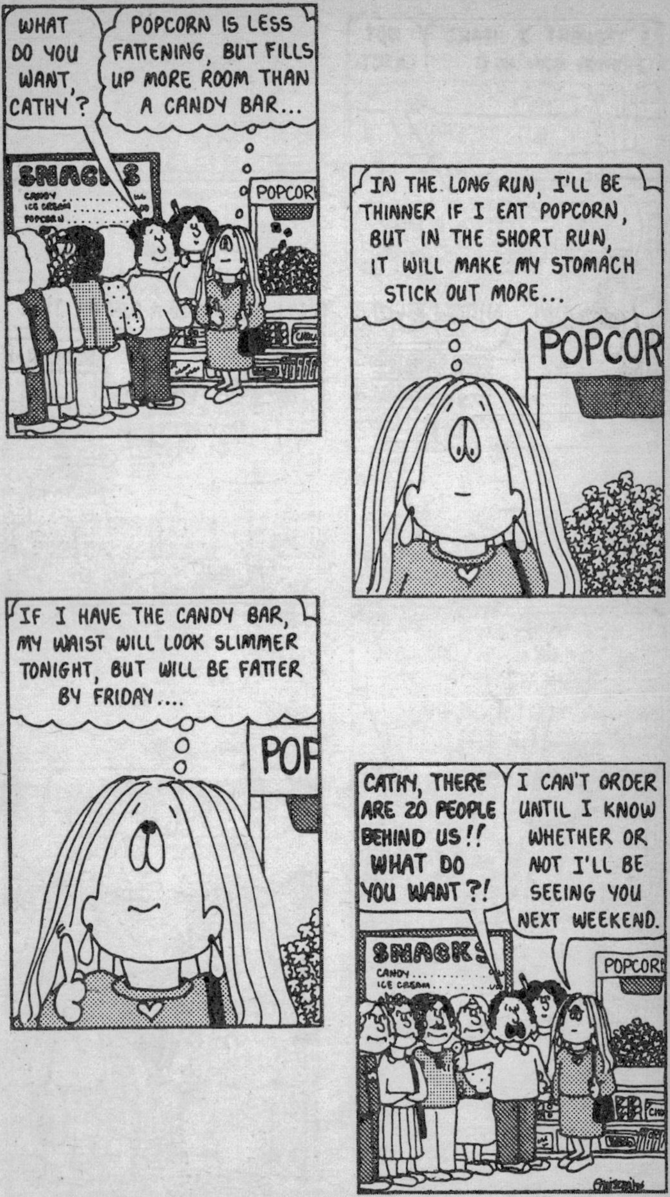
WHAT DO YOU WANT, CATHY?
POPCORN IS LESS FATTENING, BUT FILLS UP MORE ROOM THAN A CANDY BAR...
IN THE LONG RUN, I'LL BE THINNER IF I EAT POPCORN, BUT IN THE SHORT RUN, IT WILL MAKE MY STOMACH STICK OUT MORE...
IF I HAVE THE CANDY BAR, MY WAIST WILL LOOK SLIMMER TONIGHT, BUT WILL BE FATTER BY FRIDAY....
CATHY, THERE ARE 20 PEOPLE BEHIND US!! WHAT DO YOU WANT?!
I CAN'T ORDER UNTIL I KNOW WHETHER OR NOT I'LL BE SEEING YOU NEXT WEEKEND.

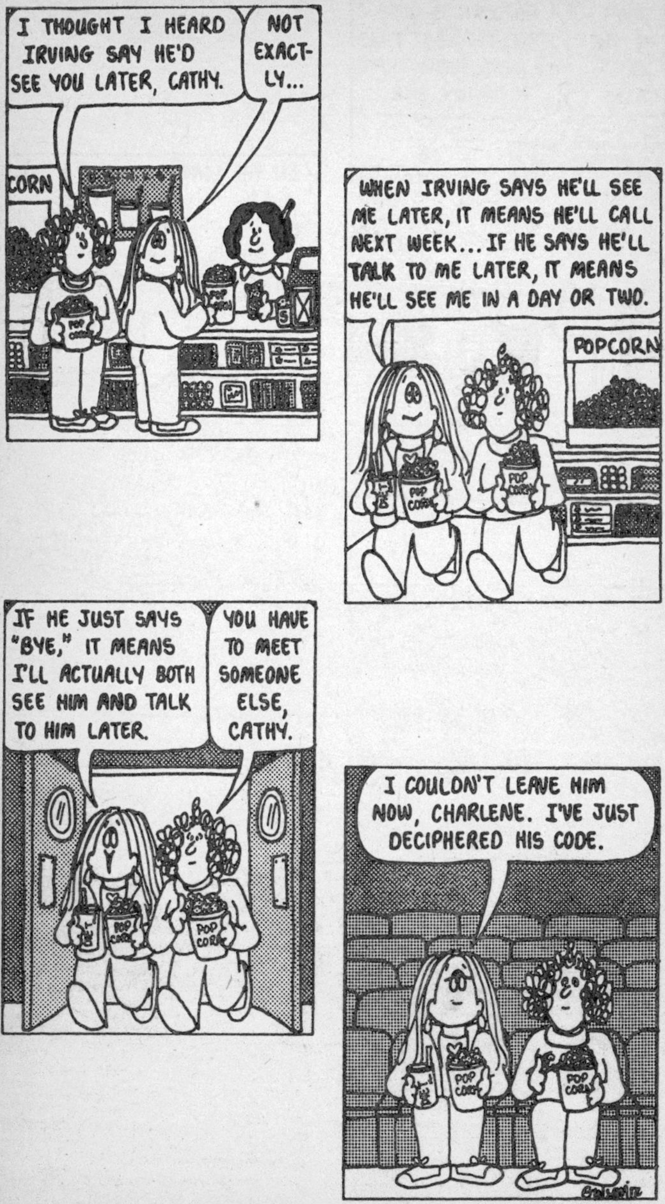
I THOUGHT I HEARD IRVING SAY HE'D SEE YOU LATER, CATHY.
NOT EXACT-LY...
CORN
POP CORN
WHEN IRVING SAYS HE'LL SEE ME LATER, IT MEANS HE'LL CALL NEXT WEEK... IF HE SAYS HE'LL TALK TO ME LATER, IT MEANS HE'LL SEE ME IN A DAY OR TWO.
POPCORN
IF HE JUST SAYS "BYE," IT MEANS I'LL ACTUALLY BOTH SEE HIM AND TALK TO HIM LATER.
YOU HAVE TO MEET SOMEONE ELSE, CATHY.
I COULDN'T LEAVE HIM NOW, CHARLENE. I'VE JUST DECIPHERED HIS CODE.

CATHY'S AT IT AGAIN!!

...juggling jobs, jealous boyfriends, and jelly doughnuts...

Cathy Guisewite at Fawcett Books

Available at your bookstore or use this coupon.

___ THE SALESCLERK MADE ME BUY IT	20926	2.50
___ SORRY I'M LATE. MY HAIR WON'T START	20925	2.50
___ STRESSED FOR SUCCESS – Vol. I of MEN SHOULD COME WITH INSTRUCTION BOOKLETS	21017	2.50
___ MY COLOGNE BACKFIRED – Vol. II of MEN SHOULD COME WITH INSTRUCTION BOOKLETS	21505	2.95
___ I'LL PAY $5,000 FOR A SWIMSUIT THAT FITS ME!!!	21248	2.95
___ TWO PIES. ONE FORK.	21249	2.95

FAWCETT MAIL SALES
Dept. TAF, 201 E. 50th St., New York, N.Y. 10022

Please send me the FAWCETT BOOKS I have checked above. I am enclosing $..................(add 50¢ per copy to cover postage and handling). Send check or money order—no cash or C.O.D.'s please. Prices and numbers are subject to change without notice. Valid in U.S. only. All orders are subject to availability of books.

Name_____

Address_____

City_____State_____Zip Code_____

30   Allow at least 4 weeks for delivery.   **TAF-92**